THE INNOCENT GIRL

ALEX COOMBS

First published in Great Britain in 2021 by Boldwood Books Ltd.

Cover Design by Nick Castle Design

Cover photography: Shutterstock

A CIP catalogue record for this book is available from the British Library.

Paperback ISBN 978-1-80048-816-8

Large Print ISBN 978-1-80048-815-1

Ebook ISBN 978-1-80048-818-2

Kindle ISBN 978-1-80048-817-5

Audio CD ISBN 978-1-80048-810-6

MP3 CD ISBN 978-1-80048-811-3

Digital audio download ISBN 978-1-80048-813-7

Boldwood Books Ltd
23 Bowerdean Street
London SW6 3TN
www.boldwoodbooks.com

1

In her student bedsit, Hannah opened her eyes and allowed the fantasy to gently drift away as recommended by *Catching Your Dreams (And Making Them Come True)*, the self-help guide she was studying.

According to the book, visualization was the first step to actualization. There was no point in wanting to be a famous journalist, as Hannah did, until you felt you were a famous journalist, at least in your own head. If you don't believe in you, how can anyone else? That was the message of the chapter she was reading.

In the private theatre of her mind, with herself as appreciative audience, Hannah had just graciously received a BAFTA for journalism. She held the award aloft and waved to her adoring public. Soon she'd have her own TV series. She'd get to meet celebrities, no, she'd be a celebrity. She'd, well, the possibilities were practically endless. She now allowed the dream to disperse. Reality took hold.

She sighed, stretched and shifted her weight on her narrow, cramped bed in the small, dilapidated room off Gower Street in Bloomsbury, central London, that was her temporary home. The walls were marked by small circles where a succession of students had Blu-tacked posters of their idols. Their ghostly residue defied repainting.

Traffic rumbled by outside. She looked at her Facebook page open on her laptop. On her wall she had written, *Am seeing sexy married man tonight ;)* and added, after a moment's thought, *But that's not all ;D have decided to explore my inner chick feelings with some girl on girl (well, this girl on one married lady, why do these people bother to get hitched!) action! Will let you know how it's going later ;) Don't forget to check my blog! :D.*

That'll get tongues wagging, she thought. More to the point, that'll get people reading. Sex sells, or so they say. No point writing without an audience. That'd be the sound of one hand clapping.

She was pleased with the Zen allusion. It was classy.

She repeated to herself, 'I am classy, I am a success,' three times, aloud. It was important to raise your self-esteem, the book said.

She closed her eyes for a minute and settled down to allow herself another brief, momentary fantasy of fame.

Her phone beeped and she checked it. One of her two lovers was on their way round. Hannah felt a surge of sexual anticipation coupled with professional, journalistic excitement. She had spent hours tracking people down to check a theory she had about the relationship of one of her lovers with Dr Fuller; tonight she would have it confirmed.

Hannah was no fool. She knew wishful thinking alone, no matter how directed, would not get her a job on *The Huffington Post* or the *Sunday Times* or the BBC. Exposing a famous (well, semi-well-known) academic as a serious philanderer, abusing his position of trust as well as potentially killing one of his lovers, and writing about her investigative work online, now that just might. At least it was a start. And Hannah was prepared to do whatever it took to realize her ambitions. Whatever it took.

She typed her revelation about her lover into her blog. It had a disappointingly low number of readers at the moment, but that would soon change. Very few people had heard of her, but lots of people knew Dr Fuller. Soon they'd all have to log in to get the lurid details. Later she'd think of a suitable headline.

She heard the entry-phone buzzer. Her partner had arrived. She pressed the button to open the door downstairs, opened her own door a crack and then lay face down submissively on her bed, as she'd been instructed to do.

'Don't look at me tonight,' he'd ordered.

Hannah slipped the black velvet hood over her head. Her lover liked her blindfolded, passive and quiescent.

She heard footsteps in her room and the door closed. All her senses were heightened now in the velvet darkness of the hood. Sound was magnified. Sensations were amplified. The click of the door as it shut had an ominous finality.

She could hear his breathing, the traffic noise in the street outside, someone's TV down the hall. She heard the faint noise of an iPod being attached to her docking station and old-fashioned dance music filled the room. Hannah's pulse quickened when she felt the mattress on the bed move as her lover sat beside her and started stroking her head through the material of the hood.

She felt her skirt being pulled up and then she heard her lover say softly, 'I thought I told you. White underwear, not black.' There was a pause and then he murmured, 'Now I'll have to punish you.'

'I'm sorry, Teacher!' she said. Her lover insisted on her using the title. Not to do so was to be punished. At the start of their relationship he'd made her write a contract out, detailing her slave duties. Everything they did together was rigorously, relentlessly planned and choreographed. There was a script written by him that she had to follow. Nothing was left to chance. Everything was controlled, even down to the music playing in the background.

Especially down to the music in the background. He was insistent upon it. Always dance music. She guessed that it meant more to him than simply a soundtrack or just something to drown out the noise of their lovemaking. The intensity of his expression was sometimes frightening.

'Sorry doesn't cut it,' the voice said.

'I'll do anything you say,' she said, her voice muffled by the material of the hood.

'Yes, you will, won't you,' said the voice, calm and in control.

Always in control. 'Arms behind your back.'

She did as she was told. Now her wrists were secured behind her back with handcuffs, depriving her of the use of her arms. She felt her underwear being pulled down and then a searing pain across her buttocks as the riding crop swished down. She bit her lip in pleasure at the stinging sensation. Her laptop pinged as someone emailed her; she felt a twinge of irritation that she'd forgotten to log off. Bloody thing.

She felt the weight of the other leaning across her body momentarily. Was he reading the blog? Surely it had moved to screen save?

She felt the familiar, strong fingers close around her throat. She arced her neck upwards submissively to allow him a better grip, the index finger against her jawbone. She felt the pressure closing, tightening, then her airways constricting as she heard the voice whispering, 'Who's been a naughty girl then?'

The artist changed on the iPod and the music shifted up a gear. A voice from way back when, a voice from long before she was born, Donna Summer's voice, ethereal and urgent, sang how she felt love, over and over again, floating above the robotic, synthesized drums.

The fingers closed around her again, but it was not like it had been before, not gentle, not fun at all, and she bucked beneath the other body, now pressing down on top of hers so she couldn't move, in genuine alarm but to no avail.

They had a code word to use to stop any activity, but she couldn't speak.

This wasn't part of the script. This wasn't how it should be.

Now her alarm changed to fear, and as the pressure continued, naked terror.

Please God, she prayed, make this stop! She could hear the song in her ears about how it felt good, so good, so good, but it didn't feel good. Not good at all.

She was choking. She couldn't breathe. It was like a night- mare and fear changed to terror. Now she could hear the blood hammering in her ears, as insistent as the music, and wild patches of iridescent colour seemed to explode in the darkness behind the hood. The music swelled to a crescendo and still the iron grip tightened.

Above her, straddling her body that was trying so hard and so ineffectually to buck him off, he hummed along to the music, his head nodding in time with the beat while his grip never slackened.

Gradually he felt her movements slowing and ceasing, and her body relaxed as her life departed.

Her killer rolled off her body and stood momentarily looking down at Hannah with genuine regret, then leaned forward and with gloved fingers delicately deleted the last section of the blog.

2

At the central ring in the large, vaulted space of Bob's Gym in Bermondsey the fighters were training in the background; around them, almost centre stage, the multilayered noise of a boxing gym.

The decibel levels were high. There was the thud of gloves on the heavy bags, on bodies and on pads, the grunts of explosive effort as the punches were launched, the swishing of skipping ropes, the *tacketa-tacketa-tacketa* noise of the speed bags, the squeak of training shoes on polished wood and the shouts of instruction or encouragement.

Freddie Laidlaw, the owner and trainer at Bob's Gym, looked at Hanlon speculatively. His eyes ran over her as she stood before him. He was looking for weakness. He could see none. Hanlon's gaze was as steady and imperious as ever.

The last time he'd seen her was when he'd visited her once briefly in hospital, hiding behind the expensive bunch of flowers he had brought with him like a shield.

Hanlon had been in bed, her head and arm bandaged, the springs of her thick, dark hair emphasizing the pallor of her skin. His heart had felt heavy at the sight of her vulnerability.

Then with her eyes still closed, she'd said, 'Put the flowers on the table, Freddie.'

'How did you know it was me?'

She opened her grey eyes and looked at him sardonically. 'White lilies are for funerals, Freddie,' she said. 'I could smell them coming down the corridor.'

'Oh,' he said lamely.

'I'm not dead yet, Freddie, but when I am, I'll be sure to let you know.'

He smiled at her. 'You do that, Hanlon.'

She propped herself up on one elbow. It hurt, but she took care not to let the pain show; she even refused her eyes permission to narrow.

'I'm a hard woman to kill,' she told him.

That evening was Hanlon's first time back in the gym since her fight with Conquest on the island. Laidlaw had watched her earlier, jumping rope with effortless ease. As she skipped, following up with basic jumps, shuffles and side swings, Hanlon was graceful and fluid in motion, her body concealed by a baggy old tracksuit. Laidlaw noticed several of the other boxers stealing surreptitious glances at her movements. She was the only female boxer in the gym. Hanlon usually worked out and sparred with the handful of professionals and semi-pros who trained at the gym on the evenings when it was closed to amateurs. This was the first time most of them had ever seen her. Aware of the attention and just for the hell of it, she finished off her half-hour workout with some showy rope tricks, cross- overs, double-unders and double cross-overs, the rope a blur of movement, haloing her slim body. She moved so fast the rope audibly swished through the air and cracked whip-like against the floor.

Beat that, she thought triumphantly.

Laidlaw went over to her, noticing the faint sheen of sweat

shining on her skin. She pushed her unruly hair back from her forehead. Laidlaw saw lines that he was sure hadn't existed before her struggle to the death with Conquest. He guessed it had cost her more than she would ever admit.

'Ready?' he asked. She nodded and held her hands out, fingers splayed. With speed born of decades of practice, Laidlaw taped her long, strong fingers. She flexed them, nodded in satisfaction and Laidlaw slipped on her boxing gloves.

He had agreed with Hanlon on just one three-minute spar- ring round with one of the other boxers. Laidlaw had chosen Jay. He was a good, promising middleweight. At eleven and a half stone he was a stone and a half heavier than she was, so a challenge but not a mismatch.

Hanlon hadn't been in the ring for nearly two months. She was keen to check her fitness levels and the extent to which her arm had recovered. Laidlaw knew too that she would be desperate to release some of the aggression that had built up inside her. Hanlon was one of those boxers who need to release their aggression and she knew it. It was one of the reasons why she did triathlons. She wasn't competing just against a clock; she wanted to smash her rivals.

Eight weeks of inaction were bottled up inside her.

The trainer got into the ring after her and motioned to Jay, who followed suit. His black skin looked as though it had been carefully painted over an anatomically perfect body.

Laidlaw waved them together to the centre of the ring. Jay had a broad sceptical grin on his face. For a start, as well as being a woman, Hanlon was almost twice his age, though little was visible of her beneath her headguard and baggy tracksuit. They tapped gloves. Jay's smile froze and vanished as he saw Hanlon's eyes, hard and watchful. Until now he'd thought the whole thing might be some practical joke. He'd made a mental note not to hit her too hard, to go easy on her. Not now. Not after that look. The two of them circled each other and then Jay moved in.

Three minutes sounds like no time at all, the length of a song on the radio or the time it takes to clean your teeth. Three minutes.

Now, consider this.

Try leaning against someone the same weight as you. Put your head on the other person's shoulder, neck bent so the top of your head is pressing just above their collarbone and you're staring at the floor. Let them do the same. Interlink the fingers of each hand with your partner's and take it in turns to push. When the other person pushes forward with their arms, resist as hard as you can, with all your strength. Then it's your turn to push, theirs to resist. Like pistons working against a heavy mass. Use your legs as well to drive yourself forward, as does your opponent. Do this for three minutes without a break, as hard and as fast as you can, without a pause to draw breath. That's one round.

That gives some idea of the physical effort inside the ring. Now, imagine too, the other person is trying to hit you in the face and body as hard as they possibly can, as viciously as they can, and they are strong and quick and practised.

All there is, is the ring. That is the world.

You can't turn away, there's nowhere to hide; you just have to face them until the round is over. Your eyes fill with sweat, occasionally tears, sometimes blood. You can't hear anything except your own laboured breathing, sometimes not even the bell.

All there is, is the ring. All there is, is the pain. All there is, is the effort.

You're unaware of the crowd, unaware of your surroundings. It's just you and your opponent and those gloves coming at you. And there's no respite, no let-up, no remorse.

Time seems endless.

Hanlon loved boxing. She was made for it. Being back in the

ring just felt so good, like slipping into the sea when she swam, gloriously right.

Her reflexes were as sharp as ever. She let Jay do the work, jerking her head out of the way of his fast jab, which was accurate but not quick enough to catch her. He favoured a sharp right-cross, Hanlon used her fast footwork and ring-craft to circle him. Occasionally she flicked out a lightning-fast left of her own. Jay hadn't expected this vicious jab and the first one caught him under his right eye, which within seconds had started to swell. Not only did he begin losing all-round vision, but it affected his calculation of distance.

He shook his head in baffled surprise. I'm losing, he thought incredulously.

He dropped his guard slightly and that was enough for Hanlon. Another punch rode over the protective gloves in front of Jay's face, catching him off balance, and then as his feet moved awkwardly to restore his equilibrium, Hanlon was on him, sending what would have been rib-breaking body shots into his lower body, if she hadn't pulled the power of the punches. 'Break,' said Laidlaw, moving between them, pushing them aside with his hands. He covered his mouth to hide his grin of delight. The old Hanlon was back. Lean and mean, he thought, lean and mean.

Hanlon moved over to a corner and rested against the ropes. She listened critically to her body. She was pleased, her breathing was perfect, her legs felt like steel. Jay came up to her pulling his headguard off and they sportingly touched gloves. She could smell his short, cropped hair and youthful perspiration. He grinned at her, taking his mouthguard out as he did so, his teeth startlingly white against his black face. Hanlon thought, he's ridiculously good-looking.

'Respect,' he said. Hanlon smiled at him. Good boxers are, paradoxically, usually gentlemen. Jay nodded and rejoined his companions.

Hanlon took her gum shield out and rinsed and spat into the bucket that Laidlaw was holding. The water was tinged pink with her blood where one of Jay's head shots had damaged her mouth. Perspiration soaked through the faded grey fabric of her baggy, sleeveless top and Laidlaw could smell a hint of scent through her sweat.

'Are you wearing perfume?' he asked. He'd never known her to do that. Hanlon's unfriendly gaze met his.

'I was seeing someone I know earlier,' she said. 'A friend.' Her expression dared him to ask another question. Laidlaw had plenty of experience of reading hostility in faces and body posture; he wasn't going to make that mistake. He knew the high price she put on her privacy.

He watched Hanlon's back, her head held high, as she walked back across the gym. Several of the other fighters touched her shoulder gently as she passed. Laidlaw shook his head with rueful affection and sighed. She was back.

As she left, a figure in the shadows of the viewing gallery above the ring, who had been watching the fight unobserved from the darkness under the roof eaves, quietly got to his feet and slipped away towards the exit.

Hanlon showered in Laidlaw's personal bathroom and pulled her clothes on. She felt elated. She had won; he had lost. The best of feelings.

She winced as she dressed. She studied her half-naked body in the mirror and could see the skin around her ribs changing colour, darkening, as she began to bruise. Her left eye, too, was puffy and swollen where Jay had caught it with a punch she couldn't avoid. By the morning it would be black.

Later that night she knew she'd be in considerable discomfort from the beating her body had taken from Jay's gloves, but Hanlon didn't mind that kind of pain. It was there because of what she'd achieved. No pain, no gain. If there's no charge, it's not worth attending the show.

She was pleased overall with her performance. It was the first time she had been in a fight since her struggle with Conquest on the island, which was a couple of months ago. Her arm had healed perfectly and her fitness levels were better than ever.

She walked out of the fire door at the rear of the building, sure-footed and silent on the metal steps of the fire escape. Her sports bag in her left hand was partially unzipped and jutting out from it was the handle of a standard-issue police telescopic baton. Hanlon had made a fair number of enemies in her time and she suspected one of them would come looking for her some day. She also didn't trust the dark streets of Bermondsey at the best of times, no matter how up-and-coming its image. Either way, she was ready.

As she exited the narrow alleyway into the dark, dimly lit street she saw a tall figure step out of the gloom.

With one fluid movement, she drew the carbon-steel baton as a familiar voice said, 'It's me, DI Hanlon. You can put the baton away now, unless you want to be arrested for assaulting a senior officer.'

'Yes, sir,' said Hanlon. Her hand moved away from the comforting metal handle. 'How can I help you?' she asked.

'You can join me for dinner, Detective Inspector,' said the assistant commissioner, stepping into the soft halo of a street light. 'I've got a job offer for you.'

3

Hanlon and Corrigan sat together at a small table at the rear of the Sultan Ahmet restaurant near the brutalist sprawl of the South Bank complex, home of Lasdun's hymn to concrete, the National Theatre and the Hayward Gallery by the Thames, just across the river from Westminster.

The restaurant was owned by relatives of Hanlon's former partner in the Met, Enver Demirel. His aunt, Demet, ran the place. Hanlon could see her, standing behind the bar, organizing everything with tight-lipped efficiency. Short, beaky-nosed, and whippet thin with a shock of dyed brown hair, she looked like a small, angry bird. Enver, and the other relatives of his who Hanlon had met, were all placid by temperament and good- natured. Neither adjective applied to Aunt Demet.

She watched the waiters moving with professional grace, and as they exited and entered the kitchen she caught glimpses of the chefs toiling away. She reflected how much Enver had hated the catering world, how he had once told her that boxing and the police force were relatively stress free compared to working for the family-run restaurant business that the Demirels had. Mind you, she thought, I got Enver shot and nearly killed, a charge that couldn't be levelled at his family.

Corrigan's six-foot-five frame was uncomfortably wedged between banquette seat and table. His huge hands made the knife and fork he was holding look child-sized. He poured himself another Efes Pilsen and emptied half of it down his throat.

If Demet Gul looked bird-like, thought Hanlon, then Corrigan with his slab-like builder's features was more like an ox or a bull. It had led many people to think him slow-witted, a huge mistake. Corrigan had a consummate political aware- ness that had kept him at the top table of the Met for about a decade now, and she felt uncomfortable under his shrewd, calculating gaze.

Hanlon and Corrigan were sharing a mezze-style starter, a selection of salads and various kebabs. Corrigan's eyes brightened at the sight of the food.

'What's this again?' he asked, pointing at a salad. Most of the mezze he could recognize, falafel, hummus, mini-kebabs, even Baba Ghanoush. Hanlon glanced at the plate.

'Kisir, sir. It's a salad with nuts in.'

'It's very good.' He had another forkful. 'What kind of nuts?'
'Hazelnuts, I believe, sir.'

'Ingenious,' said Corrigan.

'I'm glad you're enjoying it, sir.'

Hanlon ate sparingly. She could at least pretend to be enthusiastic about her food, Corrigan thought, food that was extremely good. From the expression on her face, she might as well have been eating cardboard. Her mouth seemed to attack the mezze as if eating were some sort of unpalatable duty. She never lightens up, he thought.

'I see you're keeping yourself fit, Detective Inspector.' Conversations with Hanlon often ended up as a series of sarcastic interchanges.

'A healthy mind in a healthy body, sir,' said Hanlon, pointedly eyeing the AC's prominent gut.

Pictures of the great mosque in Istanbul covered the walls, along with stylized portraits of various Ottoman emperors.

'Have you been there?' asked Corrigan, changing the subject and pointing to a framed photo of the mosque's enormous courtyard, lit up at night.

'Yes,' said Hanlon. Corrigan waited for more information. None was forthcoming. Hanlon looked back at him silently, unemotionally. Her eye was swelling up and her face was puffy. You need to get some ice on that, he thought. He had a mouthful of his Efes Pilsen beer and waved the waiter over to order another one.

He was beginning to feel thoroughly annoyed with Hanlon, a not uncommon sensation. This silent treatment from her had everything to do with Whiteside. Corrigan knew that she visited him in hospital three times a week. She had been there earlier that evening, before the gym.

Sergeant Mark Whiteside was in a coma, as a result of a shooting. Neither he, Corrigan, personally nor the Metropolitan Police had anything to do with the circumstances relating to it. Corrigan suspected that Whiteside was where he was because of Hanlon and he had the innocent person's natural resentment at being blamed for something of which he was not guilty. Hanlon was always convinced she was in the right, thought Corrigan. The fact that she often was had given her a messianic belief in herself. It was a source of huge strength but one day, thought Corrigan, it'll go horribly wrong. In one

sense, it already had.

Hanlon was very much of the 'act immediately, think later' school. Corrigan suspected that she herself knew that, which is why she relied upon cooler heads like Whiteside and now Demirel.

Not that there was any point raising this with her.

'Do you know Dame Elizabeth Saunders?' he asked now. 'The philosopher?' said Hanlon, surprised.

She did indeed. Dame Elizabeth was someone she revered. Hanlon never read fiction, regarding it as a pointless waste of time, but she was interested in history and philosophy and Dame Elizabeth, an expert on moral and existential philosophy, was one of her favourite writers. And she always felt better educated after reading a Saunders book, even if she disagreed with it.

She also admired how Dame Elizabeth had shouldered her way up the male-dominated world of academia, crunching through glass ceilings like an Arctic ice-breaker. She was high profile too. Dame Elizabeth appeared on book-judging panels, arts programmes, politics and media items on various TV stations.

Corrigan nodded. The Saunders name seemed to have jolted Hanlon out of her foul mood.

'What do you know of her?' he asked.

Hanlon frowned. 'Well, she's a well-known popular philosopher and broadcaster. She taught at Oxford and I've seen her on the TV. She specializes in moral philosophy, what is good and what is bad, that kind of thing, but also she's done quite a bit of government work. I guess that's a result of the moral philosophy. Most recently she was on that inquiry held by the IPCC on how we evaluate mental illness in arrested suspects.' 'I know,' said Corrigan through gritted teeth. 'We're police, not mental-health experts, for heaven's sake.' One of Corrigan's duties was to handle the media and he'd had a grim time recently. Accusations of racism in the Met, corruption, systemic perjury and, as if that wasn't enough, both they and the prison service were facing the consequences of a mental-health policy that left people in need of treatment rather than punishment out at large for the police to deal with.

'Well, we do get more than our fair share of nutters, sir,' said Hanlon.

Corrigan snorted derisively. 'I hadn't realized you had such a caring side, Detective Inspector. You certainly keep it well hidden.'

'Oh, I care, sir,' said Hanlon quietly. 'I care about justice, something Dame Elizabeth has written extensively about.' She paused. 'Do you, sir?'

Hanlon's mind was on Whiteside. Mark Whiteside kept alive by machinery, drips, tubing and a colostomy bag. Whiteside would have particularly hated that last demeaning touch. Even though the perpetrators were dead, she couldn't help but feel they'd got off lightly compared to him. The innocent were punished, the guilty roamed free. Where was the justice in that? Hanlon was hurting, and like any hurt animal she wanted to lash out. Her tone was one of barely veiled anger.

Corrigan restrained a childish urge to kick the table over and storm out. He'd had a terrible day and he really did not need this shit from Hanlon. He closed his eyes and counted to ten. He was on beta blockers for his high blood pressure and he could feel a vein throbbing ominously in his forehead. Ironic if I keeled over here, face down in the hummus, felled by a Hanlon-induced stroke, he thought.

Something must have shown in his face because Hanlon asked, almost meekly for her, 'What about Dame Elizabeth, sir?' It was as close to contrition as she was likely to get.

'Dame Elizabeth, as you may or may not know, is the professor of philosophy at Queen's College here in London,' said Corrigan.

'No, I didn't know that, sir.' 'Well, now you do. She is.'

'Why this interest in philosophy, sir?' asked Hanlon. 'It's very Zen of you.'

Corrigan stifled a smile. Hanlon was one of the few people who dared to tease him. His work persona was one of angry efficiency.

He took the tablet he had on the table next to him and the screen brightened as he searched for something. A photo of a man filled the screen and Corrigan swivelled it round so Hanlon could see.

He was in his mid-thirties, she guessed, with longish, floppy hair, a linen jacket and a scarf that was probably from some Oxford or Cambridge college. It was thrown casually around his neck. She disliked him immediately. He was confident and good-looking, but to Hanlon's eye there was a hint of weakness in the face, the self-deprecating grin a little too forced, with that air that some people have of trying slightly too hard. It was the kind of face that begged people to like him, the kind of person who would smile too much. It was a puzzling mix, arrogance tinged with desperation.

She looked quizzically at Corrigan.

'That,' he said, 'is Dr Gideon Orlando Fuller, who also lectures in philosophy on a five-year contract at Queen's College. Hired by Dame Elizabeth herself. He is a suspect, the main suspect, in the death of this girl, Hannah Moore, who was strangled – either by accident or design – during some sort of S&M-style sex, a week ago. This photo is from her Facebook page.'

Hannah Moore pouted at them provocatively from the screen. It was an attempt to appear sexually alluring, but her face and body were not the stuff of male fantasy. Hanlon looked at her dispassionately.

She was obviously overweight and her heavily made-up eyes were small and piggy in the generous expanse of her face.

She had dyed her hair blonde, but not her dark eyebrows, and at the front the roots showed their true colour. Yet in those eyes, framed by inexpertly applied make-up, was a real look of intelligence. Hanlon shook her head with irritation.

The girl must have known that she looked both slightly pathetic and ridiculous. That *FHM/Loaded* look was not for her, but she'd been desperate enough to try. Why could she not just have settled for quiet dignity; she was a student, not a Page-3 girl.

She looked again at Corrigan. 'And?'

'Hannah Moore was in one of Fuller's evening classes. Dame Elizabeth, who has a lot of clout in the government and civil service, has demanded and received assurances that our investigation will be discreet and low-key.'

'Is that right?' said Hanlon contemptuously. Much as she admired Dame Elizabeth, she didn't see why the Met should be forced to dance to a civil servant's tune, no matter how distinguished.

'Why on earth should we care what Dame Elizabeth thinks?' she asked.

Corrigan looked at her sharply. 'Dame Elizabeth taught the PM at university and also the leader of the Opposition. Oh, and the mayor too. Philosophy was very much in vogue then, it would seem.' He paused, allowing time to absorb the fact that the request for discretion had come from on high. 'She's also a non-exec director of a major newspaper and she is adviser to the civil service pay-review body. Let me repeat myself, Detective Inspector, our investigation will be discreet and low-key.'

'Yes, sir,' she said mutinously.

'Not boring you, am I, DI Hanlon,' said Corrigan sarcastic- ally. 'You don't seem to be concentrating.' He raised his eyebrows and leaned his head forward across the table close to Hanlon's to emphasize the point. He suddenly looked very menacing. Decades ago, when Corrigan had walked the beat, and later in the flying squad, policing had been a lot more physical. He'd always been first choice if a ruck seemed inevitable. 'How do we want the investigation to proceed?'

'Low-key and discreet, sir.'

'Exactly. You will join Fuller's evening class and gather any relevant information that may shed light on this girl's death.'

'And he's the prime suspect?'

Corrigan nodded. 'There's forensic evidence linking him to the scene, and circumstantial evidence. He has no alibi for the time in question. But the officer in charge will fill you in better than I can.'

Hanlon looked sceptical. 'Won't my turning up at his evening class at this point seem a bit suspicious?'

'Not particularly,' said Corrigan. 'Fuller's evening class has to be at least fifteen in number to pay for itself, or it'll be axed. The students will be told that you were at the head of a waiting list, should a vacancy occur, which it manifestly has.' He drank some more of his Efes Pilsen lager, the half-pint glass looking dainty in his huge hand. He beckoned the waiter for another one. He looked at Hanlon's strong-featured, intelligent face. Nobody would question her intellectual capability and he could rest assured that she'd keep her mouth shut. Hanlon never confided in anyone, no risk of any leaks from her. 'That happens to be true. The finance part. Times are tough. Everyone will be pleased with you for saving their class. You're also one of the few officers we have who would look remotely credible on a philosophy course.'

'Really?' said Hanlon sceptically.

'Really,' said Corrigan. 'They'll think you are a militant feminist.'

Hanlon raised her dark, curved eyebrows in surprise.

Corrigan beamed at her.

'Exactly, Hanlon, that's the kind of look we want. Just the ticket. Aggressive scepticism. I knew you'd be perfect. You will be a civil service adviser on a quango for women's equality. That's dull enough as jobs go to stop any questions and you're intimidating enough to block most enquiries. Queen Anne's Gate Human Resources department will authenticate any queries about Ms Rachel Gallagher.'

'That's my name, is it?' said Hanlon.

'That's your name,' said Corrigan. 'Not a million miles removed from your own surname.'

It could be worse, thought Hanlon. And it's not as if I'm being asked to live a part. All I need to do is be a Gallagher for a few hours a week. I can do that. Anything's better than sitting around at home on this endless sick leave.

'And you recommended me for this job, sir? May I ask why?'

'It's a murder investigation, Hanlon,' said Corrigan. 'I thought you'd like it. Also, I find the idea of people using their senior positions to coerce others into having sex with them against their will, as Fuller is alleged to have done, repellent, even if murder is not involved. Do you, DI Hanlon?'

Touché, thought Hanlon. You messed with Corrigan at your peril. One moment you were facing a ponderous, slow-moving, easy-to-predict relic; the next you were lying on your back, wondering just where that punch had come from.

He stood up and gave her a folded piece of paper. 'That's the name of the investigating officer, his nick and the time of your appointment.' He looked around the restaurant with approval. 'Very good food,' he said. 'You can get the bill, Hanlon. I'll be in touch.'

He towered above her. 'Oh, and Hanlon, one more thing.' 'Yes, sir.'

'You're now DCI Hanlon, acting rank until the official confirmation.'

Good God, thought Hanlon, and I suspected I was being measured for the axe. She looked at Corrigan's impassive face. It's down to you, you old bastard, she thought, in a rare moment of affection.

Corrigan saw her left eyebrow rise quizzically, as she digested the news of her promotion. He thought he would spare Hanlon the ordeal of having to express, or not express, gratitude. Both would be equally problematic for her.

'I'll be in touch,' he said.

She shook her head with affectionate irritation, watching his broad back as he threaded his way carefully through the restaurant. He didn't look back.

She unfolded the paper and looked at the name of the investigating officer and his DI and, despite herself, she smiled. You cunning old bastard, she thought.

4

He had woken up wet again. He lay in his bed staring fearfully at the ceiling. There was a clock in his room on the bedside table. It was a little travel clock with a hinge and a case that had belonged to his grandmother. It was one of the few things he did have. The hour and minute hands glowed greenly in the dark with a faint luminosity. The clock had no LED display. It was old, mechanical rather than electronic; you had to wind it up. In order to make it glow properly you had to put it in direct sunlight all day. But he loved it.

The clock told him it was seven in the morning. Please, God, let her not be up. Please, please, God. I'll do anything.

There wasn't a great deal else in his room. His mother had confiscated most of his toys. He had hidden Vulture, a rubber bird he'd won as a prize at a fair, so she couldn't take him away.

He could smell urine, overlaid with the rubberized odour of the special sheet she put on his bed to protect the mattress. He hated the smell of that sheet and its cold, sticky feel. He got up and lifted the duvet. There was an oval-shaped wet patch, but it really wasn't too bad. She probably wouldn't notice.

His pyjama bottoms were sodden, however. He pulled on a pair of underpants. They were too large for him and the elastic had gone in the waist. His mother didn't believe in wasting money on new clothes for him and that included underwear. Everything he wore was second hand.

Holding the Y-fronts up with one hand, the bundled-up pyjamas in the other, he pushed open his bedroom door.

The flat, just off Gloucester Place in central London, was small with two bedrooms, a galley kitchen and a bathroom, all opening on to a central living area. She had been up late with his 'Uncle' Phil, the producer of the show she presented, the BBC's *Let's Dance*. Monica Fuller was one of the arts correspondents. She specialized in dance. 'Big' was Uncle Phil's nickname for her. It stood, as he liked to put it ('and I do like to put it, as the actress said to the bishop,' Phil liked to say), for big hair, big tits, big glasses. His colleagues found the nickname very funny. Uncle Phil was famous for his sense of humour at the Corporation. He was very popular there. He was one of the lads.

The boy looked nervously out at the lounge, where the table was covered with several wine glasses, some half full. She must have had more than one friend round. Hers were easy to identify; they were marked with crescent moons from the very red lipstick she favoured. They'd used a couple of the glasses as an ashtray. Now they were full of a greying mass of sludge and cigarette ends and a couple of roaches from smoked joints. She must still be asleep, he thought, good. I can bury these in the washing basket and wash them later, when she's at work.

He was halfway across the room when the door to her bedroom opened and she appeared.

'What are you doing sneaking around?' she demanded. 'Nothing, Mummy,' he said defensively.

'What's that you've got, give it me.' He handed over the wet trousers, his stomach knotting in fear and misery. Please, God, please let her not be too angry, he prayed. He could smell the stale alcohol and cigarettes on her breath as she leaned over him.

'God, you sicken me, you dirty little sod,' she said with genuine disgust. 'It's no wonder your father left.'

She had on a housecoat with nothing underneath, showing a lot of cleavage. He stared at her large, heavy breasts, blue- veined, with fascinated repulsion.

'I'll have to punish you now,' she said. 'I should have been firmer with you from the word go. Phil says I mollycoddle you.'

She turned and opened the sideboard drawer and took out a heavy, old-fashioned wooden ruler.

'Hold your hand out,' she commanded.

He did as he was told, and six times the pain flared up his arm from his palm as she beat him, making him count out the strokes. Although he was in agony, he refused to cry. He would do that later.

'Now, go to your room so I don't have to look at you, and stop trembling, you pathetic little girl. It's sickening. And don't forget it's your dance class after school. I'd better see some improvement, you're supposed to be my son, for God's sake. You could at least learn to stick to a basic rhythm. It's not exactly difficult, it's not rocket science. Just fucking try, will you, if that's not too much to ask.'

He did as he was told, closing the door gently behind him. He sank down on the floor and cradled Vulture. Now he would let himself cry.

'I hate you,' he whispered to his absent mother. But it wasn't true. He didn't hate her at all. It was himself he knew he should hate. He was bad; he deserved to be punished. He was worthless. It's what he'd been taught and he was a good pupil. He was very diligent.

In the flap of his school satchel was the letter he'd been given from school. It began: Dear Mr and Mrs Fuller, I am delighted to tell you that Gideon has won the class award for outstanding ability.

5

Laura sat at her desk in her room on Staircase Five and looked out of the antique, small, leaded window, its glass divided into diamond shapes, on to the clipped lawns of the inner quad at St Wulfstan's College.

It was her second year at Oxford and Room 2B, Staircase Five, was quite simply the most wonderful place she had ever stayed in her nineteen years on the planet. The college rooms were seventeenth century and she often thought wonderingly, there has been a student like me in here for four hundred years, although obviously not female (the college had only been co-ed for ten years and that was in the teeth of stiff opposition from the dons) and certainly not from a comprehensive school in Northampton. It was like a fairy tale come true, being here. Neot's Avenue where she lived in Northampton was a perfectly pleasant road, wide and relatively traffic-free, the early seventies' houses quite spacious, but my God, was it dull. St Wulfstan's was exciting and not in some kind of unpleasant, semi-fascistic Bullingdon Club way.

She loved her studies, drank endless coffees with her friends, stayed up late and talked and talked. Her college valued her and had given her these rooms as a reward for her tireless good works, foremost in organizing and running the Philosophy Society. Laura was a formidably good organizer.

Laura was quite short and her feet barely reached the floor in the chair she was sitting in. In front of her on the desk was a list of those who would be attending the Philosophy Soc. Seminar she was busy arranging. Some, the keynote speakers, other VIPs and the women attending would get college accommodation. It was a long weekend at St Wulfstan's, in honour of some age-old benefactor, and several students had agreed to let her use their rooms for a small fee. So she was able to dangle cheap college accommodation as an extra incentive to the invitees, particularly the Londoners. She felt sorry for the London students. They had to pay huge amounts of money to live in grotty accommodation; not that Oxford itself was cheap, far from it, so it was a good balancing act to give them this opportunity to stay somewhere nice for once.

Fair, she thought.

She unzipped her Scooby Doo pencil case and took out some brightly coloured felt pens that she carefully lined up in front of her Apple Mac. Some work she preferred doing the old-fashioned way. She got a piece of paper and wrote in her firm, graceful hand, *Dr Gideon Fuller*.

She was so excited that he'd be coming; she had a bit of a crush on Dr Fuller.

6

DI Enver Demirel opened the bedroom door in the student flat off Gower Street. He ushered Hanlon into the small room and gently closed the door behind them.

'This is her room, Hannah's room,' he said. Hanlon looked around her. It was quite spartan. The room had a bed with a table beside it, a built-in wardrobe, a sink and another table that would serve as a desk. There was a bookcase and Hanlon bent forward to examine its contents. There were a few philosophy books, that was to be expected, and a shelf full of self-help books. There was Deepak Chopra, Coelho, Anthony Robbins, *Men Are From Mars*, that kind of thing. There were books about how to organize your day, your life, your relationships and your career. The optimism of the books' subject matter emphasized the sad squalor of Hannah's death. It was the library of a hopeful optimist, of someone determined to get ahead. Hanlon hated murderers. She despised their overwhelming, shallow egotism.

She wanted revenge for Hannah Moore.

There was an open book on the shelf. 'Can I look at this?' she asked.

'Sure, ma'am,' said Enver. 'We're done here.' Enver was delighted with Hanlon's promotion. His own increase in rank, to DI, had put him temporarily on a par with her and he had secretly been dreading the unlooked-for equality.

He couldn't work out what that meant; was he slavishly addicted to following the woman around or was it because it showed their relationship could be rekindled? Oh, who cares, he thought. He did know he felt radiantly happy to be back in the presence of the monosyllabic Hanlon, currently sporting a vicious-looking black eye.

He leaned against the closed door, his muscular arms folded across his expanding midriff, with almost proprietorial pride.

The inquiry into the deaths of the child traffickers in Norfolk had completely exonerated him, and the rescue of the kidnapped child had resulted in his promotion to Detective Inspector. Hanlon's evidence had cast him in a heroic light while taking any blame for breaches of procedure upon herself. Enver had kept Assistant Commissioner Corrigan's part in the matter to himself. He had been rewarded with this promotion. It was deserved, he knew that, but he still had to contend with snide remarks from some of his colleagues that he'd only got it because he was a Muslim, or because he was non-white. Enver placidly asked them if they'd been shot in the line of duty, or how many paedophile rings they had broken up.

Hanlon picked up the Dr Suzy Kirschbaum book that Hannah had been reading. Self-realization through the power of dreams. The contrast between the hopes of Hannah Moore and her sad, undignified death was total. Hanlon felt again a surge of almost homicidal rage against her killer. How dare they do this. It wasn't just the crime, it was the arrogance behind it. It was the way Hannah had been swatted out of existence like an insect.

I'm like the Duracell bunny, she thought, except I'm powered by anger, not by a battery, and I'll keep on going.

I want you, she thought of Hannah's killer, I want you and I'm going to get you.

Enver studied Hanlon covertly while she leafed through the book. She looked fully recovered now from the killing fields that the island had become, he thought. Since that night he had only seen her a couple of times and in all honesty that had hurt. He had felt she was evading him and he didn't know why. But here they were back together as if nothing had happened. He was pleased to see her looking so well and overjoyed to be working with her again.

The dark, tight trousers she was wearing emphasized her long, slim legs. Her white blouse was partially unbuttoned and he could see her collarbone and the sharply defined muscles in her neck as she bent her head. Stray corkscrew curls of her dark, coarse hair fell over her face.

She closed the book and looked at Enver expectantly. He cleared his throat.

'She was found face down here, ma'am, on the bed.' He showed her the relevant photograph on his laptop.

Hanlon looked at the image of the dead girl. Enver stared at the photo mournfully and used the end of a biro as a pointer to indicate the relevant features. Her head was invisible, covered in a black velvet hood like a bag.

'We found several hairs on the outside of the bag that didn't belong to the victim. We have Fuller's DNA on file after a drink-driving conviction five years ago; the hairs were a match.' Hanlon nodded. All of this was in the report she'd read, but she liked to hear it to confirm she'd processed the important facts. Reports tended to be over-detailed in her view, officers worried that they may not have spelled something out clearly enough and so erred in the opposite direction, burying you in a pile of unnecessary details. 'Cause of death?' 'Strangulation, ma'am. Not with a ligature, manually.

There's no sign of any struggle and we're assuming that the killing took place during some sex game. A consensual sex game. There were marks on the victim's buttocks consistent with being beaten, whipped, with something narrow, a cane maybe or a riding crop. There is no evidence of penetration, however, and no semen or other bodily fluids.'

Hanlon looked at Enver for clarification.

He said, 'According to her Facebook wall, her status was that she was in a relationship with two people, male and female, both married. The killing could have been committed by a woman. I'm assuming the victim was face down, the killer sitting on top of the body. She couldn't really struggle. Death wouldn't have taken long, according to the pathologist. Unconsciousness through strangulation can be as quick as fifteen seconds, a minute would be ample.'

'Any ideas as to whether it might be murder, or a sex game gone tragically wrong?' asked Hanlon.

Enver shook his head. 'No. I'd like to think if it was an accident then the other party would have come forward, but these days that'd be too much to ask. Taking responsibility for your actions seems very old-fashioned these days.'

He was an old-fashioned kind of man. Because he had once been a boxer, people assumed he'd be aggressive, in your face. Enver was neither. He'd drifted into boxing as a youth because he'd been shy and timid and his father, a traditionalist from the countryside, a man of simple views, had thought it would make a man of his quiet son. He'd been a very good fighter, a rock-solid chin and a formidable puncher, but never quite good enough. Deep in his heart he knew he lacked that vital something to ever be a champion. He was a good journeyman fighter, top ten maybe, but he'd never strap a belt on. When injury, a detached retina, forced his retirement, he'd gone into the police. Anything but the family restaurant business.

Hanlon nodded. 'Do we have anything else on Fuller?' A sudden image of the man's good-looking but essentially weak face came into her mind. He looked just the kind of person who'd try and evade responsibility.

Enver nodded. 'Hannah Moore was writing a blog about Fuller, claiming that he was an active sexual predator and she was going to stop him. She said that Fuller is into S&M and that he was partly responsible for the death of another student, an Abigail Vickery, some seven years ago. Either a sex game gone wrong or murder, she claimed.'

'So, like this,' said Hanlon.

Enver nodded and continued. 'She also said that when Fuller has sex with a girl he likes to keep a trophy, a cutting of pubic hair and underwear.'

Hanlon looked questioningly at Enver.

'The dead girl had a section of pubic hair absent that had obviously been cut away. Her pants were missing too.'

'Does Fuller have an alibi?' asked Hanlon.

Enver shook his head. 'The murder took place in the afternoon; Fuller says he usually has a siesta at that time. So, no alibi there. Anyway, to cut a long story short, we took him in for questioning, but he lawyered up and we had to release him without charge.'

'So no other evidence, forensic or otherwise?'

'No, ma'am. There used to be a CCTV camera that recorded the street door to this place, but that was removed as an infringement of civil liberties, after a student complained. So, we've no way of knowing who came and went. As for forensic, no. Nothing.'

Enver stroked his moustache. It was full and drooping. He looked at Hanlon. 'Fuller did not dispute the fact that the hood was his, but he said it had gone missing from his briefcase which he keeps unlocked in his office, to which most of the faculty, staff and students have access. He would neither confirm nor deny rumours of his sexual habits, but he emphatically denied having Hannah Moore as a sexual partner. I would have dearly loved a search warrant for his house, to see if that underwear/souvenir collection existed, and if so, was there anything traceable to Hannah? But no way would I have got it.'

'And what about this Abigail Vickery allegation?' asked Hanlon.

'I looked into it, ma'am. The history is appended to the report.' He shrugged. 'It's as Hannah said, but the coroner recorded an open verdict. She was found hanged and she did have a taste for S&M-style bondage sex, but whether or not it was suicide, or a sex game gone wrong, well, who knows? Fuller was her lecturer; he was said to be having an affair with her. Her father kicked up a stink, claimed Fuller had murdered her, but no one seriously believed that.'

Hanlon said speculatively, 'And do you think he did it?' She had a very high estimation of Enver's intelligence.

Enver shrugged. 'I really don't know.' He paused. 'I've interviewed a fair few people and I like to think I'm good at it, but he seemed more outraged than anything that we should think he'd be having sex with Hannah Moore. It was as if she wasn't good enough for him. He certainly showed no sense of pity or sadness that a girl he knew had died, more irritation at having his day disrupted. I do think that if he had done it, he'd have maybe tried harder to cut a more sympathetic figure. Well, you'll be able to judge for yourself tomorrow, anyway.'

'Anything else about him worth mentioning?'

Enver shook his head. 'For what it's worth, I think we should have breath-tested him before we interviewed him. He stank of booze. It would have potentially made anything he did say inadmissible. As it was, his brief took a while to arrive and he didn't say anything anyway, but if he does have a drink problem, it could be relevant. The drink-driving could be symptomatic. It would explain an accident or, if he had a propensity to violence, it might heighten it.'

'That's true,' said Hanlon. 'Well, anyway, I get to meet him soon enough. I'll come back with you now and we'll go through my story again. Corrigan has arranged some business cards and other Home Office related stuff for me, like my work pass and things, so I'll look the part.'

'What are you going to say about your eye, ma'am?' said Enver. Hanlon's left eye was badly swollen and the skin under- neath it turning an interesting colour. Enver guessed more or less correctly what had happened, but it was undoubtedly unfortunate timing.

Hanlon raised a shapely dark eyebrow. 'Nobody will dare ask, Detective Inspector. Believe me.'

7

The philosophy course that Dr Gideon Fuller taught was for part-time students, two hours on Monday, Tuesday and Thursday evenings, and it led to a qualification, a diploma awarded by Queen's College, London, a kind of mini-degree. Dame Elizabeth was a proselytizer. She was a passionate believer in the value of philosophy and wanted to share its virtues with an almost messianic zeal. She was also aware of falling student numbers, probably because of the high cost of tuition fees and a perception that philosophy would have little relevance to finding postgrad. employment. Hence her creation of a reasonably priced year-long course that came with an impressive accreditation.

She had needed a good lecturer, and not only that, one who physically looked good. Ideally she'd have had someone like the French intellectual Bernard Henri Levy, the one with the tousled locks and unbuttoned shirt, but younger. She needed a poster- boy for the department. Fuller, young, gifted, charismatic, had seemed the answer to a prayer.

Academically he was superb. A starred first in philosophy from

Magdalen College, Oxford, a Ph.D. supervised by one of Cambridge University's leading philosophers, two books and articles in *Mind*, the prestigious academic journal, as well as popular journalism and guest spots on *Start the Week* and *The Moral Maze.* Later, of course, she'd been reminded of the old cliché, be careful what you wish for.

Everyone has their flip side. Fuller was no exception. She knew of his background troubles; Fuller had brought the Abigail Vickery allegation up himself. She liked that. He was either very honest or savvy enough to know that it was the kind of story she would have eventually heard about. Either suited Dame Elizabeth just fine.

Besides, she was firmly of the opinion that to produce a pearl, you need grit. Show me someone who has never made a mistake and I'll show you someone who has never tried to do anything difficult or important was a credo she believed in.

One of his colleagues had warned her about rumours of his drinking, but Dame Elizabeth was broad-minded and Fuller was relatively cheap to hire. And until this Hannah Moore business, he'd performed extremely well.

So when he was accused of the murder, Dame Elizabeth pulled strings and arranged for what was, in effect, an internal investigation to take place. She was sure that it would exonerate him.

Hanlon, after attending the first of his lecture/tutorials, could see why he had been hired. Despite what she knew about Fuller, Hanlon was impressed with his teaching abilities in the few lectures she had attended. He was genuinely talented. He managed to be informative and witty without being patronizing. His lessons were that rare combination of being fun and extremely educational. Her classmates, veterans of years of study in one form or another, were uniformly supportive of Fuller. When word had leaked out about his arrest following the Moore murder, more or less everyone took his side.

'That girl was such a bitch.' This comment was from Jessica McIntyre, the alpha-female student. Tall, blonde, wealthy and opinionated, she was the class leader. Most of the other students deferred to her.

It was a predominately female class; there were only three men amongst the students and it was more or less the class opinion.

Hanlon fulfilled another stereotype, the class loner. The group had accepted Hanlon as the kind of oddity that you get in every classroom, yet cool by virtue of not wanting to belong, not caring if she were liked or not.

Hanlon had stamped her authority on the class from the moment she opened her mouth. Fuller had asked her name.

'My name is Gallagher,' she had said.

'I know your surname,' said Fuller mildly, 'Would you like to tell us your first name?'

'No,' said Hanlon simply. She spoke quietly but there was no mistaking the forceful resolve. The class started to pay close attention now. It was a direct challenge to Fuller's authority, to his control of the class, and everyone knew it. A ripple of interest ran through the students. Hanlon stared intimidatingly at Fuller, her swollen black eye adding a threatening note.

'Would you care to share your reasons with us?' said Fuller. He smoothed his hair with the palm of his hand as he spoke, as if to reassure himself it was still there. It was a gesture he often made when he was nervous. Teachers hate having their authority tested. If you start to lose that, everything can unravel. The question was an attempt to wrest his hold over the students back from Hanlon. The strain between the two of them was palpable, like the electrical charge in the air before a thunderstorm.

'My name was given to me by a man,' said Hanlon, keeping to the feminist script provided by Corrigan. 'It's a phallocentric gender construct. I chose to reject it.'

Relief washed through Fuller. Thank God, he thought. He could debate gender politics till the cows came home. He had done so on numerous occasions. He could do it on autopilot. It was safe, familiar ground. Familiar comforting names like Luce Irigaray, Bordo and Lloyd swirled round his head. This was much more like it. Not like naked disobedience from stu- dents. He'd dreaded being told to mind his own business. A dozen years in the lecture hall and tutorial room had left him with a keen sense of which battles to fight and which to bow gracefully out of. He just knew that Hanlon would never back down. Fuller was a good judge of character and he could tell that she was a fighter.

The Hannah Moore business had shaken him and he was not as self-confident as usual. He felt twitchy and paranoid, that people were discussing him behind his back. These weren't unusual feelings but they were magnified greatly as a result of the police questioning. The last thing he wanted was a trouble- making student. Just one could ruin the comfortable dynamic of his class.

'Fine,' he said with one of his winning smiles. 'We'll be covering gender isssues later in the term. Now,' he clicked a key on his laptop and a selection of quotations appeared on the interactive whiteboard screen, 'could you work with your neighbour and match these quotes on the nature of reality with,' another keyboard click, 'these names of philosophers. Five minutes. Go!'

Hanlon too was pleased with her answer, but it established her credentials, gave her a reputation as one not to be messed around with and neatly avoided her having to give her name, something she never did in her own life. She happily settled down with her neighbour, a woman from legal, ensuring compliance in the energy sector, to discuss their questions.

Across the classroom a shrewd pair of hard, brown eyes studied Hanlon appraisingly. Stephen Michaels, a man used to judging quality points, in his work, liked very much what he saw.

At the end of the first lesson some of the class had elected to go for drinks in a pub locally. Hanlon was invited, her colleagues in slight awe of the mysterious stranger and wanting to get to know her better, but she declined.

Socializing could wait. She was keen to observe Fuller.

Hanlon was a great believer in following people, something she was very good at, and she intended to follow Fuller. You could learn a huge amount about their character from the way a person behaved when they thought they were unobserved.

She had watched as Fuller had dropped his briefcase off in his small room that adjoined the classroom. The two were connected by a door that she noticed he didn't bother locking, then he headed off towards the lifts. It was a significant indicator that he might have told Enver the truth. Anyone could have had access to Fuller's office. Anyone could have searched his bag and desk.

Hanlon had run down the stairs ahead of the lift, which was showing its age in lack of speed, and waited outside the huge art deco building that was Queen's College, designed by Charles Holden in the thirties and looking like a gigantic, elongated Mayan pyramid thrusting into the sky, a backdrop straight from Fritz Lang's *Metropolis*. Inside it still had many of its vintage fittings; it was like being inside a thirties' ocean liner. It was a hymn to plywood, concrete and tubular steel.

Students of all nationalities, shapes and sizes walked past her, and for a moment she wondered if she'd managed to miss him. Then she saw his Byronic profile appear. More than a few students greeted him as he strolled across the square towards the main road. He was obviously well known.

She followed Fuller as he turned into Gower Street and walked northwards, head bowed as if tired and depressed, towards King's Cross.

Despite its refurbishment, King's Cross, to Hanlon's jaded police eyes, meant cheap prostitutes, very much down on what- ever little luck they had, dodgy drug deals and alcohol-fuelled violence in the grotty pubs that surrounded the station. The kind of pubs that had low-level blue lighting in the toilets, so junkies would find it harder to jack up in the cubicles. Great strides had been made to clean the place up and the restored St Pancras Hotel and British Library lent a welcome touch of class to the area, but it was still King's Cross. You might situate Google's new headquarters here, but it was still King's Cross. You can put lipstick on a pig, but it's still a pig.

It's an ancient part of London. It had been inhabited from time immemorial; there had even been an ancient river cros- sing of the Fleet River here. The river is now bricked over and culverted, but its filthy waters still flow below the shiny new buildings and Hanlon, who knew her subterranean London, thought it wouldn't surprise her at all if the whole area wasn't slightly cursed.

As below, so above.

Hanlon hoped that cheap sex was the reason for him being there, but Fuller had ignored the whores and the few sex stores that managed to linger despite the steep rental rises in the area, and then disappeared into the Uunderground, followed by Hanlon.

He caught the Piccadilly Line, to where he lived in Finsbury Park. She'd cycled through it just a few days before.

A blameless academic returning home at the end of a worthy day.

She followed him from the station, back to his nondescript flat, and watched from across the road as he let himself in. The journey had taken about thirty minutes, door to door. It would take about the same time from Hannah's bedsit, easily done. An hour out of his day would be all the time that Fuller would need to kill and get safely back home.

. . .

After the lesson the following Tuesday, Hanlon went for a drink with several of her classmates to a nearby pub. They'd by now become characters as well as known faces to her. The legal woman she sat next to was there, as was alpha woman, Jessica. They were all women apart from one man. He rarely spoke in class and she couldn't remember his name, apart from the fact it was unremarkable. Someone asked her what she did and Hanlon replied, 'I'm a consultant on EU Proposed Directive on Gender Equality Rights (491).' She was wearing her Home Office security pass on its lanyard as if it were a talisman to ward off awkward questions. It worked. As Corrigan had predicted, everyone's eyes glazed over.

The hot topic was still the murder of Hannah Moore, which was being picked over with the kind of relish only reserved for the death of someone whom nobody had really liked. The general consensus was that the police were baffled, Fuller was innocent, if foolish, and that Hannah probably had herself to blame. Her blog was at last being read and discussed, but not in a way she would have wanted.

Hanlon noticed that the only person not to join in the general character assassination was also the only man in the group. He was tall, slim, dark and balding, with a closely trimmed beard. She guessed he might have Spanish blood in him because his eyes were a Mediterranean brown, as was his skin. He was ascetic-looking, with slightly saturnine features. He was dressed for the office in a suit and tie, but Hanlon's eyes, sharp as ever, were drawn to his hands. They were slim and strong-looking, the wrists below the cuffs of his striped shirt, powerful. His fingernails were trimmed very short, and on his hands there were several deep, ugly cuts; on the inside of his left wrist, a painful-looking red weal where the new skin had regrown.

She also noticed his body, which had a swimmer's build – tall, rangy, with muscular shoulders. He's very powerfully built, she thought.

He caught her eye looking at him and he smiled warmly. 'I'm Stephen Michaels. I work at Queen's.'

His voice was deep and he had a northern accent she couldn't place – accents were not something she was good at – a cross she thought between Liverpool and Manchester.

'Are you a lecturer?' she asked. He certainly didn't look like one. He shook his head and opened his hands in a rueful, revealing kind of gesture. 'I'm one of the chefs here. This is my chance to get some culture.'

He smiled again. 'I get staff discount,' he said.

He had startlingly attractive eyes, assured and watchful. Hanlon found herself warming to him. He had that kind of hard, self-deprecating self-confidence that she found very attractive. She spent her life dealing with people, both police and criminals, who seemed to feel the need to act tough. She was so tired of people's lies and that included the image that people liked to project. Sometimes she felt like screaming, just stop it will you. Stop the bullshit. It was refreshingly unusual to be with someone free of macho bluster. Hanlon hated it. If you

can walk the walk, you simply don't need to talk the talk.

She looked more closely at him. Like calls to like, type to type. Hanlon had issues herself and she sensed that Michaels really wasn't the kind of man you wanted to argue with.

When she was a child she could remember there'd been a craze for T-shirts with slogans. 'Just Do It,' had been one. Just do it. It was a sentiment she believed in absolutely. She felt instinctively that Michaels was in the same camp.

Don't talk about it, just do it. And if you can't do it, as her old boss DCI Tremayne had succinctly put it, 'Give up and get a fucking paper round.'

Jessica McIntyre was still on the subject of Hannah Moore. 'And my God, that girl was a liar, and a fantasist too. You can't believe a word she ever said. All this nonsense on her blog about Gideon being some sort of bondage addict.' She shook her head disapprovingly. 'They say you can't libel the dead, they should have added something about the dead not being allowed to libel the living. She was sex-obsessed. She'd jump

on anything that moved.'

'I liked her,' said Stephen Michaels.

Jessica gave him a baleful look, her eyes a glacial blue under the waterfall of platinum blonde hair. She was extremely attract- ive in a highly manicured, cared-for way. Michaels returned her look evenly and carried on.

'She had a good heart,' Michaels continued, unmoved by Jessica McIntyre's disapproval. 'Did you know she used to volunteer for one day a week at Battersea Dogs Home?'

'Well, she'd have felt quite at home there then,' said Jessica unpleasantly. She stood up to leave, swinging her expensive handbag, its *LV* initials shining in the light of the pub, on to her cashmere-adorned shoulder with easy grace.

Hanlon looked at her in a calculating way. Two lovers, Hannah had mentioned, one a woman and married. There was a wedding band on Jessica's finger. She was about forty, Hanlon guessed, but lithe and athletic, the kind of girl who'd have been games captain and probably head of house while Hannah languished on the subs bench or was sent for a cross- country run with the other no-hopers. She had the air of being very much the kind of woman who was used to getting her own way, to being in control.

She could well imagine Jessica tying someone up; she was naturally dominant.

'Well, I'm off. My husband'll be back from the trading floor soon, I'd better go and rustle him up some food. See you all next week.' She tossed her head and her long, blonde hair swished imperiously.

'Bye-bye, Mrs McIntyre,' said Michaels. His voice emphasized the 'Mrs' in a pointed way. She glared at him venomously and strode off and out of the pub, her heels clicking on the tiled floor. Momentarily, Hanlon wondered if the two of them had some kind of history together. It was that kind of look, enraged familiarity with a hint of carnality. Stephen took a mouthful of Peroni beer and shook his head. 'What a bitch.' he said quietly for Hanlon's ears only. 'The trading floor! Will you listen to the woman.' He mimicked her voice. 'Rustle up some food.'

'You two don't much like each other then,' said Hanlon. He took another mouthful of beer and shook his head.

'No,' said Michaels, 'I think she's a snob. Maybe it's because she's a teacher at some exclusive girls' school and she looks down her nose at me. I do, let's not forget, work in a kitchen. I'm one of the hoi polloi.' He laughed easily but there was an edge to it. 'Let's put it this way, Hannah was not the only sex- obsessed one around here. Or who reputedly swings both ways.' 'Oh,' said Hanlon. It was surprisingly easy to imagine Jessica

McIntyre as sexually rapacious.

They sat together in a companionable silence for a while and then Michaels asked her some easy-to-answer questions about her work, more out of politeness than interest. Hanlon asked him about his. He was in charge of supervising the banqueting and canteen chefs, and worked with the head chef on the fine- dining evenings. Hanlon wasn't paying much attention either. Nothing about food, other than its dietary value, interested her. She particularly disliked cookery programmes and people who described themselves as 'foodies'. She had her own descriptive words for them.

She let him go on, until finally she got the chance to ask, 'What do you think of Fuller?'

'Well,' said Michaels, 'he's good at his job and that's the main thing, but I think he's a creep personally and if I was a woman I wouldn't want to be alone in the same room as him.' 'Why's that then?' asked Hanlon, with feigned, lazy

curiosity.

Michaels said offhandedly, 'Hannah mentioned once or twice that he belonged to some kind of weird bondage club that he went to on a Thursday evening. I don't think it's the kind of club that specializes in middle-age swingers. Hannah said it was hard-core. Jessica McIntyre may say it's a load of old hooey but if you ask me, Fuller looks like just the sort of sad-sack pervert who'd be into that kind of thing. I mean, I'm all in favour of live and let live and God alone knows, I've met enough weirdos in kitchens in my time, but who cares what a chef gets up to, it's not relevant, unless it becomes a hygiene issue, but I think there should be standards for teachers. It's a position of responsibility and it's open to abuse.'

He drained the bottle of Peroni and stood up.

'Not that anyone gives a monkey's what I think, particularly not Dame Elizabeth. She's full of the rights of man, but try getting a pay rise for you and your staff and it's a different standard altogether.' He grinned and shook his head ruefully. 'Anyway,' he said, 'I'll be off.' He yawned. 'I've got a canapé party for fifty members of the philosophy faculty to prepare for tomorrow, I'd better go.'

Hanlon watched him walk out of the pub with a long-legged easy grace. His jacket was closely tailored and Hanlon could see that he had an excellent figure. She wondered why he disliked Fuller quite so much. Maybe it was simply a reaction to Jessica's endorsement of the man but she felt there was more to it than that. There was a real undercurrent of hostility in his voice.

She shook her head and gently ran a finger along the ridge of scar tissue under her thick hair. It was where she'd had the skin split open a few months ago when she'd been knocked unconscious. She found herself touching the healed wound whenever she was deep in thought. She had also managed to get her friend and partner Whiteside shot in the head and Enver Demirel nearly killed.

She smiled bitterly to herself. At least during this investigation things should be risk-free.

8

Dr Gideon Fuller shrugged up the collar of his raincoat and stepped quickly along Gower Street; it ran arrow straight from the Euston Road in the centre of London down to the British Museum. This was university land. More or less every building of the featureless, ugly street was connected with academia.

It was the land of Bloomsbury, spiritual and physical home of Virginia Woolf and her sister Vanessa Bell, the artist, of Maynard Keynes, Lytton Strachey and Roger Fry, the art critic. Fuller always felt uplifted by their rarefied ghosts. Like them, he felt morally, intellectually and spiritually superior to the mere mortals who surrounded him.

It was also the street where Hannah Moore had lived, dreamed, loved and died. That was something Fuller managed to successfully ignore. Compassion was not part of his vocabulary.

Fuller didn't believe in love.

He didn't notice the slim figure of Hanlon following him, with her customary expertise. She had a natural ability to blend in with the background when it suited her. They had now reached the top end of Gower Street and she could see the British Museum, its great dome floodlit against the inhospitable dark of the wet night. Cars and black taxis swished by on the rain-drenched road. Fuller crossed the road into Store Street, heading for the major thoroughfare of the Tottenham Court Road, Hanlon a dark, insubstantial wraith behind him. Now she could see the lights of Centre Point, the landmark sixties' office block, glistening through the rain.

She had nearly caught up with him and she was forced to conceal herself in the shadows of Heal's Furniture Store. Then, once Fuller had crossed the road, she ran after him as he disappeared down one of the side streets into Fitzrovia.

If Bloomsbury was famous as a kind of dessicated, intellectual powerhouse, then Fitzrovia, a warren of narrow streets and restaurants and pubs, had been well known for hellraising, famous for drunken writers, drunken artists and generally dissolute behaviour. Like everywhere in London now, money was having a sterilizing effect and it was becoming sanitized, characterless.

On one level, Hanlon disapproved, but London was a city of permanent change, so it made little sense to complain. Nevertheless the steady erosion of the past saddened her. She didn't have any relatives and she often wondered if her love of London history was an attempt to forge some kind of identity. I've created a family of historical ghosts, she thought, following Fuller at a ten-metre distance from the opposite pavement.

Fuller didn't linger. He was moving south towards Oxford Street and Hanlon noticed that his stride had lengthened, his back straightened and he'd started playing with his hair again, like he did in class. He radiated excitement. She guessed that the end of their journey was near in the gathering darkness.

What Hanlon didn't know was that while her thoughts were full of Fuller, by some strange parallel symmetry, his thoughts were full of Hanlon.

As he walked the slick, wet streets of central London, Fuller was involved in a sexual fantasy, in which he brutally ordered Hanlon to undergo various painful and humiliating acts. Fuller had a very vivid imagination. He was still smarting from his run-in with Hanlon over her name.

Bloody lesbian civil servant, he thought angrily, I'll show you retribution. Women are all the same, they need disciplining. You need a good Teacher. That's how he liked to think of himself. As a Teacher. The word 'lecturer' was arid, sterile. It gave an image of someone standing behind a lectern, reading from notes. He didn't lecture; he taught. He taught people things in class and he liked to think he taught the women in his life to respect him. And if they didn't, they needed correction. He liked the word 'correction'. He corrected essays, he corrected mistakes, he corrected women when they needed it.

His thoughts moved away from the pornographic fantasies, to the practicality of how to get a good few photos of her on his phone. Once he'd done that, he'd be able to transfer them to his PC and Photoshop her head on to suitable-looking images from his S&M pornography collection. How best to take the photos, though? He waited in the rain for a break in the traffic and for inspiration.

She was no idiot, that was for sure. He'd have to blindfold her, or make her wear a hood. He couldn't take those hard, grey eyes looking at him; it would unman him.

Hanlon watched Fuller's back as he crossed Oxford Street from Rathbone Place into the seedy underworld of Soho. This was London at its most bohemian and raffish. She followed Fuller across the small, green expanse of Soho Square and into Dean Street. Hanlon knew the area in incredible detail. She could almost have found her way around Soho blindfold. Despite the bad weather, Soho's narrow streets were full, its pavements crowded and noisy with chatter, its myriad restaurants busy. The pubs they passed, the Pillars of Hercules, the Carlisle Arms, the Crown and

Two Chairmen, the Dog and Duck, were busy and gaggles of hipsters with beards and tight trousers and women from the production and media companies of Soho, drawn here for an evening out, were hanging outside the bars smoking, and not just cigarettes. Several times she wrinkled her nose against the strong smell of skunk drifting through the wet night air; she passed laughing and chattering groups of businessmen and women staggering along the streets. Older media types – balding, fat, offsetting the advancing years with expensive glasses, too-tight red trousers emphasizing their paunches, and pointy shoes – drank too heavily and laughed too loud and too desperately.

Down the road was Old Compton Street, with its gay bars and discos, where she occasionally used to go with Mark. Bouncers were standing outside the gay clubs, the same shape and build, and with the same haircuts as a lot of their muscle- Mary clients. There was a transgender bar in Brewer Street where she used to drink occasionally and Madame JoJo's, the famous drag bar.

Open doorways with handwritten signs promised massages upstairs with young models.

Strip clubs designed for the expense-accounted businessman, like Stringfellows or the Windmill.

Clip joints for the unwary Soho tourist.

Soho whispered *sex* the way the City whispered *money*. And it spoke in many languages and many accents, and right now it was speaking to Fuller.

Loud and clear.

Fuller disappeared into an alleyway just off Dean Street. It was journey's end, Fuller's destination. Hanlon knew the alley went nowhere. Once, years ago, as a rookie PC, she'd hidden in the alley waiting to nick street drug dealers. A tramp had pissed over her shoe. Very little had changed. Now she noted the three cameras pointing their electronic eyes to cover its entrance and immediately decided to return the following day. She did not want Fuller catching sight of her on a monitor inside the building.

She lingered just long enough to see which of the three doors facing on to the alley Fuller used, and then she disappeared into the neon-rich Soho night, with its explicit promise of sleaze, sex, drugs, alcohol and oblivion.

9

Like a raddled, old whore or an ageing rent boy, a brothel at ten o'clock in the morning is not at its best. Even Soho itself had felt tired and lethargic, with hardly anyone around. Bleary- eyed front-of-house staff stood outside pubs and restaurants, smoking and drinking coffee, delivery vans blocked streets and the only people looking as if they weren't nursing hangovers were the cyclists.

Hanlon wrinkled her nose at the strong smell of urine in the alleyway where Fuller had disappeared the night before. It had taken her about five minutes of intermittent pounding on the heavy red-painted door to get anyone to open it.

A burly, unshaven man, smelling of stale sweat, cheap, penetrating cologne and cigarette smoke, dressed in a tracksuit, stood with his aggressive, stubbled face revealed in the gap between door and frame. He said something unintelligible in heavily accented English. Hanlon was in no mood to waste time. Warrant card in her right hand, she shouldered the door aside, its heavy base scraping the man's hairy, naked feet. He protested angrily, rubbing his injured foot with an expression of outrage.

'Police, you big Eastern European baby,' Hanlon said to him. 'I want to speak to the manager.'

She shook her head in mild disbelief at what she'd just said.

The manager. She sounded like she was in John Lewis. She looked around her.

She wasn't in John Lewis.

She was standing in a small entrance hall with a front desk and a couple of armchairs against the wall opposite. There were three monitors on the wall showing the alleyway, the images clicking jerkily this way and that as the cameras changed angle, on the other side of the door.

Beyond the desk were a couple of ormolu chairs and a rug on the floor; in front of them a richly carpeted staircase twisted upwards. The colours of the furniture and wallpaper were dark, black, gold, crimson. Hanlon guessed that at night the place would look mysterious, darkly erotic. At this time of day, however, the cracks showed.

You could see where the paint was peeling, where the Persian rug was frayed, the odd cobweb in the cornice. The place reeked of stale smoke, alcohol, cheap perfume and sex. It smelled of what it was.

The man stood there still, rubbing his sore foot against his other leg in an aggrieved way.

'Vot are you vanting?' The accent was Eastern European, the tone unhelpful.

'I want to speak to whoever's in charge and I want to do it now, or I'll nick you,' said Hanlon, annoyed.

'On vot charge!' protested the man.

'Obstructing a Police Officer in the Execution of His Duty,' said Hanlon. She leaned over the desk. Amongst the paper- work, there was an ashtray with several cigarette ends and a half-smoked joint. 'And knowingly permitting the consumption of drugs on licensed premises contrary to the 1971 Misuse of Drugs Act.' She straightened up. 'That good enough for you?'

There was a heavy silence for a minute or so while the Slav pondered what to do about Hanlon. She started drumming her fingers on the top of the desk impatiently.

A door by the side of the stairs concealed by a mirror opened. 'I'm in charge,' said a woman quietly, standing framed in the now revealed doorway. Hanlon looked at her. She was an imposing sight. Tall and bulky, she was dressed in a pink, silk dressing gown. She was wearing fluffy slippers to match. Hanlon introduced herself and the big woman scrutinized her proffered ID carefully.

'Do come through and join me, Officer,' she said. Her accent was London, through and through, and her tone imperious.

She ushered Hanlon into the room behind her. Hanlon felt like Alice in Wonderland following this apparition into the concealed back room. Her host gestured in a make-yourself- comfortable kind of way and Hanlon sat down in a small, lace- draped armchair in an overly chintzy small room, looking at the 'Manager and Proprietress, dearie,' of the Krafft Club, Soho.

It was a strange room, more like the drawing room of an old lady than of a manageress in the vice trade.

Copies of Victorian sentimental pictures, like *Bubbles* and some depressed-looking Highland cattle *On Rannoch Moor* hung on the walls, and there were shelves of porcelain figures, shepherdesses, twenties-style flappers, that kind of kitsch. Once again, it struck Hanlon that it was the sort of room that should have belonged to an elderly spinster. Knowing it was on the premises of a sex business made it seem sinister. It was as if the rosebud and cupid statuary were masking some unpleasant secret.

At first glance, Hanlon had mistaken the madam for a drag queen. It was an easy mistake to make. The woman in front of her was not conventionally feminine. Iris Campion – 'Like the flower, but not as pretty' – was at least six foot tall and burly with it. She had massive, flabby arms, revealed by the short-sleeved dressing gown, like a shot-putter gone to seed. Hanlon, though, a good judge of physique, guessed there was still a great deal of strength under there. Her hair was close-cropped and dyed a henna-red; her face, mannish, good-naturedly brutal. Two deep scars, one on each cheek, were clearly visible. Hanlon guessed they'd been put there as a punishment, at some stage in her life.

Campion must have divined what Hanlon was thinking because she laughed. It was a self-mocking laugh, designed to deflect any sympathy, but Hanlon could feel the sadness underlying it.

'Looking at my beauty marks are you, DCI? I was sixteen when that was done. Bit of a career handicap for a young tart, eh? Damaged goods, you might say.'

Her voice was hard, and so were her brown eyes, but just momentarily, a flicker of pain ran across the woman's face and Hanlon felt she had a sudden glimpse of a terrified sixteen- year-old, a child, being held down by at least one man, while another carefully sliced through the flesh on her cheeks. The scars were ruler-straight, sharp-edged. It showed practice.

He'd have used something like a Stanley knife or even an old-fashioned cut-throat razor, thought Hanlon. 'Striping', it was called. She remembered, years ago, being in a north London pub with an old-fashioned DCI – DCI Norman Tremayne, that was his name – who'd been her boss at the time. One of the regulars had been striped for trying to stop some kids vandalizing his car. Which one was it? Hanlon had asked in all innocence. The DCI had rolled his eyes and pointed at a bunch of guys standing by the bar, one of them with both cheeks covered with wadded surgical dressings taped into place.

'Take a wild guess, Hanlon,' he'd said wearily.

Then the madam's professional face, a face as concealing as any mask, was clamped on again. Hanlon suddenly knew, with a flash of clarity, that she'd be furious if she thought Hanlon might pity her.

'So you moved into bondage then,' said Hanlon briskly. It made a great deal of sense, sex where your face could be covered, or where facial scarring itself would be arousing for some.

There's a market for everything.

Iris nodded. 'You're not thick are you, dear,' she said. She reached behind her to a small table and undid a bottle of Macallan whisky, adding a quadruple to the coffee in its china cup. Breakfast of champions, thought Hanlon.

'There's a market for everything,' Iris said, as if reading her thoughts. It was the Scotch that had done for Tremayne, she thought. Towards the end, you could smell him coming from fifty metres away. She wondered if they'd ever known each other, they were of a similar generation.

'Now, tell mother what brings you here.' She smiled sardonically at Hanlon. 'Please tell me you'd like a job, you'd be a fantastic domme. I saw the way you handled Yuri.'

'Dr Gideon Fuller,' said Hanlon, not wasting any time. 'I'm not sure I feel like discussing our clients, if indeed we have anyone by that name on our books. We're not a knocking shop, dearie. We're a private members' club, Detective Chief Inspector. Surely you know I'm not going to discuss my membership lists.'

Hanlon nodded. What else was Campion going to say. 'It's up to you,' Hanlon said with a shrug. 'But if you want

a full Health and Safety audit, including fire regs, if you want me to get the council to check that you're complying fully, without deviation, with whatever licence you're operating under, if you want a couple of uniforms posted in the street outside to "reassure" your clients and, of course, I'd be dropping by regularly, then you go right ahead and not discuss him. It's a free country. The choice is yours.'

Campion looked at Hanlon. She was a good judge of character and she could see from the other woman's face she would not back down. A fight with Hanlon would mean trouble. Campion knew what trouble looked like when she saw it looming.

She made her mind up. It wasn't a fight worth having. She nodded. 'OK. Fair enough. What do you want to know?'

'General background,' said Hanlon. 'That'll do for now.'

Campion sipped her whisky-freighted coffee. 'Well, our good doctor is a classic dom. That means, as you can guess, he likes to be totally in charge. That's in general.'

'So the women do what they're told,' said Hanlon. Campion nodded.

'They do what they're told, or he punishes them. And of course it goes without saying that the girls make sure he gets to punish them. He also has his own special preferences. He's really into AgePlay, which for him means teacher/student relationships and also breath control.'

'Do you mean strangulation?' asked Hanlon. It was obvious she wasn't talking about yoga. *Pranayama*, that was the term, she thought.

The madam nodded. 'Exactly. Just make-believe, obviously. But he does like to be dominant, which is not always the case. Particularly with teachers. They usually get enough of that at work. We get all sorts here, obviously,' she said, shrugging her shoulders. 'But you'd be surprised how many bottoms or subs we get.' Hanlon looked puzzled.

'Submissives,' Campion explained. 'We get a lot of them. Dr Fuller, though, well, let's just say I've had to have a word with him on occasion. He's certainly not submissive. Some of the girls complained; he can get a little too rough. Is that what this is about?'

'In a sense,' said Hanlon guardedly. 'You mentioned AgePlay, student/teacher role-play. Might that include peculiar sexual favours for higher marks, that kind of thing? In a role-play sense.'

She was thinking of Abigail Vickery, Fuller's possible first victim. Had he blackmailed her into sex? Could that have happened with Hannah Moore?

'But of course,' said Campion, matter-of-factly. 'Art reflects life, so does sex. You should know that, DCI Hanlon. If it happens in real life, it will absolutely happen here, and if it happens here it'll probably happen in reality.' She sipped her Scotch. 'It's the circle of life.'

Hanlon nodded thoughtfully. 'How plausible would it be to suggest someone like Dr Fuller would strangle someone accidentally?'

'Very unlikely,' said the madam firmly. 'S&M fans are big on contracts and consensus. We use safe-words a lot. There's no mystique to it, just common sense.'

'But accidents happen?'

'Very few in S&M, Detective Chief Inspector Hanlon.' There was a knock on the door and Campion said, 'Come.'

A tall man, naked but for a leather thong and a black face mask, shuffled into the room. His feet were shackled together with a section of chain. The mouth of the mask was closed with a zip.

Campion was watching Hanlon. The policewoman's face remained expressionless.

'Have you cleaned my bedroom?' asked Campion menacingly. The cowled figure nodded. 'The bathroom?' A shake of the head, then a gesture towards its mouth. It, Hanlon thought, not he. Reification it was called, she seemed to remember, treating people as things.

She wondered if Fuller thought of his women in the same way. Things not people. Was that why Hannah Moore had been hooded, so he hadn't found it necessary to look at her face as he killed her?

Would he have been unable to meet her gaze as his fingers crushed her windpipe? Did the simulated violence mask a desire for real violence? Like taking off a mask to reveal another mask.

She guessed that the appearance of this man was a lesson from Campion, a window into her world.

It was a stage-managed world, the realm of S&M. It was a world devoid of chance, a scripted world like an intricate, violent sexual dance with its own steps and its own music, the music of pain, the rhythm of control.

'Oh, of course,' Campion said and the figure leaned forward, while she unzipped its mouth. It bowed in gratitude and disappeared. The door closed gently behind it.

Hanlon looked at the madam.

'He'll need his tongue to clean properly,' Campion said, looking challengingly at Hanlon. 'Does that shock you, Detective Chief Inspector?'

She leaned forward in her chair, so their faces were almost touching. Hanlon could smell the whisky on her breath, her stale perfume and a faint sheen of perspiration. Campion reached out a finger and gently touched Hanlon's swollen eye.

'And how did you get that beauty?' she asked softly, almost tenderly.

Hanlon didn't move. She returned the other woman's stare dispassionately, her grey eyes looking into the slightly bloodshot brown ones of her host. It was like some kind of test, a peculiar kind of intimacy, the iron wills of the two women almost audibly clashing. Then suddenly, as quickly as it started, it was over. Campion nodded. The test was over. Hanlon stood up; it was time to go.

'I'd be very careful with Dr Fuller if I were you,' she said to the madam.

'If I were you,' repeated the other woman scornfully. 'If I were you.' There was no mistaking the bitterness in the intonation now.

She suddenly stood up with a speed and a lightness of which Hanlon would never have imagined her capable. 'You,' she said contemptuously, pointing a forefinger at Hanlon, 'you have no fucking idea what it's like to be me, no fucking idea at all, and pray to God you never will.' Her voice was very quiet, very threatening. She looked down at Hanlon; she was a good few inches taller.

'Before you leave, DCI Hanlon, do me a favour.' Hanlon looked at her. 'Just lift your shirt up for me a few inches.'

Hanlon unzipped the light jacket she was wearing, reached down and pulled up her blouse, exposing the skin from the waistband of her trousers to the base of her ribs. It was a riot of blue and purple bruising. Sparring or no sparring, Jay had certainly left his mark. She pulled her shirt back down.

The other woman nodded to herself, as if having had a suspicion confirmed and asked, 'What happened to the person who did that?' Hanlon shrugged, her silence eloquent. As she turned and left the room, she heard the sound of the whisky bottle being opened and Campion's voice.

'It's not just Fuller that likes hurting people is it, DCI Hanlon? Who are you to judge us? Eh? Who the fuck are you to decide?' Hanlon walked out of the Dean Street brothel into a bright

Soho morning that did not reflect her thoughts.

Who am I? she thought. I wish I knew.

10

Hanlon decided to eat in the university canteen on Tuesday lunchtime. She'd put in a couple of hours at the gym, followed by a five-mile run, and wanted something different to eat to vary her monotonous diet of lightly grilled chicken, pasta and salads. She also had an ulterior motive. She was hoping she might come across Michaels.

Hanlon had developed a keen interest in the chef. She liked the way he seemed to view the world, with a wry yet tough amusement. She felt he would make an admirable witness, reliable and trustworthy. She was also conscious of the fact that they were getting nowhere with the Hannah Moore killing. Michaels was someone who had known Hannah. He knew the philosophy class and he knew Fuller. Indeed, technically, both employed by the university, they were colleagues. She felt that his input could prove very useful. He knew Fuller's work reputation and since so much time is spent in the workplace, he would be aware not only of his own dealings with the man but those of other staff members. She fully intended to benefit from this.

The university canteen was better than she'd envisaged. It was large, airy and open-plan, with a kitchen that gleamed in a space-age way, where you could see the chefs working. The food was far better than anything available at a police canteen, where everything seemed stodgy or fried, despite endless initiatives designed to help those in the Met lose weight.

There must have been a couple of hundred students in the hall and it made her feel old and dowdy. She'd never particularly cared about clothes and she suddenly realized that the students probably thought she was somebody's mother. She found the idea disquieting. Hanlon was used to being the centre of attention. At work, her reputation preceded her and as a woman she was in a minority. Not here, at Queen's College. Here she was a nobody. She felt slightly deflated and began to wish she hadn't come.

It wasn't just the age difference, although most of the students looked absurdly young with unlined faces and gravity-defying bodies. Hanlon thought, the main difference between me and them is really one of optimism. They're looking forward to everything, but what have I got? Job satisfaction at best. I arrest people, she thought gloomily, and I spend my time with lowlifes and criminals. The rest of the time I spend with the police. It was sometimes hard to tell which was more dispiriting.

She had chosen a table nearest the open-plan kitchen, so that if Michaels did show up, he could see her. Although the canteen was crowded, her table was empty. She had attributed this to the fact that she was older than the students, looking like someone's mother. Most of them, however, found the sight of Hanlon – haughty, grim, with a black eye where Jay's gloves had caught her during their sparring session, and sitting ramrod straight – intimidating at best, or at worst, genuinely frightening. Nobody wanted to sit next to her, because nobody dared.

Michaels appeared from the back of the kitchen, saw her and waved from across the pass, the steel dividing counter between kitchen and dining area. He was not the kind of man to be intimidated by people or situations.

He was wearing chef's whites with the sleeves rolled up and the whiteness of the jacket accentuated his Mediterranean colouring. He had a striped butcher's apron on and a kitchen skullcap, which gave him a priestly air. He was wearing highly polished, black, steel-toed Caterpillar boots on his feet and appeared, to Hanlon's eyes, ready to rise to any challenge. He looked intensely competent.

She watched him moving swiftly round the kitchen, tasting, testing food, bobbing up and down as he checked fridges. The other chefs quickened their pace, looked more alert, adjusted their posture. It was like a general reviewing the troops.

She got up and went over to him.

'Gallagher, nice to see you. Everything OK with your food, I hope?' he asked, leaning over the barrier between canteen and kitchen.

'Yes, fine,' she said. She couldn't actually remember what she was eating, simply because she didn't care what she ate.

'Good. Good.' He hesitated, glanced round the busy kitchen. 'Look, I'm a bit up to my eyes in it right now.'

'That's a shame,' said Hanlon, lying with practised ease. 'I was hoping to get some input on Dr Fuller's attitudes to women. I know that Dame Elizabeth is keen to have my feedback, given what I do for a living.'

For a second he looked puzzled, then nodded and said, 'Oh, I see, that EU thing.'

'Exactly,' said Hanlon. 'Gender equality?'

'Gender equality,' confirmed Hanlon. 'Particularly in adult education, it's a fertile ground.'

She thought that the bait, the lure, of being given the opportunity to criticize Fuller, a man whom she suspected Michaels couldn't stand, would prove irresistible. She was right. He nodded his head again in agreement. He glanced up at the clock on the wall.

'I have to go and cook in the executive dining-room kitchen right now. Come and keep me company and I'll let you know what I think of our esteemed tutor.'

The last three words were heavily seasoned with sarcasm. 'That'd be great,' said Hanlon. She was particularly keen to learn more about Hannah and her love life. Hannah had given herself up to her killer, that much was obvious. There was no struggle, no fight. Hanlon wanted to know if Hannah's lovers were restricted to the philosophy circle, or had she spread her favours wider as Jessica had implied.

Michaels could help with this. Now his attention was on the canteen kitchen.

'Just give me a couple of minutes,' he said, glancing around. 'I need to make sure this lot are OK.'

He turned his attention to the team of chefs and called out, 'Molly! Here a minute.' A hugely overweight girl came running over.

Molly was enormous. Her blonde, wispy hair was tucked under a headscarf and she had slightly bulging psychotic eyes. She looked very pale beside Michaels. Her forearms were like slabs of veal. She had a huge chest under her chef's jacket and apron.

'She's bloody good,' said Michaels to Hanlon. He spoke quietly so Molly wouldn't hear.

Molly arrived in front of them. She stared at Hanlon, a non-chef, with obvious disapproval.

'Yes, chef!' She looked at Michaels with slavish devotion, like a human Labrador.

'Righto, Molly,' said Michaels briskly, 'you're in charge down here. I'll be upstairs with Kieran.'

Molly nodded. Michaels' eyes suddenly narrowed with genuine anger as he looked at the young chef. Hanlon wondered what could have caused it.

'I'm sorry, I must have missed that,' said Michaels. Hanlon noticed that he spoke lightly but there was a genuine hint of steel in his voice, harsh and threatening.

Molly blinked. 'Yes, *chef*.' She stressed the word.

'That's better,' said Michaels. 'We don't want to forget who's in charge, do we?'

'No, chef.'

Michaels nodded, satisfied his authority had been properly acknowledged. He turned to Hanlon and motioned with his head to her.

Hanlon felt faintly shocked at Michaels' peremptory rude- ness. She had no problem with the chef's desire to stamp his authority on his workforce, but she wouldn't have done that in front of a stranger. She decided there was a cruel streak somewhere inside the man before her.

'We'd better go. It'll be hellish up there,' he said quietly and laughed. He didn't look remotely concerned.

Hanlon followed Michaels out of the canteen and up and down corridors, many of which were marked *Staff Only*, until she was thoroughly lost. Eventually they emerged in a kitchen space in a part of the university she'd never been in.

It was at moments like this that Hanlon appreciated just how vast a building Queen's was. It was labyrinthine, almost nightmarish. Like many public buildings there was a kind of parallel world built for the staff and functionaries. It was an unseen world of shabby and secretive service corridors and windowless rooms, an underworld known only to the initiated.

The kitchen was quite small and compact. Michaels pointed to an area at the end of the pass where the waiting staff would collect the dishes.

'If you stand there, Gallagher, we can talk and you won't be in anyone's way. I'll introduce you to Kieran.'

He called out and a young chef with a fluffy, ill-developed beard appeared. He smiled politely at Hanlon.

'All set?'

'Yes, chef.' Service began.

As the orders rolled in from the waitresses in the dining room, sent wirelessly to the small, black plastic cheque machine, she watched while Kieran did the simple stuff. He put the pre- cooked vegetables in boat-shaped, eared dishes and microwaved them, or arranged and dressed the pre-prepared salad ingredients on a plate according to photos pinned up on a wall.

'Spec sheets,' Kieran said over his shoulder, practised fingers moving speedily, expertly. 'Just follow the photos, simple as.' He deep-fried Parmentier potatoes, similar to chips in cube form, or pommes soufflé, which were like puffed-up crisps. He also had the two large Hobart ovens. They were dual function, and could be set with the turn of a knob, to steam as well as to bake. One of them was set on the steam function and when he opened it to put something in, vast clouds of superheated vapour surrounded him.

And so it went. Fast, pressurized, relentless.

One hour later, Hanlon had a great deal more respect for the catering trade than she had ever thought likely. The speed at which they worked was breathtaking.

While they discussed the course and their fellow students, Michaels was a blur of movement.

In the time that Kieran took to make one salad – for example, pear, goat's cheese, curly endive and hazelnut with a hazel- nut vinaigrette – he had started chargrilling duck, pan-seared blackened chicken breasts, laid out Parma ham-wrapped cod loin and set a steak on the go, while doing other starters, more complicated vegetables than Kieran was allowed to, and arranging and saucing.

His concentration was absolute, his movements deft, exact and amazingly quick. She had never seen anyone work so fast or so neatly. His coordination was precise and balletic. Occasion- ally she saw his lips moving as he repeated an order to himself, making sure that all the parts of the dishes were ready.

Michaels could obviously separate the cooking from the conversational part of his mind. He managed to carry on a conversation in spite of the stress he was under. She learned that he regarded Hannah as someone to be protected. He found her startlingly naive and above all over-anxious to please.

'I felt sorry for her,' he yelled over the noise of the kitchen. 'She seemed so, well, pathetic.'

It was incredibly hot in the small kitchen; everything seemed to generate heat. The six-burner stove, the ovens, the flat-top stove, the grill (or salamander as she learned to call it), the metal pass with its scaldingly hot lights and its capacious metal storage cabinet for plates and bowls, all were roasting.

Hanlon's hair was heavy and sodden, sweat trickled down her face in the forty- to fifty-degree-Celsius heat. She could feel her clothes sticking to her. Michaels seemed cool and unaffected.

'I think that's why she ended up with a reputation as the class bike. She couldn't say no to people,' he said, slicing and arranging two pink duck breasts on beds of dark Puy lentils.

'And Fuller?'

'Exploited it,' said Michaels. 'I think, no, I know, he's the kind of man who preys on women.'

The noise of the kitchen was intense and Michaels had to practically shout. The roar of the extractor fans was like being on an airport runway. All the pans were of course metal, so they clanged as they got bashed around on the stove, and there was a continuous percussive beat to the rhythm of the kitchen as oven and fridge doors were opened and slammed shut.

'You really think that's true?' shouted Hanlon. 'Absolutely, hang on.' He barked instructions to an attentive

waitress standing next to her. 'Table Five away, Ellie. Now, where were we. Anyway, Hannah told me about a girl called Abigail Vickery. She died because of him. Either he killed her or he encouraged the S&M stuff that did her in.'

The printer on the pass, connected to the waitresses' electronic order pads, made a high-pitched, tearing noise while it operated, and this would translate into a food order which Kieran would detach from the machine, keep one copy for himself and put the other on the cheque grabber above the pass for Michaels to read.

'Dessert cheque, Kieran,' he said, then turned his attention back to her. 'He really doesn't like women, did you know that? He's always running them down, at least that's what I've been told. Oh, and he's got a huge porn collection by all accounts. I heard him boast about it once. He was smashed at some do and let it slip.'

'Really?' said Hanlon.

Michaels nodded. 'Doesn't like women, he's a pervert, drink problem, past history and now another dead girl. Whichever way you look at it, he's guilty.'

'Why are you in his class then, if you dislike him so much?' As she asked the question, the machine printed off several cheques, one after another, each a separate food order. Michaels

rolled his eyes.

'I'll tell you later,' he said. He busied himself at the stove.

Eventually, like a water main gradually being turned off, the gaps between orders grew longer and longer, the pile of completed cheques grew higher on the metal spike and Hanlon heard Michaels say, 'Right. That's the last order out. Come on, Gallagher, let's get some air.'

Thank God, she thought, that's all over. She'd had quite enough of the kitchen. She wondered how they could bear it in there for fifty to sixty hours a week. She looked up at the clock on the wall: two thirty p.m. Kieran and Michaels had done about forty meals in a couple of hours.

She did a quick calculation. Twenty mains per hour plus thirty starters, seventy plated meals, thirty-five an hour, one meal every two minutes, all done by two people. And it was all done to order, all expertly cooked, all perfectly arranged. It was staggering really. Michaels was extremely good.

She followed him out through a side door, past a room marked *Dry Store* and down a corridor lined with several bags of potatoes, then through a beaded, chain curtain, a fly screen to a small roof terrace outside.

By the fly screen Michaels pointed to a staircase. 'That'll take you out down to the main corridor below.'

They stood side by side, looking out at the rooftops of central London. She could see the sparkplug-like shape of the Telecom Tower from here. It was amazingly tranquil.

The terrace was small and intimate, a secret place high up in the ziggurat of the Senate building. Michaels grinned at her. He had grabbed a couple of bottles of Nastro Azzurro out of one of his fridges and he prised the tops off, using a cigarette lighter that he kept for the stove. He handed one to Hanlon and then sat down with his back against the wall, looking out through the railings at the city stretching away westwards.

'Why am I in his class?' He drank some beer thoughtfully. 'I didn't know anything about him until Hannah filled me in. She was trying to pump me for information. She thought that because we worked for the same uni we'd mix.' Just like I did, thought Hanlon. He gave a bitter laugh. 'God, she was naive. She'd have made a terrible journalist. As if he'd mix with a peasant like me.'

'Are you saying he's a snob?' asked Hanlon.

'Too right,' said Michaels. 'They all are. Intellectual snobs.'

Hanlon could hear the bitterness in his voice. 'I'd love to see them try and cope in the real world.' He shook his head disparagingly. 'Ivory towers, Gallagher, ivory towers.' Hanlon decided to change the subject.

'It's not always that busy, is it?' she said. Michaels shook his head.

'We're one chef down.' he answered. 'Normally we'd have one on starters and desserts and one on veg and sauces, leaving me with just the mains and the plating up, and of course we'd have a KP for the washing up. But not today. Never mind, it all went well.'

Michaels stood up and stretched his arms. His jacket rode up, and Hanlon caught a glimpse of his washboard stomach and a trim line of hair descending southwards from his navel into the very white waistband of his Armani under- wear. She could see that some women might find him very attractive.

'Nothing like a bit of action to get the adrenaline going,' he said. 'Eh, Gallagher.'

Now she did smile, albeit ruefully. 'That's what they say.' 'Right, well, I'd better go and sort that kitchen out,' said

Michaels. She looked surprised. 'Don't you have cleaners?' she said.

'Not in a kitchen, are you mad?' Michaels grinned and shook his head. 'No, we get all the excitement, us chefs. Cooking, cleaning, it's a fun-packed world. Shall I see you this evening?'

Hanlon nodded. 'Yes. See you tonight,' she said.

She watched as Michaels disappeared back the way they had come.

Fuller was obviously not quite the man of the people he liked to portray himself as, and, if Michaels was to be believed, dangerous to women.

She drank her beer thoughtfully.

11

Laura logged off Outlook Express, with a well-deserved feeling of satisfaction. She had confirmed the lecture hall, she had double-checked that the JCR dining room would be reset for the buffet meal at half past eight and she had confirmed that Dr Gideon Fuller would indeed be giving, in person, the second of the two lectures, on Nietzsche, the controversial German philosopher.

Fuller was an acknowledged Nietzsche expert. She thought about Fuller for a moment. She'd met him once and been highly impressed. She found him very attractive. Despite his good looks there was something haunting in his eyes, a hint of danger that hung over him like a dark perfume. She wondered what she would do if he made a pass at her; she rather hoped he would.

She ticked the last item on her to-do list. Laura was a big believer in lists.

She stood up, stretched and studied her reflection in the antique mirror that was said to have belonged to Ludwig Wittgenstein. Laura doubted this. Wittgenstein was surely more of a Cambridge philosopher, but it was a nice story and it could have happened. If it had, it would be strange to think of the tormented

Viennese philosopher being reflected in its polished surface just as she was now.

Laura had long, dark hair and a slim figure, and to her own eyes she looked about fourteen rather than the sexy under- graduate she aspired to be. Only her mouth, full and sensuous, matched her dreams. That and her neck, long and elegant. She took her glasses off and peered at the mirror. She grinned goofily at herself and made her eyes go crossed. Oh, it was hopeless. She may as well face it: people were going to spend the next few years, as they had the last few years, saying she looked really sweet.

It'll be written on my grave, she thought. *Here lies Laura, she was really sweet.*

I don't want to be really sweet, thought Laura. I want to be sophisticated and elegant. Oh well.

She kicked off her shoes, lay down on her narrow bed and picked up her copy of *Twilight of the Idols.*

12

Laura was not the only person with Nietzsche in mind. *Thou goest to woman, do not forget to take thy whip!* His pen circled the passage in *Thus Spake Zarathustra,* as memory called up the beautiful face, the intelligent, wide eyes. There would be no need of a hood when they met again at the college.

This time he wanted to see her face as she went, as she slipped away into darkness. Hannah was simply not the kind of person you would want to see die. In life she'd been clumsy, gauche. As he choked her, she would probably have looked off-putting.

That wouldn't be the case with his next encounter. She was beautiful, vital. She had a great body and he couldn't wait to see her wide, generous mouth, the full lips parting sensuously, the tip of her tongue provocatively visible, as she breathed her last.

Revenge, he thought, revenge.

They say it is a dish best eaten cold.

He also knew the secret of Wittgenstein's mirror. Soon it would have something truly remarkable to reflect.

He didn't know that much about Wittgenstein, his ideas were a bit too mathematical, but he did know the famous quote, *Whereof one cannot speak, thereof one must be silent*.

Soon, witness and victim, mirror and woman, would prove the truth of this dictum.

He knew the college well. There were few premier-league colleges in Oxford that he hadn't worked in at one time or another. He even knew the room intimately. It couldn't have been better chosen, if he'd done it himself. It was perfect for the purpose.

All would go according to plan. The music for their final meeting had been selected. 'You Make Me Feel (Mighty Real).' The song was particularly apposite; her death would indeed make him feel mighty real.

The long, delicate fingers underlined another passage by the German philosopher. *To live is to suffer, to survive is to find some meaning in the suffering*. He felt he knew a great deal about suffering.

Now it would be someone else's turn.

13

Hanlon met Enver at his new office in Euston. The area was still menacingly sleazy. The enormous red-brick building of the British Library with its windswept, rain-drenched piazza, where litter blew like tumbleweed in a Western, made Hanlon almost nostalgic for the old days. She could remember the giant gasworks that used to be there, the gasometers rising out of the ground like enormous, circular, filigreed napkin rings designed for a race of giants. It was round here that the then DPP had been nicked years ago, for picking up prostitutes. That the Director of Public Prosecutions should be using prostitutes was no real surprise, but a King's Cross prostitute? The area by the gasworks was a kind of elephants' graveyard for clapped-out whores, famously dreadful. There had been a piece of prominent graffiti on a wall after the event, *The DPP kerb crawled here*. Maybe, thought Hanlon, they could put a blue plaque up in his honour.

Enver had a space in a quiet corner of the station. To Hanlon's eyes his desk was irritatingly cluttered. He bustled around and fetched her a cup of coffee, which she sniffed suspiciously. It had that over-stewed scent of filter coffee which has been hanging around too long. It smelled horrible.

Enver looked content in his new job. Hanlon thought he could never be described as happy; he was a worrier by nature.

He worried about case details, leaks to the press, his mobile phone being hacked, and he was always concerned about his weight, although he never seemed to do anything about it.

It was a common problem with ex-athletes, she thought, particularly boxers who have to make a certain weight. Once they stop they tend to go the other way.

He was looking quite trim today, she noted, his good- looking, sad face brightening at the sight of her. His very dark hair was sleek and glossy. Thank God for that, she thought. It was bad enough him obsessing about his stomach without adding a baldness crisis to the equation.

Briefly, succinctly, Hanlon ran through what she'd learned about Fuller, both in person and from the other students and Iris Campion.

'So Dr Fuller enjoys pretending to strangle women, enjoys hurting them, basically,' said Enver.

'Exactly,' said Hanlon. 'We're unusually privileged to have this kind of information, face it, Enver, most people's sex lives are pretty mysterious. And we have it on good authority that he is not the kind of person to slip up while he's doing it, he's had plenty of practice. So if it was Fuller then it was murder, not some sex game gone wrong. It's not like it was some kind of first-time mistake.'

Enver nodded. 'I looked into the story about the girl, his former student, the one who killed herself, or was killed by Fuller in some sort of S&M game. Abigail Vickery,' he said.

'And?'

Enver scratched his heavy moustache. His sleeves were rolled up and Hanlon could see the powerful muscles in his forearm move as he did so. Promotion definitely suited him, she decided. As a sergeant, he'd been depressed-looking, the problem, maybe, of responsibility without power. Now he seemed more confident, easier in his own skin. The trouble with Enver, she thought, was that he was a very decent man who cared a bit too much. Now he had a lot more latitude in the way he operated. Corrigan would see to that. To the politically minded assistant commissioner, having a photogenic non- European, particularly of Turkish origin, in a senior position was a godsend. It would play well with the gallery and in North London, with a Turkish community of an estimated four hundred thousand, Enver was worth his weight in gold. He'll go far, she suddenly realized. Not like me. I'm too untrustworthy.

I wouldn't promote me any further than I am now, she thought.

'It's maddeningly inconclusive,' he said. 'Murray had me check further. She'd been treated for depression', he flicked through his notebook, 'with SSRIs, which are a kind of drug they use for that sort of thing. It's quite a controversial treatment, seemingly. Anyway, she'd made a previous suicide attempt, there was a history of mental illness. The coroner put it down as an open verdict, I guess maybe to spare the family, but it was a good verdict. She was found hanging from a doorknob. Could have been a sex game, could have been suicide.'

He drank a mouthful of the revolting coffee, not seeming to mind the taste. 'It was only later that stories started to sur- face about Fuller and the girl. He told a colleague they were kindred spirits.'

He shrugged helplessly. His mournful brown eyes reminded Hanlon of a seal.

'Hannah's Facebook entry said she was having a relationship with a married man and a married woman,' said Enver. 'Do you think Fuller was that person? Wouldn't she have been more specific?'

Hanlon shrugged. My turn now, she thought.

Her face, decided Enver, had become even more mask-like since the last time they'd worked together. He was having trouble getting used to Hanlon's stylishly cut hair. Previously it had no attention lavished on it whatsoever. Enver, who much to his own irritation, was deeply obsessed with her, was busy wondering if she had done it to please another. He could see that the idea was slightly crazy, that Hanlon would do such a thing seemed out of character, but Enver was jealous; it was that simple, and he couldn't hide it from himself. Perhaps he should try following her. He'd done it before, disastrously. He smiled at the memory.

'Stop grinning like an idiot,' said Hanlon, annoyed. 'Sorry, ma'am,' apologized Enver, slightly slavishly. He liked it when Hanlon was cross – the pugnacious cast to her jaw, the angry look in her eye, the way her hair seemed to bristle. Anger suited her.

'Hannah Moore wanted people to read her blog, Enver,' said Hanlon. 'She wasn't necessarily telling the truth. Yes, she was having a relationship with someone and yes, it does look as if it contained an S&M dimension and yes, that is Fuller's thing. The removal of her underwear, presumably as some sort of souvenir or memento or trophy, is also linked to Fuller, but all of this is circumstantial.'

She pushed the coffee away from her so she didn't have to smell it.

'Fuller is not married any more,' she said. 'That lasted a couple of years and finished five years ago. He was working in the USA at the time, Harvard, so it could have simply been a visa thing, to get green-carded, who knows. But Hannah might not have known that the marriage had ended. Having a wife is a useful excuse for men who have no wish to take a relationship beyond the bedroom.' She made a gesture of dismissal. 'It could mean nothing, it could mean a lot, we don't know. Remember, we do have a married woman classmate of hers certainly strong enough to do it, and with a reputation for being sexually liberal.'

Enver looked startled. 'We hadn't thought about that,' he said. 'Do you think she was. . .' He searched for a suitable word. Hanlon rolled her eyes. 'Polysexual,' she said, 'or poly- amorous, that covers wider ground, possibly. You shouldn't

be so cut and dried in these things.'

Enver shifted in his seat. He was old-fashioned and disliked talking about sex, particularly with a woman.

Hanlon was thinking of what Michaels had told her about Jessica McIntyre. 'Have you checked the alibis of her other classmates?'

Enver shook his head. 'It didn't seem relevant at the time.' 'I would,' said Hanlon, 'particularly Jessica McIntyre.' Enver raised an interrogative eyebrow and she briefly explained why. 'Do you know if Fuller gets off on music?' asked Enver unexpectedly.

Hanlon looked puzzled. 'No, I've got no idea. Why?'

'We've had a witness come forward,' said Enver. 'He's a student who lives just above Hannah. He's been away, but was around on the day of the murder. He says the walls and floors are quite thin in that Hall of Residence, sound travels. It's quite common for students who are . . .' he looked embarrassed, 'having sex, to play loud music. To drown other noises out, if you see what I mean.'

'Yes, I have grasped the concept,' said Hanlon acidly.

Enver continued. 'Well, anyway, he said that on the day of the murder he was trying to write an essay about three o'clock in the afternoon and was put off by, and I quote, "cheesy" disco music. He says it was Donna Summer, his dad likes her. That's how he knew who it was. I just wondered if Fuller had given any hint as to his musical tastes. The same student says he's heard similar music from her room at other times.'

Hanlon shrugged. 'I've no idea but it's something to bear in mind.' She frowned thoughtfully.

Enver took the opportunity to look at her properly. He saw her long, powerful fingers, the nails cut short and painted with clear varnish. Wisps of dark, curly hair snaked down over her forehead. Hanlon had made no attempt to conceal her bruised eye and its startling colouring seemed to enhance the integrity of her face. He saw faint lines on her forehead that hadn't been there when he had first met her. As always, she looked tired, but it suited her, in a strange way. He tried to picture her laughing or looking carefree, but it defeated his imagination.

He'd once fought an opponent who had come into the ring to the music of a band performing a song called, 'Born under a Bad Sign', and he thought the title would suit Hanlon.

His surname, Demirel, meant Iron Hand in Turkish. When he'd been boxing his manager, who came from Birmingham, had wanted him to walk to the ring to Black Sabbath's 'Iron Man'. Enver had firmly vetoed the idea. It was bad enough that he shared the name with a former Turkish president.

He cleared his throat to try and pull himself together, disentangling his mind from the whirl of memories. 'So, what next, ma'am?'

'I've got to meet Dame Elizabeth, Fuller's boss – the one with all the connections, who specifically requested a low-key investigation. There's no class tonight, Fuller and the Queen's College Philosophy Society are off to some Oxford College, St Wulfstan's, for a seminar. It's an overnight thing. How about you?'

'I've got a meeting with DCI Murray, who's the SIO on this.' Enver looked mournful again. 'I'll bring up interviewing the classmates. To be honest, if we don't get some sort of break, ma'am, it's all looking pretty futile. We've got a suspect, but no evidence.'

She nodded. 'I'll call you tomorrow.'

Hanlon stood up to leave. The bruised skin around her ribs felt tight and constrictive. She put her hands on her hips and leaned backwards, stretching her spine with a supple grace that left Enver sickeningly jealous. His own back had been causing him a great deal of trouble. Bending down to tie his shoelaces was painful; he had to put his foot on something high up. I can't touch my toes any more, he thought. Of course, his growing girth didn't help. He could feel his belly folds rippling upwards when he leaned forward. Fatso, he thought bitterly.

He couldn't rid himself of the image of his fingers groping helplessly towards his shoelaces, now tantalizingly out of reach. On impulse he asked, 'Can you touch your toes, ma'am?'

Hanlon zipped her jacket up and looked at him with irritation. With one fluid movement she bent from the hips, her legs straight, and placed both palms effortlessly flat on the floor, her nose touching her knees, her hair tumbling forward, then she straightened up. Again it was a smooth, effortless motion.

'Yes,' she said.

Enver watched her admiringly as she walked away from him towards the office door. Perhaps I ought to take up yoga or something, he thought, secure in the knowledge it wasn't going to happen.

14

Later that afternoon Hanlon sat at the back of the small lecture hall, watching Dame Elizabeth give a talk on Kant, the German philosopher.

Hanlon rarely read books. She occasionally bought *Triathlon* magazine or *The Economist* if she had to make Tube journeys, but fiction she found pointless. Sometimes she studied history, or books on art, and philosophy had always interested her. It was why she'd read some of Dame Elizabeth's books. She had that rare skill of being able to make a subject intelligible to the layperson. It was also, Hanlon guessed, the mental equivalent of a healthy snack. You felt a glow of virtue afterwards, for doing something not too arduous, but which was generally agreed to be good for you. At least that was how Hanlon, who subjected her body to endless workouts, felt. She should at least attempt something similar mentally, exercise for the brain.

She was annoyed that she was finding philosophy in class so difficult and simultaneously annoyed with herself at being annoyed.

Like anything, it had its own special vocabulary, terminology and shorthand, so she knew it was ridiculous to think that she could just come in cold and pick it up. Nevertheless, that's how it was. She was used to being the expert, she guessed, to having people, even those who couldn't stand her, defer to her. To be the weakest in the class was an unpleasant shock. Hanlon was big enough to recognize this. Maybe I need taking down a peg or two, she thought. Maybe I've grown too big-headed. Dame Elizabeth was proving everything Hanlon hoped she'd be. She stood in front of the desk, speaking without notes to the students in the raked seating of the auditorium. Although not tall, her personality dominated the large room, making it hard to look elsewhere. She was eye-catching, controlling, authoritative.

Hanlon guessed she must be in her mid-sixties now. Her snow-white hair was cut expertly and expensively short and contrasted with her tanned skin and piercing blue eyes, visible even at this distance. She was wearing a beautifully cut skirt and jacket. She looked immaculate, like an ex-*Vogue* cover girl, and she had a larger-than-life aura that commanded attention. True beauty is timeless and Dame Elizabeth was still beautiful, but Hanlon could imagine that when she was young she would have been effortlessly desirable. She was a world away from the hackneyed image of the smelly old lecturer, looking unwashed, in twinset tweeds and Oxfam jewellery.

She easily held the students' attention as she talked about the Categorical Imperative and Synthetic and Analytic propositions. Hanlon hadn't got a clue what she was on about, but it somehow didn't matter. You don't have to read music, or play an instrument yourself, to enjoy the sound it makes.

At the end of the lecture, there was a Q&A session and one part of this Hanlon did understand. The question of whether or not it was ever permissible to lie. In many ways, Hanlon's whole life was taken up with lies, half-truths and evasions. Endless memories of interviews came instantly to mind.

'Did you do it?'

'No, I swear . . .'

'Did you do it?'

'No. Maybe. It depends what you mean by . . .'

'I didn't actually . . . I wouldn't have unless . . . He/She/It made me . . .'

And all possible permutations of that theme. And her own job at the moment. She wasn't Gallagher, working for the Home Office. That was a lie too. She lived her life surrounded by falsehood.

Was Fuller a killer, or was he innocent?

Was it truth, or lie?

It was a philosophical question and a very real one.

Dame Elizabeth said that, according to Kant, lying was never justified. Indeed could never be justified.

A student put her hand up and asked, what about if you were in Holland in 1942, sheltering a Jew in your attic and the Gestapo came to your house? Should you tell the truth about your guest, knowing they'd be taken to a death camp?

Yes, said Dame Elizabeth, you should, you must, tell the truth. She had been anticipating this question; it invariably came up. According to Kant, she explained, there can be no exceptions. There are no ifs and buts. It's not up to you to decide which bit of a moral law you decide to obey. If you start tinkering around with the main premise, you're left with nothing.

'I hope that answers your question,' she said. The student, who was Jewish, looked far from convinced. Dame Elizabeth continued. 'For example, killing. If you kill, you have a very shaky right to condemn others.'

Hanlon frowned her disagreement.

Killing, for Hanlon, was not an abstract notion.

'And I'll leave you with this thought,' said Dame Elizabeth. 'All actions, all decisions have consequences whether seen or unforeseen. In choosing to do what you regard as the right thing, rather than obey a moral, universal law, you might be doing something terribly wrong.' She paused. 'Think about it! See you all next week.'

The audience, with the exception of Hanlon, got to their feet with the usual rustling of papers, conversations initiated or restarted, bags being moved, zipped up, tablets and laptops closing, goodbyes being said. Soon there was just Hanlon left, her elbows on the shelf in front of her, chin resting on the bridge formed by her interlaced fingers.

Her grey eyes studied Dame Elizabeth dispassionately. Hanlon was almost certainly the only person in the room to have killed other people. One purely in self-defence, one for vengeance and one for justice. Is my conscience clear? she thought. Yes. To you, Professor, and to you, Herr Kant, these are just theories.

Not for me.

I know what it's like to have a life in the balance. Iris Campion's words returned to her memory. *Who are you to judge?* Answer me that, Professor.

The professor looked up at Hanlon, the only person left in the room. She had requested the meeting and guessed this was the policewoman sent by Corrigan. Gallagher, she remembered, was the name that the assistant commissioner had given her. She thought with affection of the huge figure of the AC. Corrigan was one of those people who seemed to enjoy hiding their light under a bushel. Most academics in her experience pretended to be much brighter than they were. Corrigan pretended to be slow on the uptake and then, just as you relaxed, unleashed a salvo of expertly chosen fact and tight, analytical reasoning. She knew him well from her civil service committee work and advisory positions she had held. When the murder had happened, she turned to him immediately. Now he had sent her this unlikely-looking figure. Whatever she had been expecting, it wasn't this woman.

Dame Elizabeth was not a superstitious woman, but the motionless figure sitting near the back of the auditorium looked very much as she would have imagined the Angel of Death to appear – dark, brooding, implacable.

She mentally shook herself in irritation at this atypical flight of fancy.

'Do come down,' she called, with an authority she didn't really feel. 'Come and join me in my office.'

She watched as, with an easy grace, Hanlon descended the stairs towards her. Dame Elizabeth shivered. Something about the policewoman was very disturbing indeed.

15

Hi, Mum! I'm so excited about tonight. All the Phil. Soc. are coming and some of the dons from the other colleges, and I spoke to the college chef and he's got a couple of mates in to help with the extra catering so it's all good. Yay! Anyway, am sooo looking forward to meeting Dr Fuller. Will be in touch, love you heaps, Laura. PS Say hi to Dad!

Laura pressed send on her iPhone and glanced round her room. It looked perfect. It was almost like a stage set. Even the old stone-flagged steps of Staircase Five had been mopped clean earlier in the day. Generations of student feet had worn them away so they sloped upwards at a slight angle. They shone where the light hit them.

Laura was an optimistic girl; why not? She was nineteen, just gone, and things usually went well for her. She knew that tonight would be a wonderful night, one to cherish and remember. Behind her geek-chic glasses, her eyes were shining with the happiness of the moment.

16

Dame Elizabeth looked at the woman across the desk from her. She had spent her whole working life grading and assessing people – students, civil servants, university lecturers, lovers – and she knew she was good at it.

How, she wondered would she judge the policewoman? First of all, she thought, Corrigan had obviously made an excellent choice. Dame Elizabeth had specified she did not want anyone who would stand out. She didn't want students, or faculty for that matter, protesting they were being spied on by the authorities. Universities were a breeding ground for silly, paranoid fantasies, not helped by organizations like Special Branch occasionally launching fantastically stupid undercover investigations. Now there were the torrent of unauthorized incidents of surveillance as revealed by Bradley Manning and Edward Snowden. Undercover policewomen at a strongly left-wing university, it could so easily go disastrously wrong.

Gallagher, or whoever she really was, certainly did not look like she was in the police. She didn't look groomed enough. With her springy, slightly unkempt hair, the black eye and the rather expensive blouse she was wearing, she reminded Dame Elizabeth of the radical student activists of her youth. There was something about the cast of the face that was anti-authoritarian. She could easily imagine Gallagher petrol- bombing the US Embassy in protest against the Vietnam War or leading a Baader-Meinhof protest march in what was then West Germany. It was a fanatic's face. But if you looked closely, you could see she was surprisingly good-looking. She had high cheekbones, a full mouth, dark, curved eyebrows, and her figure was excellent.

She also looked like trouble. It was spelled out in the combative set of the jaw and the far from friendly expression on her face.

Her estimation of Corrigan, already quite high, rose another notch. She wouldn't be brave enough to employ this woman, no matter how good her qualities. He was a bloody good judge of character. I'm getting old, she thought, annoyed at herself. I'm choosing the easy route and I'm getting risk averse.

Hanlon also reminded her of someone she'd once known back in her youth. The face hung tantalizingly at the back of her mind, but Dame Elizabeth had met a lot of people and she didn't follow the thought up.

'So, have you found anything relevant to add to DCI Murray's investigation?' she asked.

'Yes,' said Hanlon. She made no attempt to elaborate or say more. It was this unusually abrupt reply that triggered Dame Elizabeth's formidable memory. Now she knew who Hanlon reminded her of.

The possibility alarmed her, almost like meeting a ghost. It's not so, she told herself. There is something almost horrific about the past returning to haunt you. It's ill omened. It never presages good.

Her face, schooled in a thousand meetings, showed nothing of her inner turmoil. It cannot be.

She moved the thought to one side for later inspection. There is no point getting sidetracked in a meeting, particularly if you're the one doing the distracting. She concentrated on the business in hand.

'I'm waiting,' she said. Time to remind the policewoman who was in charge here.

'I've established that Dr Fuller is a habitual customer of a brothel specializing in S&M. That there is quite compelling circumstantial evidence linking him to the death of Hannah Moore,' Hanlon said.

Dame Elizabeth rolled her eyes. 'Dr Fuller's sexual inclinations are his business,' she said. She looked with hostility at Hanlon. 'How many of your fellow male officers use pornography, have affairs or take favours from prostitutes on their patch?' she demanded. She would not accept a lecture about morality from someone in the police.

Hillsborough, the Lawrence affair, Plebgate, the police federation, frivolous personal-injury claims involving kerbs and papercuts. And those were just what sprang immediately to mind.

'More than I'd care to admit,' said Hanlon, ruthlessly honest. 'Fortunately, I don't have to work with any bent policemen.' Thank God for Enver, she thought, even DCI Murray for that matter, a perfectly happily married man, who bored his colleagues rigid with tedious stories and photos of his children.

Dame Elizabeth nodded, surprised at Hanlon's candid answer.

'There you are then,' she said.

'There is the possibility that he may have been pressuring students into sex for better grades,' said Hanlon. It was a rumour she'd heard from a woman in her class, and one substantiated by

Michaels, but she thought she'd air it, just to see the professor's reaction.

Dame Elizabeth raised a questioning eyebrow. 'The possibility,' she said with heavy emphasis. 'All sorts of things are possible; let's try and confine ourselves to the empirically verifiable. Dr Fuller seems to be the victim of a certain amount of rumour and innuendo, none of which would warrant disciplinary proceedings, let alone police interest. Wouldn't you agree?'

'May I remind you a girl is dead, Dame Elizabeth. That's why the police are interested. It's not out of a prurient interest in Dr Fuller's sex life.'

Prurient, thought Dame Elizabeth. Not a word you hear every day. She looked into Hanlon's menacing, cold eyes.

'And that's why we all want to find out who did it,' she parried briskly. 'Now, what do your fellow students have to say about him?'

'That he's hard-working, a good teacher, they like him,' admitted Hanlon.

'And what do you think?' Dame Elizabeth tilted her open palms towards Hanlon in an over-to-you gesture.

Hanlon hesitated, unusual for her. 'I don't know,' she said. She was thinking back to Iris Campion, to her statement that *some of the girls say he can get a little too rough*.

She pushed a hand through her unruly hair and the sleeve of her dark jacket slipped backwards revealing her slim, muscular forearm. She was wearing a very geometric, severe silver and platinum bracelet. Its unadorned simplicity and austerity seemed chosen to mirror Hanlon's personality. Dame Elizabeth stared at it, aghast. Veteran as she was of the need to keep a public face on at all times, her features remained impassive.

'Oh well,' she said faintly, her mind almost hypnotized by the ornament, then, 'Do you mind if I ask you what your real name is? I'm assuming Gallagher isn't it.'

'No, not at all. I'm DCI Hanlon.'

Dame Elizabeth's heart sank. Of course it is. I knew that, she thought. What else could it be. Hanlon gave her a business card with her rank and mobile number. Dame Elizabeth took it. There was just one more test, one more thing of which she had to satisfy herself.

'That's a very unusual bracelet you're wearing.'

'It's German, from the Bauhaus movement,' Hanlon said. 'It belonged to my mother.'

Walter Gropius, the founder of Bauhaus, designed it, thought Dame Elizabeth. It's so rare, it's practically unique. And no, it didn't belong to your mother, DCI Hanlon. And yes, that is empirically verifiable.

Let's verify the hypothesis.

So be it. *Alea iacta est*. The die is cast. 'May I see it?'

Hanlon gave her a puzzled look but undid the clasp and handed the small bracelet to Dame Elizabeth. It was surprisingly heavy and very well made.

'Walter Gropius, the founder of Bauhaus, designed it,' said Hanlon. 'It's very rare.'

Dame Elizabeth turned the piece of jewellery over between her fingers. There was a small message engraved on the inside. She couldn't read the letters, they were too small, but she didn't need to. Her eyes had been a lot sharper when she'd first read the inscription, her face then softening with love and delight.

That was in another country. In another century. In another city.

Her literary mind added, *And besides, the wench is dead.*

And she shivered.

That was in Berlin. She knew what was written there: *Jann and L 1976*. The seven was written continental style with a bar through the stem.

She gave it back to Hanlon. 'Thank you, it's very distinctive.' Hanlon nodded and placed it back on her wrist. She could have said, my mother left it to me after she died. She could have said, my mother's name was Jennifer but the engraver, presumably German, got it wrong. He put Jann instead.

She could have said, I never knew who my father was, but I guess maybe his name began with L and maybe that's why I choose not to have a first name.

The false reason she'd given Fuller in class, for not having a first name, was not too far removed from the reality. She could have told Dame Elizabeth that the name she was given came from her adoptive parents. She could have said, I want nothing to do with them or it. I'm Hanlon; I'm not that other girl. But she didn't.

Hanlon never talked about herself. Like Iris Campion, she had rejected the idea of victimhood.

And Dame Elizabeth Saunders could have told her the truth, then and there, but she didn't.

Dame Elizabeth seemed lost in thought as Hanlon stood up. 'I've got a question for you,' Hanlon said.

'Go ahead.'

Hanlon looked at her, puzzled. The dame seemed suddenly very distant, as if totally lost in thought.

'You seemed to believe that Kant was right, that we should obey moral laws, like do not lie, come hell or high water. Do you seriously believe that?' Hanlon's face showed barely concealed anger.

Something to be debated.

Dame Elizabeth nodded. 'I do believe that, yes,' she said, almost sadly.

'Even if it would result in the death of an innocent person?' The professor nodded. 'Yes,' she said, 'even if someone were to be killed. Some things are worth dying for.' Her voice was very quiet.

Hanlon shook her head contemptuously and turned and left the office.

Dame Elizabeth watched the door close and then buried her face in her hands, as a wave of self-revulsion engulfed her. I didn't lie to you, DCI Hanlon, she thought to herself, but I sure as hell avoided the facts.

You can't escape the truth, thought Dame Elizabeth. It catches us all up in the end. Kant knew that, and so do I.

17

Forty miles away, west of London, he ran a gentle but firm hand over the light Oxford stone of the seventeenth-century college building that ran along three sides of the quad. The fourth side was where the large vaulted arch led to the gatehouse and the outside doors of the college.

The manicured, rectangular lawn of the inner quadrangle was bordered by a low, knee-high hedge of box that he guessed to be maybe as old as the college. It was a beautiful, tranquil place, the busy, noisy streets of Oxford outside its walls unheard and unseen. Here there were the three colours, the green of the grass, the honey-coloured Oxford stone of the buildings and the blue of the sky overhead. It was very soothing.

He knew the college well, intimately even. He had worked there for a few terms on a temporary basis and had got to know every inch of its ancient fabric. He always made a habit of knowing the topography of wherever he worked in precise detail. He liked the feeling of freedom it brought. Years ago he had come across the phrase used on security passes the world over, *Access all areas*. He loved that expression. It was exactly what he liked to do, to be able to access all areas, to go where he pleased.

In this college, he knew, for example, that there was a hatch on the outside pavement that flapped outwards and led to the college buttery where beer and wine were stored. He still had a copy of the key. He knew there was a small and rarely used concealed gate, which led from the street to the Master's private garden. He knew where there was a street light close to the wall of the college that students used to help themselves climb over, when the college gates were closed.

He usually took copies of master keys with him when he left a workplace, or in today's increasingly electronic security, he stole swipe cards and password details. These days it was information, rather than hardware, that counted. He wouldn't need keys for what he was about to do.

He checked that the iPod was cued correctly and that the leather gloves were in their correct pocket. Above his head, *Staircafe V* was carved into the lintel stone in antique, lettering, the lower case 's' written as an elongated 'f' and the Roman 'V' for 5.

The steps were worn and shallow; they must have been cleaned recently, because they gleamed gently in the light. They spiralled upwards and he followed them to a heavy oak door, with *2B* on it in brass. The door was open, revealing a further door inside, and he knocked gently on this, while pulling on the supple, black leather gloves.

She opened the door almost immediately. 'Oh, it's you,' she said, her large eyes widening in surprise. 'What do you want?' She looked radiantly beautiful. Her mouth was full-lipped and inviting.

'I just need to check on a couple of things about tonight.'

'Well, do come on in,' she said.

And he did. It was that easy.

Twenty minutes later, Ben Protheroe, a physics student who had the room above, passed by Laura's room. The outside door was closed, 'sporting the oak' it was called in Oxford, and it meant you didn't want to be disturbed. He could hear music coming faintly from her room, music with a heavy dance beat. He stood there for a moment, listening.

Ben Protheroe had never heard 'You Make Me Feel (Mighty Real)' in his life. Neither had the girl inside, until now. He felt a stab of jealousy. He really fancied Laura. He found the thought of her in someone else's arms unbearable.

Inside the room, sightless eyes stared at the ceiling while her killer danced gracefully to Sylvester. It had taken him a long time to learn to dance, but master it he had.

The carefully choreographed dance movements, lovingly practised, were now reflected endlessly in Wittgenstein's mirror.

Whereof one cannot speak, thereof one must be silent.

18

'And who found the body?' asked Hanlon. She and Enver were driving down the A40 towards Oxford. The horizon was low and grey. Enver sat in the passenger seat. Hanlon reckoned it would take a good hour and a half at least to reach the Summertown police station near central Oxford, where Fuller was being held.

'A student called Laura Thomson. It's her room that Jessica McIntyre was staying in,' said Enver. 'She organized the seminar, the philosophy evening, and those students from Queen's, about ten of them, had been given accommodation belonging to St Wulfstan students, as part of the arrangements.'

Hanlon swore angrily as a car pulled out in front of her without indicating. They hadn't reached Northolt yet and were travelling ridiculously slowly, due to the pressure of traffic. Enver looked around him with interest at the nondescript housing sprawl. He rarely travelled outside London, had never been to Oxford. Today was a day out, like a treat at school.

I must travel more, he thought, all I know is North London and Rize. Rainiest place in Turkey. Well, Oxford here we come, I can broaden my horizons.

'So what do we know?' asked Hanlon, scowling at the traffic. Enver shook thoughts of his father's home city from his mind.

'McIntyre checked in at the college lodge at three o'clock. We know that. The proctor, that's what they call the gate-keeper—'

'I know what a proctor is, Detective Inspector,' said Hanlon with ominous calm. Of course you do, thought Enver, you know everything. He felt a touch of guilt at this mutinous thought. My promotion has gone to my head, he said to himself.

'Yes, ma'am. He gave her the room key, noted the time, she signed for it. That's the last she was seen alive. Her phone wasn't used subsequently. The coroner estimates the time of death at around five in the afternoon. Plus or minus, obviously. She was strangled, manually, as opposed to ligature; the bruising is quite clear, right-handed assailant. And strong. There was no sign of a struggle, so it's a reasonable assumption she knew her killer well enough to let them get close.'

Hanlon nodded. The traffic was speeding up now and she changed gear on her new Audi TTS Coupé, enjoying the noise from under the bonnet and the kick of the two-litre engine. The car handled beautifully.

'Is there any sign of S&M-style sex?'

'No, ma'am,' said Enver.

'So what's the evidence against Fuller then? Why is Oxford holding him?'

Enver scratched his thick, drooping moustache. 'DCI Templeman, who's the SIO on this, had heard of Fuller through the Hannah Moore investigation. I suppose he's interested in crimes against students, with him being at Oxford.'

Hanlon made a derisive noise. 'You're based in Euston, Enver. You've got UCL, Queen's, bits of Westminster Uni, language schools. Are you particularly interested in students? Or trains come to that, what with being near two major stations. Or books – you've got the British Library too.'

Enver remained unruffled by Hanlon's sarcasm. She had washed her hair and he could smell her shampoo. The diagonal slash of her seat belt against her white cotton blouse, pulling the material in, emphasized her figure.

His own stomach strained against his seat belt; he guessed it too, emphasized his figure, but not in a good way. I'm starting to ripple, he thought unhappily, like a fleshy waterbed. However, he almost enjoyed the sensation of support the seat belt gave him. He'd been finding belts too tight lately; they were leaving terrible red marks when he took his clothes off at night. Soon he'd have to wear braces.

He had to slim down. Losing weight was imperative. Thinking of Rize made him think of his father; he'd died of a massive heart attack aged fifty when Enver was a teenager. The warning signs were there.

But there was always tomorrow.

Losing weight was proving a failure, so he decided, as a temporary measure, to disguise his weight gain rather than fight it. He was wearing a new jacket he'd bought. That in itself had been stressful. He'd read in a *Grazia* magazine belonging to a WPC that stripes were slimming and had bought, at considerable cost, a blue and cream striped linen jacket from an expensive shop in Covent Garden. It had provoked sniggering at work. The same PC, Liz Mallowan, the unwitting *Grazia* owner, had begged him to take it back to the shop, over a quiet drink in a local pub. 'People are laughing at you, sir. They say you look like an ice-cream salesman.'

She adored Enver; she hated her colleagues for making fun of him.

He had been wondering about the hummed snatches, behind

his back, of 'O Sole Mio', or 'Just One Cornetto' as it's better known in Britain. Now he knew the reason why.

The new jacket had a check design. He wondered if it suited him. At least no one had said anything. He took a packet of Jelly Snakes out of his pocket and offered one to Hanlon.

'Jelly Snake, ma'am?'

She turned her gaze away from the road. They were exiting the A40 and joining the motorway. She looked at him incredulously.

'Do I look like a woman who eats Jelly Snakes?' she demanded.

'They're organic,' said Enver defensively. 'Made with real fruit juice. They're probably good for you.'

Hanlon shook her head wonderingly. 'Put the Snakes away and concentrate on Dr Fuller, please.'

The car surged forward and Enver caught sight of the speedometer as they hit both the M40 and ninety miles an hour. Oh well, he thought.

'According to DI Huss, she works for the SIO, he lied about his movements that afternoon. He claimed to be in his hotel room at the Blenheim between three and six p.m, but the room key is linked to a computer and it shows that he was absent from three to five fifty. The Blenheim Hotel is about a five- minute walk from the college.'

He was going to say that the Blenheim was a big hotel in the middle of Oxford, but he felt it would draw a sarcastic comment from Hanlon.

Hanlon nodded. Fuller's inability to provide an alibi had echoes of the Hannah Moore case, compounded here by the fact that it was a total lie.

'So plenty of time for Fuller to have killed McIntyre and returned to the hotel.'

'Exactly, ma'am,' said Enver and continued. 'His hotel room was searched and a pair of black leather gloves were found. He could give no coherent explanation for the gloves. It was twenty-one degrees Celsius in Oxford the day of the murder; not exactly glove weather. The gloves are now with forensics, as are his clothes. They also found an item of women's clothing, whatever that may be.'

'I think we can guess,' said Hanlon grimly. 'So presumably they'll hold him without charge, until they get the results back from the lab.' Thirty-six hours was the length of time the Oxford police could hold him without formally charging him, from the moment the custody clock started ticking.

'Any other potential souvenirs?' she asked.

'Yes, ma'am. A swatch of pubic hair, and yes, there was hair missing from the deceased.'

She fell silent as they drove, thinking of the dead Jessica McIntyre, so tough, competent and abrasive in life. Hannah Moore had been one of those people who had 'victim' almost tattooed on their forehead. You couldn't say that about McIntyre. Hanlon was surprised there hadn't been more signs of a struggle; she wasn't the kind of woman who would go meekly to her death.

She'd been a champion of Fuller, had stood up for him. Had she, Hanlon wondered, been Hannah Moore's female married lover and if so, did that have any relevance? Had she been Fuller's lover, come to that?

They reached Headington, on the outskirts of Oxford, and Enver explained about the meeting he'd arranged with the DCI in charge of the McIntyre investigation. DCI Templeman wanted to hear from the two of them face-to-face before he restarted his interview with Fuller.

'It should only take half an hour or so, ma'am,' said Enver. 'I hope so,' said Hanlon. She hadn't visited Whiteside for

two days and was beginning to feel guilty.

She thought of him now, alone and unconscious in the airy hospital room in Seven Sisters in North London. It was like *Sleeping*

Beauty in reverse, Whiteside the handsome prince and she the very-much-awake maiden.

She had tried to remember if she'd ever actually read *Sleeping Beauty*. She doubted it. Mark's parents had never read it to him. He said they didn't like any books except the Bible. Perhaps one day they'd tackle *Sleeping Beauty* together.

The Audi threaded its way through the complex street system into the centre of Oxford where the colleges were. Enver hadn't realized that Oxford was such a large place.

It seemed prosperous and smugly pleased with itself. The traffic was gridlocked. It took nearly three-quarters of an hour to drive the relatively short distance across town to the police station.

Hanlon parked and they went into reception. Both she and Enver were aware of the curious glances they attracted and the fact that when they walked in the place seemed prac- tically deserted, yet a few minutes later there was quite a bit of traffic as officers tried to catch a glimpse of the notorious Hanlon.

She had become a minor celebrity within the force, after the island killings. Before that she had been mainly known in the Met for a controversial policing incident when she'd rescued a fellow officer and hospitalized several of his attackers (or innocent bystanders, depending upon who you believed). But now her fame had reached a larger audience.

The Met had clamped as many reporting restrictions on Hanlon's last case as it could, and she herself never spoke about it, but people talk. If anything, the tale had grown in the telling, unhampered by truth, fed on rumour. Now here she was in person, accompanied by her bulky, scary-looking minder, Enver Demirel, the ex-boxer turned cop. Enver looked as if he could wrestle bears and still come out on top.

A competent-looking, burly young woman came up to them. 'Hello. I'm DI Melinda Huss. You must be DCI Hanlon, DI

Demirel.' She had a pleasant, open face with blonde hair and a scattering of freckles. There was a healthy look about her as if she worked on a smallholding, out in the open air. Her shrewd blue eyes assessed the two of them.

The legendary Hanlon seemed a bit of a let-down, if she were honest. She looked tired, careworn, and the remains of a black eye didn't help. Her face was sour and unwelcoming. Quite frankly, thought Melinda, she seemed a bit of a bitch.

Her colleague, though, was a different story. Melinda liked her men to be men. She had no time at all for the effete metro- sexual kind, or for the urban chav. Central Oxford was packed with the first type, scrawny men in skinny jeans and beards. The outskirts of Oxford – Cowley, Headington, Iffley and Botley – were packed with the other, tattooed youths in stonewashed jeans, gold chains, sovereign rings and hoodies.

She found both equally unappealing.

Her eyes drank in Enver's powerful neck and shoulders, the large, strong hands. He wouldn't have a man-bag, or wear moisturizer or use words like 'spritz', or try to get seconded to police the Glastonbury or Reading festivals so he could watch the bands.

He wouldn't use expressions involving the word 'artisanal'. He wouldn't eat or make sourdough, thank God. He certainly wasn't Superman. You couldn't imagine him bounding over a building, or wearing tights, but he absolutely looked more than capable of running through a wall, even if he couldn't hurdle it.

Melinda wished to God she could have him by her side in some of the grim places she had to work. Oxford is much more than the Dreaming Spires; it's also the Blackbird Leys estate and rough pubs in Cowley. She found herself thinking dreamily, I bet he wouldn't just be good in a fight.

She liked his drooping moustache, the sleepy, slightly sexy

bedroom eyes. She liked the ridge of his broken nose and the scar tissue by the side of his eyes. She swallowed hungrily.

'Please follow me,' she said and as she did so, she caught Hanlon looking at her with sardonic amusement and she knew, with a terrible flash of clarity, that the witchlike DCI had more or less read her mind. Hanlon watched, expressionless as an Easter Island statue, while a hot, crimson flush of embarrass- ment spread over DI Huss's face from her neck up, like mercury rising in a thermometer.

I hate you, you cow, thought Huss venomously. Coming up here from London, telling us what to do in Thames Valley CID where you obviously think we don't know our arse from our elbow.

'DCI Templeman started without you,' she said as they walked down the blue-carpeted corridor. She smiled warmly at Enver.

Huss led them through a door into a small room that adjoined the interview room. There was a one-way mirror separating the two rooms and through it they could see Fuller, accompanied by a lawyer – presumably the duty solicitor, thought Hanlon – opposite them an owl-faced, overweight policeman in his late fifties and a much younger colleague.

'DCI Templeman,' said Huss, pointing towards the older man. He had a monotonous, Scottish accent that betrayed no emotion as he spoke.

'You lied to us about being in your hotel room at the time of the murder of your student, Jessica McIntyre. You are unable to account for the presence of gloves in your possession similar to those we believe the killer may have used. Is there anything else that may have slipped your memory, Dr Fuller?'

Hanlon was used to seeing Fuller confident and in control of his class. Here he looked understandably nervous. Even his bouffant-style hair looked lank and lifeless, and when he bowed his head, Hanlon could see the pale scalp beneath. She could see deep lines on his face and suddenly realized that Fuller must have been wearing some form of foundation make-up in class. Here, in the police station, he seemed to have aged ten years.

Fuller said something inaudible to his lawyer, who nodded. 'No comment,' said Fuller.

Templeman nodded. He took his glasses off, cleaned then replaced them. He continued the investigation in his robot- like Scottish voice, leaving almost palpable pauses between sentences. You could almost count to three in the silent gap between the end of one sentence and the beginning of another. His enunciation was very precise. It was the kind of voice that after a while would drive you mad with its grinding monotony. 'And you weren't in the college when the crime was

committed?'

His lawyer intervened. 'None of us, DCI Templeman, knows exactly when that was,' he said. 'How can my client possibly be expected to answer that?'

'I'll rephrase the question. When did you arrive at the college, Dr Fuller?'

'About seven o'clock.'

Templeman nodded. 'Were you anywhere near the college prior to that?'

Fuller shook his head. Templeman pointed to the small microphone between them. 'Please answer audibly, Dr Fuller.'

'No.'

Templeman produced a black-and-white photo from the blue file in front of him. It was sealed in a transparent evidence bag. With maddening slowness, Templeman made a point of carefully locating the identifying tag.

'We are now looking at exhibit 5 AC. This was taken by the college CCTV at four fifty p.m. It clearly shows you, Dr Fuller, outside the college gates. Would you care to elaborate?'

'No comment,' said Fuller.

'It would help us to believe you, Dr Fuller, if you cared to share with us the reason for your presence. May I remind you why we are here. One of your students has been murdered. I would have thought you might want to cooperate with us.'

'No comment.'

'But you were there, Dr Fuller, and a minute or so ago you said you weren't. It's difficult for us to work out what happened, when you keep changing your story.'

'No comment.'

The interview carried on. It was obvious that Fuller was evading the truth. The relentless, monotonous questioning continued, until Templeman produced another photo, this time of a pair of black bikini briefs and some brown hairs in a small plastic bag, the kind used for change in a bank.

'We are now looking at exhibits 8 ED and 12 ED, a pair of ladies' black bikini briefs, size 8, and a plastic bag, containing a swatch of brown body hair. And these were found in your hotel room, Dr Fuller. Could you explain?'

Templeman didn't alter the pitch of his voice, but the tension in the room increased. Fuller's lawyer looked questioningly at him.

In the adjoining room, Hanlon and Enver looked questioningly at DI Huss. 'The McIntyre woman was missing her pants and a section of pubic hair had been removed.' She smiled at Enver, blanking Hanlon out. 'I'd say Dr Fuller has some explaining to do.'

Hanlon was unimpressed. She herself was size eight. I knew McIntyre, she thought. I knew her shape. That woman was five eleven and no way was she a size eight; more like a twelve. When those come back from forensics it won't be her DNA on them.

Fuller leaned forward. He showed no sign of emotion other than profound weariness as he spoke into the microphone.

'No comment,' he said.

. . .

On the drive back from Oxford to London, Enver tried to engage Hanlon in conversation but she was in a foul mood.

'Well, where did he get those pants then?' said Enver. 'Why won't he say where he was that afternoon?'

London's not the only place with brothels, thought Hanlon. 'I bet you fifty quid they're not hers,' was all she'd say. That and, 'If you choose to prefer Miss Barnyard's judgement over

mine,' spoken with real vitriol, 'that's your business.'

Enver was hurt by Hanlon's tone. He couldn't for the life of him see what he'd done, or said, to warrant her evident rage. Or DI Huss come to that. Presumably she was Miss Barnyard.

As they'd reached the car, Hanlon had flung her jacket into the back, crumpling up the innocent material with real venom. She'd rolled her sleeves up and was gripping the steering wheel so hard that her knuckles showed white through the skin. Even her hair seemed to bristle with anger, and as she drove she kept pushing it back and upwards with her left hand so it stood up in manic corkscrews. Her lips were compressed tight as the powerful car reached a hundred down the motorway. He didn't question her competence as a driver; she was perfectly in control. The muscles stood out in her forearms. Enver watched her admiringly. She looked incredibly attractive when she was angry, he thought.

Enver sighed at their speed. If Traffic stopped her, God knows what would happen. An automatic ban maybe. He badly wanted a Jelly Snake to soothe his nerves but feared her reaction.

I must stop comfort eating, he thought.

Before they'd got in the car, Hanlon had checked the messages on her phone. One, unknown caller, had read simply:

They want to pull the plug on Whiteside. See Lansdale, union rep.

19

Dame Elizabeth sat in her office, thinking about Hanlon and thinking about Kant. She didn't know it, but she had come to the same conclusion as Hanlon. Most of her life, she had been advocating, and believing in, ruthless honesty, and now she suspected that it had all been easy because she had never needed to make a difficult decision.

Now that time had come, she'd flunked it.

Nearly forty years ago – God, so long ago, she thought – she'd been a young postgraduate student doing research for her Ph.D. at Berlin's Humboldt University. One of the lecturers, not that much older than herself, had been a man called Jonathan Hanlon. His field was the philosophy of art and aesthetics and he epitomized the title of his discipline. He was devastatingly attractive.

That wasn't hyperbole on her part. People stared at him surreptitiously in public. He had done modelling work, highly unusual in the seventies, but his beauty marked him out. There was something of his looks in Hanlon's face – the cheekbones, the set of the jaw, the full mouth, above all the grey eyes. But where hers were cold and unforgiving, his had been warm, life-affirming.

Most of all, Jann Hanlon had charm.

He also had a beautiful wife who he said looked very much like Ophelia in Rossetti's painting. That's where Hanlon would have got her corkscrew curly hair from.

Dame Elizabeth had flung herself at him. She hadn't cared that he was married. She hadn't cared about anything; she was like a woman possessed. She was burning with lust. Not that she'd needed to do much flinging; it would have been like charging at an open door. Jonathan, Jann as everyone called him, was an intense womanizer and Dame Elizabeth had been very attractive. And for six wonderful months, he was hers.

It was the best time of her life. It was exhilarating. They went to wild parties with the Fluxus crowd (Jann was a friend of the famous artist Joseph Beuys), they held court at the Adlon Hotel, they went to openings at Berlin's galleries, they did soft drugs with avant-garde Berlin musicians, they went to decadent thirties-style nightclubs where Jann was a big hit with the drag queens.

This was the seventies before Berlin had become the fashionable place to be in Europe, and the shadow of post-1945 destruction still hung heavily. Jann introduced her to Grunkohl with smoked sausage, Eisbein and Konigsberger Klopse, beef dumplings with capers in cheap restaurants. They drank huge quantities of beer and wine.

They hung out with Andy Warhol, when Jann had helped organize an exhibition of his work at the Kunsthalle, and they had endless sex in her cheap apartment, that smelled of hash, patchouli oil and incense, in Alexanderplatz, overlooking the Berlin Wall.

The pace that he lived his life was feverish; there was never any time to reflect or consider. Any money he earned he would squander. Jann never saved or worried about the future. She remembered him saying, *Zeit ist Geld und Geld ist gut*. Time is money and money is good. An unfashionable view at the time.

She remembered lying naked in bed with Jann in January while outside a bitterly cold wind blew in from the east and snow gently and silently fell, her bedroom warmed by an old thirties stove and his heat. He had a marvellous body; she guessed that was something else Hanlon had inherited from her father.

She remembered a particularly groundbreaking Anselm Kiefer exhibition. Afterwards they'd walked hand in hand down the Unter den Linden to the Brandenburger Tor. She had been so much in love with Jann at that moment in time it was almost ecstatically painful.

She remembered shopping in the flea market at Rathaus Schöneburg, where Kennedy had made his *Ich bin ein Berliner* speech. And Jann had bought her the bracelet that now Hanlon was wearing.

Then came the inevitable split. A huge row, Jann had a terrible temper. Unforgivable things were said on both sides, the typical, lacerating wounds of love gone wrong. Jann went back to Ophelia (Catherine, that was her name, Dame Elizabeth remembered now); angrily and dismissively, she returned the jewellery he'd given her and came back to England, back to Oxford. Jann was a distant memory, a footnote on one of the many pages in the book of her life.

Then two years later, in the late seventies, 1979 it would have been, came a shocked phone call from Germany one night. Jann was dead, a stupid, perfectly avoidable, car crash. Not murdered by a jealous husband, or dead of a romantic disease. A car crash. A stupid, stupid car crash. Jann had always driven too fast, too aggressively. He drove like he lived, without evaluating risk properly, heedless of consequences. In some ways it was typically Jann, infuriating and thoughtless.

It was such a waste, a dumb, pointless way to die.

She wondered if DCI Hanlon had the same tendency to charge in without thinking.

Dame Elizabeth was a good judge of character. She rather suspected she had.

Until two days ago she had hardly thought of him in years. Earlier that day, she'd phoned the man who'd given her the news of the fatal car crash, another academic, now at Belfast University. He'd told her of Catherine's unravelling after Jann's death, the depression that settled over her like a thick, impenetrable fog. There had been one botched suicide attempt then, one evening, she strode out in front of an Inter City 125 train. No mistakes there. No cry for help. The real thing. The daughter, given up for adoption, had now resurfaced

before her very eyes, in her university.

Dame Elizabeth was technically unsure where she stood on the subject of fate, but what she did know was that she had a duty to tell Hanlon what she knew of her parents. Well, about her father anyway. What Hanlon chose to do with that information would be up to her, but Dame Elizabeth would have acted properly.

With a sinking heart, she took Hanlon's card from her purse and texted to ask her to meet her in the lecture hall where they had first met, at seven p.m on Sunday. The terse reply came almost immediately, a graceless yes.

20

Hanlon looked out of her window at the commuters hurrying eagerly away from the City and at the traders standing in noisy, expensively suited groups outside pubs. I need a distraction, she thought.

Endless images of Whiteside in his hospital bed mixed with thoughts of Jessica McIntyre and Fuller, like some crazy snow-globe of memory. She remembered how McIntyre's engagement ring, below her wedding band, had sparkled in the light when she had moved her left hand. No, no, it hadn't sparkled, it had blazed, almost as if it had supernatural powers. Hanlon had never really thought about diamonds before, except in crime terms; now she did. It must have been unbelievably expensive, she thought.

She wondered what Hannah had made of Jessica, with her Mulberry handbag and Manolo Blahniks, her leggy beauty, her poise and her wealth, all that Hannah was not or did not have. The two of them united in death. The two of them victims of the same killer.

Oh, this is hopeless, she realized. She suddenly thought of Michaels. Perhaps he could shed some light on the relationship between Fuller and McIntyre. He had disliked McIntyre, she knew that, and he was no friend of Fuller's. But once the chip on his shoulder had been taken into consideration, he could well provide some valuable insights.

I wonder, mused Hanlon.

Will be in Bloomsbury. Fancy a quick drink? she texted him.

White Horse, 5.30, half an hour, have to be back at work for 6 p.m., came the reply.

Perfect, thought Hanlon, texting back a *yes*. Let's see what the chef has to say.

21

Hanlon met the union rep, Derek Lansdale, on Saturday morning. He made it clear that Hanlon had absolutely no say in Whiteside's fate. He made it more than clear; he positively revelled in telling her.

He reiterated that Hanlon had no claim on Whiteside; she wasn't family or in a relationship with him. Unlike his parents, who were the ones who had decided that enough was enough, that it was time to let their son go. He even brought up the cost of keeping Whiteside alive. Besides, he said, maybe Whiteside would prefer to be dispatched cleanly, food and drink withheld until Nature had run her course, than languish in this hospitalized limbo.

Lansdale strongly disliked Hanlon. He also was entirely happy to let his feelings show. For more or less the first time in his unionized police life, he wished that management would sack someone. Her. He didn't like women in the police force in general and he disliked her in particular.

He rationalized his thinking to read that she was a bad example to the police force and that if individual police made a habit of recklessly endangering their own lives, it would create a dangerous precedent. The obvious implication, although he didn't actually say it, was that it was Hanlon's fault Whiteside was where he was.

It didn't help her feelings that she often did blame herself for his condition. He was where he was because she had put him in the firing line. The fact that she hadn't ordered him to go, having no authority at the time, but that he had volunteered because he liked and admired her, only made things worse.

Hanlon felt her temper rising dangerously, but managed to control it. The arguments about quality of life and parental rights left her unmoved. The first was a temporary issue in Hanlon's mind anyway. As for the second, Whiteside was not on speaking terms with his mother and father. Lansdale himself, Hanlon despised as a gutless desk-jockey.

She longed to drive her fist repeatedly into Lansdale's pasty white face. Instead, she went home, changed, and ran a punishing five miles, deliberately upping her pace until her body cried out with cleansing pain, then, back home, her body slick with sweat, worked on her abs with endless sit-ups, crunches and abdominal twists. She tortured the muscles until they practically screamed. She showered, checked her phone, and found another message from the unknown caller, the one who had told her about Whiteside, this time giving Whiteside's parents' address in Borough, South London.

She lay on the unrolled futon that was her bed, staring up at the ceiling. She had phoned the number of the mystery caller back, but there was no reply, as she expected. She thought she must know the caller and guessed it was almost certainly a colleague. The motive behind the information provider was far from obvious, though.

Hanlon was notoriously short-fused. Was he – she was sure it was a he – hoping she would create some sort of incident to discredit herself? Anyone who knew Hanlon would quite reasonably assume that she might well turn up at the parents and create some massive, alarming scene.

Momentarily she considered doing just that. Going round to his parents and warning them off. Maybe break something, and she wasn't thinking of a vase. Then she thought of DCI Tremayne, warning her when she was a trainee, 'Don't hit the fuck-it button, Hanlon,' and she rejected the idea.

Or were they trying genuinely to help her, to give her the chance to save Whiteside's life? She had toyed with the idea of getting the phone traced by GPS. Getting the mobile phone service provider's permission would be simplicity itself, but she suspected that whoever had the phone would merely keep it at whichever station he worked out of. She was already sure it was a copper doing this. What good would it do to know where he worked? It's not as if they would have the phone in their uniform pocket. In their place, she'd have stashed it at the back of a cupboard that wasn't used often. An old Nokia or brick – no one would give it a second glance. It would sit there gathering dust until it was next needed.

I've lived too long in a half-world of lies and suspicion, she thought. Absent-mindedly she clenched her fist and tightened her left bicep. The long, sinewy muscle arced obediently. At least there's something I can rely on in this life. I need physical action, she thought. I'm not designed for introspection.

Her phone rang. It was Enver. She felt a huge surge of affection for the man wash over her. She almost snatched at the phone as she picked it up.

'Hello, ma'am, sorry to bother you. There's been a development on the Fuller case.' His voice was as excited as Enver's could be, not a great deal.

'What exactly?'

He hated talking about important things on the phone. He was convinced they were all bugged. 'I don't want to talk about it on the phone,' said the ever-cautious Enver, 'but if you could come over to Euston, I'll fill you in.'

'Give me half an hour,' said Hanlon. She pulled on some cycling gear and trainers, and she was ready. Thank God for Enver Demirel, she thought.

The first thing Hanlon noticed as she strode across the floor of the open-plan office to Enver's desk was a familiar figure sitting opposite the DI. Detective Inspector Melinda Huss, no less.

If Hanlon was less than enthused by the sight of Huss, the flicker of distaste that ran across the latter's face suggested the feeling was mutual. Oblivious to the tension, Enver beamed happily at the two of them.

He can be incredibly obtuse, thought Hanlon. He will never grasp that we can't stand each other.

Hanlon sat down opposite Huss. Her slim, muscled body outlined in Lycra was in marked contrast to the more generous form of DI Huss. Huss was showing quite a bit of cleavage, thought Hanlon, eyeing her up and down, no prizes for guessing whose benefit that was for. Any minute now she'd be staring at Enver and playing with her hair.

Good luck with that, she thought. Enver's so shy of women it's not true. In his own mind he's convinced no woman could possibly find him attractive.

Enver had something on a plate. 'We've got coffee cake, ma'am,' he said. 'DI Huss made it specially. It's got walnuts in.' Hanlon looked at the cake. Much as she hated to admit it, it could have come from an upmarket patisserie. It was the kind of cake that won prizes. It looked superb and was presented on a china plate that certainly did not come from the scabby kitchen area in the corner of the office. Huss had even brought a doily for the cake to sit on.

Hanlon wondered crazily if Huss were baking her way to the

top, her rivals in promotion on the Oxford CID ladder failing medicals left, right and centre, felled by carb- and cholesterol-induced heart problems and Type 2 diabetes.

'Do you bake, ma'am?' asked Huss smugly.

'No,' said Hanlon irritably. She didn't even own an oven. There were shops for that kind of thing. She watched as Enver cut the cake, refusing a slice herself, and then said, 'So, what's this development then?'

Enver, mouth full of coffee and walnut gateau, butter icing and mocha filling, gestured at Huss to explain. His eyes gleamed with pleasure. It was delicious cake, highly flavoured, the sponge moist but firm.

His family background in catering always surfaced at moments like this. He was by far the most talented Demirel in a kitchen. His not going into the family business had been a bitter blow to his father.

'We'd obviously conducted one search of Fuller's room at the Blenheim, but DCI Templeman wanted a secondary search doing, just in case we'd missed something, and sure enough, hidden in the mattress itself, we found another pair of women's pants and some more pubic hair clippings,' she said.

'What size were they?' asked Hanlon.

DI Huss gave her a suspicious look. 'Ten,' she said.

'And the other ones, the size eight?' continued Hanlon, rather enjoying her role as Fuller's barrister in absentia. 'Have you had the results back?'

'We have,' said Huss. 'The DNA is no match for the victim, but the new pants are.'

'And the gloves?'

'No useful results,' conceded Huss.

'So that's when Templeman had the second search done, is it, when the original one exonerated Fuller?' said Hanlon.

Enver had been watching the conversation between the women as it went to and fro like a spectator at a tennis match. 'What does Fuller say?' he asked.

'No comment. That's more or less it. He won't tell us where he was at the time of the murder other than out for a walk to plan his lecture. He cannot explain the presence of the victim's clothing in his room.' Huss looked at them with an air of triumph.

'Presumably he says that they were planted there,' said Hanlon.

'Well, he would, wouldn't he, ma'am,' countered Huss.

Hanlon said acidly, 'And how secure was Fuller's room during his time down at your nick?'

'The door was locked, obviously. It was securely taped. So yes, the area was secure,' said Huss defensively. Hanlon rolled her eyes.

'We hadn't gone overboard with sealing the area. It's Oxford's most famous hotel for heaven's sake,' said Huss defensively. 'We can't go round draping it in crime-scene tape. But yes, the room was sealed.'

'Did anyone think to photograph the seals? Or at least check that their validity hadn't been compromised?' asked Hanlon. There was an uncomfortable pause from DI Huss who said,

'I don't have that information to hand.'

I'll take that as a no, thought Hanlon. If this comes to court, Fuller's lawyer is going to rip you lot to shreds.

'So, what's the state of play with Fuller, have you actually charged him then?' she asked.

DI Huss shook her head. 'He's been bailed pending further enquiries and is due to return to Summertown in three weeks' time, by when the CPS will have decided what to do.'

'And what do you think?' said Hanlon to the DI. 'Do you think he's guilty?'

'Absolutely,' said Huss. 'He's not exactly behaving like an innocent person. He's lied to us, he's evasive, there's a stack of circumstantial evidence around him. He fits the profile.' She paused angrily. 'If he's not guilty he's doing a bloody good job of acting like he is. And I think he's a danger to the public. He's been involved in two murders, possibly three, that we know about. For all we know this is the tip of an iceberg. And if that underwear wasn't Jessica McIntyre's, whose was it? Answer me that!'

I certainly intend to, thought Hanlon. Oh yes, I am going to make that a priority. If Fuller is not the killer, then it's time to start looking elsewhere.

Huss continued, 'If anyone else dies, the press and public are going to be down on us like a ton of bricks. Rightly so.'

Hanlon said nothing, then stood up. God, she's got a great body, thought Huss bitterly, staring enviously at the Lycra- clad form.

'What do you think, ma'am?' she asked.

Hanlon shrugged. 'I'll be in touch,' she said to Enver and nodded coldly to DI Huss.

Huss and Enver watched Hanlon stride across the office floor. Huss noticed that Enver's eyes had lost their sleepy, good- natured look. They were watchful, guarded. He was thinking over Hanlon's position on Fuller.

Huss had been making discreet enquiries about Enver from colleagues. One or two knew him or of him. He was highly regarded, a coming man, and they were all impressed with Enver's ability to handle himself in a brawl. I want him, she thought. I wonder what he's thinking.

Enver wasn't thinking of Huss. He thought she was very attractive, too attractive for him. He moved his mind to the case.

Hanlon obviously had doubts about Fuller's guilt. Huss, on the other hand, was convinced of it. Enver was thinking to himself, Hanlon had a track record of being right. The thing is, he thought gloomily, if Fuller was not the killer, then they were left entirely without a suspect.

'What do you think, Enver?' she said.

'I think, DI Huss, that this is exceptional cake.'

She'd been hoping he would call her Melinda. She'd been so close, maybe a drink after work. Not now. Just her surname. She felt a surge of resentment towards Hanlon.

The woman had ruined her day.

22

He was thinking of the last thirty seconds of Jessica McIntyre's life. Killing her had been a real pleasure. She was an unpleasant, snobbish, domineering, sex-crazed bitch and thoroughly deserved it. It was so much better than killing Hannah Moore, which had been more like drowning a puppy, a trusting puppy at that. Still, he reasoned, we often have to do what we don't want to.

It's all a question of control. Life is inherently unfair. Only through imposing order upon chaos can we hope to progress. And when life attacks us, we have to fight back. And when we lose we can return to the fight, coldly, dispassionately.

For our self-respect depends upon our ability to make requital, for good or for evil, as Nietzsche said.

He thought about McIntyre some more. All too often in his life, he had suffered unfairly, he had taken too much grief. It was a very pleasant change indeed to be dishing some out. McIntyre with her silly upper-class ways, and her equally deluded intellectual arrogance, was better off dead. Well, the world was most certainly better off without her, anyway.

He guessed that he had two more killings to go before he could stop and relax. Two more women, both powerful characters in their own way, Dame Elizabeth and Gallagher.

It would be a particular shame to kill Dame Elizabeth. She had after all employed him and he had always prided himself on his good relationships with his previous employers, but he had little choice. At least, he thought, he could take pride in the fact that in the period he had worked for her, she'd had nothing but good things to say about him. He had always taken a great deal of care with his work; he had always been highly regarded.

He had the music for Dame Elizabeth's departure planned. Nietzsche of course had a ready quote for music. He really was an incredible thinker.

Without music, life would be a mistake.

'D.I.S.C.O.' by Ottowan. That would dictate how she would die, the movements of her final dance on this earth. He had choreographed the killing meticulously.

At least with Dame Elizabeth he would not have to rush things too much. McIntyre was a strong woman; he had been forced to be quick. Luckily he'd had the element of surprise. Dame Elizabeth was in remarkable shape for a woman of her years, but she would be unable to put up much of a struggle. He hummed a phrase of the song to himself.

He had a very pleasant singing voice.

23

Ask most people in Tottenham or Arsenal, North London in general, if they'd heard of the Andersons and you would get a yes. The Andersons were a well-known crime family, second generation now, currently led by Dave 'Jesus' Anderson. Jesus was his nickname since he'd crucified a rival to a door with a nail gun.

Drugs and prostitution were the Andersons' core businesses, these days. Malcolm, Dave's father, had started off in the seven- ties with armed robbery. Then most wages were paid in cash and there'd been whole fleets of vans carrying money for payday on Fridays. Technology changes had put an end to that.

Security vans delivering to banks had become too hard to target what with explosive-propelled dyes and other technological improvements to mark the cash. Malcolm Anderson's choice of crime seemed as quaint and old-fashioned as being a highwayman. But drugs and prostitution had remained stable, although increased Internet traffic, together with cloned copies of drugs from China and the super-abundance of legal highs freely available, were denting the drugs trade.

Hanlon had sent Dave Anderson down once. She'd also

perverted the course of justice to get him freed, in return for information to save a child's life. Now she was going to ask for his help again.

Hanlon felt she knew without a shadow of doubt where Fuller would have been on the Thursday afternoon, assuming that he hadn't been murdering Jessica McIntyre. Oxford would have its brothels too. Fuller, though, with his very specialist tastes, would have looked to visit a definite S&M place, and his reluctance to speak on the subject suggested that a certain code of silence was expected. In other words, Fuller was more frightened of whoever ran the brothel than he was of the police.

Hanlon took this as a personal affront. She wanted criminals to know who was boss. She wanted them afraid of the police in general, herself in particular. If Fuller wasn't going to give their names for questioning, she'd find out herself. She'd bet Campion would know.

S&M brothels aren't that common. It was a restricted world and they would all know each other by reputation, if nothing else.

Campion wouldn't tell her. 'Me, grass someone up, dearie, I should coco,' she'd say, or words to that effect. She hadn't minded throwing Fuller to the wolves but a fellow criminal, that'd be different.

We'll see how Jesus Anderson's name will play with you, thought Hanlon grimly. I'll bet you won't say no to him.

Few people did. And they were all dead.

She had texted Anderson upon leaving the police station in Euston. She hadn't seen him in person since prison where he'd been on remand for what should have been an open-and- shut case of possession with intent to supply. She'd followed the subsequent dropping of charges against him and she had kept his phone number. She'd always suspected she would use it at some stage.

She returned home to the one-room flat where she lived in the City. Her flat was as solitary as its owner.

It had originally been designed as a kind of executive penthouse for the small four-storey office block it stood in, but had fallen foul of planning regulations. One of Hanlon's admirers had tipped her off about it. He worked for the investment company that owned the property. The flat was redesignated as a security office and leased to Hanlon under an assumed name as a business premises. It had a separate entrance to the offices; none of the workers had ever registered her presence. She had never brought anyone home.

Officially she lived in a terrace in Bow. It was where she was listed on police records; it was where her mail was sent. The woman who actually lived there was a seventy-year-old ex-pub landlady who Hanlon had known for years. Gloria was her name and she too liked anonymity, hugging her solitariness close to her. She trusted no one, the ideal gatekeeper between Hanlon and the outside world.

Hanlon showered, changed and checked her phone. Anderson said he'd meet her at seven p.m. in a pub, The Three Compasses in Edmonton, north of Tottenham.

It was five to seven when Hanlon pulled up outside the pub. It was a simple drive, more or less direct, up through the intriguing strata of London. From the shiny temple of mammon that was the City, through hip Hoxton and the middle-class enclave of Stoke Newington, through orthodox Jewish Stamford Hill to the Turkish foothills of North Tottenham and beyond. She checked the clock on the car. She was always punctual.

Being late was a sign of grave moral weakness in Hanlon's eyes. Edmonton wasn't an area she knew well. She'd been on a team that had recovered a body from the reservoir years before, but that was about it. She also knew it had Britain's largest incinerator. Greenpeace called it London's Cancer Factory. LondonWaste, its current owners, call it London EcoPark.

A rose by any other name, thought Hanlon. Doubtless the Andersons had made use of its facilities on more than one occasion. She could see its huge, slim tower thrusting into the sky from here, like a minatory finger.

The street that the pub was in looked poor and rough. The cars parked by the side of the road were old, most of the tax discs out of date. The tarmac was worn, the pavement cracked and the terraced houses that lined the street, each with a satellite dish pointed hopefully at the sky above, were in urgent need of repair. Curtains sagged, paint peeled. Front gardens were unkempt, with weeds and uncut grass, breeze blocks, mattresses and other detritus. It was an unloved street, in an unloved part of London. Several windows had right-wing flyers displayed and there were a couple of ragged St George flags, hanging from rudimentary poles out of top windows.

There was a group of kids, all of them white, although it was a very ethnically diverse neighbourhood, playing football on the pavement. The street, Gilpin Road, was a cul de sac. Outside the pub, two large, shaven-headed men stood, menacingly watchful. They weren't smoking, they didn't have drinks; part of Anderson's Praetorian guard, thought Hanlon. They were wearing a bouncer's off-duty uniform of crombie coat and shiny DMs. Hanlon could see the faint bulge at the front of the shoes that indicated they were steel-toed. The Three Compasses was not a pub you went to for a drink, unless you had dealings with the Andersons. It was a business premises, not a licensed premises.

The kids, seven of them, formed a little semi-circle round Hanlon as she got out of the Audi and locked it. One of them, aged she guessed about eleven or twelve, took a pace forward. He was small and stocky, his blond hair cut short. He exuded confidence.

'Nice car, miss,' he said, with mock politeness. He was wearing a very new pair of Air Jordan Nike trainers. Hanlon guessed they cost over three figures. He had a Lonsdale T-shirt and a gold chain. The eyes looking at Hanlon were those of an adult, not those of a child. They were disconcertingly vicious. He was the kind of child who would find it amusing to throw bricks at a cat, she thought.

'Mind your car for you, can we?'

Hanlon wondered what the going rate for her Audi would be, if she didn't want to return and find it keyed and the tyres let down, or punctured.

Her silence and impassive face were beginning to annoy the kid. He glared at her with an expression no child should have. It belonged to a much older head. He wondered if she spoke English.

'Twenty quid,' he said.

Hanlon pointed at the pub. 'You know Dave Anderson, don't you?' Her voice was quiet, but the kid flinched. He knew a threat when he heard it. Her face was sinister in the gathering gloom of the evening.

The kid nodded; he didn't look so tough now. He looked worried. Hanlon carried on, menacingly. 'I'm meeting him over there. Anything happens to my car, if so much as a leaf blows on it, I'll ask him to sort it out with you. I'm holding you personally responsible. You got that?'

The kid nodded.

'You know what he'll do to you.' The kid nodded again.

'Good,' said Hanlon.

She crossed the road to the pub. The kids resumed their game of football, but this time much further down the street. No one wanted to accidentally kick the ball against her car.

* * *

Anderson hadn't changed since she'd last seen him. His hair was still long and slightly ratty, the face still thin and the mouth narrow-lipped. He always looked slightly malnourished, she thought. Then again, perhaps he was.

She'd seen pictures of his father leaving court thirty years ago. He had been a bit of a ladies' man. He'd looked like a seventies' footballer, leather bomber jacket, big-collared shirt, sideburns and tight, flared trousers with zip-up ankle boots. He'd have worn Brut and driven a souped-up Ford Capri.

Dave Anderson made no such concessions to the fairer sex or 'the ladies, God bless 'em', as his dad would have put it. He was just violence in human form, dangerous and highly intelligent. They sat in a room at the back of the small pub, a poolroom with two tables, the baize scuffed and stained. His personal worth, as they say in Rich List terms, must have been several million but financial success, thought Hanlon sardonically, hadn't changed him. He was still the man who'd nailed someone to a door, the kind of man who would methodically torture you then knock your teeth out with a brick for fun, the kind of man whose only publicized regret, in a particularly brutal

killing, was that the victim had died far too soon. 'Hello, DCI Hanlon,' he said.

Hanlon nodded politely. Very few people could have known about her promotion. It was Anderson's way of letting her know how powerful he was; his way of telling her he had an informant in the force. She had expected nothing less. You'd always find a bent copper somewhere or other. They're like rats; you're never less than a few feet away from one. She looked around her, making the usual, careful inventory of her surroundings. The back bar room they were in had no natural light, no windows, and was dimly lit by cheap imitation-candle wall fittings, with dirty, brown shades. Most of the fittings were crooked and the wallpaper old and nicotine-stained. It had been there for years. Some of the marks on the green of the pool-table baize looked suspiciously like blood. She guessed it was in here that Anderson would mete out punishments.

It looked that sort of place.

There was a strong element of theatricality in Anderson's brutality, thought Hanlon. If you were brought in here against your will, just his reputation would suffice. And this room was like a stage set. It looked like the kind of place where a London hard man would kick you to death. Just looking around would lower anyone's spirits.

Anything in here would look like an instrument of torture or death, from the stained pool table, to the small plumber's blow-torch standing on the end of the bar next to a pair of pliers. In a workman's toolbox, pliers were an innocent, useful device, but with Anderson, pliers conjured up images of teeth, nipples, genitalia, any soft tissue, in their metal jaws.

Even the pool balls ceased to look innocent and more like something useful to be stuffed inside a sock and used as a makeshift club.

'Mr Anderson would like a word.' Not what you would want breathed into your shell-like.

Anderson indicated a table with two chairs. She'd forgotten how big his hands were. They sat down and he offered her a drink. She declined with a shake of the head. One of Anderson's employees stood attentively behind the chair that he was sitting on, like a large, none-too-bright Alsatian, at his master's heel. 'So, what did you want to talk about?' asked Anderson.

He had immediately agreed to see Hanlon. She intrigued him, maybe not least because she was one of the very few people he'd ever met who wasn't afraid of him. Others in that category had been either criminally insane or unbelievably stupid. He didn't wonder at all how she got her black eye. Such things were commonplace in his world.

'A specialist S&M brothel in Oxford. It'll be centrally located off St Giles, I'd guess off the Banbury or Woodstock Road,' she said.

He smiled, or rather his mouth did. 'It's a bit off my manor.' 'I realize that. But Iris Campion would know, wouldn't she.' Anderson laughed. 'Soho Iris. You move in peculiar circles, DCI Hanlon.' He turned to the bodyguard behind him. 'Danny, go and tell my dad I've got a copper here asking about Soho

Iris. That'll give him a laugh.'

Danny gave Hanlon a warning glance, as if to say don't you dare do anything while I'm gone, although quite what he had in mind she couldn't begin to imagine. He turned and left the room.

'So how's your sergeant then, the one that was in a coma?' 'Still in a coma,' Hanlon replied. Then she asked, 'And your dad?'

Anderson shrugged. 'Still dying.' He smiled thinly. 'Busy planning his funeral. It's going to be huge. He's working out seating arrangements now. For the meal afterwards. People get very touchy about things like that. He was always good at planning, Dad. He never felt he got the credit he deserved for his jobs. He was always Mad Malc, oh fuck, it's Malcy with a sawn-off, Malcy'll break your legs, but I tell you something for nothing. Seventeen armoured vans before he got caught, he was the brains and it was only because he was grassed up by that Maltese Alex, that he ever did serious time.'

Nothing like a stroll down memory lane, thought Hanlon. Happy days, blags, the Sweeney, armoured cars, shooters. Dave Anderson would have been a baby when all this was going on.

She knew the names only from old-timers she'd worked with. DCI Tremayne would have recognized the name. She'd been thinking a lot about him of late.

'Disappeared didn't he, Maltese Alex,' said Hanlon.

'Did you know that Edmonton incinerator's chimney is a

hundred metres high,' said Anderson elliptically. 'They started it up in 1971. Lot of things have been burned there over the years. Gone up in smoke. Cremated.' The two of them contemplated Maltese Alex's demise, his dust particles scattered to the North London winds. 'He wasn't even Maltese, you know, he was from fucking Pinner.' He shook his head in contempt. 'What a tosser,' he added with real scorn.

Danny appeared at the door. 'He wants to come down, boss.' Anderson rolled his eyes and stood up. 'He won't have a stair lift put in. He says it's for old people. I'll be back in a minute.' A short while later he reappeared, carrying his father in his arms, as you would a child. He didn't look much heavier than one now. The old man had one arm around his son's neck. Hanlon guessed the skeletal Malcolm Anderson would weigh in now at under six stone. Danny was behind with a small oxygen tank and, with a free hand, pulled an old armchair forward that was in the corner. Dave Anderson settled his father down in it. The old man gestured for the oxygen and put the ends of the clips from the tubing connected to the cylinder in his

nose. He closed his eyes and breathed as deeply as he could.

His skin was waxy, translucent, and his breathing was laboured from the cancer. He'd had one lung removed and the other was barely functioning. His pupils were dilated from opiates, but his eyes still had the same angry look as his son's. Hanlon had stood up out of respect. Now the old man indicated she should sit down. She waited until he'd caught his breath. Malcolm Anderson looked at her appreciatively and spoke. 'Always a pleasure when David brings a nice girl home.' He gave a kind of wheezing laugh. 'And I hear you've got a steady job too.'

Hanlon found herself grudgingly drawn to the terminally ill old criminal, who could still keep a sense of humour in the face of death, now only kissing distance away. Grace under pressure. 'It's only our second date. Don't get your hopes up,' said Hanlon.

Malcolm Anderson smiled and grimaced, as a wave of pain struck him. He adjusted something on a belt around his waist. Hanlon guessed it was a pump for morphine.

'So, tell me about Iris, I haven't seen her for ages.' His voice was little louder than a whisper.

Hanlon told him about the brothel without mentioning Fuller. He was particularly amused by her description of Iris's maid.

He closed his eyes and fell silent. 'I knew her before, before you know.' He brushed one sunken cheek with his fingertips, miming a cutting action. 'Razor Lewis, he was called. Obvious reasons really. I was glad I killed that cunt for her.' He gave a wheezy, faint laugh. 'I can say that now, no one's going to nick me. I've done a few things I regret now, too late of course, but not that. Razor Lewis, that takes me back.' He closed his eyes momentarily and a smile both wistful and ominous played over his lips. For a second Hanlon could imagine him as he was before the illness.

He opened his eyes and now they were hard and unforgiving. 'I hated that bloke. He was so fucking . . .' he paused, searching for the right word, 'uncouth.'

His eyes closed again. 'You go and see her, see Iris. Tell her I told you she'd help. Give her my love, darling.' He hissed to himself from the pain. 'Up we go, David.'

Gently, Dave Anderson lifted his father up, much as he in his turn had been carried up the same stairs as a sleepy child by his dad years ago.

The door closed behind them and Hanlon stood up. 'Say thank you to your boss,' she said to Danny. She looked round the empty pool room. The impassive Danny, hands folded in front of him, stood quietly in a corner. He nodded and watched Hanlon leave the back bar.

Out in the street the kids were gone and her Audi was unscathed. She got in and drove slowly home through the North London streets.

Hanlon thought to herself, that's the first time anyone has called me darling in a very long time.

24

Sunday morning and the City, London's financial square mile, was practically empty. It always felt strange to her, the eerie silence that enveloped the district at weekends, like being in a zombie film or some post-apocalyptic disaster movie.

Hanlon rode through the deserted streets on her Fuji triathlon bike, enjoying the freedom and the absence of traffic. Tomorrow, Monday, three hundred thousand workers would be decanted into the area. Today, on a Sunday, there'd be fewer than seven thousand and most of those would be invisible. Weekends were a great time to cycle around the City, particularly a Sunday, when she had no training to be done. Sunday was a rest day and she limited herself to light exercise, like cycling around just for fun. Sometimes she just liked to enjoy her body for a change.

She ate breakfast at a café, chewing her way without enthusiasm through an omelette, and returned home. She felt restless and irritable. The following day she'd decided to go and see Campion at the brothel.

Fuller was preying on her mind.

She couldn't work out if he was a killer or if, as he claimed, someone else was doing the crimes and framing him. DI Huss, however, had irritatingly put the problem very well. If Fuller was the killer, he was still at large and if anyone else died they were going to look increasingly negligent. The press would certainly have a field day. She could almost see the headlines now.

Why was this man free to kill again? Incompetent cops bungle investigation. The real Dr Evil.

She was mildly surprised that there had been nothing yet in the papers, almost certainly because the second murder had happened down in Oxford and no connection had yet been made.

In one of his last classes she'd been to, Fuller had touched on Utilitarianism, the theory that you can measure if something's good by its impact on society. On that basis, they should put Fuller behind bars immediately for the public good. If he was guilty, the murders would stop, because he could no longer commit them. If someone were trying to frame him, the murders would have to stop too.

When she found the brothel in Oxford that she was sure Fuller had attended, she could maybe get confirmation one way or another. They'd never be able to use it in court, but it'd help clarify her mind. She knew that this was a very arrogant way of looking at things, but she was getting increasingly disillusioned with the police force. She decided that if her superiors discovered what she was up to and tried to discipline her, then she would resign. She would resign very publicly too.

Hanlon had never sold information or stories to the press; she despised them. But she did know several journalists she had a grudging respect for and she was sure they would leap at the opportunity to publish any Hanlon-led revelation. And she did know a lot of dirt.

She looked around her one-room apartment for inspiration as to what to do with her day. Hanlon was terrible at killing time. In truth, work was her drug. Her boss, Corrigan, had once wondered to himself what motivated Hanlon. The answer was simple. It was work. It gave her something interesting to do. It filled time. She didn't have the kind of distractions that most people have. She didn't have any friends to see, any real hobbies other than triathlon, if that could be called a hobby, and today was supposed to be a rest day. The triathlon was more a way of mortifying the flesh than a desire for sporting achievement. Six days a week she worked her body till it screamed in pain, Sundays she deliberately did nothing, to let it recover. It was the hardest part of her training.

She had no TV. Television annoyed her, as did film and music. In fact, most things annoyed Hanlon. She could have gone out for lunch, but eating was not done for fun. In truth restaurants slightly sickened her. She particularly disliked the elevation of food to a quasi-religious experience with its own hagiography, its own priesthood and its own liturgy. It had got seriously out of hand, in her opinion. Even the process of eating, moving food around in her mouth, she found faintly disgusting.

She had a book to finish on the Spanish Civil War but didn't feel like it at the moment. It was hard to work out who was what, through the thick forests of acronyms – the POUM, the CNT-FAI, the UGT, the PSUC, it was bewildering. The book was, however, one of the few things in her flat to read; the picture on the wall, a signed black-and-white photo of the German artist Joseph Beuys, the only thing to look at.

The only link to a father she never knew.

Art was one of the few things she did enjoy and she was surprisingly knowledgeable about it. When she was young, a man had come to the house where she lived with her adoptive parents and left the photo, signed and framed, of the artist sitting in a corner of his studio wearing work boots, jeans and his trademark fisherman's vest. Under the brim of his hat, Beuys looked sad and slightly worried. His eyes had a haunted look. Her adoptive parents had told her that the photo had belonged to her father and that she should have it. It was the only thing of his that she owned.

She unrolled her futon mattress and lay on it, staring at the ceiling. She ought to be visiting Whiteside's parents to try to talk them out of their decision, but she feared her temper. There were times when she envied Anderson's freedom of action. He would have made them an offer they couldn't refuse. But Hanlon knew she could never physically assault a couple in their sixties. That being the case, there was no point threatening them. Like Anderson, Hanlon didn't make threats. Their method was to point out to the other person the consequences of non- obedience.

It was then up to that person to choose their fate.

For lack of anything better to do, she took her phone out and texted Dame Elizabeth to see if they were still OK for their meeting.

Dame Elizabeth responded almost immediately in the affirmative, seven p.m., then she added casually:

I think I might be able to tell you something about your father, if you're interested.

Hanlon stared in disbelief at the screen. She read the message again to make sure there was no confusion on her part, that she hadn't somehow misunderstood.

. . . if you're interested.

Well, that would be a classic understatement.

All her conscious life, since she could remember, she'd wanted to know more about the man whose surname she bore and, paradoxically, almost just as strong was the desire not to know. Everyone else knew where they came from it seemed, but she did not. She had no parents, no siblings, no family. Nothing.

Sometimes this was a thing of pride, sometimes a source of unhappiness.

Then again, she was honest enough to realize that she almost certainly could have found out if she'd so chosen. There would be public records to consult, established procedures for this kind of thing, existing protocols. She could even have used police resources, blind eyes would have been turned, and lastly she could have utilized the network of people who owed her favours, or simply did her bidding.

She'd done none of those things. She wondered if at the back of this lay cowardice. The worry that she might discover some highly unpalatable truth about her parentage. What if her father had turned out to be a rapist, a worthless junkie, insane? She already knew she had a mother crazed enough to commit suicide, that much her adoptive parents had told her.

Even worse maybe, depressingly normal. An accounts clerk with hairy ears and a cardigan.

She'd turned her back on her past, but now the past had risen to claim her. As Dame Elizabeth had found out, you can ignore the truth but it won't go away.

'Fine,' replied Hanlon, tapping the word in. She lay back down on the mattress. Her grey eyes for once lacked their usual angry certainty. Tonight would be the first time in her life that anybody had told her anything about her father.

If I'm interested, of course, she thought.

25

DCI Hanlon was not the only person with family on their mind. Fuller too lay on his bed, a bottle of vodka on the table beside it, thinking about the past. He'd got to Oxford like Laura, but by a very different route.

He was sixteen when he did his A levels, nearly two years younger than everyone else in his class. Big's career at the BBC had crashed and burned. Uncle Phil, steadily climbing the corporate ladder, had ditched her for younger meat.

Big was axed from TV. She'd been judged by the Corporation as too old and unattractive to be in the public eye. The flat in central London was now gone and Monica Fuller spent most of her days and nights drowning her sorrows at The Queen's Head pub round the corner from their new flat in Acton, in a far from glamorous part of West London. She told the regulars that she was involved in community dance projects. They didn't care. Nobody who drank there cared about anything any more. To be a regular at the Queen's was to be a card-carrying failure. It was a truly terrible pub.

Gideon Fuller's academic career was beginning to unfurl like a triumphant banner.

When they left central London, he had left the private school where he'd been a scholarship student and had wound up at the local comprehensive. Learning moved at a more sedate pace there. Fuller, through a mix of streaming, and a headmaster worried that the new kid whose public-school accent marked him out so dramatically might come to an unpleasant end, was fast-tracked.

Fuller, lost in unhappy memories of the past, poured himself another vodka. He picked away at the recollections of the past like a scab. His eyes narrowed. He was remembering his last day at home. His ability to recall events was amazingly good. He must have relived this event thousands of times. His free hand held Vulture gently. Vulture had been there too.

It must have been in August, twenty years ago. The results had come in the post, which would have been nine thirty a.m. There were two letters, one for him, one for Big, as he had come to think of her.

He remembered holding the envelope that contained the key to his future. He knew he had done well, but how well remained to be seen. He had opened the buff envelope with his name on, four grade As. If he passed the Oxford University entrance exam which he was signed up for in the autumn (and he knew he would – fish swim, birds fly, I pass exams, thought Gideon), he'd be in and away from all this mess. That was the expression he used to himself, mess. Gideon never swore. He didn't want to be like Big, with her foul mouth, and he would never drink for the same reason.

He showed Vulture his results. Vulture was delighted for him. He waggled his neck and his beak jumped up and down with excitement. Gideon felt a surge of happiness. It was an unusual feeling and one he had learned to associate with achievement, with things, not people.

Things make you happy; people just hurt you. It was an axiom.

In the present day, his phone started ringing. Fuller ignored it.

He was reliving his past in every excruciating detail. His memories were startlingly vivid and detailed.

As if on cue, Monica Fuller's bedroom door had opened. 'Morning, Mum,' he said. His mother gave him a look of

angry disgust.

'What's that you've got there?' she demanded. Big was still drunk from the night before, but only too aware of how bedraggled she was looking. She'd slept in the clothes she'd been wearing and a residual smell of The Queen's Head, the ghost of Christmas Past, lingered on the fabric. She noticed Gideon wrinkle his nose slightly and a wave of anger against her prissy, goody-goody son surged through her. Who did he think he was to judge her, the little bastard. She badly wanted to hurt him. Let him share her pain. Do you think it's fun being me, she thought, does it look like I'm having a laugh? She took a cigarette from the packet on the table and lit one. She knew he hated smoking.

She snatched the letter from him, holding it at arm's length so she could focus, one eye half closed against the smoke rising from the cigarette in her mouth, and read through it. Well, no joy there. Her lips curled. Academic results, big deal, what use are they in the real world?

She opened the other letter. It was from his drama and dance teacher at the stage academy Big sent him to. It was disastrous, an unambiguous demolition of Big's hopes to see Gideon in the West End. It might as well have said, Two Left Feet and can't act. She knew, deep down, that he was not cut out for life as an actor but she was unwilling to let go of her dreams. There was no place in life for her as an academic's mother. There was, however, a role for her as a stage mother; indeed she might build a second career on its back. She could be an agent or maybe get a choreographic role. She knew he could act, she knew he could dance, it was in his genes. He'd just chosen not to. She was furious, and still very drunk.

'Look at this,' she said. 'And after all the sacrifices I made for you. You ungrateful little bastard.'

Gideon stared at the floor in misery. 'You didn't even try, did you?'

'I promise I'll learn to dance, Mummy. I'll make you proud of me.' He wasn't sixteen any more. He was ten. His mother snorted in derision. Vulture was still sitting on the kitchen table. Big's eyes alighted on it.

'God, you've still got that horrible thing,' she said, picking Vulture up.

'Give him to me,' said Gideon. Big laughed, gratified by his obvious distress. Got your attention now, haven't I? she thought. It felt good.

'Playing with toys at your age, you little poof,' she said.

Then it happened. She took her cigarette out of her mouth and stubbed it out in Vulture's left eye. There was a hiss, a plume of thin smoke and a smell of burning rubber.

'Give him to me,' repeated Gideon.

If Big hadn't still been half-cut from her three a.m. session she would have noticed the change in his voice. Big sneered. She had noticed there was a deep cut in the rubber where the wing of the bird joined the body. With one brutal, downward motion, she tore the wing off the bird and threw Vulture out through the open kitchen window of the second-floor flat. The wing followed.

She turned to look at her son in triumph and was sent flying, as Gideon's open palm slammed into her cheek. Her glasses flew off and Gideon stamped on them as if he was crushing a venomous insect. He looked at her cowering from him. His hand hurt; God knows what her cheek must have felt like. He felt the triumph spreading through his body as he saw her pain.

Big was no coward, nor was she a stranger to being knocked around by men, but this unexpected attack seemed to paralyse her.

She steadied herself on the table and Gideon slapped her again. It felt even better. Big whimpered. He liked that. In fact, it was the sweetest sound he'd ever heard.

Then he grabbed hold of her throat with his right hand and squeezed. Now he could see the pain and terror in her eyes. How do you like it? he thought. Sixteen years I've had of this, you drunk old bitch. Now it's payback time.

He increased the pressure on her throat and her bloodshot, slightly yellow eyes bulged. If I keep going, thought Gideon, she'll die. It was a tempting thought. He pushed her away roughly and his mother staggered across the kitchen.

'Get out,' he said. 'Get out. When you come back I'll be gone and don't even think of looking for me.'

'Fine,' hissed his mother. 'That's just fine by me.' And with as much dignity as she could muster, she left the flat in her stockinged feet.

It wasn't the first time she had done the walk of shame, but usually, of course, it was homeward bound. Ten a.m, walking to the pub through the streets of Acton, half-dressed and without shoes or money was a first. As she rounded the corner her nose started bleeding. A woman passer-by stared at her in a concerned way.

'What the fuck are you looking at?' snarled Monica.

Gideon packed a sports bag with his best second-hand clothes. It didn't take long. Then he picked up his school ruck- sack, much heavier. He'd need that. He closed the door of the flat behind him and went down the stairs, then out of the rear door to the service road where he found Vulture lying on the tarmac. His sightless eye was a puckered socket, but the good one still looked at Gideon with unstinting affection.

Gideon picked him up, kissed him and said, 'I'll make sure nothing bad happens to you again.' He couldn't see Vulture's wing anywhere. He put the bird inside his shirt and walked off to the Tube station. He had nowhere to go.

The first night he climbed over the railings into Holland Park in central London, near Notting Hill, and slept under a bush. He was woken up at seven a.m. by an angry parks employee and told never to be found there again. The second night found him on Hampstead Heath. He was cold, shivering and very hungry. A man came up to him and asked if he was OK. Fine, said Gideon. Do you want to come home with me, said the man. Gideon nodded.

He knew there would be a price to pay, but it would be worth it.

The first time the pain was intense, agonizing, but he got used to it and it was better than being at home.

Anything was.

In October he passed his entrance exam to Oxford.

He was on his way.

26

DI Huss looked at the crime-scene photos from the Jessica McIntyre murder with increasing puzzlement and irritation. She'd been infuriated by Hanlon's sceptical attitude at first, but was growing more and more uncomfortable with some of the points she'd raised, both directly and indirectly.

She had tried ignoring Hanlon's objections, but she was too honest and too good a policewoman to succeed. She would have to deal with them somehow; she couldn't sweep them under the carpet.

Could Fuller's room have been accessed after his arrest? The brutal answer was yes, it could. The discovery of McIntyre's underwear after the room had been searched once was worrying. It could have been planted. It was certainly what any defence lawyer would argue. So the admissibility of the underwear as evidence was highly problematic.

Then there was this other problem. There were two doors to the room where Jessica's body had been found: the heavy outside one, the 'oak' as they called it, and the internal one. She looked at Laura's statement again.

The outside door had been locked, as had the inside one. But the inside one had a Yale lock, you could just pull it closed. The oak door had an old-fashioned mortice key. And there was the key, clearly photographed by forensics, lying on the desk in front of the window. How had the killer locked the door, from the outside, and made the key appear back inside the room?

She hunted for Laura's mobile number and called her. Per- haps the girl could help.

Half an hour later she was in the Junior Common Room with the absurdly young-looking philosophy student.

'It was so strange,' the girl said to Melinda Huss. 'I thought it was a joke at first, well, momentarily anyway.' She would make a great witness, thought DI Huss. Laura's replies to questions were measured and thought out; she considered her words before she spoke. She was utterly credible. 'Then it was more like something from a horror film, those bruises around her neck.' She shook her head in disbelief, her eyes large and serious behind the severe frames of her glasses. 'I haven't been back in the room since. Well, obviously. I don't think I really want to. Do we have to go back right now?'

Huss shook her head. 'No, Laura, no, we don't, but if you would I'd be very grateful. A couple of things don't really add up.' Laura stood up. She really was remarkably small, thought DI Huss, who rose too, feeling large and lumbering by contrast.

She put a determined face on.

'Oh well, DI Huss, maybe no time like the present.'

The two women walked together round the cloisters that surrounded the quad and then stopped outside the staircase. The college was projecting its usual aura of deep calm. It was hard to imagine a more unlikely setting for a murder. To Huss, her surroundings radiated an almost tangible sense of privilege. Huss, despite her reasonably privileged background on a large, commercially successful farm twenty miles from Oxford, felt the familiar stab of resentment that the non-student population of Oxford usually feel towards the student body. It was the Hooray Henry mentality. The percentage of students who belonged to the Bullingdon Club was statistically negligible, but they cast a very long shadow indeed. Privilege rather than ability was suggested by the Oxford brand.

The university students all seemed so smug, although she exempted Laura from this.

They stopped outside the staircase and Laura's fingers pushed at the mortar between the honey-coloured bricks. She worked a small fragment of cement loose and looked at it critically.

'It needs repointing,' she said to Huss. 'Sorry, Dad's a builder.

I was brought up to notice these things.'

Huss felt a stab of contrition. She had written Laura off as the by-product of privilege. It hadn't occurred to her that her background might be one of good old-fashioned proletarian graft.

They walked up the stairs and stood in front of the heavy outside door. 'This was closed and locked when I arrived,' said Laura. 'Is it OK to go in?'

'Yes, we're finished here,' said Huss. Laura unlocked it with her key. 'How many keys are there to this door?' Huss asked. 'Two,' said Laura. 'I left one for Jessica McIntyre at reception;

I had the other one. I guess they keep a master copy there too.' They entered the room via the secondary, internal door. 'What are the things that are troubling you?' she asked

Huss. She shivered slightly. She didn't know if she'd ever want to return here again.

DI Huss indicated the window desk. 'That mortice key, or rather its twin, was found lying there on that desk. So it's an interesting question as to how the killer left the room, other than by climbing out of the window.'

Laura raised a conspiratorial dark eyebrow. 'It's easy if you know how,' she said. Huss looked puzzled. 'Let me show you,' Laura said.

The study walls were panelled with wood and Laura walked over to where the mirror hung. 'Can you give me a hand to move this?' she asked Huss.

The two women propped the mirror up against the other wall. The panel behind it had a small circular knob. Laura tugged at this and the panel, which was obviously some kind of cupboard door, opened on its hinges. The edges of the door were so well tailored to the panelling they were practically invisible.

We should have found this, thought Huss angrily. Which dumb ass was in charge here? For some reason she thought of Hanlon. It's not the sort of thing Hanlon would have missed.

Inside the cupboard a rope suspended from a pulley hung down, disappearing into the depths below. 'It's a dumb waiter,' said Laura. 'This room used to be for one of the dons here; they had to live in college by university law. Anyway, this connects down to the kitchens. I think it was so that the don could get food and drink any time he wanted, otherwise he'd have been stuck with High Table in the Senior Common Room.'

Huss noticed a faint flush of embarrassment to her cheeks.

'How do you know where it goes?' asked Huss.

'Well, you can fit in it, you see,' said Laura, glowing red with shame. 'And get lowered down and maybe, well, liberate some food and get hauled back up again.'

'Not booze then?' asked Huss. Laura shook her head. 'No,' she said, with a tinge of sadness. 'They store that locked up in a kind of cage to keep the chefs away from it. You won't tell the college, will you, I only did it a couple of times.' She looked anguished.

Huss shook her head. 'No, I'm not going to tell the college. But I will need you to make a statement and I do want you to show me where the thing comes out at the bottom in the kitchens.'

As they walked down the stairs Huss got on her phone to set the wheels turning to bring back a forensic team to examine the dumb waiter and help for interviewing all the kitchen personnel.

Fuller had been lecturing from seven o'clock that evening, but if he had threaded his way through the kitchen, he'd have blatantly stood out from the chefs in their whites or the waiting staff, who for a start, were almost all half his age. He would have stood out like a sore thumb. How on earth could he have got away without being noticed? What else have we missed? thought Huss angrily.

27

Back in London, he finalized his plans for Dame Elizabeth. Her hero, Kant, was famous for never having left Königsberg and for having a routine so punctual and unvarying you could set your watch by him. Dame Elizabeth liked to emulate him.

This addiction to routine would be partly her downfall. He was counting on it.

He was looking forward to her death, to seeing her die.

The atmosphere rare and pure, danger near and the spirit full of a joyful wickedness: thus are things well matched.

Also sprach Zarathustra.

Every Sunday night, from six thirty to eight thirty, Dame Elizabeth was to be found in the small lecture hall near her office, marking essays and doing paperwork. She also let it be known that she would be there for any student needing help or advice. She was a strong believer in lecturers having a visible presence, particularly philosophy dons. They should be there, like beacons of sanity in a disturbed world. That's what was most disturbing to her about the deaths, the notion that philosophy itself would be mocked. She could imagine the philistine jeering headlines in the red-top press, or the legion of adverse Twitter comments and noticeboard pages making sarcastic remarks about her subject. The British were fond of mocking anything intellectual, jeering at culture.

He knew that the booking list for students was empty; he'd seen it. He knew that she'd be alone on this Sunday night. Five minutes was all he would need with her, that's more or less how long 'D.I.S.C.O.' lasted. He'd have to use his iPod, though, he could hardly play the music through the lecture hall speakers. Nobody would be around on a Sunday night, except for the old security guy at the desk in the foyer, but better safe than sorry.

His preparations were complete. He had bought a dog collar and lead from a pet store, south of the river. It was a dog choke-chain collar, essentially designed to strangle the animal into submission. He slipped it experimentally over a cushion and pulled it tight. The steel links bit into the fabric with a satisfying solidity and strength. It would be marvellous to see and feel it in action on smooth, human flesh.

He put the song on his stereo and cranked up the volume. First came the rhythm and the pan-pipe intro, breathy and urgent, then the song kicked off. He put the choke chain back round the cushion. He imagined the chain around Dame Elizabeth's neck, D, the chain bit, I, he pulled harder, S, now he was pulling as hard as he could, and holding for two beats, C, O and repeat.

He was breathing hard now, with excitement, not exertion. 'D.I.S.C.O.'

Then he undid the chain and lead and put them into his dishwasher, to remove any stray fabric or trace. He would leave the chain around her neck when he had finished and didn't want anything there for forensics to find.

He would be wearing latex gloves tonight. Leather was a more pleasing material but latex, well, you had a much better tactile sensation.

He looked at his watch. Four hours. Like Kant, he was obsessive about time.

Dame Elizabeth would have appreciated the irony.

28

Hanlon, atypically, decided to wear a dress for her meeting with Dame Elizabeth. Her wardrobe was far from extensive, but she really only had a few kinds of situations to be catered for. Work meant practical, in case it got damaged, and non- provocative – she didn't want her colleagues surreptitiously ogling her. For court appearances, she wore a dark suit, and this doubled for funerals. Then she had her sports clothing. None of these seemed particularly suitable for what was going to be a momentous meeting. So the dress it was, bought to take Whiteside out for a birthday dinner. He'd been very amused and secretly very flattered. He knew that she wouldn't have made the gesture for anyone but him.

It was grey, tight-fitting and came to just above her knees. It showed off her legs and flattered her slim figure. She remembered being concerned at the time that it would restrict her movements. Whiteside had laughed. 'We're having dinner, not arresting someone. We're not going to have a punch-up.'

Now, of course, Whiteside was not having dinners any more. He was being fed nutrients through tubing. That would be one of the arguments used to hasten the end of his life, its lack of quality. But

Hanlon, with all the mulish stubbornness she was capable of, believed that he might recover. Such things had happened before; they might happen again. Besides, who was to say he wasn't actually conscious? Admittedly there was no brain activity to measure, but you couldn't say with absolute certainty that he wasn't still thinking, in some form.

She still didn't know what to do about his parents. Without their intervention, the status quo could go on for a long time. No one would be rushing to end the life of a policeman injured in the line of duty. The fact it was a civil-service matter, too, would help prolong any decision. Nobody in government employ rushes to do that, to make a difficult decision, if they can possibly help it. Form a committee, that would be the default position.

She put Whiteside from her mind and concentrated on the here and now.

She mentally calculated the time it would take to get to Bloomsbury. Like all Londoners she didn't think of distance in the capital in terms of mileage, but in journey time, in minutes or hours. Parking wouldn't be an issue, she could use the staff car park. Seven o'clock they'd agreed. She'd get there at quarter to and kill time outside. Hanlon was never late.

She was feeling unusually nervous. No one had ever given her any information about her father and now, well, she didn't believe in God, but it was like some form of Providence, some kind of Fate, had intervened. Whatever happened it would be life-changing.

29

He checked the contents of the bag he'd packed. He was nothing if not methodical. Latex gloves, four pairs. He'd double glove his hands to minimize the risk of them splitting. Rubber S&M mask. This was one of the simpler designs, like a ski mask made of black latex. Some of the ones he'd seen were extraordinary, looking like pilot's oxygen masks or thirties-style military anti- gas hoods, complete with arcane, mysterious attachments. In his view, they went a step too far. You can gild the lily too much.

Then the choke chain and lead. Last of all, his iPod, the song 'D.I.S.C.O.' cued and ready. He hummed the chorus to himself and executed a couple of the moves he'd use later. He was a great dancer, all the practice his mother had forced upon him was coming in useful.

Six thirty, that's when Dame Elizabeth Saunders would arrive. Seven o'clock, that's when she would depart.

30

Dame Elizabeth looked around her with approval. When she'd been an undergraduate at Girton College in Cambridge, she'd been appalled by the show-off techniques in tutorials, the one- to-one, or small-group time, that dons had with their students.

She hated the faux Brideshead fetishism, the emphasis of eccentricity over professionalism. There was the tutor with a pronounced hygiene problem, who would lie theatrically on a chaise longue, another whose room was full of cats, another who would insist on a sherry break. Lots of sherry breaks, judging by the state of his nose. At his funeral he'd been described as convivial. Yeah, right, thought Dame Elizabeth, in the same way that George Best or Oliver Reed suffered from conviviality.

The lack of respect shown to students who had worked extremely hard to get there, and the unbridled egomania, disgusted her. Dining at High Table was the worst. It would have been amusing, the high regard in which the dons valued their intellectual abilities if it hadn't been so risible. Did knowledge of the Saffavid dynasty, for example, qualify you to hold forth on the state of the British economy in the twenty-first century? No.

Dame Elizabeth was far from left wing, but something about the smugness of the lecturers brought out the revolutionary in her and she would have liked to herd them, Cambodian Pol Pot style, out into the flat fenland fields around Cambridge for forcible re-education.

The small auditorium was the antithesis of the cosy tutor's room. It was her reaction to the closeted Oxbridge world. Marking her work here, in full view of anyone who happened to poke their head in, was Dame Elizabeth's way of saying, we work at this university. This is what we do and I'm in charge, I'm accountable, the buck stops here.

She was a very visible head of department.

She was grading essays at the moment, or at least going through the motions. Her mind was mainly full of Hanlon and Hanlon's father. She had dreamed about him last night, his unnervingly intense grey eyes, his superb body, his arrogant grace. Jann Hanlon. His daughter seemed to have inherited these traits, but not his charm. Admittedly, she didn't know her well, but Hanlon seemed noticeably deficient in this quality.

If you Googled Dame Elizabeth, you would find she'd writ- ten about twenty books on philosophy and philosophers and meta-ethics. There were nearly a hundred articles cited. If you searched for Jann Hanlon it would get you nowhere.

He was supposed to be writing, or have written, the defining work on the philosophy of art. She'd never seen it. His lazy brilliance might never have been. It was as if he had never existed.

It was as if he had left no trace whatsoever on history, other than his daughter.

To redress the balance, she'd written Hanlon a letter, a memoir of the man she'd known. Writing was easier for Dame Elizabeth than speech. It was short, about five pages, and was in a buff envelope, together with some photographs she had found of Jann. It contained everything she could think of that Hanlon might want to know about her father. She had just finished rereading it. She was pleased with what she'd written.

When she saved the document on her PC, she labelled the file *Accounts Due*. That more or less summed up how she felt about Jann.

She'd written *DCI Hanlon* on the envelope; she realized she didn't know Hanlon's first name.

And what, she wondered, would Jann have made of his daughter? He would have been a terrible father, no doubt about it. Leopards don't change their spots, thought Dame Elizabeth, somewhat unphilosophically. He wouldn't have changed nappies or done any of the school runs. He'd have been out at parties. He wouldn't have done any housework. No nanny or au pair, no attractive mother at playgroup would have been safe from his attentions, from his charm. He had that inner glow particular to men who women find attractive. Women certainly loved him, and the daughter would have too. She'd have forgiven him his affairs. Jann was beloved.

Maybe, she thought, he wasn't meant to make old bones. Jann defined himself enormously through his physical attractive- ness and that's not a quality that lasts. Maybe an old Jann would have been dreadful to behold.

She looked at the clock on the wall to her right. Ten to seven. Hanlon would be here soon, she wasn't the kind of person to be late.

The auditorium was in semi-darkness; only the lights above the small stage provided for the lecturer were switched on. There was a door to the left of the stage where the lecturer could exit. Stairs ran down the raked seating, twelve rows, seating for sixty, dividing it in two.

She felt stupidly nervous and to settle her mind she typed *Jann Hanlon: Born Dublin 1939–Died Berlin 1979* on the keyboard, then pressed return, and the words flashed up on the interactive whiteboard behind her. It was as good a way to start as any.

Dame Elizabeth had always been able to hold an audience. She'd begin with that, hold Hanlon's attention, give her the letter to read and then a Q&A session. Perfect. She had a lesson plan.

She saved it and clicked on the menu icon. The screen was now blank, apart from the toolbars.

There was a sudden bright glow as the auditorium door opened and when she looked up, a figure was outlined in the light. Hanlon had arrived, she thought.

31

Hanlon reversed her car in a perfect arc into a tight parking space off Gower Street. A car to Hanlon was like an extension of her own skin; she had complete spatial awareness. She grinned suddenly to herself at memories of Enver parking, the worried frown of concentration, the more or less random movements of the steering wheel. The way he would drive to the furthest end of a car park to have a bay free on either side, and then when he did finally stop the car it would invariably be parked at some strange angle, or with the bonnet or boot poking out.

The entrance to the staff car park had been dug up by workmen and coned off, meaning that she had to go round in a tortuous loop because of the one-way system. This had added a lot more time to her journey than she had anticipated.

She took her phone and texted Dame Elizabeth to say she'd be ten minutes late.

. . .

He stood looking at her, across the desk. His eyes were slightly unfocused, dreamy almost. She wondered momentarily if he'd been drinking.

'What are you doing here?' she asked curiously.

'Oh, I just wanted to run something past you,' he said. He unzipped a small rucksack he had with him and took out a plastic wallet with a small, battered black book inside. He put it on the desk between them.

She looked closely at it.

Die fröliche Wissenschaft; The Gay Science, the title read.

By Friedrich Nietzsche.

He pulled on a pair of latex gloves. 'It's a first edition,' he said. 'From1883. The first English translation. I promised the library I'd be very careful with it.' He indicated the gloves. 'I'll just slip these on. They don't want it damaged. It's so easy to damage or break things. I just wanted your opinion on this.' He opened the book to a passage near the beginning.

She looked up at the clock. Five past seven. 'If you're quick.' She was thinking of Hanlon; she wasn't the kind of woman who'd be late.

'Oh, I will be,' he promised.

Hanlon walked across the deserted square to the main university building and banged on the glass door, until the security guard at reception ambled over and let her in. She showed her student pass, explained she was here to see Dame Elizabeth and he signed her in. It took a while. English wasn't his first language. He logged the time, 19.05.

. . .

He opened the book and stood behind her. 'Could you read this?' he said, indicating the relevant passage. She cleared her throat and started to read aloud.

'One holds that what is called good preserves the species, while what is called evil harms the species. In truth, however, the evil instincts are expedient, species-preserving, and indispensable to as high a degree as the good ones; their function is merely different.'

As she finished reading, she became aware of what sounded like the tinny noise of the repetitive beat of a dance song, leaking out from an iPod's earphones. She wondered what he could be doing. She turned her head.

Looking down at her was not his face but a featureless, black leather mask through which she could just see his eyes. His head swayed to the beat. She opened her mouth incredulously. She'd never seen anything like it in her life. It was a mix of the terrifying, like an executioner's hood, and disgusting. Some- thing that belonged in a nightmarish, perverted sex game.

She wondered what on earth he thought he was playing at.

It was like some sick practical joke.

Her lips started to form the circular shape of the syllable 'Wh—' but before she was able to finish forming the final '—at' of the word, his left, latexed hand, with terrible speed, was around her throat, crushing her windpipe. She fought for breath, but no air could enter her screaming lungs.

His hand forced her backwards, against her chair. Her eyes bulged, the small blood vessels starting to rupture as the pressure rose, then she could see in front of her the glint of metal, as he slipped the choke chain over her head.

Her hands clawed ineffectually at the metal links, as he stood behind her, one knee braced on the back of her chair while he sang along to the song. 'D.I.S.C.O.'

With every letter he uttered he yanked back savagely on the

chain and then relaxed it slightly. D. Yank. I. Yank. S. Yank. C. Yank. O. Yank. Each time he did that, her head flew backwards and then forwards, so it looked as if she were nodding along with the infectious beat, like he was. The word was repeated twice in the intro. He hummed along in ecstasy.

The chain had completely crushed her trachea and her hands had fallen away from her throat to hang by her sides. Her neck muscles were now completely slack and her head lolled forward.

He let go of the chain, did a little shimmy, spun round gracefully in a complete circle and laced his gloved fingers into her thick, white hair. Dancing was such a liberating experience.

He rocked her head from side to side with the music as he sang along.

The music in his ears swelled and reached a crescendo before the infectious chorus kicked in. It was a tune he'd learned to move to, as a kid, in his dance class.

At this point, he slammed her head forward as hard as he could into the desk in front of him. Skin broke, bone cracked, her face was now a bloody wreck. He pulled her inert head back up in time with the beat.

'Dee, dee, dee dee

She is Ohhhh, ohhh, ohhhh D.I.S.' Slam again of the head into the blood-spattered wooden surface. '*C.O.*'

The sound of her head striking the desk was loud and percussive. Blood stained its surface.

The door at the top of the auditorium opened.

Hanlon had arrived.

32

As soon as she opened the door that led into the lecture room, heavy and resistant on its hinges, Hanlon saw, far below her, the bloodsoaked face of Dame Elizabeth. Standing directly behind her at the desk was the masked figure of a man.

Hanlon didn't stop or hesitate. She started running down the steps towards them.

'Police!' she shouted. The tight dress hampered her movements, as did her shoes. She kicked these off as she ran and, keeping her eyes on the masked man, reached into her handbag for the knife that she habitually carried.

For a second, the man didn't move. Then he did. He pushed Dame Elizabeth away from him, scooped up a small red ruck- sack with one hand and the beige envelope with the other. The name on the letter meant nothing to him, but any letter for the police was not going to be left lying around.

Dame Elizabeth's head fell heavily on to the computer keyboard, pressing several keys as it struck, and the lines of Hanlon's father's birth and death dates flashed up on the white-board screen.

Hanlon paused momentarily on the stairs. It disconcerted her seeing her father's name there and the dates of his life. Her swift mind made the connections instantly. Dame Elizabeth obviously knew her father well and this knowledge, so tantalizingly about to be imparted, had died with her.

For Hanlon this was a graphic reminder of what she would now never know. She gave a cry of pure rage like the howl of an animal.

She sprinted down the stairs.

The man had disappeared through the door to the left of the stage. Hanlon stopped momentarily to check on the professor. The elderly woman's eyes were half-open, staring glassily into nothingness. Hanlon pressed down on the neck, searching for a pulse in the carotid artery, but there was nothing. Hanlon didn't have time to do any more but she'd have been amazed if there'd been any life left.

Throwing her bag to the floor, she took out her knife and chased after the masked man. She depressed the switch to release the blade, which sprang out silently on its well-oiled mechanism. She stopped momentarily to slash open the fabric of the skirt of the dress, so her legs could move. That was so much better. She could run properly now instead of hobble.

The exit led to the corridor a floor below where she'd entered the auditorium. The corridors at Queen's College were extremely long and straight, and as she burst through the doors, she could see the back of her quarry nearly at the end, heading for the lifts. Hanlon put her head down and sprinted, arms pumping, the flick-knife blade in her right hand flashing in the dim lighting overhead.

The man she was chasing was fast, but Hanlon was a good sprinter. She could run a hundred metres in twelve to thirteen seconds. She had great technique and a lot of her exercise work included plyometric exercise, squats and box jumps, which helped explosive speed. She saw him look over his shoulder as she gained on him ominously, the distance closing fast, her snake-like hair bouncing as she ran.

At the end of the corridor, around the corner, were the lifts. They were the original thirties' design, endlessly repaired over the years, and although they worked, they took a long time to arrive. Unless the man was extremely lucky, she'd catch him as he waited. If he tried to outpace her, he was hers. She found it hard to believe that he would have anything like her fitness levels. Hanlon had no doubt either about who would win in a fight.

If the worst came to the worst, she would have no hesitation whatsoever in using the knife. She knew how effective it could be. It had once been used on her. She still had a small, centimetre scar to the left of her navel where it had gone in as far as the handle. She'd kept the weapon as a souvenir.

He disappeared around the corner closely followed by Hanlon, who was just in time to see the doors of one of the three elevators close and the lift indicator, an art deco sunburst effect, light up. Going down.

There was a staircase to the right of the lifts and Hanlon ran down, keeping more or less the same speed as the lift. Occasionally she would leap down the bottom four steps, saving even more time.

But fast as she was, the lift was faster. Third, second, first, ground floors as the lift descended, then the basement.

The stairs dog-legged here, adding a couple of seconds' time penalty to Hanlon's pursuit. She burst into the basement corridor just in time to see two large double doors flapping shut a little further ahead. Hanlon ran up to them, brushing her hair back from her sweat-soaked forehead with her forearm. She approached the doors cautiously and peered through the glass panel.

The killer was somewhere inside.

She guessed she should really call for assistance, but her phone was in her bag five floors up. She toyed with the idea of smashing the fire alarm to summon help. Presumably the security guard was completely ignorant of what was going on. There were very few internal CCTV cameras in the university because of student objections over privacy and data protection issues.

But more to the point, she wanted the killer for herself. He hadn't just killed Hannah Moore and Jessica McIntyre. He hadn't just deprived Dame Elizabeth Saunders of her life; he'd deprived Hanlon of the only chance to get to know her father. She wanted answers, she wanted revenge, and she wanted these things free of witnesses and PACE regulations.

Hanlon knew she would be most vulnerable coming through the doors. In the past she'd been attacked while doing just that and she wasn't keen to repeat the experience. She appreciated too that she was facing a very level-headed, very violent man.

She pushed one door open with her left arm, the right holding the knife. She moved fast and in a low crouch.

She was through, unscathed and standing in one of the university kitchens. She looked around her; there was no one in sight. This particular university kitchen was not just big, it was huge.

She knew from her conversations with Stephen Michaels, the chef, that there were quite a few kitchens dotted throughout the huge edifice that was the main university building. There was the open-plan one for the main refectory, where she'd eaten her lunch, and there were several satellite ones, like the one that serviced the executive dining room or other eating areas. There were also kitchens for functions either academic or civil (the university was rather cannily hiring itself out as a venue for conferences and weddings, trading on its art- deco good looks), and there was this one for the university restaurant.

It was the first time she'd been inside a large, commercial

kitchen. She made a quick inventory: three six-burner gas stoves, a bank of sizeable ovens built into the wall, steel prep tables. Like all commercial kitchens it was brightly lit, and this one was high-ceilinged and airy. Its clinical lines, white tiling and steel tables reminded her of a morgue.

On one of the prep tables was a large machine for slicing meat. It was missing its guard. Its razor-sharp cutting edge gleamed in the overhead kitchen light. It was plugged into a waist-high socket on the wall. Some kitchen artist had decorated it with a sign featuring a vividly drawn skull and crossbones and the words *Be careful. I'm dangerous!* written on it. Hanlon eyed it sardonically. So am I, she thought.

She guessed that somewhere there would be a walk-in freezer and a walk-in fridge. And there would be a storeroom, a dry store, for the pasta, rice, oil and so on. Right now, she was looking for hiding places.

He had to be here somewhere. She was so tense, so much adrenaline fuelling her body, that the atmosphere was almost surreal, hyper-real. She could feel her heart thudding, sweat beading her lean body from the chase.

There were three pillars supporting the ceiling, rectangular tiled blocks, which ran down the length of the kitchen. They were not wide enough to hide behind, so she was able to discount those. She turned her attention elsewhere.

The ovens were big enough to climb inside, but glass-doored. She looked hard. He wasn't there. There was a huge stockpot, the size of a dustbin, standing on its own gas ring on a reinforced plinth. She stood on tiptoe and looked inside. Nothing.

She moved slowly and silently on her stockinged feet, the tiles cold against her skin, her ears straining for any noise. All she could hear was the hum of the refrigerators.

She walked past a knife rack on the wall, its collection of chefs' knives and a couple of Chinese cleavers making her own knife look stupidly inadequate. She picked up a rolling pin from under one of the prep tables. It was a cylinder of heavy plastic a metre long. It was hard and as heavy as a baseball bat. That felt better. She retracted the blade of her knife and held it loosely in her other hand. She walked down the centre of the long room, swinging the rolling pin menacingly.

Come out, come out, wherever you are! she said to herself.

In the centre of the kitchen the floor was wet and there were a couple of yellow, plastic A-board signs warning of slippery surfaces. There was a drain-like plughole recessed into the floor. Water had collected around it in a two metre-wide lake. Close to the puddle was a walk-in fridge.

From the outside it looked like a long refrigerated container from the back of an HGV. It more or less was that. From where she was standing, Hanlon could see down the rest of the kitchen to the fly chains hanging inside what would be the double doors, opened by a lever mechanism that led to the yard outside. Nobody was visible.

She walked further into the kitchen, all her acute senses straining for a hint of his presence. Hanlon had assumed from her vantage point that the fridge was fully recessed into the walls of the kitchen. It was, however, a free-standing unit and its rear was not flush with the wall at the end. Instead there was a half-metre gap between wall and fridge, where the kitchen staff normally left the several mops and brushes used for cleaning the floor. He wasn't there.

Now she was running out of places to search. There was a door that led to a walk-in freezer; she checked it just in case: nothing. Just neat shelving containing tubs and boxes of frozen food. She checked the fire door at the end of the kitchen. The lever-action bar to open it was still secure; he couldn't have got out that way.

She looked back down the kitchen. It had to be the fridge. She looked dubiously at its heavy door. *Come into my parlour, said the spider to the fly*, she thought.

Enver would have called for backup. Hanlon, supremely confident and spoiling for a fight, had absolutely no intention of doing so.

The rolling pin would be useless in a confined space. She put it down, clicked her knife open and pulled the door with her left hand. It swung outward into the kitchen, and she stepped inside and into the fridge.

From the corridor, through the perspex door panel, he had watched Hanlon as she moved slowly down the kitchen. Unknown to Hanlon and unnoticed by her in the excitement of the chase, there was a large cupboard used for storing the floor cleaner next to the kitchen entrance. Its door had been made to look like the panelling of the walls. He'd had time to push the heavy, hinged kitchen doors open, then release them so they'd still be in motion and conceal himself.

Distracting her by their motion, the tactic had worked. He had considered slipping away up the stairs and immediately rejected the possibility. He didn't want to encounter the security guard and for all he knew, the police were on their way. No, the kitchen-door exit would be the best bet.

Hanlon had thought the danger to her would lie in entering the kitchen. The opposite was true.

Now she was in the fridge, he immediately changed his plans. Gallagher was obviously highly competent. He didn't want to kill her now; it didn't fit in with his plans. He was also worried about leaving a DNA trace if he got scratched or cut in the inevitable struggle. Gallagher certainly wouldn't go down without a fight, that was for sure. The chase down here had certainly proved that. The gleamingly clean surfaces of the kitchen with their shiny metal worktops were the ideal hunting grounds for a forensic team. The same could be said about the spotless corridor.

He wanted urgently to neutralize the woman and get out. He had toyed with the idea of running for the far door, but Gallagher would be on him, and by God, could she run. He also had no idea if the door was locked. It shouldn't be. It was clearly marked as a fire exit, but you never could tell.

Back in the fridge, adrenaline was coursing around Hanlon's body and her heart was pumping. It was a good feeling. It was what she had been missing for the last couple of months.

Hanlon loved action. It stripped away all worries, all concerns, all the futilities of daily life. It was the here and now, a glorious kind of freedom.

Lights came on inside as the door opened fully. She stood in the doorway, looking down the length of the fridge. Tubular, steel shelving ran down both sides to the end where a noisy compressor blew chilled air. It was incredibly neatly organized and the tubs of prepared food all bore colour-coded date and product labels. There was nowhere to conceal a person that she could see.

He opened the kitchen door and slipped inside. He saw the tips of her fingers on the door jamb. It was now or never. He ran for the open door of the fridge.

His original plan was to throw all his weight at the door and send it smashing into her outstretched fingers, breaking them all. He'd forgotten about the wet floor. As he reached the metal of the door, his foot slipped beneath him and he skidded, depriving himself of momentum. The noise from the compressor inside the fridge was extremely loud, but Hanlon must have been aware of something subliminally because she straightened her arm fractionally, so that when the heavy door slammed to, it struck her just above the wrist of her right hand.

The force of the blow fractured the bone with an immediate, agonizing pain. Hanlon snatched her arm back in an unthinking, automatic reaction and as soon as her hand was out of the way, there was a loud click as the fridge door slammed. Then she heard a dry scraping noise as he forced the steel of the cylindrical-shaped knife sharpener he'd picked up from the wall-mounted rack through the metal bracket designed to take a padlock, so the fridge and its contents could be secured. Hanlon was locked in.

The fridge's internal temperature stabilized, the compressor cut out, and she could hear the rattle of the fly chain and the metal clang of the bar that operated the kitchen fire doors leading to the yard, as he let himself out.

She was alive, but trapped. She clutched her injured arm to her chest with her left hand and her eyes narrowed with the pain. But that was only the initial shock. Then a second wave of agony broke over her and she felt her knees buckle beneath her.

She nearly blacked out with the pain. A wave of nausea crashed over her. It was the kind of pain you felt deep down inside your gut, in the pit of your stomach. She sat down heavily on a sack of Yukon Gold potatoes, trying to control her breathing.

Blood was trickling through the fingers coiled around the wrist and she rested her forearm on her knees as she carefully let go and assessed the damage. The skin was already rising like bread dough as the swelling increased, and each beat of her heart amplified the pain as the blood was forced through the constricted vessels.

She suddenly shivered violently from the cold. Hanlon was wearing the grey silk dress and it had short sleeves. Fine for a hot, summer's night; not so good as fridge wear.

She watched the goosebumps rising on her arms. She could see a temperature gauge on the wall opposite, telling her it was six degrees. It had been twenty-two Celsius outside when she'd parked her car.

She wondered how long it would take them to find her.

However soon it was, it was going to feel like a long, long time.

33

'Four hours, I was in that fridge before they found me,' fumed Hanlon to Enver. It was midnight and they were sitting in the Euston police station where Enver was based. He looked at her thoughtfully. It obviously wasn't the fridge that was bothering her, he thought. If anyone could sit locked in a fridge with a fractured, bleeding wrist for hours without worrying about it, that person was Hanlon. And he thought her attitude was uncalled for. The response, once the body of Dame Elizabeth had been found by the security man doing his rounds, had been extremely efficient.

The police really could not have done a better job. The university building was vast, labyrinthine, and once the dog team had arrived, they'd led them straight to Hanlon, while their colleagues, who'd started at the top of the building, were still working their slow way down, floor by painstaking floor.

More or less every square metre had to be checked out.

She'd had her arm X-rayed and strapped up at nearby University College Hospital. She'd given a statement and Enver had filled her in on what they had so far on the progress of the murder investigation. It was getting nowhere fast. Nothing on what few internal cameras there were. No trace evidence left by the killer.

Hanlon was more shaken than she cared to admit by Dame Elizabeth's death. She'd always been profoundly affected not so much by the waste of a life inherent in murder, but by the incredible selfishness of the murderer. Dame Elizabeth had been a woman whose life had been a beacon to others. She had touched maybe thousands of people for the good. Hanlon didn't doubt she had flaws, but her life had been extinguished by some creep with less worth in her mind than a cockroach. Three women, possibly four, if the theory of Abigail Vickery's death as a sex killing proved correct, were dead. To add insult to injury, she'd seen the killer playing with the body of Dame Elizabeth as if it were some sort of toy. And it was an insult. It was deliberately degrading to the corpse.

Then of course there was the personal aspect. Hanlon had expected the evening to end with a sense of finally knowing who she was and where she came from, and now this had been snatched away from her by the murderer. He'd killed Dame Elizabeth and he'd killed her dreams.

Hanlon wanted revenge.

She had been unable to identify anything about the man in the mask. No forensic trace had been found. Gloved, masked, careful as ever, it could have been anyone.

Fuller was another dead end. Murray had gone round to Fuller's flat in person. Fuller had answered the door. He'd been drinking. Murray told Hanlon he'd looked considerably the worse for wear, unshaven and bellicose. He refused to allow them in; they had no warrant. He'd said, 'Yeah, I'm really going to let you in so you can fit me up like you did in Oxford.' Or words to that effect. *Arrest me or go away* was the gist of his message.

Familiarity with the police was obviously breeding contempt in Fuller's mind.

As a defence it worked well. Murray had no grounds to arrest Fuller. Even if he had, he would have been unable to question Fuller until the man was legally sober enough, and by then his solicitor would have got him out. There was really very little he could do.

Murray was far from assertive as a policeman and he decided to let Fuller come to the station in the morning to give a statement, although he did put a plain-clothes in the street just in case Fuller emerged from his flat.

When this officer was relieved the following day, Murray gave instructions that Fuller be escorted round the back entrance of the station. There'd be quite a media scrum out there on Monday, he guessed.

Meanwhile the phone calls and emails to the station about Dame Elizabeth were accumulating rapidly. Her murder was very much in the public domain now, and was tweeted and retweeted as well as being hot news on other social network sites. She had touched thousands of lives and her students and legions of ex-students were media savvy. TV was now getting involved.

Murray was the ideal choice to handle this kind of thing. Unassertive he may have been, but he was unflappable and possessed of a certainty that everything would be all right in the end. He gave a mini press conference, confirming no details other than that the police were investigating a suspicious death. The press knew Murray; they knew he could stonewall indefinitely.

Well, Hanlon thought, my involvement is practically at an end. Fuller's philosophy course would be suspended indefinitely, so her undercover role was over. She had Murray's blessing to tie up the loose ends regarding Fuller's potential whereabouts in Oxford on the day of the murder, and that was more or less it. By Friday, it would all be history.

34

He opened another bottle of wine and reread Dame Elizabeth's letter that he had snatched from her desk. It was very moving. How sad never to have known your parents. Even if you couldn't stand them, it was important to know where you came from. And the father sounded so interesting too. But it was the mother that was vital; the mother was the key to everything. Nietzsche had understood this. He had written:

'Everyone carries within him an image of woman that he gets from his mother; that determines whether he will honour women in general, or despise them, or be generally indifferent to them.'

He despised them.

He recognized now that DCI Hanlon was the woman he had previously known as Gallagher. He sipped his wine and thought of how he could best use this unexpected development to his advantage. Nothing sprang immediately to mind, but that didn't matter. Time was not particularly pressing at the moment. It did amuse him, though, that he knew practically everything there was to know about her father, while she knew nothing. It was like a Norse myth. By killing Dame Elizabeth he had somehow gained control of her memories, like Odin, drinking some magical potion brewed by dwarves or giants, able almost to see the future.

Well, he could see Hanlon's future and it was bleak. He would be seeing to that personally. But maybe it would be more merciful for Hanlon to die a violent, glorious death rather than get old and withered. He had the consolations of philosophy; he doubted if they would do much for Hanlon. He found this God-like image of himself entirely fitting. He was an exceptional person. It was only fitting that he do exceptional things.

So, it was Hanlon then. That was her real name. The name suited her, its twin syllables short and hard. He had been thinking a great deal about her of late and not just about her death. He found her very attractive. Maybe he would have a chance to do something about that.

35

The following morning, after the rush hour had died down, Hanlon got off the Underground train at Lambeth North. She left the Tube station and looked around her, orienting herself with the twin landmarks of the Shard and the London Eye. It was nine thirty a.m.

Her arm was in a sling, the wrist heavily strapped up, and the traces of her black eye gently disfigured one side of her face. She caught a glimpse of her reflection in a shop window and smiled grimly.

Lambeth seemed very light and open in the morning sun. If the colour scheme of Euston and Bloomsbury was dark and forbidding, then this part of London seemed light grey, palely reflecting the clouds above. The sky seemed huge. The roads were wider than she was used to; the traffic was light. It was surprisingly nice.

She remembered a music-hall song she knew about the place and it ran briefly through her head.

Any time you're Lambeth way
Any evening any day
You'll find us all, doin' the Lambeth walk.

. . .

Its jaunty air, as dated as a boater hat and Max Miller, was at odds with her angry mood.

She remembered that the Imperial War Museum was near here. Perhaps fittingly, it had been a mental hospital in a previous incarnation. The *Mutiny on the Bounty*'s Captain Bligh's house was opposite. Hanlon was pleased to remember these disparate facts, even though South London was a bit of a mystery to her, a North Londoner.

She checked Whiteside's parents' names and address on her phone – Anna and Peter Whiteside. She crossed a couple of roads until she was in the right street. It was quiet and a long, low block of flats ran down one side of it. A blue plaque stated that William Blake, Poet and Visionary, had once lived there, or rather in a house on the site of the flats.

She walked round the back of the building and found the door of the ground-floor flat that the Whitesides lived in. In the window was a crucifix and a framed religious text that had been painstakingly embroidered.

I am the Way, the Truth and the Light.

Hanlon's heart sank. She rang the bell and the door was opened by a short, rather attractive woman of about sixty. She had a similar nose to her son but that was the only resemblance that Hanlon could see. She looked Hanlon up and down.

'Can I help you?' 'I'm DCI Hanlon.'

'Yes?' she said enquiringly.

'I'm here to talk about Mark,' said Hanlon. 'I'm a friend of his.'

The woman nodded. 'You'd better come in then. I'll put the kettle on.'

Hanlon followed her into the flat. It smelled of polish and stale air. The smell of sanctity.

* * *

An hour later Hanlon was drinking another cup of tea, this time with Anna Whiteside's polar opposite, Iris Campion.

The madam sipped her Scotch, while she waited for her tea to cool, and studied the policewoman opposite. She was wearing a dark jacket and trousers and an expensive-looking cotton flowery shirt. As if mocking the feminine floral design, she had a strapped-up wrist that had been bandaged halfway up her forearm. Her unmarked eye had dark bags underneath it almost as severe as the bruising on the other had been. Her face was set and hard. Hanlon looked dangerous and viciously attractive, thought the madam.

'Well, you look royally pissed off, dear,' said Campion cheerily.

'I am,' said Hanlon.

The conversation with Whiteside's parents had been as bad as she could have imagined. Maybe even worse. Whiteside's father had sat next to his wife on the sofa, a balder, fatter version of his son. Like his son, he was heavily built, old muscle now, but still formidably strong. His sleeves were rolled up and his forearms were covered in fading tattoos. Hanlon guessed he had been a builder when he was younger. Maybe he still was. Something manual anyway. He had the physique that came from years of hard graft, not sculpted gym muscle. His sparse hair was carefully stuck to the top of his head in a comb-over. He was holding his wife's hand in a visible display of unity.

Their front room was eerily reminiscent of Campion's. There were occasional tables with hand-embroidered cloths covering them, antimacassars on the backs of chairs, but unlike Campion's room, everything had a biblical motif. There was a reproduction of Holman Hunt's *Light of the World*, a bearded, hippy-looking Jesus, lantern in hand, his head haloed by a distant moon, knocking symbolically on a closed, weed-choked door, that gave on to this world. Jesus reminded Hanlon of a drugs squad officer she'd once worked with.

'I can give you five minutes, no longer,' Whiteside senior said. His tone made it clear that his time was valuable.

'John preaches down at the market on a Monday,' Anna said proudly.

'I am a voice, crying in the wilderness!' John Whiteside said. 'Make straight the paths of the Lord!' Presumably, thought Hanlon, for my benefit.

The following conversation had been utterly pointless. She asked them, in as near as she had ever come in her life to begging, to grant Mark a stay of execution. John Whiteside's position was clear.

First of all, God's will was to be done. For whatever reason, He had decided that Mark should be in a coma.

Who was she to question the Lord?

Second, there was Mark Whiteside's homosexuality. Rather to Hanlon's surprise, his father raised it himself.

'We must all answer to the Lord in the fullness of time, DCI Hanlon, and Mark is no exception. Possibly the Lord has gathered Mark to his bosom to save his soul from straying. You know what I'm talking about,' he said accusingly. *You evil fag hag*, Hanlon could imagine him thinking. He continued:

'Thou shalt not lie with mankind as with womankind: It is abomination. As Leviticus says.'

'Amen,' said his mother, her eyes downcast.

'Well,' said Hanlon. John Whiteside had obviously given the subject some considered thought.

'If there is a man who lies with a male as a man lieth with a woman, both of them have committed a detestable act; they shall surely be put to death,' added John Whiteside sonorously.

'Leviticus 20,' said Anna, like a good student.

And that was more or less that. Hanlon could see no point in continuing the farce. Icily polite, she thanked them for the tea. In the hall was a large wooden crate filled with leaflets of a religious nature and an A-board; *REPENT!* it said.

Anna, who was showing Hanlon out, said proudly, 'My husband carries them down to the market to stand on when he testifies. He's ever so strong.' Her voice caught on the word *strong*, and her eyes flooded with tears. 'Just like . . . You'd better go,' she said suddenly, too proud to break down in front of Hanlon. She held the door open and Hanlon heard it click shut behind her back as she left.

Hanlon jerked herself back to the here and now in Campion's office. The madam was wearing a great deal of make-up this morning and looked huge, in a sleeveless black dress that emphasized her doughy, muscular arms.

'Finished thinking, have we, dearie?' she asked mockingly. 'You can almost see the wheels turning.'

Hanlon sipped her tea and looked steadily back at Campion.

The latter pointed at Hanlon's wrist.

'Did you get the bloke that done that?' she asked.

'No,' said Hanlon. Campion nodded, not unsympathetically.

An almost friendly silence descended, then Hanlon spoke. 'In central Oxford there's a brothel that will provide S&M

sex and is used by Dr Fuller.'

'Surely not,' said Campion with heavy sarcasm. 'Not in Oxford, not in the city of dreaming spires.'

Hanlon carried on. 'Despite considerable pressure, even though he's facing a possible murder trial, Dr Fuller has declined to name this place. So, I'm looking for a brothel with truly frightening management. Does any of this ring any bells?'

Campion reached behind her and took out another bottle of Macallan. She poured herself a generous measure. 'The sun is over the yard-arm,' she said. She squinted at the cuckoo clock on the wall. 'Somewhere in the world anyway. I don't know anything about Oxford. I can't help you.'

Hanlon could smell the Scotch from where she sat.

'I was talking to Dave Anderson the other day,' she said. Campion's back stiffened and she looked at Hanlon with new respect.

'You do get around, duckie,' she said neutrally.

'I met his father too. He told me to send his regards.' The two women looked steadily at each other, both powerful, both intimidating.

'Malcolm Anderson,' said Campion wonderingly. 'I'd heard he was dying.'

'He is,' said Hanlon simply.

'I didn't want to go and see him,' said Campion quietly. 'I want to think of Big Mal as he used to be. In his car coat, you won't remember those, you're too young. He was very good- looking. Does he still have those sideburns?'

Hanlon shook her head, 'Chemo,' she said.

'Poor fucker,' said Campion, sighing deeply. 'Mind you, a lot of people would be glad to see him burn in hell.'

'Like Maltese Alex?' asked Hanlon innocently.

Campion looked suddenly very angry. 'Don't you push your luck, Hanlon.'

'He asked after you.'

Campion sat up very straight and stared in a hostile way at Hanlon. 'And just why, exactly, did my name come up, DCI Hanlon?'

Hanlon ignored the question. 'He mentioned someone called Razor Lewis.' Campion blinked and her hand involuntarily went to the scars that ran down her face.

'Mind yer own fucking business, Hanlon.'

'He said that you should help me,' Hanlon carried on, undaunted.

'Malcolm Anderson said that?' 'Yes.'

Campion sipped her malt whisky and looked at Hanlon with

narrowed eyes. Perfectly relaxed and unmoving, Hanlon levelly returned her gaze. The policewoman had that rare gift of almost complete immobility that animals have, and humans rarely do. Hanlon's eye had virtually healed but Campion remembered the heavy bruising to her body and now the strapped wrist. Her cold grey eyes were fixed expressionlessly on Campion. Somehow she seemed to have the Andersons, God forbid, on her side. Campion wondered how on earth she'd managed that. The boy, as she still thought of Dave Anderson, was psychotic.

Hanlon must be odder than she had at first believed. The flowery blouse under her tailored jacket somehow added to the sinister effect of the policewoman's presence. Campion knew tough people when she met them, it had been her life. Hanlon was that unusual mix that you hardly ever came across. Violence and high intelligence.

Well, she wasn't going to cross Dave Anderson, that was for sure.

She picked her phone up from the table and scrolled down, punched a button.

'Tatiana. Downstairs, now please.'

'You'll get what you want,' Campion said to Hanlon.

'I know that,' said Hanlon. Her face was expressionless. 'I usually do.'

Campion looked at her, her emotions a mix of contempt, sympathy and respect. 'I'd be careful what you wish for, dearie. It might just come true.'

36

Gideon Fuller came to on his sofa. His mouth was furred and dry, there were two empty bottles of wine next to the sofa and he guessed there would be more lying around in the kitchen.

His head ached as he pieced together the events of the previous night. Dimly he remembered his conversation with the policeman. So they wanted to talk about Dame Elizabeth, did they? Well they would have to wait a bit. He was now, he guessed, more or less on leave from the university. He could hardly turn up for work as though nothing had happened.

He wandered, yawning, into the kitchen of his flat. There were the other two empty bottles by the sink. He put his coffee maker on. He sat down on a chair while he waited.

The press would be round. He'd better look good for them. The last philosopher he could think of who'd killed anyone was Althusser, a Frenchman, who had strangled his wife in 1980. Fuller recalled he had got three years in a psychiatric hospital. More to the point, people still knew his name, which was more than could be said about his Marxist theories, which

now seemed pointless and very dated.

Foucault, another French philosopher specializing in society's attitude to madness, was rumoured to have knowingly carried on having unprotected sex while diagnosed with Aids. Murder by proxy, death by virus. Fuller didn't believe the story, but it certainly hadn't done Foucault's reputation any harm.

Maybe being linked to a series of murders would do his own career some good.

Fame at last, he thought bitterly.

After his shower he would call his solicitor. He was sure he would get the police off his back soon enough; they'd got no evidence. They couldn't have. After that he'd have to think hard about his future. Well, he wasn't going to buckle, that was for sure. He hadn't survived childhood to be kicked to death on the shores of adulthood. He'd turned his unhappiness into strength before and he would do it again.

What does not kill me makes me stronger.

He made his coffee, strong, black, and went into his bed- room. On the pillow next to his was a familiar face. He was a lot older now and the paint had faded from his feathers so he was virtually monochrome, a dark greenish-black. His one eye looked lovingly at Fuller, and of course he still had only one wing. Fuller automatically pulled the duvet slightly higher so Vulture was covered. He gently patted him on the head. You could always trust Vulture.

He turned on his computer and checked his emails, then he opened his photo files to the one marked *Gallagher*.

He had built up a file of about fifty images of Animal Play and Pup Play. These were women dressed in dog-style outfits, collar, lead and so on, and an anal plug with a tail. They were engaged in dog-style activities, many of a hard-core sexual nature.

The true man wants two things: danger and play. For that reason he wants woman, as the most dangerous plaything.

Nietzsche had nailed it again, he thought. That man was a genius.

His personal favourite was the girl on a choke chain being led to a dog bowl. He opened his wardrobe. Half of it was devoted to his S&M gear. He took down a choke chain and tightened it experimentally round his arm. It felt good. He loved choke chains, the feel of the metal links, the pattern they made on the skin, the sensation of total control. He imagined slipping it round Gallagher's neck and pulling it taut.

He was becoming obsessed by Gallagher.

Now all he had to do was to get into the classroom where he could place a camera in the interactive whiteboard, grab some good head shots of her and Photoshop them on to his image collection. Then he'd have a better idea of how she'd look as he wanted her, tied up, submissive, helpless.

He wondered, as he stripped off to shower, how he was going to do that, but he smiled grimly to himself. He hadn't got a first from Magdalen and a Ph.D. for being stupid.

Gallagher should feel honoured. As Nietzsche said: He desires his enemy for himself, as his mark of distinction.

He washed his hair carefully with the shampoo that claimed to thicken and volumize. He felt his mood brightening.

37

The door opened and a tall, slim, Slavic-looking girl with short, brown hair entered. She had enormous blue eyes. She was wearing a towelling dressing gown and she smiled nervously at Hanlon. She probably thinks I'm a client, thought Hanlon sadly. Campion indicated a chair and the girl sat down.

'Tell this lady about Arkady Belanov,' said Campion. The girl's eyes widened slightly. 'Actually,' Campion added, 'show her what Arkady likes to do.'

Tatiana stood up and shrugged off the dressing gown. Underneath she was wearing a Minnie Mouse T-shirt and a pair of girl-boxer shorts. She turned her back on Hanlon and pulled up the material of her underwear. She put a hand on her glutes and lifted. The skin there in the crease below each buttock, which would normally be unseen, was a mass of angry scar tissue, a semi-circular crescent of former agony and perpetual humiliation. Hanlon leaned forward and examined the scarring. It wasn't from cuts, it was burns, probably from a blowtorch. It was also, in its strategic placing, ingeniously placed to cause pain and discomfort long afterwards. It would have taken forever to heal. No air could really get to it. And for a working girl like Tatiana, the bulk of her clients would never see it. Unless, of course, they wanted to. Unless, of course, it was the kind of thing that excited them. And every time she lay on her back to please them, the friction would have been utterly agonizing.

I think I can have a fair guess as to the character of Arkady, thought Hanlon.

'Fire-play, it's called,' said Campion dispassionately. 'OK, darling, you can get dressed now.'

'He likes this,' Tatiana said. 'He likes very much.'

'What else does he like?' said Hanlon. Tatiana looked confused.

'Why do you want to know?'

'I think,' said Campion, 'I think she would very much like to meet him.'

'Are you crazy woman?' demanded Tatiana. 'No,' said Hanlon evenly.

That's a matter of opinion, thought Campion. Then she spoke to Tatiana. 'Tell her where the house is, tell her how to get inside, tell her how to get to meet Arkady.'

Tatiana looked at Hanlon fearfully. 'If he knows I spoke with you he will kill me. This,' she indicated her backside, 'was just for fun.'

'If you don't help,' said Hanlon, 'I'll find him anyway and I'll tell him where he can find you.' She spoke very quietly. Her face was half in shadow, her black eye partially obscured by some unruly curls of her thick dark hair. One grey eye gleamed menacingly at the Russian girl.

'Tell her what she wants,' said Campion warningly.

Tatiana looked at Hanlon with utter disgust. 'You are not crazy, you are bitch.'

'I'm waiting,' said Hanlon. Tatiana sat upright in her chair, as if she were at school, and told Hanlon what she needed to know.

38

Fuller had managed his morning well. The police interview was farcical. He was getting used to what had once been a novel situation, police interrogation, with surprising ease. Then again, essentially a police interview was not too different from a viva or oral exam, which he'd had to do as part of his Ph.D. The subject matter was different, in this case the murder of Dame Elizabeth Saunders and his innocence thereof, but the principle was the same. He'd always done well in exams; this was no different. He walked it. They had nothing to tie him to Dame Elizabeth's murder. He knew it and they knew it.

Suck on that, DCI Murray, he thought to himself.

The expected press scrum had failed to materialize. There had been two or three photographers outside the police station, but the magic needed to grab a paper's imagination seemed to be missing.

Fuller thought wryly how upset Dame Elizabeth would have been. In many ways she had thought extraordinarily highly of herself. And the world she inhabited had reflected the image back to her.

This public indifference to her fate would have been most galling.

It was an official world Dame Elizabeth lived in and so she was forever in London's heartland. The Houses of Parliament for committee work, the Mansion House, the London Assembly, the RA, Whitehall. It was against London's finest and most imposing backdrops that Dame Elizabeth flourished. But it was a world that meant little to most people, one of cosy civil service patronage, agreeable long lunches and formal dinners, prestigious but undemanding meetings, albeit in the most spectacular of surroundings. The fact that most people didn't care about these things and nor would they shed a tear that she would never now take her seat in the House of Lords, or become the head of the BBC Trust, would have upset her greatly.

Fuller looked as if he was from that world, but he wasn't.

He was very much an outsider and was made to feel one. The establishment's rules were as codified as S&M and its motives every bit as self-gratifying, just as self-satisfying. Just as ridiculous in many ways.

Ironically, it was also a world of which the Home Office bitch Gallagher was part, although she was but an insignificant cog in the machine.

The woman preyed on his mind. There was some quality about Gallagher that attracted Fuller hugely. When he closed his eyes at night, he thought of her face. He felt somehow, no, he knew, that deep down, she was like him. He was certain of it. He hadn't felt so sure of being with a kindred spirit since he had met Abigail Vickery.

If you're gay, you're supposed to have a gay radar. Sado-Masochism is similar. He felt he could tell fellow S&M spirits, and by that he meant people who didn't simply play at suffering, but people who knew what suffering was. People who didn't fear hell;

people who'd experienced it. Gallagher had, somewhere, somehow, he knew it. She was damaged like he was.

Like calls to like.

Fuller was obsessed with her.

Well, tonight he would find out. Tonight he would tell her everything. It was time to gamble, as if he was in a casino, playing roulette. He would take the pile of chips he had amassed during his life and put them all on one number, then spin the wheel.

He typed the email address he had from the university for her into the address section of the Compose Mail box.

My office 8 p.m. tonight. We need to talk.

He pressed send.

He'd get there for seven. Rig his digital camera up to film them. That way he'd have some record of what happened, even if things didn't go according to plan. If things did go the way he wanted, he would of course have more tangible souvenirs. He had absolutely no doubt that she would be there.

OK came the reply.

He nodded. It was all going to work out fine.

39

Hanlon looked thoughtfully at her phone. Fuller's was an invitation she couldn't turn down. It was possible that he might make a clean breast of the killings; it was equally possible that he might attack her. Hanlon felt more than equal to the challenge.

She dismissed Fuller from her mind and looked around the police station office. After the Whitesides and Campion, she had felt the need to see someone she trusted, someone normal, and was now sitting at Enver's desk, waiting for him to come out of a meeting with Murray.

She took in the details of the crowded office with jealousy. Everyone, naturally, knew each other. There was the typically low-key noise of such a place, quiet conversation, phones ringing, the chatter of printers, laughter. It must have been at least a year since she'd been part of station life and although she'd never been exactly popular, she'd been accepted. It had enabled her to have her cake and eat it. She'd managed to be both solitary and part of the herd.

She shook her head angrily, annoyed with herself for feeling self-pity.

The staff around the office were virtually all staring surreptitiously at Hanlon, whose status was approaching legendary. The newly bandaged arm added to the mystique.

She had seen the murderer.

She had pursued the murderer.

She had been attacked by the murderer and locked in a fridge. There was a general feeling of jealousy towards Enver from his male colleagues, for being so close to the most talked about woman in the Metropolitan Police.

Now Enver crossed the room and joined Hanlon at his desk. He thought she looked haggard, more tired than usual. Perhaps she over-exercises, he thought, all that running around can't be good for you. His chair creaked ominously beneath him as he sat down.

'How did it go with Fuller?' she asked.

Enver rolled his eyes. 'It was a disaster,' he said. 'His solicitor's very good, for a start, but we had absolutely nothing on him.'

'Alibi?' asked Hanlon. Enver shook his head.

'Between you and me, I have a feeling that Dr Fuller is a bit of a recluse,' he said. 'I spoke to a couple of colleagues of his and Fuller doesn't attend functions or parties, not unless practically ordered to. He's quite antisocial. He doesn't even have Facebook. That's pretty odd these days for a university lecturer.' He looked directly at Hanlon. 'What about last night, do you think it was him?'

'I wish I knew,' she said. 'I keep changing my mind about him. He's very contradictory.' She paused, then continued. 'When I first saw him, when Corrigan showed me his photo, I thought he was a kind of weak-looking individual, that he wouldn't have the balls for this kind of thing. But I'm beginning to wonder. I think he's very bright and he learns quickly. I've listened to the recording of that first interview, he was shitting himself. Now he's self-possessed. I think I was wrong about him. He does have balls.'

Enver nodded. 'Well, that pattern, I mean the ability to adapt to a learning curve, would fit the killings too. An initial fail-safe strangulation, the victim willingly subdued, and then the McIntyre woman, a ratcheting up of violence, and after that the Dame Elizabeth murder. It's a clear progression in confidence and technique.'

'I still find it hard', said Hanlon, 'to work out the forensic evidence that was found in the first murder, the hairs, and the underwear in the second, given the level of sophistication of the planning.'

Enver shrugged. 'Maybe he wants to be caught. One thing we do know with certainty about Fuller is he likes Sado-Masochism. What could be more sadistic than murder? And what could be more masochistic than making sure you got punished for it? I read your report on what he was doing to that professor, that's pretty crazy stuff. Perhaps that's the explanation for his carelessness, he's just crazy.'

We need to talk. Hanlon thought about her email from Fuller. *We need to talk*. Maybe he does want to be caught, or maybe he's crazy, or, possibly, he's innocent.

She wondered whether or not to tell Enver about her meeting with Fuller and immediately decided against it. Enver would be horrified and would insist on coming with her.

She looked at Enver over the desk. He was like an old mother hen. She smiled, remembering his inept attempt to trail her once in a Corrigan-inspired desire to watch her back, to stop her doing anything stupid. He'd do the same again if he had any idea of what she was about to do.

If he told Murray, it would be officially cancelled. Either that, or turned into some form of police circus with surveillance, recording equipment and some form of SWAT team lurking in a broom cupboard.

'Speaking of Dame Elizabeth,' she said casually, 'she knew my father and was going to give me something of his.' Like details of his life, she thought grimly. 'I don't suppose crime scene found anything?'

Enver had, of course, no idea what she was talking about.

His own family story was textbook immigrant. Father arrives in the early seventies, gets job in a restaurant in Turkish North London, where language skills aren't an issue, works his way up to head chef and opens a successful kebab house, marries local Tottenham girl; the business is transformed by Enver's two brothers, Aunt Demet and some cousins into three upmarket Turkish restaurants. It was a life short on family drama, long on back-breaking work. Everyone was too busy for introspection. If anything, Enver felt he knew rather more about the family history of the Demirel family than he wanted to, from his great-grandfather's role at Gallipoli to his grandfather's achievements in secondary education in Rize province, to his father's early struggles in the restaurant trade. 'No. Just those dates about your father,' he said.

When he'd seen the short text, the name *Hanlon*, the words *born* and *died*, he had shivered inside. It didn't make him think or wonder about her family history. It made him horribly aware of the fact that he might well be writing something similar for the woman in front of him. Her obituary. He'd have to order her tombstone too, if she wanted a church burial. DCI Hanlon born . . . died . . . He looked at the slim figure of Hanlon opposite, so tough and yet so fragile.

I worry about you, he wanted to say. Hanlon would go crazy with rage if he said that. She was always pushing her luck and Enver didn't believe in good luck lasting forever. Things revert to an average mean, he thought. Every bit of good luck has a corresponding amount of bad.

'And what about her computer?' said Hanlon. 'Any leads there?' Again, what she really wanted to know was if they'd found a folder marked with her name, rather than the unlikely existence of a folder marked *Killer: Definitive Proof*. Dame Elizabeth was a woman with forty years' experience of note- taking and the written word. Writing was as natural to her as breathing. Hanlon found it unthinkable that she would have called her over to what was essentially a meeting without some sort of agenda. There would have been at least a list of what she'd got to say.

The eye-catching announcement of her father's death on the interactive whiteboard had been a demonstration of how the professor had planned to treat their meeting, as much a lecture as a confidential talk.

Her mind went back to the moment when she stood at the top of the stairs looking down at Dame Elizabeth, her face a ruined sheet of blood, the masked figure standing executioner- style behind her. She forced herself to think, to remember. He had scooped up a small red bag, and something else, something beige – an envelope?

It wasn't the kind of thing she could swear to in a court of law. She couldn't deny the possibility that her mind was imagining it, but it's what she believed she had seen, and it fitted her theory perfectly. A letter, to her. Perhaps even now, Fuller was reading it, if it had been him there the night before.

Was that why he wanted to meet with her now? She had to know.

Again, Enver shook his head. 'Sergeant Gustafson has made a start on her PC, but it's full of philosophy notes, ideas for lectures, old emails and memos. Quite frankly, I think the case will be closed one way or another by the time he gets through it. I guess it will all end up with her executors.'

'Oh well,' said Hanlon. So it's down to you, Fuller, she thought.

Down to you to tell me about Dame Elizabeth. Down to you to hand me over what was in that envelope. Down to you to give me back my past.

40

It was when Fuller first grabbed hold of her that Hanlon decided to headbutt him.

As he reached his hands towards her, seizing the lapels of her jacket, it was a decision that made itself. The cast on her damaged right wrist had effectively immobilized it. She couldn't use that hand. She knew that if she hit him, not only would the pain be excruciating, but she wouldn't be able to get enough power behind the punch.

Fuller's handsome face was covered in a faint sheen of sweat and she could smell the sweet, sickly residue of alcohol on his breath, as he brought his face closer and closer to hers.

They had been standing at the front of the classroom, the plastic chairs for sixteen students laid out in a classic semi-circle, facing the interactive whiteboard that dominated the front of the room. It was mounted on its high-tech metal frame and had a metre-long projector boom jutting out from the top at right angles. It looked a bit like a street lamp welded on to the top of the whiteboard.

Hanlon had known from the moment she received Fuller's

cryptic email, telling her it was urgent they meet up, that it would probably end in trouble, but she couldn't afford not to. She also felt more than able to rise to whatever threat Fuller posed. Hanlon's self-confidence was reckless. Enver would have pointed out that only a few hours ago her attitude had got her attacked and locked in a fridge. Hanlon wouldn't have listened.

If Fuller was the man who had killed Dame Elizabeth, then he had already run away from her once and hadn't had the guts to tackle her in the kitchen. If he wasn't the killer, then he was just an ineffectual university lecturer with a sad sex life. But she had to meet him. She had to know. There was too much to risk losing had she refused. She hadn't, however, been expecting this.

Fuller's office and the adjoining classroom were on the fourth floor, above what had been Dame Elizabeth's lecture hall. Memories of the previous night flashed through her mind.

A deserted public building at night is an eerie place. The space, designed for large numbers of people, is unsettling when you are the only one in it. Noises are magnified; shadows proliferate. As she walked down the long, wide, empty corridors, lit by recessed bronze art-deco light fittings in the shape of bas-reliefs, reminiscent of Roman torches, she half expected a masked figure, like she had seen the previous night, to leap out at her.

She was fully prepared for that. It was a possibility she actively welcomed.

Hanlon was wearing a loose jacket and her strapped right hand was inside the diagonal slash of the pocket holding her knife. To bring it out would take under a second. In some ways Hanlon was itching for a violent confrontation. She had held herself in check for the union rep and for Whiteside's parents; she'd had dreams and hopes created for her only to see them destroyed in front of her; she'd been attacked and imprisoned. It was a sizeable debit column and only a great deal of hurt to a guilty party would wipe it out.

She was tired of self-restraint. She wanted action.

As she approached Fuller's office, she could see the door open, a light inside. She wondered again about the man. It wasn't that he was a mass of contradictions; it was as if Fuller was hiding some vital part of his personality, putting on an act. Everyone has a public face and she wondered what the real face of Fuller would look like under the public mask. She found it hard to believe that violence lay under his skin; God knows she'd seen enough of that over the years, it was commonplace to her. Fuller managed to project something more like a terrible despair. There was a little-boy-lost quality about the man that she felt, but couldn't understand.

Hanlon wasn't quite sure how she knew this. She had never regarded herself as empathetic, or gifted with the ability to see people's souls; generally speaking she couldn't care less, but something about Fuller called to her.

It was undeniable but true. There was something compelling about the man.

Fuller was sitting on the table in front of the whiteboard in chinos, patterned shirt and polished brogues. He was looking very Sunday supplement trendy lecturer. He was Boden man, staring at the floor, lost in thought. He raised his head, to see her framed in the doorway.

'Do come in,' he said. He sounded a little strange, his speech slightly strangulated. It was only as Hanlon approached him and smelled the alcohol that she realized Fuller was very drunk. 'You said you wanted to see?' she said. The hand in her pocket toyed idly with her knife. She was expecting Fuller to produce the letter that she was sure Dame Elizabeth would have written to her.

'That's right.'

She walked up to him, mentally downgrading Fuller's threat

level. He stood up and swayed gently, his eyes unfocused. He didn't look as if he'd be able to stand unaided, much less attack anyone. That's where she was wrong.

As she came within reach, moving with surprising speed and grace, almost like a dancer, propelling himself forward, Fuller grabbed hold of her jacket. Using the momentum of attack, he swung her round.

'Come here,' said Fuller thickly, his voice low and vibrant. He could smell her hair, feel her surprisingly solid body in his hands. She looked insubstantial, but it was only now that he realized how strong she probably was.

'I want you,' he whispered, his mouth against her face.

He pushed her back so she could feel the edges of the teacher's table in front of the whiteboard against the back of her legs. His face moved closer to hers as he tried to kiss her. The grey eyes under her dark, shapely eyebrows narrowed. She was nearly his, he thought.

It was then that Hanlon struck.

When you headbutt someone, it helps if they're taller than you, otherwise you run a high risk of a clash of heads. That achieves little. It's the softer, more vulnerable areas of the face that you want, the nose, the mouth, the cheekbones. Fuller, two inches taller than Hanlon, was an ideal height.

She stepped in towards him and swung her arms upwards, breaking the hold he had on her clothing. Now it was her turn. She seized the lapels on his jacket and pulled him suddenly towards her. For one delirious second Fuller thought she wanted to embrace him. As she did so, she drove her head forward with all the strength in her sleek, powerful neck muscles. Headbutting someone is a real art and she did it perfectly.

Fuller was taken completely by surprise; the speed with which Hanlon's head descended was awesome. The iron-hard bone of her forehead smashed into the soft tissue of Fuller's nose. It caught him just on the bridge.

The bone broke with a thud and Fuller instinctively brought both hands up to his ruined face. Just as instinctively, as not everyone who's headbutted goes down and it's always best to have a backup plan, Hanlon kicked Fuller as hard as she could between the legs.

The force of the kick was tremendous. To kick someone successfully is quite a difficult thing to do. It's a clumsy way of going about things and it's usually easy to avoid, but when it works, it really works. Until the tip of Hanlon's shoe thudded into his testicles like a sledgehammer, Fuller was totally pre- occupied with his nose. All the strength of Hanlon's legs – legs that were capable of carrying her over a marathon, a hundred and eighty kilometre cycle race and a three point eight kilometre swim – went into the movement.

Fuller staggered back and collapsed on the floor, one hand cradling his crotch, the other his bleeding nose. His shirt, decorated with small roses, was stained with blood. His whole body was convulsed with agony. Tears poured from his eyes. Hanlon stood looking grimly down at her attacker. She wondered idly whether or not to tell him she was a police officer.

Fuller moaned in pain. Maybe now wasn't a good time, she thought to herself.

Then she noticed something on the table behind them that made her change her mind about Fuller. There was a dog's choke chain, more or less identical to the one that had been embedded in the neck and throat of Dame Elizabeth, and a pair of functional-looking chain handcuffs. She picked them up and examined them. They weren't the fluffy pretend kind used in sex games. They were professional restraints. She recognized the brand; some of her colleagues swore by them.

Were you going to use that on me? she thought. Well, we'll see, shall we.

Hanlon wrapped her left hand in Fuller's sweat-stained hair and yanked him to his feet. He was still dazed and compliant. She attached one end of the cuffs to his right wrist, pushed his arm upwards, threw the chain-metal links of the handcuffs over the metal projector boom that jutted out slightly above his head height, and fastened it to the other wrist. Fuller was now standing shackled to the interactive whiteboard. His eyes flickered and opened fully.

While she was doing this, she noticed what would have otherwise been invisible. She would never have had any reason to look so closely at the top of the overhead projector. A small Lumix digital camera had been carefully gaffer-taped to the side of the boom. The duct tape was a metallic grey in colour and was a perfect match for the colour of the boom. The camera was practically invisible.

Hanlon reached into her pocket and took out her knife. Fuller had his eyes open now and was watching her nervously. She clicked the blade open and sawed through the tape. She removed the camera and examined it.

The screen at the back showed it to be set to one-minute time lapses. She scrolled back through the images and there on the small screen at the back of the camera, were the two of them in a succession of reasonable-quality photos. It was like some strange flick book, Fuller standing by the table, Fuller grabbing her jacket, her pushed against the table, her headbutting Fuller, Fuller collapsed, most of him now out of camera shot.

Hanlon walked over to the whiteboard. Fuller was still oddly silent, watching, seemingly resigned to his fate. The projector boom was mounted on a vertical metal track so that it could be raised or lowered. Hanlon clicked its catch off and pushed it upwards a couple of centimetres, forcing Fuller to stand on tiptoe. If he relaxed his stance, the metal links of the handcuffs would bite into his wrist as he hung from them. She clicked the catch back on.

Hanlon lined up the exhibits on the table. The choke chain and the camera. The handcuffs were obviously being modelled by Fuller.

'Well?' she said interrogatively.

'I find you incredibly attractive,' said Fuller by way of explanation, with what, to Hanlon's ears, sounded like worrying sincerity.

'I beg your pardon?' she said incredulously.

'I'm sorry I alarmed you,' he said. His nose was running like a tap, the blood rolling down his shirt now that the fabric was saturated, unable to absorb any more.

'Really? What were you trying to do then?' she asked. Fuller rolled his eyes. 'I was trying to make a pass at you,' he explained. 'And if you'd responded, favourably, I mean,' he added hastily, 'we could have maybe taken it up a gear. That's why I brought the cuffs and the chain.'

Hanlon picked up the choke chain. 'So you like choke chains?'

'Yes,' said Fuller. 'Well, it depends.'

'OK then, so what's the idea behind the camera?'

'I wanted some photos of you,' said Fuller. 'Please can you lower me down a bit, this is starting to hurt.'

'Why did you want photos of me?' continued Hanlon remorselessly.

Fuller sighed. 'For masturbatory reasons.' Hanlon stared at him, startled. 'What!'

'Oh, for heaven's sake,' said Fuller, trying to look as dignified as a man could who was chained to a whiteboard, with face and shirt covered in clotting and drying blood. She had to hand it to him, though, it did sound like a remarkably candid answer. 'Is it so hard to understand?' he said in an almost irritated way. 'I wanted to create sexual images of you so I could have a wank.' Hanlon shook her head in disbelief. I've heard everything now, she thought.

'Obviously,' said Fuller, with masterful understatement, 'things have not gone according to plan.'

'So you weren't trying to assault me at all,' said Hanlon. 'I must have jumped to the wrong conclusion.'

'Exactly,' said Fuller, before adding hurriedly, 'I can quite see how you made that mistake, though.'

'Mm hm.' Hanlon's voice was low and measured. 'And if I take this evidence to the police,' she pointed at the camera, 'who do you think they'll believe, Dr Fuller?'

'I had nothing to do with those killings,' said Fuller wearily. 'Someone is trying to frame me.'

'And you don't have sex with your students?'

'Not generally, no. I don't like people, OK?' Fuller's voice was angry. 'I don't like them in my life, I don't like them in my flat, I don't like them in my bed. I like fucking whores, so I don't have to socialize.'

Once again Fuller was confusing Hanlon. He was terribly plausible. She began to feel angry with herself. Nearly twenty years' experience in the police and she hadn't got a clue if the major suspect was innocent or guilty.

'You tried to have sex with me, though. I'm one of your students,' pointed out Hanlon.

He shook his head in exasperation. 'You're not listening to me. I said, generally. In fifteen years there've been two, you and a girl called Abigail Vickery. She was like me, just like I thought you were.'

'What, into S&M?'

'No,' said Fuller irritably. 'Fucked up mentally, like I am. Damaged goods.'

Well, Dr Fuller, you certainly know how to romance a girl,

thought Hanlon. Tell them you want to wank over them then imply, no, wrong verb, state they were mentally impaired. It was undeniably a novel approach.

Hanlon looked at him thoughtfully, then made her mind up. Tomorrow would tell if Fuller had or had not been involved in the Oxford killing. If he had, or she had any doubt whatsoever of his guilt, she'd take tonight's evidence to Murray.

She took two evidence bags out of her inside jacket pocket and dropped the chain in one, the camera in another.

'What are you doing?' asked Fuller nervously. Hanlon stood up and stretched.

'I'm going home.'

'And me?' Fuller looked understandably agitated as she walked towards the door. His legs did a kind of jig. 'My calves are on fire. You can't just leave me here.'

'Can't I?' said Hanlon.

'What will people think?' wailed Fuller.

'They already think you're a murderer,' said Hanlon. 'Perhaps they'll just think you're eccentric.'

She switched the light off as she left and closed the classroom door behind her.

41

If you had two to three million pounds to spend on property, you too could own the house that Arkady Mikhailovich Belanov had on the Woodstock Road in Oxford. Its eight bedrooms were in more or less continual use throughout the afternoon and evenings, seven days a week. The client list was extensive and carefully vetted. Arkady and his minder, Dimitri, always took the trouble to meet each of their customers. This had a twofold purpose. Arkady was genuinely proud of the quality of the service he provided and liked the customer to know that every whim, no matter how strange, would be catered for.

He also liked to give a little pep talk to explain what might happen should his privacy be breached or his name mentioned. Dimitri, sleeves rolled up, displaying some of his many prison tattoos, mainly related to the right-wing SS, *Slavyanski Soyuz* group, a Russian neo-Nazi party, showed them photos on a tablet. These illustrated the punishment he had inflicted on various people foolhardy enough to cross Arkady Mikhailovich. As a result, none of the clients ever dared mention his name or the address of the property.

In many ways the clients felt more secure knowing their confidentiality was so well protected. Arkady had a high customer-satisfaction rate.

Hanlon arrived at eleven a.m. She knew from Tatiana that this was the best time to catch Arkady. The brothel didn't open until twelve and Belanov would be catching up with his paperwork.

'He is creature of habit,' she said.

Hanlon had parked in the street round the corner, in an old Lexus she'd borrowed from a dodgy car dealer she knew. She'd specified something fast and anonymous. The plates were false. Hanlon knew that when she left number 41 she might well be followed or at the very least be leaving in a hurry.

She rang the doorbell and waited for a moment. She heard footsteps echo on the tiles in the hall and then the door opened.

The man standing in front of her was huge. Hanlon guessed he was at least six foot six and he had the over-developed bulk of a bodybuilder. He was wearing a tight T-shirt to emphasize his enormous arms. His skin was a swirly mass of inky tattoos.

They were incredibly ornate, beautifully executed. Each had a criminal meaning. Hanlon found herself gazing at the onion domes of an intricate Russian church peeping over the scooped neck of his T-shirt. She didn't know that for Russian criminals each of the domes meant a period in prison. That didn't matter. She didn't have to be an expert in body-art semiotics to work out she was dealing with a violent thug.

His pectoral muscles looked like hot-water bottles under the Lycra fabric. An inky spider was visible crawling upwards through the neck of the T-shirt. Hanlon thought to herself contemptuously, you'd last about two minutes if they put you in a ring with Enver. All that pointless bulk. This had to be Dimitri, Dima to his friends, not that he had any. He was Arkady's minder and bodyguard.

He is balbesy, a thug, Tatiana 'Tanya' had said, Arkady Mikhailovich is avtoritet, criminal leader.

She ran her eyes over him speculatively. Like a lot of body-builders, as opposed to weightlifters, he over-favoured the top half of his body, the chest, biceps and lats. The lats stretched upwards and outwards like vestigial wings. He smelled of cheap eau de cologne.

'Yes,' he said, looking down at Hanlon with curiosity. He saw a tall, slim woman with dark, curly hair. Despite the warm, early autumn weather, she was wearing a Burberry-style raincoat, belted tightly around the waist.

She looked him in the eyes, undoing the belt of the raincoat to allow the Burberry to fall open. Dimitri ran his eyes greedily over the figure-hugging black stripper's basque. It belonged to Tatiana, who was slightly smaller than Hanlon, and it was extremely tight.

'Paul Molloy sent me,' she said demurely. 'I'm a present for Mr Belanov.'

Dimitri grinned. 'You'd better come in then.'

Hanlon followed the enormous kite-shaped back of the Russian into the house. The floor tiles were Victorian, but the pictures hanging in the gold picture frames in the hall were not of that period, like Landseer's *Monarch of the Glen* or the *Death of Gordon*, but showed hyper-real pornographic sex, mainly of a violent nature.

'Stop here,' said Dimitri coldly, in the middle of the entrance hall. 'Hands on head.'

She did as she was told and Dimitri unbuttoned her coat and looked at her. 'Very nice,' he said. She felt his eyes moving up and down over every curve of her body.

Quickly and professionally he ran his hands over her, searching for concealed weapons. He made her turn out her pockets, then remove her stiletto-heeled boots so he could check inside. He ran his fingers down the seams of her raincoat. He even had a quick look through her thick, curly hair to make sure there wasn't a razor blade tucked away. It was like being groomed by an unpleasant ape.

The downstairs front room had been turned into a bar area and here Dimitri stopped and pointed. 'You, wait there. What is your name?'

'Candice,' said Hanlon. 'But you can call me Kandi, with a K.'

'OK, Kandi, with K. Take seat. I'll be back soon.'

Hanlon sat down in the small bar area, making an inventory, as she always did, of her surroundings. She kept her hands demurely folded in her lap. She was very careful not to touch anything. She counted eight small round tables, a mahogany- topped bar and a high ceiling with an elaborately moulded central rose for the chandelier and moulded cornices.

She was satisfied with the way things had gone so far. Enver would have gone crazy if he'd known what she was doing, but Hanlon had no doubts she was doing the right thing. She was, by nature, a risk-taker and prone to over-confidence. But so far she had always triumphed and the game was worth the cost. One day, she knew, her luck would run out, just let it not be today. Each table had a drinks menu with eye-wateringly expensive spirits, Grey Goose vodka, Courvoisier, malt whiskies, premier cru wines and champagne. There was also a laminated menu

of a different sort.

Ten photographs of skimpily dressed girls with names, ages and potted biographies. The girls described their sexual pref- erences and areas of expertise. Hanlon repressed a shudder.

According to Campion, Paul Molloy was a vicious little pimp who had clashed with Arkady Belanov over money. Molloy had a couple of pubs in Cowley, legitimate businesses where he could launder his vice earnings, and Dimitri and some hired help had trashed one of them. Sending a girl for his approval would be exactly the kind of peace offering Molloy would make. Hanlon was characteristically trusting to luck that Arkady wouldn't contact him to check. Tanya had said that would be beneath his dignity.

Dimitri reappeared in the bar a couple of minutes later and jerked his head at Hanlon to follow him. She did so and they crossed the hall into Arkady's office.

Tatiana had explained in detail Arkady's sexual preferences but she had omitted to tell Hanlon what he looked like. For some reason she had imagined a man rather like Dimitri, or Campion's Yuri, in other words, an unshaven Slavic thug.

She hadn't expected the mound of flab that was Arkady. He looked like a giant baby, in a turquoise velour tracksuit. He had an enormous double chin, or rather a single wattle of fat, that hung from the underside of his face. He smiled beatifically at Hanlon. His lips were huge, pendulous.

'This is Kandi,' said Dimitri.

'Show me what you can do, Kandi,' Arkady commanded. The first thing she did was put her hands in her pockets and take out a pair of black, elbow-length suede gloves and put them on. That was the fingerprint issue sorted, she thought. I certainly don't want to leave any prints. Arkady practically purred with pleasure. He loved gloves. Particularly long ones. In his office, as well as his desk and a workstation with a semi-circular groove cut in it to accommodate his swollen belly,

was a couch such as you find in a doctor's surgery.

Hanlon shrugged herself out of her trench coat. Arkady greedily drank in the lines of her body as revealed by the skin- tight basque.

Dimitri was standing, watching impassively, leaning against the far wall. While Arkady's body stiffened, Hanlon could sense the bodyguard relaxing. There was nowhere she could possibly be concealing a weapon.

Hanlon patted the doctor's couch invitingly, coaxingly, and

Arkady stood up with alacrity and stripped naked. His very pallid, white flesh hung in folds from his heavy, short frame. He rubbed his large, pudgy hands over the straining flesh of his paunch and his pendulous breasts in happy anticipation. Unlike Dimitri his body was tattoo-free apart from an eight- pointed star on his shoulder. Tatiana had explained to Hanlon that this meant he was a high-ranking criminal.

He is one of the new crime bosses, *novye vory v zakone*, not tattooed so much as old ones, she had said.

Arkady hadn't made his money the soft way. His pale skin bore many angry scars. Life had certainly left its mark on him. He climbed on to the black, padded sofa, doggy-style, and looked at Hanlon.

'Call me Starshi,' he said. 'Yes, Starshi,' she said meekly.

Starshi meant old one. It was used to refer to the leader in a cell block. Another thing she'd learned from Tatiana.

Wordlessly, Dimitri handed her a length of rope and resumed his position, leaning against the wall.

'Are you staying?' asked Hanlon. She really could have done without him there, she thought. Dimitri nodded.

'After Arkady Mikhailovich finishes with you, is my turn,' he said, matter-of-factly. It was the prison way, where they'd both grown up. In a corrective labour institution, an ITU, in Perm region where in winter the temperature averages minus twenty degrees Celsius. In your dreams, thought Hanlon grimly.

She folded the rope in half and trussed Arkady up, more or less in the same way as a butcher would a chicken. The rope wound around his hands in front of him, running back down his body, around his ankles, back again on itself and around his armpits, secured with a tight reef knot on his broad, fleshy back. The Russian was kneeling on the couch, supported by his elbows and forehead, his huge backside, dimpled with cellulite, pointing to the ceiling. She made sure that the rope passed around the couch so Arkady was tied to it. He was going nowhere.

The rope bit cruelly into Arkady's ample flesh until it was practically invisible in places, buried in the flab. He flexed his body against it and groaned against its constrictive pleasure. He was enormously well-endowed and the pleasure he was finding in this rope-play was extremely obvious.

While Hanlon was doing this she had been surreptitiously scanning Arkady's office for something to use against Dimitri. The bodyguard was probably not much bigger than opponents who she had demolished in a boxing ring, but this was no boxing ring. There were no rules and no referee. No one to say 'Break!' All Dimitri would need to do to defeat her, would be to fall on top of her. She'd be pinned to the ground under that bulk and he could beat her to unconsciousness or worse.

Similarly, if he got those massive arms of his round her and squeezed hard, he could break her bones.

Ideally, she could have done with a baseball bat and Dimitri looking the other way. What she did see was something nearly as good.

Propped against Arkady's desk was a double-barrelled shotgun. On top of the desk, next to the monitor, was a box of cartridges.

Hanlon had no intention of shooting anyone. She didn't even know if the gun was loaded, but she did know that a shotgun usually weighs four to five kilos and she knew what it felt like when someone hit you with one like a club. She unconsciously rubbed her left arm; it's how that had been broken, by a rifle butt.

She walked up to Dimitri. His hair was closely cropped and stood up like coarse bristles.

'Can I have some more rope, please?' she asked, with a salacious smile.

He nodded, went over to the desk, opened a drawer and handed her another couple of metres of rope. It looked like the kind you could get in specialist sports shops for climbing. Hanlon took it with a murmured thanks and turned away, breaking eye contact with Dimitri in case he got an inkling of what was coming.

There are two types of headbutt. Using your forehead, as she had on Fuller, and the side-head strike. She had moved her head to one side, so Dimitri was looking at the dark, tight, curly hair on the side of her head. That is the beauty of a side headbutt; there's no eye contact, so the recipient has no idea it's coming. Now she whipped her head round with a mighty flick of her neck, so the top of her forehead smashed into his face. Hanlon was lucky with the blow. Her tough skull made contact with Dimitri's eye socket, fracturing the bone beneath the skin. It hurt the Russian like hell.

'*Suka*', bitch, he hissed.

Hanlon had hoped that Dimitri would instinctively put his hands up to his face, allowing her a split second in which to grab the shotgun by the end of its metal barrel and swing it into his head. No point even trying it against his body.

This didn't happen. The big man gasped with pain, but he'd been hurt too many times before, in fights, to allow his opponent to dictate terms. Unlike Fuller, he was no pushover. He swore viciously in Russian and lashed out at Hanlon with his left arm. She ducked and his meaty fist swung over her head, grazing her hair. Then it was her turn to gasp with pain, as his strong fingers closed over her bandaged right wrist. He yanked her hard towards him. She knew that in a nano- second, his left hand would clamp on to her, probably in her hair, and she'd be his, unable to escape.

The power in the Russian's huge arms was immense. Hanlon threw herself forward to break free. Dimitri grinned, as he tugged her backwards as hard as he could. He was expecting her to resist, but Hanlon half-spun herself back into his body, using the power in her legs. They were now both facing the same way, like in some extreme tango dance, and she slammed her left elbow as hard as she could into his solar plexus.

It drove the wind out of the Russian and he gasped for breath. He literally couldn't breathe. He tried to suck in a lungful of air, but nothing happened. He was on the edge of blacking out. Now Dimitri let go of Hanlon's wrist, as he attempted to steady himself with his hand on the edge of the desk. He was momentarily bent double, trying desperately to get some oxygen into his body and also trying to disregard the terrible pain.

Hanlon snatched up the shotgun and brought the butt smashing down and round in an arc on the side of Dimitri's jawline just where it met his chin. It drove the Russian's head sideways with massive force. The impact to his brain, as it was driven against the wall of his skull, must have been terrific.

Dimitri collapsed on to the floor, temporarily unconscious. He was still stirring, though, and Hanlon straddled him and tied him up with the climbing rope. She did this with extreme speed. Even now his eyes were fluttering and any second consciousness might return.

This time there was no finesse, no artistry. She lashed his wrists together and brought the rope down to secure his ankles.

He was now completely immobilized. In one of the desk drawers she found a reel of Sellotape and this she used to wind round and round Dimitri's mouth so the bottom half of his head looked like a badly wrapped parcel.

Only then did Hanlon allow herself a thirty-second rest, while she assessed the situation.

Arkady was immobile. Lashed as he was to the couch with Hanlon's beautifully executed rope-work, this was hardly surprising. She crouched over Dimitri to take a better look. He was very pale but she pressed her index and middle finger down by the hugely defined muscle in his neck and windpipe, and felt a good strong pulse from the carotid artery. In all honesty, Hanlon didn't particularly care one way or another about Dimitri's fate. Arkady was not the kind of man who would dream of involving the police. Neither would he have any particularly strong feelings regarding Dimitri. Still, on balance, Hanlon was pleased the man was still alive.

The door to the study had been bolted shut earlier by Dimitri and there was a large sash window which overlooked a well- tended lawn. That's my exit, she thought.

'Who sent you?' Arkady had up till now been completely silent. Now, naked and bound, utterly helpless, he exuded a kind of impressive aura of calm. He had spent a lot of time in prison and in the army. He'd endured a lot of pain. He had been officially classed as an *Osobo opasnyi retsidivist*. Nobody had ever broken his spirit. Hanlon looked at him.

'It wasn't Paul Molloy,' he said speculatively. 'None of his people are your quality.'

Hanlon ignored him. She continued her investigation of the office. She picked up the shotgun and broke it open. The circular brass ends of two cartridges stared back at her. The blow to Dimitri could well have caused the hammer to fall, even though, as she noticed, the safety catch was on. She took the two cartridges out and examined them. SG shot. A typical twelve-bore cartridge, say a Number 4, 3.1 mm, will have about thirty to forty tiny spherical metal balls inside. That's the kind of shot you'd use for a bird. SG shot is much larger. You'd get eight or nine pieces of lead in there. You could kill a deer with SG shot.

Hanlon automatically looked up at the ceiling. If the gun had gone off, there would be a huge great hole up into the bedroom above.

She opened the drawer where she had found the tape she'd

used on Dimitri, and took out a Swiss army penknife she'd seen in there. She also took out a cigarette lighter that caught her attention.

She opened the main blade of the penknife and ran it down the outer layer of adhesive bandage strapping her right wrist. She peeled this back and took out the carefully folded piece of paper that had been hidden underneath. She unfolded it and held it in front of Arkady.

'This is Dr Gideon Fuller,' she said.

'I do not know this man.' Arkady's voice was perfectly level.

Hanlon sighed. 'This is Dr Gideon Fuller,' she repeated. 'I just need to know if he was here last week.'

There was silence from the Russian. Hanlon sat down in the chair by the desk. Arkady's eyes stared at her balefully. He watched as, with the penknife blade, she carefully cut open the crimped end of the shotgun cartridge and shook the shot out on to the polished wooden surface of the desk.

'What on earth could you be wanting to shoot with this, Mr Belanov?' she asked, holding up a piece of shot. 'Planning a trip to Magdalen College deer park, are you? Or had you planned on something more two-footed?'

She did the same with the other cartridge.

She now had eighteen pieces of shot in front of her.

Next, she removed the wadding out of the cartridges and dropped it neatly in the bin.

She surveyed her handiwork critically. 'If anyone else had said that they couldn't remember a customer, well, I'd probably believe them. But you're famous for three things, aren't you. Your retentive memory, Mr Belanov, the fact that you like to hurt women, and your enormous penis. The last one's true, obviously. I can well believe the second, and that gives me hope for the first.'

Hanlon took Arkady's iPhone from its docking station and prised it apart with the blade of her knife. She dropped the back cover in the bin and placed the other half in front of her. She now had what was in effect a shallow plastic tray filled with circuitry. 'I have nothing to say. I do not know this doctor,' spat Arkady. Fuller was nothing to him, but his pride was a different

matter. Arkady didn't talk. It was hardwired into him. 'Oh well,' said Hanlon indifferently. 'If you say so.'

She tipped the contents of the cartridge into the shallow tray of the half iPhone and then added the back cover.

'Hope you've got all your information backed up, Belanov,' she said solicitously. The nitro gunpowder was made up of lots of tiny blue rectangles like confetti. They reminded Hanlon of microtabs of acid that she'd seen once in a drugs bust.

Arkady was starting to look nervous. 'There's no point trying to hurt me,' he said. 'I like pain. It's my friend.'

Hanlon shrugged. She looked down at the pile of nitro- glycerin gunpowder, then she picked up the lighter and struck it, staring momentarily at the flame. Its burning light reflected in her eyes as she looked at Arkady. They reminded him of the eyes of a wolf. She smiled horribly at him.

She placed the explosive-filled half-phone, now a shallow tray full of gunpowder, carefully underneath his groin.

'I'm not going to hurt you, Arkady. I'm going to blow your balls off,' she said conversationally.

From the floor Dimitri moaned faintly. Hanlon took a tissue from a box on the desk and rolled it into a spill to light the gunpowder.

Arkady was very conscious of the explosive just below his heavy, dangling balls. His scrotum visibly tightened. He reached a decision.

'Thursday. Two weeks ago. Three to five thirty. He was here, with Oksana,' he said.

Hanlon lit the paper she was holding and looked at the flame. 'Are you sure?'

'Yes. Now, please . . .'

Hanlon looked at his face. She was fairly sure that he was telling the truth. He certainly looked anguished enough.

Hanlon dropped the lighted spill into the gunpowder. Arkady screwed his eyes tightly shut, in anticipation. Instead of the explosion he had been dreading, the little pile of blue rectangles caught fire and burned with a hot yellow flame. It licked upwards. Arkady let out a stream of what Hanlon took to be Russian swear words as the flames singed the pubic hairs off his scrotum and perinaeum. A horrible smell of burned hair filled the room. 'You should learn something about how ballistics work,' said Hanlon, 'given your fondness for firearms.'

'You bitch,' said Arkady. 'Who sent you?'

For some reason Hanlon suddenly thought of the quiet, dignified old man in his archaic uniform, selling *The Watchtower*, outside Mark Whiteside's hospital. There was an air almost of sanctity about him and Hanlon, despite her lack of religious beliefs, always bought a copy.

If only Mark had been here, she thought.

She picked up Arkady's Y-fronts, held his nose, and when Arkady opened his mouth to breathe, she stuffed them inside, careful not to let him bite her through the fabric. She secured them with tape.

She leaned forward and whispered in his ear, 'The Salvation Army.'

Then Hanlon picked up her Burberry and put it on. She opened the sash window, climbed into the garden and was gone.

42

'You did what!' said Enver, horror-struck. He remembered a saying of which his mother was particularly fond, *I was literally tearing my hair out*. That's what he was practically doing now. His powerful fingers were laced into the hair on his head, tugging at the roots as Hanlon calmly tipped another bucket of outrageous behaviour over his head.

I'm beginning to understand how Corrigan must feel, he thought.

Enver was no fool and he could sense how promotion was gradually beginning to change him. He'd had to deal with two cases of good police work being undone by methods that would not stand up in court. He was beginning to learn that unaccountable actions led to unfortunate consequences. He'd always known this, of course, but now he was responsible for the actions of others he was beginning to take a more managerial view of things: that having a system, even though it inevitably contained flaws, was better than anarchy.

And anarchy was what he was looking at now. He had seen a

couple of the photos of Fuller, looking as if he'd received the most terrible beating, with the handcuffs round his wrists.

What if this makes the papers? That was his immediate thought.

'Please tell me they weren't your cuffs, ma'am,' he said to Hanlon. She shook her head innocently.

'No, mine are SpeedCuffs. These ones are a different make.

They're his all right.'

The meeting with Fuller, the chief suspect in a murder enquiry, was bad enough. It was irregular, but it would pass muster. If it did come to trial, though, it would be a gift from heaven to the defence lawyer. Coercion would be the first thing to spring to mind, followed by police brutality.

Fuller had been found by one of the cleaners at six in the morning, still shackled to the whiteboard. Once the cleaner and his colleagues had finished staring, and, as it transpired, taking photos, they had to phone maintenance to find some bolt cutters to free him. Half an hour later the pictures, several of them, had been uploaded to the Internet. It had become the most talked about thing at the university, although so far Fuller had remained silent about what had happened and who had been involved.

Enver had hoped, when he first heard about it, that maybe the incident was related to Fuller's peculiar sex life, but deep down he had suspected Hanlon's involvement and sure enough, here it was.

'Fuller won't complain,' she said confidently.

Since the day before, when she had obtained the information she needed from Arkady, Hanlon had been feeling much more like her old confident self. In his lessons – ironically he had given one called 'Well-Being' – Fuller had provided a quotation from his beloved Nietzsche on happiness that summed up her current feelings.

A yes, a no, a straight line, a goal.

After the incident on the island, she'd been feeling not exactly depressed, but flat. Life seemed to have lost its savour.

She wondered if it could be some form of post-traumatic stress. If it was, she'd deal with it in her own way. She didn't want to see a police shrink; she had a paranoid feeling that she'd be recommended as mentally unsuited to return to active duty.

That would suit many of her colleagues.

Mind you, she felt she had reason enough to feel down. Her best friend was in a coma, for which she blamed herself. It had been her unofficial investigation into a child serial killer that had got Mark shot in the head.

Hanlon was perfectly aware that her unorthodox actions might have unexpected consequences, but it was a risk she was impelled to take. She was, at heart, a gambler and the highest stakes were when she was playing with her own life. When you won on a bet like that, the reward was tremendous. She was also prepared to pay the price for her actions herself. If it meant being sacked, so be it. If it meant being beaten up or injured, so be it. If it meant death, well, that would be that and obviously she'd be in no position to complain.

It was also a step in her quest for vengeance to punish Dame Elizabeth's killer. From a selfish point of view, she'd had the chance to learn about her father snatched away from her. Hope can be so cruel. Revenge can be so strong.

In revenge and in love woman is more barbarous than man. Another quote from the German philosopher, courtesy of Fuller. She should have reminded him of it as she tied him to the boom of the overhead projector, given him something to ponder.

Basically, she'd felt out of control of her own life, but the Arkady incident had made her feel a great deal better. Positive action at last.

A Yes.

She had managed to confirm that she was right to be suspicious of the Oxford incident, even if it did weaken the police case against Fuller.

A No.

'He won't complain,' she said again to a dubious Enver. 'You say he won't complain now,' said Enver. 'But when he's

standing in court facing a murder charge he might feel very different. Particularly, ma'am, when there's a picture of him chained to that blackboard,'

'Whiteboard,' corrected Hanlon.

'Chained to that whiteboard with his nose broken and his face covered in blood. Both of which you did.'

'Don't forget, he tried to assault me!' protested Hanlon. 'It's your word against his,' said Enver.

'I've got it on film, thanks to him and his perverted camera and porn obsession,' countered Hanlon. 'And it's his camera. He can hardly claim he was unaware his image was being recorded. I think it would be ruled in as admissible evidence.' 'What you did to him, it does look awfully like torture,

ma'am,' said Enver.

Hanlon shrugged. 'He started it,' she said mutinously. Enver thought, I won't even begin to answer that.

'Well, ma'am, I'm sure his lawyer will say, why didn't you arrest him?'

'I don't think he did those murders,' said Hanlon, simply.

Enver stared at her in amazement. 'Why not? He even had a choke chain with him when he attacked you.'

'Because he has an alibi for the time the Oxford killing was committed,' she said confidently.

Enver looked at her with surprise. 'Who alibied him?'

Hanlon went through her story of the day before with the two

Russians. Enver stared at her aghast. The Fuller business was bad enough. This was off the scale.

I'm glad I don't drink, he thought. This would drive anyone down the pub.

'So,' Hanlon said smugly, 'I have every reason to believe him, and before you say anything, I think it's highly unlikely that Arkady Belanov is going to log a complaint to the Oxford police about an assault. It's not really his style.'

'No, no, it's not, ma'am. But I'm sure that what is his style is to have some form of surveillance camera in the reception and bar area at least, and I'm also sure that there'll be at least one of our colleagues in Oxford on the Belanov payroll. That's going to be his style. Really it is. He'll know exactly who you are by the end of the week, if not sooner.'

He put his hand back into his thick hair for comfort. It was so typically Hanlon, blithely convinced of her own indestructibility. She'd been careful enough not to leave fingerprints and then almost certainly allowed herself to be filmed.

She never thinks things through, not fully, he thought. It's action, action, action, no planning.

'You might as well have taken a photo and sent it to him on SnapChat or Instagram. Or a selfie. Please tell me you didn't.'

'Oh, nonsense, Enver,' said Hanlon. 'You're such an old woman. He'll put it down to business. One of those things. It's an occupational hazard for a criminal.'

'Ma'am, you threatened to blow his balls off,' said Enver, shaking his head in disagreement. 'He's not going to forgive that in a hurry.'

'Well, we'll cross that bridge when we come to it.' Hanlon sounded flippant, but she had to admit that maybe Enver had a point. Someone from the brothel would have eventually found and released Arkady and Dimitri and while obviously no one would have dared take photos, as had happened with Fuller, it was the kind of story that would inevitably leak out. They'd been made a fool of by a woman and this would add insult to injury. A very big insult probably. They couldn't afford not to do anything.

'I don't know what Murray is going to make of this, ma'am,' said Enver.

Now it was Hanlon's turn to look alarmed.

'Surely you're not going to tell him about any of this?' she said. He looked at her mournfully. He couldn't play the them- and-us game any more. Enver shook his head.

'We'll have to tell him about Fuller, ma'am. Just in case. I think it would be better coming from you. You can claim you were upset. Get your side of the story in first.'

'I was upset, Detective Inspector. First he tried to assault me, then he said he enjoys masturbating while thinking of me. Who wouldn't be upset,' said Hanlon. 'And he questioned my sanity.'

I wonder why he'd do that? thought Enver to himself sarcastically.

'Exactly, ma'am. So upset, your judgement was clouded temporarily, but now you want to make sure everything is done by the book, now you're less upset. Luckily you've got photographic evidence showing Fuller attacking you. It's all very much out there in the public domain, isn't it, as you said. I agree that the Belanov incident shouldn't come out, but what are we going to do about the fact it points to Fuller's innocence?'

Hanlon felt that there had been some kind of seismic shift in their relationship. Although Enver was technically lower in rank, he seemed very much to be dictating the agenda. It was like talking to a junior version of Corrigan. She reluctantly conceded that he did have a point.

'Well, we'll just have to find the real killer, won't we?'

A Straight Line.

'We have no suspects. Nobody except Fuller,' pointed out Enver. 'And let's not forget that the only person who really thinks he's innocent is you, and that's based on evidence that would be totally inadmissible in court.'

Now it was Hanlon's turn to get annoyed. 'What I have managed to do is prove to my own satisfaction that Fuller, weirdo creep though he is, did not kill Jessica McIntyre and very probably, almost certainly, did not do the other murders. It may have been a bit irregular, but I think now you can put some pressure on Oxford to recheck their investigation.'

A Goal.

Enver shook his head dejectedly. It's up to me then, is it? I wonder what I can say to DI Huss.

'Well, I'll see what can be done,' he said.

Hanlon stood up and walked away from Enver's desk without a backward glance. It was a deliberate snub. Enver felt undervalued and upset as he watched her slim, elegant back leaving the office. He sighed and picked up the phone on his desk and dialled Summertown. Hopefully DI Huss might be able to help.

43

DI Huss was having troubles of her own. This problem, too, had a human face, DS Ian Joad.

Every office, every place of work, has someone who is generally universally reviled, and Summertown nick had Joad. DS Joad, with nearly thirty years' history of taking small bribes, sexual coercion of prostitutes, fiddling expenses, complaining and generally being a pain in the arse.

The last few years he had added 'stress' to his repertoire of annoying habits and two or three times a year would come down with it. He would signal these bouts of stress in advance with dramatic sighing and waving of his arms, pantomime panic attacks. Then he'd be off for a month. It was, of course, illegal to enquire too much about Joad's stress, because that in itself would be inherently stressful. No senior officer doubted Joad's ability to keep just the right side of the law, and that included employ- ment legislation. No senior officer underestimated his cunning. One memorable time he tried to submit an expense claim for overtime at a court appearance he'd scheduled for himself, when he knew it was a rostered day off and he could claim a day's extra pay for a five-minute showing. The 'stress' had got in the way of the actual court appearance, but he argued that had he not been stressed, he'd have received the money and so should be paid it.

It was the day Templeman exploded. No one had seen anything like it before or since. The mild-mannered, church- attending Scot had screamed, 'Is that meant to be some sort of fucking joke, Joad?'

'I don't know, sir. Not exactly.'

Even Joad was alarmed. He'd pushed the DCI too far. 'I've never seen a bigger disgrace than you in my life, Joad.

Now get out of my sight.'

Joad was bloodied but unbowed.

Templeman had a new prayer he added to his daily list. 'Dear God, in Thy infinite wisdom, may DI Joad apply for a transfer.' Huss looked again at the papers in front of her. The first problem, or irregularity, had been the CSI team missing the killer's escape route at the scene of crime in the college. That had been bad enough. Now there was this. Huss was looking at the Scene Attendance Log for the day of the second search of Fuller's room at the Blenheim Hotel. She corroborated this with the crime scene log, in case there were any discrepancies. The senior officer rostered was DI Joad. DS Ed Worth was also listed as present at the scene, and a forensics man called

Davies, who she didn't know.

Huss had seen Worth not ten minutes earlier in the canteen, which is where, stony-faced, she headed now.

Worth was drinking coffee with a couple of guys from Traffic.

'Hi, Melinda,' said one of them. She smiled sweetly and said, 'I need to have a word with Ed, if you don't mind.'

'Sure, no problems.' The pair from Traffic got up and gathered their things. Goodbyes were said.

'So, Melinda,' said Ed Worth, 'how can I help?'

Worth had one of those curiously old-fashioned faces, square-jawed with a broad, high forehead and matching haircut, that made him look as if he'd wandered out of a thirties-era film. He was a bright guy, though, and Melinda knew he detested Joad. Working for Joad meant doing two people's jobs. Joad's mastery of the system made getting him dismissed for incompetence very unlikely. The best they could do was cross their fingers and hope Joad committed an actual crime of a serious nature or was harvested by nature, as a result of his heavy drinking and smoking.

'It's the Fuller case,' she said.

'What about it?' asked Worth warily. Huss's attractive but no-nonsense face was wearing a frown. She could be quite frightening when she was angry. She was used to ordering stockmen who worked with cattle and farmworkers, tough, aggressive men, around. She was used to command.

Whatever it is, thought Worth, I bet Joad's got something to do with it.

'When you returned to re-examine Fuller's room, was the search scene still intact?'

'Well, the tape was still there and the door showed no signs of being tampered with, so yes.'

'And Joad didn't interfere with anything?'

'By that,' said Worth, 'I assume you're meaning plant evi- dence. No. He couldn't have. It was pretty well hidden. The slit in the mattress was maybe a centimetre and the fabric is striped, so it's not like it was some gaping slash. There was a tacking stitch holding the edges together, we bagged the complimentary sewing repair kit to check against the thread in the stitch, and the forensics guy said it looked like being a match.'

Relief ran through Huss's body. When she'd heard that Joad had found them, she'd automatically assumed something dodgy was going on. Now it looked as if she was mistaken.

Worth continued, 'If it wasn't for the DCI's suspicion that Fuller was guilty, we would never have been back a second time and he'd have got away with it.'

Huss nodded. She knew that Templeman thought the initial underwear and hair had been left by Fuller in order to confuse the investigation. The thinking was he'd come back for the real souvenir at a later date. It was unlikely that the mattress would have been changed by the time he wanted to use the room again.

'And you checked that the room hadn't been accessed?' 'I already told you. It definitely hadn't.'

'No. No, you didn't,' said Huss. 'You said the door didn't *look* tampered with.' She emphasized the word *look*. 'The hotel have got records of when rooms are accessed via the swipe-card key. Did you confirm it with them?'

Worth looked uncomfortable. 'I didn't know that. Maybe Joad checked.'

'Well, we'll see,' said Huss. Her displeasure was plain to see. Worth winced. He liked Huss.

The Blenheim Hotel was only a short distance from the police station and Huss walked there, oblivious of the tourists and students around her. She went up the imposing steps of the battleship-grey hotel, which always seemed grim and unwelcoming, scowling across the road at the Ashmolean Museum. The doorway to the hotel was in the form of an oddly pointed arch that looked as if it had come from a church.

The duty manager who saw her was a charming, good- looking young Pole. He ushered her into his office, typed in Fuller's room number and clicked on the access history to the room.

He said, in his faultless, slightly accented English, 'Well, to answer your question, no guests or cleaners have been in during time you specified.'

Huss noticed he had the Eastern European habit of dropping the word 'the' when he spoke English.

'Good,' said Huss. That cleared that up. She guessed she could now relax. The manager held his hand up, palm outwards in a warning gesture.

'I am not finished. There is manager's card like this one,' he took his wallet out and showed her a credit-card-sized piece of plastic, 'that is slightly different.'

'How so?' Huss asked. Irek, the manager, smiled. 'Cleaners' keys will allow them access to rooms and storage

areas for linen, cleaning products, stuff like that, but not for restricted areas, where food or alcohol is stored, valuable things. My card gets me in anywhere I want. More importantly, it doesn't show up on the system.'

'So, there'd be no record,' said Huss.

He nodded. 'It's a system flaw,' said Irek. 'One I pointed out, actually. We do have someone working on it now from head office. We're part of chain, and I can get them to check. But it'll take two working days.'

'But it can be done,' said Huss. 'Oh yes, it can be done.'

Huss gave him her business card. 'Please make sure it is, Irek.' 'I absolutely will do that, DI Huss. I will call you in two days.' She exited the Blenheim feeling slightly happier. With luck, she'd be able to prove incontrovertibly that the crime scene had been completely undisturbed. She couldn't see any way a manager at the Blenheim could be bribed into allowing someone intent on planting evidence access to the room. Not that it was impossible to believe, but that it would be risky.

But it was all too easy to believe that one of the cleaners on a minimum wage and a short-term contract, maybe someone not even in the country now, maybe with fake ID working illegally, could be persuaded to let someone into the room.

'Here's a hundred quid, just open this door and go away

for five minutes.'

Well, that hadn't happened. Joad hadn't misbehaved. It was all good.

But Huss came from generations of farmers. Caution and pessimism ran through her like a strand of DNA double helix.

Two days. She'd believe she was clear when it happened.

44

Arkady Belanov, as Enver had correctly predicted, was not in a forgiving mood. He was not a forgiving kind of man at the best of times. Revenge was very much on his mind, now that the immediate aftermath of Hanlon's visit had been dealt with. He was particularly infuriated that Hanlon was a woman.

Women had no place in Arkady's world except for sexual pleasure, as the butt of jokes or for public beatings and humilia- tion. His relationships with women were those of slave and master from plantation times.

Now Hanlon had turned his world on its head. He had been the butt of a joke, he had been physically attacked, he had been humiliated. Nothing short of Hanlon's death would satisfy him.

He wanted a *razborki*, a settlement of accounts.

Dimitri had been sent to a private treatment clinic in Wembley that Arkady used occasionally when people who worked for him needed patching up. The facilities and doctors were good, but more to the point, there were no awkward questions asked. They X-rayed him, suggested he might like to go somewhere for a proper CAT scan, gave him industrial- strength pain killers and sent him back.

The fortunate thing for Dimitri was that the injury (all the pain seemed to cluster at the site of the broken bone around his eye) was easy to isolate. This was not the case for Arkady.

Arkady had been treated at the clinic, too, for the second-degree burns on his groin. The major problem for him was that whatever he did put pressure on the area. Sitting, lying, even standing, the burned flesh was chafed and pressured. The fact that it was this kind of pain he had enjoyed inflicting on his girls was an irony he failed to notice.

Dimitri was making light of his injuries. He had survived much worse in the past, as had Arkady, but the humiliation really hurt. To be beaten up by a woman, that was an unwel- come first. He ran the scene over and over in his head like a video on a loop. Hanlon headbutting him, fine, who could have anticipated that? But then his stupidity, when he had a hold of her, in not finishing the job properly! A two-handed grip and she'd have been his. Instead, that elbow strike to his gut, then the wooden end of the shotgun driving into his jaw. Well, the next time they met – and there would be a next time, they would see to that – it would be very different.

Arkady concerned himself with more practical problems. Who was she? He very quickly decided that she had to be some kind of professional. Well, that much was obvious. His first thought was probably ex-army. Not many men, let alone women, would have either the ability or, maybe more to the point, the guts to tackle Dimitri. If it had happened in Russia he would have guessed maybe the FSB, the Federal Security Service, the KGB's replacement. Where Putin had come from. But they weren't in Russia and he couldn't blame Vladimir Vladimirovitch for this.

What was she? Mixed martial artist? Cage fighter? Surely not.

The only time he had seen commitment like that, bravery like that, and that fanatical look in the eye of someone perfectly prepared to die for their cause, was when he'd served with the army in Chechnya.

Svoboda ili Smert!

Freedom or death. That was a Chechen war cry he had heard many times. He could easily imagine it on her lips too. While promoting brand Belanov, Arkady had always heavily emphasized the terrible things that would happen to those who crossed him. He had learned long ago that fear paralyses people as effectively as a choke-hold. He liked people to be afraid of him and you would have to be crazy not to be. Whoever the woman was, she hadn't been deterred by his reputation.

Then there was the question of who had sent her. His first thought, when Dimitri went down, was, I'm a dead man. She had to be an assassin, a hit-woman. He had never heard of such a thing, but why not? To see was to believe and from his position he felt sure he was looking death in the face. What else could this be? When you live a gangster's life, you will probably die a gangster's death, either behind bars or violently. There was no doubt in his mind as to his fate.

He knew what violent death looked like. He had meted it out often enough.

His most coherent thought had been a desire to die well, to show her that a Russian wasn't scared of death. Dimitri had a tattoo of the Virgin and Child on his chest ready for this eventuality. It meant that his conscience was clean before his friends. Arkady's only hope had been that it would be quick. He could scarcely believe what he was hearing or seeing, when she stuck that picture of the nonentity Fuller under his nose. This peculiar request for information on probably the least important of his clients, was what he found hard to grasp. That anyone should risk their lives to find out what that ineffectual pervert was up to was bewildering.

Arkady's brain was an incredible storage system. In prison he'd occasionally do memory shows for his fellow inmates, memorizing packs of cards, that kind of thing. He had been able to provide all the details she had wanted in a nano-second, time, date, length of stay, choice of girl, but who cared about some two-bit teacher?

That made him rethink the soldier part of his theory. Police? It was such a cop kind of question, establishing an alibi, but such an unorthodox way of going about things. Still, it was something worth checking out. Indeed, realistically, it was one of the few things he could check out.

To think was to act. Arkady picked up his new mobile phone and called his contact at Oxford CID.

DS Joad looked around the bar with approval. It was only the second time that he'd been here, although he had been on Arkady's books for two years. He had been given dis- appointingly little to do. Since he was paid a retainer, plus extra for services rendered, he'd earned a lot less than he was hoping for. Plus, he'd expected to be given the run of the house, where the girls were concerned. Joad had been extorting sex from prostitutes all his life and now he had hit the mother lode, he wasn't allowed so much as a blow-job. Perhaps today his luck would change. He looked at the menu of girls. Nadezhda from the Caucasus looked very promising.

He ordered a Beluga Goldline vodka on the rocks. It was eye-wateringly expensive and he liked the stylish bottle it came in. He also liked the way that he didn't have to pay for it. He knocked it back quickly and banged the glass down on the bar so he could get another one in while the going was good.

'Make it a large one, Ivan,' he said to the barman.

He caught his reflection in the mirror and straightened his tie. He was looking good. He was glad he'd worn his best suit. He fitted in perfectly. He'd had a bit of banter with the barman about it. He was popular with barmen; he had the common touch. He sipped his drink and looked around the bar. He smiled benignly at the other customers with their girls of choice. The barman slipped away and crossed the corridor to Arkady's office. He knocked on the door and Dimitri opened it. 'Get that fuck-wit out of my bar, please, Dimitri Nikolyavitch,' begged Sergei. 'He's beginning to freak the other customers out.' Dimitri looked across the office at Arkady, who nodded.

Dimitri then accompanied the distraught barman and returned thirty seconds later with Joad, still clutching his drink.

Arkady began to reconsider his hiring policy. Surely anyone was better than this. He ran his eyes coldly over Joad, who was grinning at him, anxious to please. The policeman was wearing a terrible three-piece suit, made of some dark, artificial fabric. Even in Arkady's hometown of Tulskaya in south Moscow, notorious for being an industrial slum, a real dump, it would look like shit.

'Sit down,' he said abruptly. Joad did as he was told.

Enver had guessed that Hanlon would have been photographed on some form of internal security system. So she had.

Arkady slid a high-resolution photo of Hanlon across the top of his desk. Joad's eyes widened as he saw who it was. He immediately decided to lie for the moment. It's what he usually did.

Arkady had noticed Joad's reaction.

'Do you know who this is?' he demanded.

Joad shook his head. 'No, I was just admiring the view. Nice tits, bit small for me, not like Nadezhda,' he added hopefully. Arkady stared at him coldly. 'I'm sure I can find out for you, though,' said Joad.

'I hope you can,' said Arkady menacingly.

'If she's on our system, it might take some time,' said Joad, pulling a face.

'Then make time,' said Arkady.

Joad put his serious face on. 'I'll run her through databases for you. Do you have fingerprints? That would be a huge help.'

'No,' said Arkady.

'She sounds like a professional,' said Joad. He frowned to indicate the difficulties he would face.

'Meaning?' said Arkady.

'I mean, she might not even be on our system,' warned Joad. He was warming to his task. 'But I swear to God I'll pull all the stops out.'

'You do that,' said Arkady. 'And I will want some form of address, some knowledge of how to get hold of her.'

Joad thought carefully. 'I'm sure that can be done, if I can track her down. And I take it you'll want any other relevant information.'

'Yes.'

'What's she done, this woman?' asked Joad, curious to know how Hanlon had come to Arkady's attention.

'Pissed me off,' said Arkady.

45

Enver looked across the table at the twin figures of DCI Murray and Assistant Commissioner Corrigan. He had forgotten exactly how tall Corrigan was, and he looked even bigger in his uniform. Murray yawned and scratched his bald head.

'Sorry, sir, sorry, Enver,' he said. 'We've got this new puppy and we keep her locked up in the utility room at night because she's not house-trained, and she whines all night. Worse than the kids.'

'Yes, sir,' he said.

Corrigan said nothing, but Enver noticed a flicker of impatience running across his slab-like face. We're not here to talk about the puppy, the expression said.

'The AC is with us today for a brief assessment report on the philosophy killings,' said Murray. 'I'd be grateful to you, DI Demirel, if you could give him a brief summary.'

'Yes, sir,' said Enver. It was the kind of thing he excelled at. He had a retentive memory and a gift for precis. He also had the advantage of knowing that Corrigan was well disposed towards him. Enver had made reports to senior officers in the past, who had taken a cruel delight in deliberately misunderstanding, or misinterpreting, facts to make him look ridiculous. He guessed it was a typical power game. Belittling your juniors.

Corrigan was not like that. He was, however, immensely shrewd and a couple of times Enver noticed him raise his eye- brows and make a note on a pad of paper. After a while, the paper was annotated with short sentences in his neat hand- writing and ominous-looking question marks.

'And how has DCI Hanlon been getting on in her information-gathering role?' asked Corrigan. His eyes were fixed gently but firmly on Enver's.

It was the question that Enver had been dreading. Corrigan knew Hanlon very well. He knew that she was quite capable of acting irregularly. He was superb at evaluating data and he could see that Enver's report, while excellent, was expertly side-stepping around certain contentious issues.

Namely, Hanlon. Corrigan was extremely fond of Hanlon. He found her honesty, her incorruptibility and her integrity admirable, but above all he found her compelling. He wasn't drawn to her because of anything, he had to admit, it was more in spite of. She was cantankerous, unpredictable and a huge source of trouble. And he also knew he would go to extraordinary lengths to protect her. He knew that Enver felt the same. She'd nearly got him killed, had got him shot in the foot, he was lucky not to have been crippled, and here he was, still loyally covering her back. He would bet good money that Enver knew an awful lot more about her activities than he was letting on.

Enver, correctly, put the AC's presence here as a kind of warning not to overstep the mark. He scratched his moustache, which he did when he felt hesitant.

Telling the truth was out of the question. How could he even begin with the Belanov incident? But just for a second he felt an overwhelming desire to make a clean breast of everything, to pour his heart out to Corrigan. He resisted the temptation.

Let Hanlon deal with it, he thought. She created the situation in the first place.

'Fine, sir.' He hesitated. 'She does have some theories that may impact upon the case, I believe.'

Corrigan raised an eyebrow. 'Really, do go on, I'd be fascinated to hear a DCI Hanlon theory.' His tone was dry, ironic.

'Yes, sir.' Enver thought of Hanlon's strong, slightly arrogant features and the impossible situations she landed him in. I could strangle you, he thought.

There was a pause while he frantically racked his brains for something noncommittal to say. Murray yawned.

'I'm all ears, Detective Inspector,' Corrigan added helpfully. Enver said smoothly, 'I wouldn't like to pre-empt anything the DCI has, sir. I'm sure it'll all be in her report, a full and comprehensive account.'

'I'm sure it will,' said Corrigan with more than a hint of sarcasm. 'Until that happy day, let's hear your side of things.' Sod it, Enver thought, it's what she wanted after all. He took a deep breath. 'I rather think, though, sir, that she may have doubts as to Dr Fuller's guilt.'

Corrigan nodded. 'Ah yes, Dr Fuller. He seems to be trending quite a bit on Twitter of late. Have you followed any of the gossip yourself, DI Demirel?'

'No, sir.'

'Well, @LionofAfrica15 has posted some hair-raising images of Dr Fuller online. I think the Lion might well be a cleaner at Queen's College. Have you seen it?'

'Not as such, sir.'

'Dr Fuller is handcuffed to a whiteboard. He seems to have been beaten up. Does this ring any bells, DI Demirel?'

'I'll certainly look into it, sir,' said Enver. '#DrFullerphilosophy. That should take you there,' said Corrigan.

'Yes, sir,' said Enver. Bloody Hanlon, he thought.

'I'm sure it's got nothing to do with the Metropolitan Police,' said the assistant commissioner menacingly. 'Why don't you try asking DCI Hanlon about it? She might favour us with one of her theories.'

'Yes, sir,' said Enver unhappily.

The discussion switched to other, more mundane aspects of the case and its wider ramifications. Time passed slowly until Corrigan stood up, towering over the table. 'Well, I'd best be off. Tell DCI Hanlon I was asking after her.'

'I will, sir,' said Enver. He and DCI Murray watched him leave. Message understood, thought Enver.

Murray turned to him and said, 'Right, Fuller. I happen to share DCI Hanlon's concerns, up to a point.' Enver looked at him in surprise. 'I'm not a hundred per cent happy with the case against him as it stands and the CPS are mak- ing concerned noises about the Oxford end of things, but that's not our concern. I take it you've got nothing to add to this?'

'No, sir,' said Enver. Not unless you count DCI Hanlon beating Fuller up and then threatening to emasculate a Russian criminal, then perversely coming to the conclusion that Fuller was innocent.

Murray smiled happily.

He was by nature a glass-half-full kind of a man. He was very relaxing to work with, not like some DCIs Enver could name. Murray hadn't particularly cared that Corrigan had been down checking on the progress of the case. As far as he was

concerned, he'd done his best. His conscience was clear. 'Well,' said Murray, 'there's one thing I would like you to do.

I want you to go up to Leeds and interview Abigail Vickery's mother.'

Enver raised his eyebrows. 'Yes, sir. And to what end?'

Murray took his glasses off and polished them on the fat end of his tie. 'As of course you know, one of the theories swirling around Fuller is that Abigail was his first victim. That's seven years ago. What I really don't want to have to do, is track Fuller from then until now, looking at unsolved assaults and sex crimes in places associated with him. All that time, all that effort, all that cost.' He shook his head. 'I know you looked into the police and coroner's reports but I want you to have a word with the mother. Police reports don't always hit the mark, do they, DI Demirel?'

He spoke innocently enough, but Enver thought of the gaping holes in his own report. First Corrigan, now Murray. No one really believes me, he thought gloomily. Murray carried on.

'I contacted Alison Vickery. She'll be at home on Monday. No sense dragging her down to the local nick, maybe opening old wounds. Go and see her, find out what she thinks. It's as simple as that.'

'Yes, sir,' said Enver.

'I got DS Fremlin to book you rail travel. Go to him and he'll give you the ticket documents. I'll see you, I guess, on Tuesday or Wednesday.'

'Yes, sir.'

'At least with you, Enver,' said Murray, 'I can rely on you to be discreet and tactful. It's a terrible thing to lose a child, so handle her gently, yeah.'

'Yes, sir. I'll do my best,' said Enver.

First Oxford, now Leeds. Who said police work wasn't glamorous?

46

Joad scratched his head in annoyance. Over the weekend he had drawn a complete blank on Hanlon. His friend in personnel, HR as he now had to call it, had been transferred, and he could no longer access addresses of serving officers. The Data Protection Act seemed to be taken very seriously indeed these days. He had tried a couple of exploratory approaches but had been warned off. He'd then got in touch with an old drinking buddy in the Met, to see if he could shed any light on Hanlon's whereabouts. Again, a total blank. Hanlon was one of those people who everyone felt they knew, but nobody actually did. He couldn't go back empty-handed to Belanov.

What he did next, struck him as genius.

'Hey, Dave,' he'd said to the desk sergeant at Summertown. 'Hi, Ian, busy are you these days. Caught the St Giles flasher yet?' Someone had been exposing themselves to women, students and tourists, in the centre of Oxford and Joad had been given the case. Three of the women had said 'there was something funny' – that is, strange – about the man's genitals. Beyond that and the fact he had long hair, Joad had made little progress.

He was in no hurry.

'I think he's a foreigner, Dave,' said Joad seriously. 'But I tell you what is strange, several of the women have mentioned seeing an Audi around at the time.'

'An Audi,' said the desk sergeant. 'You amaze me, Phil. Not an Audi, oh, there's probably only, what, a few thousand in Oxford. You've practically nailed him. Promotion beckons.'

'Very funny, Dave,' said Joad. 'It was an Audi, like that bloody arsey woman from London was driving, the DCI. Here for the Fuller inquiry.'

'DCI Hanlon. A TTS Coupé?' said the desk sergeant.

'No way was it a TTS Coupé. It was an RS,' countered Joad. 'No, it bloody well wasn't.'

'RS. I used to be in Traffic.' 'So did I. It was a TTS.'

'Bet you a fiver it wasn't.' Joad dangled the offer of the money provocatively and the desk sergeant took the bait.

'Done,' said the sergeant. 'Prove it!' said Joad.

He shrugged and typed into the keyboard in front of him, calling up the CCTV images from Friday and the approximate time. Both men watched as Hanlon's scarlet Coupé rolled into the station car park and neatly reversed into an empty bay. The camera froze on the image of the bonnet and front number plate.

The desk sergeant looked at Joad in triumph. Ian Joad sighed and pulled out his wallet.

'Better luck next time,' called the sergeant.

As soon as Joad was round the corner, he pulled his notebook out and jotted down the number.

Five minutes later, he ran her plates through the PNC and had her address.

Bingo! he thought.

But if Joad was stalking Hanlon, Huss was stalking Joad. DI Huss approached the desk sergeant with her firm, steady walk and land-girl physique. She was from generations of Oxfordshire farming stock and looked it. There were three hundred years of Husses in the local churchyard. Her lineage would have stretched way back beyond then, before recorded history for the non-aristocracy.

She could drive a tractor at ten; her father's old second-hand MoD Land Rover when she was eleven. Now he relied upon her to fix it. It was a Series 2 1964 Land Rover, which made it almost a quarter of a century older than Huss.

She could repair fences, milk cows, trim hedges, plough and harvest. She could butcher a cow, pig or sheep, and her baking skills were formidable. She could do her father's tax returns and sort out his computer, apart from the occasion when he had attacked it in a fury with his powerful, scarred fists. She was also a regular finalist in the BASC twelve-bore shooting contests in Oxfordshire.

Police work was dealt with in the same can-do spirit, but like most farmers Huss had a formidable temper.

Like all her family, indeed like most country people, she also held a grudge, worrying at it like a dog with a bone. Huss hated Joad.

It was Huss's self-appointed mission to get Joad sacked. One day, please God, he would really mess up incontrovertibly.

'Hi, Dave,' she said cheerily to the desk sergeant.

'DI Huss. Are you still free for the darts night next week?'

Dave Rennison ran the police team and Huss was probably his most talented player. It was a source of grave regret to him that the younger police didn't seem interested in the game at all. Too busy farting around with stupid electronic things.

'Wouldn't miss it for all the world. What was Joady after, Dave?'

The sergeant explained. Huss thanked him, then walked off and out of the building. The desk sergeant's reply had given her plenty to think about.

* * *

Huss was now heading back to the Blenheim Hotel, where she hoped that Irek would have the information she needed on access to Fuller's room.

She arrived sooner than she wanted at the Blenheim and to kill some time, trotted up the steps of the Ashmolean Museum opposite.

She sat on a bench in the first gallery that she came to, oblivious to the paintings around her, and thought about Joad. One thing Joad did know about was cars. She'd heard him shooting his mouth off often enough, about the merits of this gearbox compared with that, where to buy the best tyres locally, the strengths and weaknesses of this new car versus that. A lot of it, she suspected, would be recycled *Top Gear* or *What Car?* gossip, but he would have known what car Hanlon drove.

That was without a shadow of a doubt.

No, he wanted that image so he could get her number plate details. It had to be that. Nothing else made sense.

Huss now jumped to the right conclusion, but the wrong reasons. Obsessed as she was by the Fuller case, she assumed that Joad would be gathering information to sell to journalists about the investigation. Hanlon's car registration could well give Joad access to more personal details. And if he was going down the press-informant route, why stop at Hanlon? She and Templeman could end up splashed across some Sunday supplement or on a TV programme.

It had to be that. Only sex or money would motivate Joad, and even Joad wouldn't be stupid enough to try it on with Hanlon.

As soon as I get back to the station, I'm pulling Joad's roster schedules, she thought. He'll want to see the journalist in person in order to get paid. With Joad, it'd be cash all the way.

He's not going to be paid in anything traceable. I'm going to follow that bastard.

She thought there was one good thing about a useless cop like Joad. She could follow him mounted on her father's prize bull and he would never notice.

Satisfied with her decision, she left the Ashmolean, crossed the road and headed up the steps of the Blenheim, to see if Irek had any information for her.

Twenty minutes later she reappeared with a face like thunder. Irek did indeed have information for her. Someone had used an executive pass key to enter Fuller's room at five past eleven on the Friday morning.

At that time, Fuller was being interviewed by DCI Temple- man. The new evidence would now be totally inadmissible. The crime scene had been irrevocably compromised.

Huss shook her head mentally in irritation at the thought of having to tell Hanlon she had been right all along.

Joad, you bastard, she thought venomously. You should have thought of this. Well, I'm going to make sure you get done for something, even if it kills me.

47

Joad left the Summertown police station at four o'clock on the dot. Oxford is a city that does its best to deter traffic from the centre and, like many of his colleagues, Joad was forced to park in one of the park-and-ride schemes out of town.

He caught a bus into the town centre, Huss dawdling along behind on her old mountain bike. Oxford is very bicycle friendly, or certainly tries to fool itself it is, strong on initiatives, short on action, but the bike remained the most sensible way to tail Joad.

Wearing a college scarf she was not entitled to, with a helmet and mask, Huss blended in perfectly with the myriad other cyclists. She was invisible.

She slowed as the bus arrived in the centre of Oxford. The road here near George Street was a bottleneck. It was a horrible cocktail of exhaust fumes, angry motorists, bewildered visitors, throbbing bus engines and coaches disgorging or collecting tourists who milled around in the road, adding to the confusion. The streets themselves here always seemed narrow and meanly proportioned. It was her least favourite part of central Oxford, a human anthill that had been poked with a stick.

Joad had spotted Huss from more or less the moment he left the police station. There was a major flaw in Huss's assessment of Joad's character. Contrary to Huss's opinion of him, Joad was far from stupid. He also had a paranoid streak, exacerbated by his own criminal activities, which led him to assume the eyes of the authorities were on him at most times. He was forever looking over his shoulder.

He did wonder why Huss was following him. The trouble was that Joad had four or five scams on the go and he wasn't sure which one had engaged her interest. The most likely one would be his expense claims for informant pay-offs. Huss's boss, Templeman, signed off on these and Joad had been sailing close to the wind with the flasher investigation. That's what he assumed this was about.

Joad always liked to have an acceptable explanation for everything, no matter how far-fetched.

He used his time on the bus to review his own explanations for payments to known prostitutes. These were, of course, for sex, but highly discounted for police rates. He would claim that he was questioning them to see if they knew the flasher. He was probably local. He probably used sex workers. He was reported as having genital malformation. Maybe the prostitutes could put a face to the penis. The prostitutes needed to be paid for their time. That sounds reasonable, he thought to himself.

Huss's fond belief that she had blended seamlessly with the student traffic was misplaced. Joad would have recognized her burly frame no matter what she'd been wearing. Huss was quite distinctive in that respect. From his vantage point on top of the double-decker bus, he was ideally situated to keep her in sight and to decide when to lose her. She was also wearing a pink cycling helmet and Joad could easily keep track of her. As the bus slowed near George Street, very close to the Blenheim Hotel, the other traffic crowded round and Joad made his move.

Huss was hanging back about ten metres from the bus when Joad slipped off the vehicle behind the sizeable bulk of an overweight woman, who had to squeeze herself past the metal pole by the middle door of the bus. Cornmarket Street was full of shoppers and he could see Huss's head swaying backwards and forwards as she tried to spy him in the crowd. She caught a glimpse of the back of his head as he slipped into a major department store on the opposite side of the road to George Street. Huss was now in a quandary. She didn't want simply to abandon the bike to its fate outside the shop and she also felt that she'd be ridiculously conspicuous in her cycling gear if she walked through a shop catering for middle-aged women, full of safe, conservative, clothing.

Continually checking that the sweating Lycra-clad form of Huss wasn't behind him, Joad strode confidently to the rear of the store, taking his warrant card out of his pocket as he went. He walked up to a cheerful-looking middle-aged woman shop assistant and said to her, 'Sorry to bother you, love. Police. No need to be alarmed. Is there a rear entrance that I can use?'

'Of course, follow me.' She smiled excitedly. This was a welcome break from routine.

She led Joad helpfully down a couple of corridors at the back of the shop to a loading-bay area.

'Go through that door, that'll take you to Turl Street.' 'Thanks very much,' said Joad.

He passed through the loading bay and, as she had said, found himself in the broad, quiet streets behind George Street. There was no sign of Huss.

Five minutes later, he was ordering what he felt was a well-deserved pint, in the pub he had chosen for his meeting with Dimitri.

Here's to informants and the Oxford flasher, he thought.

He became aware of a hulking presence at his side.

'Hello, Dimitri,' said Joad cheerily. 'What can I get you to drink?'

48

An hour later Dimitri was back at the house on the Woodstock Road in Arkady's office.

'She's police,' he said. Arkady nodded. That made sense. Of course, and presumably one acting very much of her own volition. He was no expert on British police methods, but he was sure they did not include what had happened to him and Dimitri.

'How come Joad didn't know her, Dima?' Aside from the obvious reason of wanting to rip me off, he thought.

'She's Metropolitan Police, Arkasha.' Dimitri only ever used the diminutive form of Arkady's name when they were alone. It would have been disrespectful to do otherwise. He didn't want to do anything that might anger Belanov. 'She's investigating this Fuller character for murder. We would be his alibi.'

Arkady smiled bleakly. 'Alibi, us! He would have to be so desperate.'

Dimitri shrugged. Who cared. He doubted Fuller would have given Hanlon their details. She must have worked it out herself. 'Joad gave us her address, in London.'

Arkady sipped his vodka. It was a cheap, rot-gut brand from Moscow. He preferred it to the smooth, effeminate stuff he sold in the bar. It reminded him of who he was and where he had come from. He was not one of these Russian criminals who wanted to reinvent themselves as a businessman. That put him in a minority but he didn't care. He had old-style *Vor v zakone* thinking in that respect. He was happy to remain outside the law. He didn't want a house in Rublyovka or a *dacha* in Kievskoye.

'Well, you'd better pay her visit then.'

Dimitri nodded. Arkady's word was law for him. There is a word in Russian, *opushenny*, meaning low or debased for life. Its usual use is in the context of male rape. Arkady had saved Dimitri from this in Moscow's Butyrka prison, where Dimitri was on remand for a stabbing and Arkady doing two years for drug offences.

It was Dimitri's first time in prison and it was hell. He was one of forty prisoners in a twenty-four-bunk cell. Dimitri was bottom of the pecking order and had to sleep next to the *parasha*, the communal toilet, the dirtiest, smelliest place in the cell.

Dimitri quickly fell foul of the cell leader, the *Starshi*, the Oldest. He was from North Ossetia. This technically made him a Russian but for Dimitri he wasn't. He was *rossianen*, Russian in name only. Dimitri was *russky*, a proper Russian. Full of the arrogance of youth, Dimitri insulted the *Starshi*'s homeland. Retribution was immediate and terrible.

At a barked command from the Oldest, he was held down by four of his cell mates, one man on each arm, one man on each leg, his prison trousers and underpants around his ankles, bucking and struggling, snarling abuse and threats, while a jeering queue formed in his cell, waiting their turn.

The line was headed by the *Starshi*, naked, his body a mass of prison tattoos detailing his twenty years inside in pictorial detail.

His whole life story was there, from the tattooed dagger entering his neck showing he had killed in prison and was available for hire, to the stars on his knees showing he knelt for no man. Every killing, every robbery, every sentence, all inked into his skin in a life that had taken him through Russia's grim penal system. On his stomach was written:

Death is not vengeance, The dead don't suffer.

After they finished with him they were going to tattoo Dimitri, but this would be a tattoo of shame, a tattoo of punishment. Two eyes, one on each hip, so that Dimitri's lower quarters would form a face, with his penis as the nose. It would be a symbol of homosexuality, marking Dimitri out as a designated plaything in the prison.

Arkady and two minders broke it up.

Arkady had saved Dimitri from gang rape. His body might or might not have recovered, maybe not – Aids was common, treatment only available to the rich – but his spirit wouldn't. Arkady burst into the cell, shank in one hand, shouting at the Ossetian in a language Dimitri would come to recognize as Chechen. The Ossetian might have been *Starshi* of the cell, but Arkady was *Starshi* of the block. He was a *Brigadir*, young as he was, the trusted head of muscle for the *Klitchka* or *Vor* who ran the prison. Arkady left, taking Dimitri with him.

Ever since that moment, Dimitri was Arkady's man. It had been twelve years ago, but Dimitri relived the shame and fear on a nightly basis.

'*Opushenny*.'

The Hanlon situation was nowhere near this on the scale of things, but both had been humiliated and both men were hypersensitive to any kind of ridicule. As far as they were concerned, Hanlon had signed her own death warrant. Nothing else would really do.

'When?' asked Dimitri.

'Some time soon,' said Arkady. 'I want you to do it, Dima, I don't want any mistakes made.'

Dimitri nodded. 'It will be pleasure,' he said.

49

Hanlon woke up at her usual time of around six in the morning. Bed, for Hanlon, was typically spartan. She did some warm-up stretches, pulled a tracksuit on and then headed down at a steady jog to the River Thames. The City was just starting to wake up properly now, the coffee shops and sandwich chains opening their doors, the smell of coffee spilling out into the street, traffic starting to pick up.

The day was going to be warm and full of promise. Hanlon felt unusually cheerful, as she ran over the graceful span of the Millennium Bridge to the south side of the river and headed east in the direction of Greenwich.

Neither happiness nor contentment could be called default settings for Hanlon. Her usual mental state was one of dis- satisfaction or wary aggression. Today, though, it was as if some strange drug had been administered while she slept. I feel happy, she thought. It was a peculiar sensation, but she was sure that's what it was. Once or twice before in her life she had felt it and then the floodwaters of her natural world- weariness – *weltschmertz*, she'd learned the Germans called it – had risen and joy had disappeared once again.

It wasn't that she was an unhappy person; it was more like living with a defective sense of smell or colour. You knew that these senses existed, you knew everyone else appreciated them, but for you they simply weren't there.

But right now she felt happy and it felt good.

Her feet pounded the pavements. Her body felt light and strong. I'm in fantastic shape, she thought, and allowed herself a small smile of triumph.

The Thames was huge and powerful this morning, the movement of its brown, smooth water muscular, as it ran under the piles of Tower Bridge. There was very little river traffic around at this hour, only the occasional working barge cruising up and down the river.

As she ran, she felt an unusual joy at the strength in her body. She was too used to taking it for granted, she thought. She never savoured its power and beauty. She spent hours effectively torturing it day after day, week after week, so she could run, cycle or swim a few seconds faster than some equally deranged female obsessive from, say, Vilnius or Glenrothes, at some sparsely attended triathlon meeting in the middle of nowhere. It was all utterly pointless really. She never kept trophies or cups or medals. She binned them. Whiteside had a couple of the more prestigious ones that he'd saved. 'Just so your grandchildren know you didn't make the whole thing up,' he'd said.

But today, for some reason, she was happy to feel her shapely, powerful thighs and calves pounding along the concrete walk- way, no feeling of tiredness or stress in her muscles. She felt like she could run forever.

She ran past a play-park and paused for a minute by some monkey bars. She couldn't put any stress on her damaged wrist but she jumped up, caught one of the welded tubular metal bars and performed ten, graceful, one-handed pull-ups, slowly and perfectly.

Then back to her run.

She returned to her flat an hour later. She did half an hour of yoga, her resilient body stretching and flexing, then showered. She looked critically at her body in the full-length bathroom mirror. Her long, shapely legs, her washboard stomach. Even

Hanlon was pleased with what she saw.

She pulled on some underwear and walked into her lounge.

She had a text message from Michaels.

Are you free tonight for a drink?

I wonder what he wants, she thought to herself. She checked her calendar on her phone. God, she was supposed to be Corrigan's guest at a fund-raiser to improve women's profiles and women's issues in the Metropolitan Police. It was at the Mansion House too. She'd nearly forgotten. Corrigan would have gone crazy. It started at eight p.m.

Yes, she wrote, 6 p.m.? Yes. Usual place.

She put the phone down. I hope he's got some idea of another suspect besides Fuller, she thought, and I hope he doesn't drone on about unappreciated he is.

Her thoughts turned to the Mansion House.

I'd better buy something to wear. My only good dress is now in the bin.

50

Enver walked out of Leeds station into the wide streets and the anonymous, modern architecture of Leeds city centre. Leeds, after London, seemed hugely spacious, the roads wide, the sky and horizon limitless. Even his own heavy body seemed lighter on these northern pavements. Maybe it was the air, he thought, or maybe the eight and a half million or so people who lived in the capital city generated their own kind of gravitational pull, so that walking in London was inherently harder. Whatever it was, he felt it was a far more relaxing cityscape than the one he was used to.

He had half an hour to kill before he was due to meet Alison Vickery, the dead Abigail's mother. He had a coffee in Costa and sat there quietly, marvelling to himself at the strange northern accents that he could hear all around him. It was a reminder to him of how metropolitan-fixated he had become. Everywhere outside London seemed alien. Even on the train ride north, he found things like pylons and wind turbines novel. They weren't part of his internal geography, his own sense of being.

He finished his coffee and caught a taxi out to Headingley where Alison Vickery lived, wondering at the comparatively empty roads and the free-flowing traffic. You had a feeling, too, with Leeds that it had a defined beginning and a defined end. Here was Leeds, here wasn't. He was fully aware of the green belt around London and the girdle of the M25, but the city felt endless. This was different.

It was manageable; it was explicable.

The taxi dropped him off outside a pleasant, sizeable terraced house with a neat front garden.

He rang the bell, the door opened, and he found himself facing a tall, attractive blonde woman in her early forties.

'Hello, I'm DI Enver Demirel,' he said. 'I believe you're expecting me.'

'Alison Vickery. Do come in.' Her greeting was relaxed, friendly. He had been dreading a hostile, resentful reception. They sat in Alison Vickery's front room, which was comfort- ably and classically furnished. Enver looked around him. He got to see a strange selection of living rooms in the course of his job, everything from charity-shop/found-in-a-skip-furnished to the contemporary, a puzzling (to his eyes) mix of distressed and hard-edged minimalist, to show that the peeling paint and

exposed brick was ironic, rather than born out of necessity.

Then, of course, there were the tragic wreckages of some homes. Waste piled high, the stink of rotting food and blocked drains, the smell of shit and misery. He had once been round to a flat where an old man had died and his body had lain undiscovered for several months. There was a human-shaped stain on the fabric of an armchair where he'd seeped into the material over time. It was like the Turin shroud.

This living room told him its owner had money and safe, predictable taste. That was fine by Enver. It was forthright, and looking at Alison Vickery, he felt she'd give him forthright answers.

She wouldn't go off on a tangent about politics or contemporary life.

Her sofa was huge, comfortable and just the right height, so he wouldn't need to struggle in it, thrashing around to regain his centre of equilibrium before standing up again. He was grateful for that. He strongly disliked low furniture.

Alison Vickery had very long legs and at six foot was the same height as Enver. She had long, shapely fingers, pale blue eyes, a beaky nose and a slightly sad face in repose. Her fine hair was the colour of straw. Enver thought she was very attractive.

They'd been looking at a succession of photos of her daughter on the high-definition flat-screen TV. Alison's computer was hooked up to it, so it was as if Abigail was a third person in the room.

The images came and went. In none of them did the girl look happy.

'I always knew something terrible would happen to Abi,' she said softly. 'She was always bright but so withdrawn, so quiet.'

Enver nodded sympathetically. He didn't know what to say.

What could you say? A photo now of a teenage, Goth-looking girl filled the screen. Black suited Abigail. She was darker skinned than her pale mother, with Mediterranean colouring. But there was no mistaking the bitter look of contempt and anger on her face.

Enver remembered a girl he'd once gone out with, who was a film fanatic. She was always quoting a line from a film, from the fifties, about youth rebellion, when one character asks, 'What are you rebelling against?'

To which the reply was, 'What have you got to offer?'

That seemed like the kind of thought Abigail Vickery would have.

Alison Vickery said, 'She was always angry. But mainly at herself. It was always internalized. Her father and I are long since separated but we never got round to getting divorced.' She looked at her daughter. 'Maybe that was just cowardice on my part. He had a truly evil temper, and he'd take it out on others. He never internalized his anger, he'd lamp you.' She shook her head sadly. 'He was always getting into fights. But that's Leeds for you, Detective Inspector, we're supposed to be very mean, in money terms, and tough. If you get a good kicking you don't complain.'

'It's the same where I grew up,' said Enver. 'Maybe it's a class thing. You don't involve the police. You don't grass people up.'

'Maybe it is,' she said. They both silently contemplated the British caste system.

She looked at her daughter again. 'Oh, Abigail. And you had nothing really to be sad or angry about. That was the terrible thing. She had looks, brains, everything going for her. She told me once she thought she was probably crazy because she had nothing to complain about but she still felt angry.'

'And she went to university and met Dr Fuller,' said Enver, hoping to steer the conversation more in the direction of the investigation.

'Yes,' said Alison. She shifted in her seat. He noticed again her spectacular legs. He felt a stab of guilt that he found the woman he was talking to exceptionally desirable.

'She had got a First in philosophy from Durham.' She sipped her tea and sighed, 'You'd have thought that would have helped. I think,' she frowned and corrected herself, 'no, I know, she did philosophy to try and make sense of the world as she saw it. But of course it didn't help. If you're born that way, that's the way you are, I think. When she got her First, I was so pleased, so proud. She was furious, and depressed.' She shook her head. 'Crazy, isn't it? Can you imagine that? I go to people's houses and they have graduation photos of their children on the wall, holding their degrees in their robes. They all look pleased as Punch. Why wouldn't they? Not Abi.' She drank some more tea. 'I knew she'd got a First because I found a scrunched-up letter from the uni in the bin. Anyone would have thought they'd tried to insult her.'

Her eyes filled with tears suddenly and she fished a tissue out of her sleeve. Enver started to say something, but she blinked back the tears and shook her head to indicate she'd be fine. 'She'd come down to get coffee about twelve, lunchtime, just holed herself up in her room. I remember wishing – this is going to sound crazy – that she'd been on drugs. That way I'd have had something to blame.' She shook her head sadly. 'But no, it was all her, she was naturally fucked up. She didn't need drugs or booze.' She looked sadly at the TV screen.

'So, she was mooning about the house, not this one, a different one. Still in Leeds. I was doing well financially. I run a software company. Anyway, I said, why don't you do a Ph.D., here at the uni. I can afford it. It's well-regarded. I thought she might make some new friends.' She laughed bitterly. 'In a sense she did.'

'Fuller?'

Alison nodded. 'I knew they were having an affair. It wasn't maternal instinct or anything. She told me. In John Lewis of all places. In soft furnishings.'

'It is a good shop,' said Enver solemnly. 'Never knowingly undersold.'

Alison gave him an exasperated look. It reminded him of Hanlon somehow. I never say the right thing, he thought. I'm useless with women. 'Anyway, that's how I knew. I met him a couple of times. I thought, well, if he makes her happy, who am I to judge?'

'And what did you make of him?'

She shrugged. 'I don't know. He was what you'd imagine a lecturer to look like. Unremarkable. Boden lite.'

Enver nodded. 'And when . . .' He didn't really know how to finish the sentence. Alison did it for him.

'And when she died, no, I didn't blame him. I don't think he's a murderer, not unless he's very good at pulling the wool over people's eyes. A master of deceit. Her dad – my ex – did, still does, almost certainly. He was convinced. He's sure Fuller killed her. But then again, Steve's as mad as a hatter. And he likes being angry. Me, I think it was suicide. When my dad was ill with cancer, in a lot of pain, he more or less turned his face to the wall. He wanted to die. Life had nothing left for him.

'I don't think Abigail was murdered. I think she just found being alive too painful. That's what I think. I think she just turned her face to the wall.'

'Thank you,' said Enver. Well, he thought, that's two people, her and Hanlon, convinced of Fuller's innocence.

As for himself, he wasn't so sure. A master of deceit. Could that describe Fuller? It sounded horribly possible.

Hanlon's case seemed to rest on the testimony of a Russian gangster, who thought he was going to lose his genitals and was quite likely to say anything he thought she might want to hear, and the fact that Fuller had come up with some sort of insane defence after he'd unsuccessfully tried to rape her. He began to wonder if Fuller might not be able to get away with anything. He seemed to have a strange knack of convincing people of his innocence in the most unlikely ways.

Well, Fuller was going to walk, by the looks of things.

He was lost in thought when he heard Alison say, 'Would you like more tea?'

'Yes, that'd be great.' He followed her into her sizeable kitchen. It was almost as big as Enver's one-bedroom flat. A laptop was open on the kitchen table, an Apple Mac in the corner of the room, a tablet on one of the work surfaces. Everything gleamed and sparkled. The surfaces were spotlessly clean; nothing was lying around.

'Sorry about the mess,' Alison said.

There was a baking rack with scones that had been cooling on the grey marble-effect Corian surface of the worktop. They smelled as good as they looked. Enver stared hungrily at them. Alison noticed and smiled.

'Would you like one?' He nodded. 'Yes, please.'

'Cream? Jam? It's home-made.'

Oh God, yes, he thought. 'If it's not too much trouble.'

She laughed. 'No, it's always nice to have an appreciative audience. You look like a man who likes his food.'

While Enver pondered the meaning of her sentence, she opened a large shoulder-high fridge and took out some double cream, then bent down gracefully to get a steel mixing bowl from a low cupboard. She plugged in a small hand mixer and whipped the cream.

Enver stared, watching it thicken. Her movements were deft and precise, her face frowning gently while she judged the consistency of the cream.

She noticed Enver looking at her. 'Nothing worse than over-whipped cream, don't want it turning to butter.' Her mobile phone rang and she glanced at it, picked it up.

'*Ciao. No, sono occupata adesso . . . Poi, domani . . . si . . . si . . . è vero? Non è possibile senza Claudia . . . Si, in bocca da lupo! Ciao Paolo, a domani, ciao.*'

Her face changed as she spoke in Italian. She was commanding, dominant. Her posture was different too. Her back straightened, her voice hardened. Her work face, her work persona. It made him think of Hanlon. She was very different: there was only one side to Hanlon. Work, social life, sport, be it triathlon or boxing, it was all the same to her. She was indivisible.

What you see is all there is.

Alison rolled her eyes and clicked her phone off. 'Milan,' she said. 'Like headless chickens. I'll have to go over there tomorrow now.'

She stopped the machine and dipped a finger in the cream. He watched as she held it up to her mouth and saw the pink tip of her tongue as she licked it.

There was a feeling in the room like the heavy electrical charge you get before a savage thunderstorm. He could feel the hairs on his head and arms bristle.

She took the whisk attachments off the machine and put them in the sink. Then she smiled and moved towards Enver.

He suddenly knew with a terrible clarity that she felt the same way about him as he did her.

He could imagine closing his eyes in ecstasy as he felt her arms around him, her body pressing against his.

He could imagine kissing her and tasting the cream on her tongue.

He could imagine moving upstairs with her, still clinched together, she walking backwards, step by step, their bodies pressing into each other, then, on the landing, as she said at the door of the spare room, 'In here. No one goes in my room apart from me.'

But he didn't. Alison Vickery was still a witness in a murder enquiry, but above all Enver knew he would feel, rightly or wrongly, that he had somehow taken advantage of her. He was an old-fashioned kind of man. He coughed and smiled despairingly at her and she, divining his thoughts, smiled sadly and ruefully back.

What might have been and now never was.

'More tea?' she asked again.

He nodded; he didn't trust himself to speak.

51

Hanlon walked into Room 8 of the Tate Modern in Southwark by the River Thames. Both of the Tate Galleries – indeed, now she thought about it, more or less every gallery she had ever been in – were mysterious places, like mazes, labyrinthine. And like a well-designed maze there was always something half-glimpsed in the distance that made you think you knew where you were going, until you got there and it was illusory.

The great former power station, a testimony to the glory of brick construction, was one of her regular places to visit in London. Its shape made her think of the other industrial complex she'd seen recently, in Edmonton. But Southwark, with its enormously expensive property, is a hymn to wealth, Edmonton, a London blues song of poverty and the paucity of dreams. If you did have a dream in Edmonton, it would be to get out.

This wasn't her favourite gallery. She preferred Tate Britain, always so much quieter and intimate than the assertive Tate Modern, that and more user friendly. The Tate Modern was a very shouty building. It bellowed Art at the top of its voice. She also enjoyed walking through the creamy, white stucco streets of

Pimlico, which always seemed a haven of tranquillity after the noisier parts of London. The streets often seemed strangely deserted there. At times it was almost dreamlike, particularly with the ziggurat shape of the MI6 building like a Mayan temple opposite, on the other side of the river.

Here was the reverse. Opposite was the whirlwind of activity of the City clustered round the epicentre of the Bank of England in Threadneedle Street. The river traffic was heavy, tourist boats and commercial barges ploughing through the dirty, thick water of the Thames. The huge river was the kind of nondescript grey, green-brown colour that you get when you're a kid painting in class and you keep rinsing your brush out in a jam jar. The South Bank was full of tourists wandering along from the west of London, or maybe visiting the Globe Theatre next door. There were joggers and City refugees, who'd walked across from the North side to escape the commercial hubbub. There were living statues and a Mickey Mouse, and a small stage was being prepared for a band to play later that lunchtime. Then there was the human traffic over the Millennium Bridge, from which you could see the spires and towers of

Canary Wharf in the distance.

Hanlon made her way through the immense building that was the Tate. She wanted to see again some of the work by the man she assumed her father had liked, the artist whose signed photograph hung on her wall. The gallery was fairly quiet today and the room with the Beuys sculptures was virtually empty of other gallery visitors.

After several false starts and turnings, she found the Beuys. At first glance, the sculptures themselves seemed dis- appointing, the usual kind of thing that gets modern art ridi- culed. She felt disappointed, slightly cheated. Then she looked more carefully. There were three pieces on display. Hanlon found herself drawn to

Hirschdenkmal or *Monument to Stag*, whose juxtaposition of metal frames and tubing on floor and table reminded her uncomfortably of the dead, still warm, body of Dame Elizabeth. Even the table that the sculpture lay on echoed Dame Elizabeth's blood-spattered desk. What had been a hyper-intelligent, energetic über-woman in the prime of her life, a woman with so much to give, had been reduced by the actions of some moral cretin to a bag of bones and flesh.

It wasn't so much the cruelty of her death that upset Hanlon, as the fact it had been caused by a selfish idiot.

Thinking about Dame Elizabeth's death sent a powerful current of rage surging through her body.

If she had arrived five minutes earlier, she could have prevented that. She put aside the thought. What's done is done. No use torturing herself with regrets.

She looked again at the sculpture, at its title. Someone had killed the stag. Someone had killed Dame Elizabeth, Jessica McIntyre and Hannah Moore.

Opposite the dead stag was another sculpture, this one huge, an enormous elongated triangle of pitted and corrugated black steel hanging down from a girder.

Stag with Lightning in its Glare.

It was like the flash of a vengeful thunderbolt. Hanlon stared at it, her face withdrawn and sinister. She rubbed the scar on her head, invisible under her thick hair.

She thought of lightning; she thought of revenge. Now it was time for the hunter to become the hunted. I am the Lightning, she thought. I am the storm.

She was glad now she'd visited the gallery. The Beuys sculpture was a coded message from beyond the grave.

She thought, Dame Elizabeth wouldn't approve, she hadn't believed in revenge. Kant wouldn't have approved. Tough, thought Hanlon, I do.

She walked outside the gallery and sat on one of its wide steps, looking out at the broad Thames and the flat temple-like shapes of the buildings across the water on the far bank, with the dome of St Paul's rising above them. There was a cool breeze and it caught her wiry, curly hair, blowing it across her face. Her phone vibrated and she checked the text message.

It was from the anonymous caller. *Whiteside Senior claims incapacity benefits*, it read.

Hanlon thought back to her meeting with the Whitesides. '*John preaches down at the market.*'

'*My husband carries them down to the market.*' '*He's ever so strong.*'

All said by Mrs Whiteside.

Hanlon thought of the heavy wooden crate, the A-board for the 'Repent!' signs, the bull-like chest of the father, similar to that of his son's. Whiteside senior might be incapacitated emotionally or morally, but as far as Hanlon could see, the Good Lord had seen fit to grant him perfect health.

Hanlon's secondary school had been a C of E girls' grammar school. She had come away with religion. She knew the major prayers, she could still remember the words to 'There is a Green Hill Far Away' and 'All things Bright and Beautiful'.

They hadn't covered homosexuality in RE, but theft had certainly been on the curriculum. She could still remember the dessicated, elderly Miss Ardglass saying:

'Treasures of wickedness profit nothing: but righteousness delivereth from death.'

And, more succinctly,'*Thou shalt not steal.*'

Well, well, well. She scrolled through the hundreds of her contact names on her phone, until she came to Desmond Jardine of the DWP. He was a senior Fraud Investigation Officer and he loved his work.

'Hi, Des, it's DCI Hanlon here . . . Yes, they promoted me . . .

Actually, you could. Could I call in and see you for ten minutes if you're around . . . This afternoon would be fantastic. See you then.'

A yes, a no, a straight line, a goal.

She thought to herself, well, Mr Whiteside, judge not lest ye be judged.

And the DWP will be coming to judge you. And they will be in a wrathful mood.

Hanlon's next stop was Regent Street and the revamped area incorporating Carnaby Street. It was almost the reverse side of the City. That was a place, a secular temple, devoted to the making and worship of money. Its buildings were stone, glass and concrete hymns to mammon. It was an almost spiritual place. The West End was just consumerism gone berserk. Hanlon wandered around Carnaby Street and the adjacent area. For years it had been full of shops selling tat, T-shirts with the Pope smoking a spliff, or bearing the legend *My Sister went to London and all I got was this lousy T-Shirt*. Now it had become chic again.

She missed Whiteside terribly as she looked for something to wear. He'd loved helping her whenever she'd bought anything. He loved shopping. Hanlon did not particularly enjoy clothes shopping. It seemed a frivolous waste of time. But she knew what suited her and after all, she only had to buy one dress and shoes. She thought of Mark in his room in the hospital, wired up to machinery, in the endless sleep of his coma. She tried to imagine him next to her, his powerful, shapely body, his mocking laugh.

She settled on a shimmery, tight-fitting dress for her 'Women in Policing' dinner. It was probably not formal enough but Hanlon liked it. Whiteside would have done. If Corrigan didn't he could always send her home. Then again, Corrigan would be delighted that she hadn't turned up wearing something deliberately designed to annoy him.

It was a very sixties style that suited her slim, athletic figure.

The shop assistant looked at her admiringly. She wished she had Hanlon's legs. In fact, she'd have settled happily for the rest of Hanlon, given the chance. The dress was breathtaking and Hanlon looked stunning.

She studied herself critically in the mirror.

'Is it for a date?' asked the shop assistant timidly. Serving Hanlon was unnerving. She wanted the scary, monosyllabic woman out of the shop. Startled by the question, not one she was used to being asked, Hanlon started to glare, grey eyes narrowing menacingly. The shop assistant quailed inwardly. Then Hanlon suddenly thought, yes, it is, in an odd way. I am buying it for a date with a man I like and respect. Surprising but true. She had never really thought about Corrigan except as a necessary evil, but the truth was, she suddenly realized, I really do have a lot of time for him.

He'd started as a beat copper when to be Irish was a dirty word, when houses that offered accommodation had signs up: *No blacks, No Irish, No Dogs*.

Now he was almost top dog in the Met and one of the most respected figures in British policing. And he likes me, she thought wonderingly, which considering all the trouble I've brought him, is quite amazing.

She remembered a conversation she'd had with him when she was recovering after the business with Conquest in Essex.

'What have you been doing, sir?' she'd asked.

'Digging you out of the shit, DI Hanlon. What do I spend my time doing? I'm sorry, I didn't hear your reply.'

'Digging me out of the shit, sir.' She smiled at the memory.

Tonight I'll do what normal people do. It won't be spectacular, but I'll have a nice time. I'll enjoy myself.

I'll eat, drink and be merry. I'll be a credit to the force. It can't be that hard.

'Yes,' she said, almost shyly. 'Yes, it is for a date.'

52

Dimitri and Sam Curtis, a young Oxford thug who worked for the two Russians, got out of the white van that Curtis had stolen from Coventry the previous day. It was a five-year-old Ford Transit, now fitted with false plates. Dimitri liked white vans, their anonymous ubiquity. Arkady had wanted no connections to be made at all between Oxford and the dead policewoman. He'd also been very specific on how he wanted her killed.

Dimitri had wanted to take his time; he wanted to beat her to death, slowly. Arkady vetoed that. The woman had shown herself to be more than resourceful. Besides, who knew who else might be in the house, or indeed what else. For all they knew she might have a Rottweiler or some such animal, a Doberman, for example. The point was to do the job simply, effectively, cleanly, without anything going wrong.

Arkady had several handguns at the Woodstock Road property, two SRI Gyurza 9 mm pistols and a Makarov. He also had his favourite piece, a Baikal. This was a small, snub- nose handgun and it had enough power to pierce a bulletproof jacket. They were old friends, old military service issue. He'd served his year of compulsory military service in Chechnya. It was the end of the nineties. Arkady wasn't partying like it was 1999; he was in Putin's second Chechen war. He'd learned how to kill, not just Chechens either.

Dedovschina, forcible male prostitution and rape, is commonplace for military conscripts, but Arkady was already a tough survivor of Russian state institutions. People had tried it on with him before and he'd killed the first soldier who'd tried to take him. There was no trouble after that. This soldier was what they called a 'Grandad', a conscript whose time was up and who'd soon be going home. Perpetually drunk and not caring about how they behaved now they could see the dazzling light of freedom after a year or two of terrible food, lice, stolen pay, perpetual danger and squalor, the 'Grandads' were the most feared group in the army, after the officers, of course. They could do what they wanted. In Arkady's unit punishment beatings were common, sometimes for no reason at all other than just for the hell of it. If Arkady had killed an officer, he'd never have survived.

He'd dumped the dead 'Grandad' at Konservny, the mass open grave on the edges of Grozny, the state capital. No one cared. In fact, Arkady's CO promoted him, impressed with his abilities. He was transferred to an 'Elimination Group'. They were given a list of targets and a Polaroid camera to photograph the corpse. Then either a trip back to Konservny if they were minded to return the body or, if not, 'pulverization' as they called it. This involved strapping the body to a high-explosive artillery shell. Absolutely nothing was left.

It was that experience that taught him Chechen. And it was the attempted rape that had spurred him on to rescue Dimitri a couple of years later in the prison cell.

He didn't want to use the Russian handguns. He didn't want to leave any clues as to their ethnicity. From what Joad had told them of Hanlon, there would be quite a list of people wishing her harm.

So, he thought, let's not narrow the field down. Let the Met look for home-grown killers not Russians.

The previous night he'd hacksawed off the barrels of the twelve bore, the one she'd hit Dimitri with, and given him the sawn-off. One barrel for Hanlon's body, one for the head. After that there'd be very little left of her that would be recognizable as human, apart from arms and legs. There was also very little room for error.

Dimitri and Sam Curtis had been here now, outside the end-of-terrace house in Bow, parked diagonally opposite, since twelve. Curtis stared in surreptitious fascination at Dimitri's intricate tattoos on his massive forearms. He wished he had some like that. They made his own look stupid.

'What does that one mean again?'

Dimitri looked at him and said, 'It means, *I live in sin, I die laughing*.'

Sam asked, 'Where did you have it done?'

The giant Russian said, 'In Labour Colony Number 40, in Perm.' He pointed at some characters on Curtis's arm. 'What does that mean?'

'It's Chinese. It says, *Death or honour*,' said Curtis. Dimitri suppressed a smile. 'Where did you have it done?' 'Woody's Parlour in the Iffley Road,' said Curtis. Not exactly

'The Crosses' prison in St Petersburg, thought Dimitri contemptuously. He turned his attention back to the house. Nobody had entered or left the house, apart from an old woman, who Dimitri guessed to be in her seventies. Maybe it was Hanlon's mother.

Dimitri found himself getting increasingly suspicious of this address, this house. It did not seem the kind of place a woman like Hanlon would live. The net curtains, the tiny regimented flowerbed, the cheap statue of a robin in the neat, postage- stamp-sized front garden, it just wasn't her.

He had texted Arkady to confirm the address; maybe it was a postcode error. It wasn't. He suddenly realized that it was probably a poste restante, a delivery address and noth- ing more. A cut-off point between Hanlon and the outside world.

He had an A4 padded envelope with Hanlon's name and address on. He checked that the sawn-off was loaded and clicked the safety off. He had a deep, diagonal inside pocket, sewn into his tracksuit top, which would contain most of the gun. The excess part of the butt was hidden by the folds of material of the jacket. He doubted that she was in the house, but he would look stupid if she opened the door to him and he wasn't armed.

'Hi, remember me!'

'Wait here,' he said to Curtis. He got out of the van and stretched painfully. He'd been cooped up in that Ford for hours. They'd been sitting in the back where they couldn't be seen, a mirror propped on the front seat reflecting the image of Hanlon's front door. Or to be more precise, a front door.

He crossed the road and opened the gate, rang the doorbell.

He could hear the sound resonating inside.

The door had a stained-glass panel, depicting art nouveau- style tulips. Their red heads drooped mournfully. He could make out a figure approaching slowly. Not Hanlon, the old lady. He reached inside the tracksuit jacket and slipped the safety back on.

The door opened, a pair of shrewd eyes assessed him, tak- ing in his huge, pumped bulk, his intimidating features. The enormous biceps distorted the sleeves of his jacket.

'Can I help you?'

'I have package for DCI Hanlon.'

She looked at him dubiously. For a nano-second, he toyed with the idea of simply disposing of her. One blow, that's all it would take. One blow. His fist would shatter her face, she'd go down, and then a stamp with his foot on her throat or neck, it'd be over. Her bones would break like dry twigs. It was very easy to kill old people, he knew from experience. Then he could just wait for Hanlon to arrive in comfort.

But Arkady hadn't sanctioned it.

'Do you want me to sign for it?' asked the old woman. 'No, is valuable. I must have DCI Hanlon's signature. When is she back?'

He could see the old woman didn't believe a word he was saying.

'Oh, I don't know, dear, she comes and goes. Do you have a card, I'll tell her you called, Mr . . .?'

'Is not important. My boss will call her, thanks for your help.'

'What delivery company are you, dear?'

He smiled meaninglessly at her. 'I am sorry.' He grimaced. 'My English not too good. I come back.'

He turned and retreated down the path.

Well, he realized he was beaten for now, but he knew that he had guessed correctly. The place was a poste restante and the old woman would almost certainly tell Hanlon someone suspicious had been asking after her. She'd probably be calling Hanlon in the next few minutes.

Hanlon would want a description. Eastern European, huge. She'd know it was him and she'd want to come over and check things out. She wouldn't be deterred by the thought he might be waiting.

He doubted she would be making anything official. Her actions in Woodstock were proof enough that she was working alone; she would want to keep it that way. When she turned up – and she would come, he had no doubt of that – it would be by herself.

He heard the door close behind him and he got back into the van, started the engine and moved away quickly. He knew that the woman would immediately go upstairs to check the street. The road was quiet, with two entrances at either end where Hanlon might appear. At least he knew the make of her car and he would certainly never forget what she looked like.

At the end of the street he parked and said to Curtis, 'Go to nearest car-hire place and come back with something small. Park other end of street.' He jotted down the number and the make of her Audi. 'This is her car. You see it, you call me.' He scrolled through the image gallery on his phone and sent her image to Curtis's.

'This is photo of Hanlon. You see her, you call me. Every thirty minutes, you text me.'

'Sure, boss,' said Curtis. He was eager to ingratiate himself with the huge Russian. Dimitri and Arkady were like gods to him. It was an enormous promotion to have got a job with Belanov's firm and he wanted to prove himself worthy of the honour.

As he left the van, he wondered again who had damaged Dimitri's face. He must have some balls, he thought. He must be built like a brick shit-house. It was probably some other branch of the Russian mafia that had done it, he decided. Who else would dare?

Curtis turned his attention to the job in hand. This new task would give him the chance to show how good he was. Already he was planning on Googling car-rental places in Bow; he had a fake driving licence that was registered at Swansea.

Today was his chance to shine. He fully intended to make the most of it.

53

Fuller entered the university through a back entrance that few knew about. The university, like just about every university he had worked or studied in, apart from the Oxford and Cambridge colleges, which were more like mini-fortresses with their main gates and high walls, was a jumble of buildings with a variety of approaches.

The one Fuller chose was down an alleyway and then along a cul de sac, which ended in a small barred gate hidden behind some bins. The gate should have been locked, but never had been in all the time that Fuller had worked there.

The gate led to an access road that ran round the back of the main university building and was used for deliveries and waste collection. At this time of night, six p.m., it was deserted. Fuller was wearing hipster jeans that were a bit of a squeeze to get on these days, Converse sneakers and a hooded Queen's College top which obscured his face. CCTV would show him up as a generic student.

He could easily have got into the university through the main entrance, but tonight it would very much suit his purpose to be incognito.

Around the corner was one of the smaller student-union meeting rooms. There were half a dozen in the university, to serve the ten thousand strong student body. Access to it was theoretically only possible via the internal corridors branching off the university main halls.

Tuesday nights in this particular meeting room were pre-booked all term by the al-Nahda (in Arabic it meant 'renaissance') society. They were a moderate group of Muslim intellectual students, who debated the perennial issues gripping the Arab world. Israel, American foreign policy, democracy, the Muslim Brotherhood, the usual. More importantly for Fuller, he knew their routine. He had been a guest speaker at their meetings a couple of times, and a lot of them, particularly the overseas Middle Eastern students, smoked. The emergency door was propped open to allow exit to the outside for this purpose.

Prayer time for early evening tonight was six thirty p.m. Fuller lingered in the shadows outside, until he heard the opening of the *Shihaada* in the *Adhan*, the call to prayer:

'Allah u Akbar.'

He knew this meant God is Greatest. More importantly, he also knew that it would be repeated three times and that everyone inside would be facing the Qibla, the direction of the Ka'aba in Mecca in Saudi Arabia. Fortunately for Fuller, this was opposite the door he was about to use. Everybody's back, without exception, would be turned.

He slipped through the door unseen. He was in the corridor outside the meeting room and he could see the backs of heads of about forty Islamic students engrossed in their devotions. Nobody looked round; nobody saw him.

Unseen and unnoticed, he slipped into the main university building.

In the capacious pockets of his jacket he had a choke chain and mask.

He was ready for her this time. This time he knew she wouldn't say no.

54

Enver sat in the kitchen with Alison Vickery. Her cooking was every bit as good to taste as to smell. A while ago he had started to feel major guilt pangs about eating so much and mentioned this to Alison. She was one of those people who he met occasionally that he just clicked with. Like the missing piece of a particularly irregular cut in a jigsaw. She rolled her eyes impatiently.

'Shut up, Enver,' she said. 'There's nothing wrong with a healthy appetite.'

Enver had taken his jacket off and Alison Vickery could see his powerful ridged pectoral and shoulder muscles; she could guess at the iron-hard sinew beneath the skin.

'You've got a lovely body,' she said to him. She meant it. 'I'm overweight.' said Enver gloomily. 'I eat too much.'

Sex was off the agenda, but Alison was one of those women that he felt an affinity with. Usually he was very shy with women, but not with her.

'Well, you're not size zero, that's for sure. But if girls want to date Mo Farrah, they'll hang around more athletics meetings,' said

Alison. 'You look pretty good to me. Now, have you got any more questions?'

He looked round the sizeable kitchen for inspiration. He didn't want this moment to end. He felt at ease in his skin.

The room was functional. She hadn't tried to turn it into a farmhouse kitchen, or a Sunday-supplement version of one. Enver knew that Huss's mother's kitchen, which was a real farmhouse kitchen, was full of dog baskets, bits of machinery like distributor caps, Defra correspondence and tools. It drove Huss mad.

Only Alison's utility room, seen through an open door, showed any signs of non-culinary activity. On top of the cupboards above a double sink, and extending to some ancillary shelving, were various industry awards that had been presented to her over the years, old framed photos, cups for netball and ice skating that she'd won, and even a stylized John Travolta in his trademark pose out of *Saturday Night Fever*. Things she didn't want to throw away, but equally didn't want to display. Enver was terrible at dancing. He thought he probably looked like a tormented bear. On the dance floor he felt like everyone

was pointing at him and sniggering.

'So, you dance as well,' he said aimlessly, looking at the dance trophy.

'Oh, that,' said Alison. 'That's not mine, that belongs to my ex. He loves dancing. It's an obsession.'

55

Hanlon ordered a bitter lemon at the pub near the British Museum while she waited for Michaels. She felt oddly conspicuous in her new dress and matching shoes with a slight heel. Generally speaking, she dressed so as not to be noticed, or if she was competing in a triathlon, the only thing that distinguished her from the others was usually a race number fastened to her top. Invisibility was the intended objective.

She suddenly thought, what if Michaels thinks I've made the effort for him?

So tonight was unusual. She had become aware of several men looking surreptitiously at her, when they thought she wasn't going to notice. Hanlon scowled irritably. She was beginning to feel overdressed. Had she made a mistake in wearing this to the 'Women in Policing' do? She was not a fine judge of dress code. She suddenly had a morbid fear of being laughed at. She recognized this to be stupid but there was nothing she could do about it. Well, it was far too late to go home and change.

To take her mind off this train of unproductive thought, she recalled her afternoon with the Whitesides. It was a minor victory, but it had left a taste in her mouth as sour as the slice of lemon in her drink.

The last time she had been to see the Whitesides it had been as a supplicant, a beggar. This time it was like threatening a criminal. No, it wasn't like that, it *was* that. Whiteside senior had been manifestly guilty of defrauding the Department of Work and Pensions. If he was well enough to carry his heavy crate of religious pamphlets into Lambeth market and stand for a couple of hours, haranguing the locals on the need for repentance and to call on the Lord to forgive their sins, then he was well enough to work. Well enough to realize he was lying, when he said he was suffering from crippling back pain that kept him housebound.

A five-thousand-pound fine, plus paying back what you owe, said Hanlon, that's what is coming to you. And the possibility of three months in prison. Then the public disgrace. Then the interview I will personally give to the local press, about how a policeman decorated for bravery, a role model, cut down in the line of duty was betrayed, Judas-like, by his parents. It might even go national, she said.

Mrs Whiteside had silently cried, the tears tracking down her face, while Hanlon twisted the knife with sadistic relish. Her husband had glared, with true biblical hatred, at Hanlon.

What do you want? he'd asked.

Six months, Hanlon said. I want six months of his life and then, win or lose, I'll leave you alone. You can go ahead and get your court order to kill your son and I won't try to stop you. Whitehead senior nodded. What else could he do. She saw herself out, resisting the temptation to turn round and kick

the door viciously.

To a certain extent the current crisis had forced her to act. It was actually a good thing, she thought. Up until now she had buried her head in the sand; now was the time to look reality in the face. She realized she had been hoping that, somehow, the situation might just resolve itself. That Whiteside would just sit up in bed one morning.

She recognized that there were three options. Either she got some form of treatment organized, or he recovered by some unforeseeable miracle of the sort believed in by his parents, or she let him go. It would have to be the first. She had read about Persistent Vegetative States and how people who had been written off as brain dead had made recoveries. She owed it to Whiteside. There was a hospital in New England, near Boston, that was regarded as the best in the world. All she needed was a couple of million dollars. Perhaps I should kidnap Arkady Belanov, she thought. I bet he's got it. Her phone beeped and brought her back to the here and now.

She checked her phone and saw that she had a message from Michaels. For a moment she thought he was going to cancel their drink, leaving her with the problem of killing time alone before her dinner. But it was to tell her he was running late at work and to meet him, if possible, in the main downstairs kitchen. She frowned uncomfortably. The downstairs kitchen was the one where she had endured the cold, painful and uncomfortable few hours locked in the freezer. He wouldn't know that, of course, how could he, but it seemed a strange place to choose to meet.

She texted Yes, and almost immediately he was back in touch with instructions as to how to access the kitchen via the fire doors at the rear. Seemingly there'd been a clampdown on access to the university after the murder and she would have trouble with security.

Now Hanlon was feeling puzzled. Michaels was not the kind of man who would put up with this kind of thing. The kitchens were his kingdom and he would decide who came and went on official business. Oh well, she thought, I'll ask him about it later.

She texted, See you in ten minutes.

She switched her phone off, dropped it in her bag and left the pub. She felt a dozen pairs of eyes glued to her backside as she strode through the door. She was relieved to be out of there. She walked past the British Museum with her loose-limbed athletic stride. She caught a glimpse of herself in a shop window opposite. I look good, she thought, with surprise. She started to look forward to her evening out.

I'll have fun, she thought. The police dinner will be fine. It's just a question of having the right mental attitude and being in superb shape, like for a race meeting.

Perhaps I ought to strap a number to my chest.

For the first time in weeks, she smiled a genuine smile.

56

'So,' said Enver, 'your ex is a champion dancer? What, like *Strictly?*'

'Oh no,' said Alison. 'That's not his kind of thing at all. He was a good northern soul dancer. That and disco dancing. It's how we met, in a disco. He's a bloody good dancer. I'm not bad but he's practically professional level. Personally, I much prefer northern soul to all that Hi-NRG stuff. He won loads of trophies from the weekenders at Camber Sands. He'd practise for hours, it was all really tightly choreographed.'

She folded her arms in front of her and looked up at the ceiling. 'But of course, disco, particularly Donna Summer, Sylvester, all the gay stuff – odd when he was so heterosexual – was really his thing. Stephen Michaels, the disco king.'

'Your ex-husband is called Stephen Michaels?' said Enver stupidly.

'Yes. Vickery's my maiden name. Abigail preferred it to Michaels so that's what she was called.'

Perhaps it's all just simply coincidence, thought Enver, feeling stunned. But of course, he knew it couldn't be.

'What does he do?' he asked casually.

'Oh,' she said, stifling a yawn, 'he's a chef, a very good one. Very sought after. Went down south when he was a kid. Did his apprenticeship at the Dorchester, three years there, worked up here in a couple of Michelin-starred and rossetted places, but he's down south again now, I think. The last I heard of him, he was somewhere in Oxford, some flagship hotel, the Blenheim, is it? That and doing agency for the colleges. He told me he'd worked in all the big ones.'

Enver thought of the other things she'd said about him. He had a truly bad temper.

He was always getting into fights. It's a miracle he never killed anyone.

But it looked as if he had. It really did. As he sat opposite Alison, things slotted comfortably into place.

Enver knew a great deal about working in kitchens. His family background involved catering. He'd become a boxer, and when that career finished thanks to injury, a policeman, to avoid it.

He knew the terrible, endless, grinding hours, the sixty-hour weeks, the shouting, the stress, the continual air of hysterical violence, hanging as heavy as the heat, in the kitchen. He'd grown up with it. He knew the implacable attention to detail, the concentration needed.

He thought of what Hanlon had told him of Michaels' sense of injustice, which he could see now flourishing in this febrile background. The chef brooding at the seduction and killing of his daughter by some poncey intellectual that the law refused to punish. The feeling that they were all in it together, Fuller, McIntyre, Dame Elizabeth. One law for them; one law for the likes of him.

He thought of the care with which Hannah Moore had been killed. He thought of her affair with the married man. That would technically fit Michaels, who was separated but not divorced.

Then the Donna Summer as he killed her. The Disco King.

The choreography, again the attention to detail.

The knowledge of the layout of St Wulfstan's. He'd worked in all the big colleges.

That would almost certainly have included St Wulfstan's. A chef like Michaels, a senior agency chef, would have wanted to know where a dumb waiter in his kitchen led to. And after the murder, in his chef's whites, mingling with the other chefs, he'd have been part and parcel of the kitchen furniture. Who's the bloke with the beard? Oh, some guy from the agency. In the rabbit warren of the college kitchen, he'd have been unnoticed, unchallenged.

He'd worked in the Blenheim too. The kitchen staff in a hotel always did their level best to sleep with as many waitresses and cleaners as possible. They were usually eager to reciprocate. Michaels, good-looking, charismatic, important, a god in the kitchen, could easily have persuaded some employee to help him, or even better, would have known where keys were kept and how to get them.

As a former senior chef, and a respected one, all the staff would have treated him like an honoured guest. He could bet that when Michaels popped into the Blenheim all his drinks were free, meals wildly undercharged, rooms upgraded or mysteriously never showing up on the bill. To have slipped into Fuller's room would have been simplicity itself.

Enver thought, maybe he's insane. Some imbalance that had surfaced in a different form in his daughter. Hanlon had mentioned in her report about the murder of Dame Elizabeth the way he was interacting with her corpse, almost dancing with it, the choreography again. The disco music as he had killed Hannah. Well, mental health wasn't his field. That would be for others to decide.

Maybe he just liked killing people.

Then the choice of the kitchen to hide in when being pursued by Hanlon, an instinctive choice for Michaels, safe, familiar ground.

And finally, of course, a motive. Michaels bent on revenge on the man who he saw as having killed his daughter. Death would have been too good for him. He could have killed Fuller but instead presumably wanted him broken – everything he had worked for, the career, the reputation, the livelihood, all taken away.

Fuller would find prison hellish and he would be very much at the bottom of the food chain.

Well, that would certainly be enough to bring Michaels in for questioning. Mentally, he congratulated Hanlon.

It hadn't been Fuller. She'd been proven right again.

57

Hanlon walked around the electric barrier leading to the steep ramp that dropped down to the subterranean concrete yard at the back of the huge basement kitchen. Outside the kitchen doors, she looked upwards. It was like being at the bottom of a wide, square well, and she could see the evening sky above her, framed by safety railings.

The fire doors were propped open and the silver links of the metal fly screen hung down, obscuring her view of the kitchen. Hanlon parted the chain with her left hand, careful not to snag the bandaged cast on her right wrist or her handbag in the metal curtain, and walked through into the kitchen.

The steel links jangled quietly and percussively as they parted in front of her.

She shook her head to free her hair, which had caught in a couple of the tangled links of the chain. She stood stock still, unable to move, momentarily transfixed by the sight of Fuller in front of her.

When you are faced with a sight you simply do not expect, you don't feel alarm or shock: it's a what-on-earth-is-happening sensation. The brain is trying to assimilate what the eyes are telling it.

Hanlon was having one of those moments.

Fuller was the last person she had been expecting to see that evening. After dominating her professional life for nearly a month, for once, she simply hadn't thought about him. But here he was. She stood in her short, shimmery dress, holding her handbag, dressed for her formal evening out, and stared. She had even put make-up on, dragged a comb through her protesting thick hair and sprayed a discreet amount of perfume over herself. And here was Fuller.

The philosophy lecturer was standing looking towards the door and Hanlon, who was framed by the silvery backdrop of the fly screen, as if she had just walked on stage. His skinny jeans and Calvin Klein underpants were down around his ankles. His sweatshirt and T-shirt lay in a crumpled heap by his feet.

His eyes stared imploringly at Hanlon.

58

DI Melinda Huss was annoyed with herself for about five minutes after losing Joad, but then decided not to waste emotional energy. In Huss's view there was never any point in crying over spilled milk. If something went wrong, you fixed it. Tractors, machinery, fences, bent coppers, all one and the same. As soon as she saw his thin, high shoulders and greased-back hair disappear into the department store, she realized she had lost him. She turned round and pedalled back to the station.

She chained her bike up and, helmet in hand, went in search of Worth. Fortunately, he was still at work. He looked up admiringly from his desk at the sweat-stained form of Huss. Worth found DI Huss extremely attractive. There was a lot of Huss and here she was, kind of gift-wrapped in her damp, Lycra finery.

'Melinda, can I help you?' he said eagerly.

'I hope so,' she said. 'I want Joad's username and password for his PC. Do you know them?'

Worth grinned. 'Do you really think that Joad would be thick enough to write important stuff like that down on a Post-it note and stick it underneath a drawer?'

Her face fell and his smile broadened. 'Absolutely he is.'

He pushed his chair backwards on its castors to his colleague's desk, opened a drawer, felt underneath and removed the yellow piece of paper. Huss copied down the information.

'Thanks, Ed,' she said.

Worth watched Huss's broad back disappear across the office. She was a big girl, he thought, but oh so sexy. Mentally he wished her luck in her feud with Joad.

Back at her own desk, Huss logged on as Joad and went to his history folder. There, amongst what were almost certainly porn sites, was a request for number-plate identification. Hanlon's number plate. Her address was of course listed.

Bingo, Huss thought.

She sat at her desk, thinking, tapping her strong white teeth with the end of a pen. She had the following day off, so she could stay in London if she wanted, or come back to Oxford on the last train.

Joad and Hanlon; Hanlon and Joad. What could it be about?

Well, she thought, I can discount the journalist theory. No writer would be after information like that, post-Leveson. Hanlon's disciplinary record, yes; her car registration, her address, no way. So who else would possibly want to know a policewoman's home address and why?

She could think of several reasons, none of them pleasant. Well, one thing was for sure, she'd get nothing from Joad. She wouldn't be able to do anything at all official with the information, but she could pass it on to Enver. He could act on it and say it came from an informant, which would be essentially true, and keep her name out of things.

She got her phone out and texted him.

59

Enver was on the train back from Leeds. He was in a strange mood, in which elation and sadness were mixed.

On the one hand, he had almost certainly succeeded in solving the crime. He had been over and over in his head what he had learned about Michaels. It simply had to be him.

He tried to think of a scenario in which Michaels was an innocent party. It didn't work. If Fuller was innocent, it must have been him.

Maybe just as importantly, and as Hanlon had suspected, this new information would prevent a major miscarriage of justice. On the debit side, he felt guilty because inadvertently he was about to cause Alison Vickery more unhappiness. Bad enough to have a dead daughter; now her ex was about to be charged with murder. But there was nothing he could do about that.

His phone told him he had a message and he saw that Huss had texted him. He texted her and she replied almost immediately,

Where are you? :/ she wrote.

On a train, coming back from Leeds. I'll be at King's Cross at seven. It took time for Enver to text. His fingers were long, thick and strong, and they often depressed neighbouring keys.

Are you free tonight? I need to talk to you. :/ The reply was almost instantaneous. Huss by contrast, to Enver's way of looking at things, was lightning fast.

Sure, he replied.

I'll meet your train. :)

I look forward to it, he wrote. It was true. He liked Huss.

She seemed solid and dependable.

He put his phone away and wondered what DI Huss could possibly want to see him about. It had to be Fuller.

60

Fuller was no threat to her. He was no threat to anyone. He had been cling-filmed round and round the pillar, so he looked like he'd been bound by some huge spider, as if he was a chrysalis.

More cling film had been wrapped over his face, giving him a Botoxed, face-lifted look. The skin was pulled tightly back, but she could see there was a tear in the plastic membrane around his nose, so he could breathe.

Then Hanlon felt the most tremendous blow to the side of her head and she was knocked sideways by the force of it, dropping her handbag. Her thick hair protected the skin of her scalp from splitting open with the impact of the strike, but she staggered and her left leg buckled underneath her. She was too dazed to feel any pain. As she knelt on her left knee on the kitchen floor, dark spots circled and exploded in her blurred vision.

Hanlon was very nearly unconscious. She had lost all rational thought and really didn't know where she was at all. She shook her head and out of the periphery of her vision, she saw a highly polished, black steel-toecapped boot scything towards her stomach.

There was a yellow-orange tab on the back of the boot and the legend *Caterpillar*.

The tip of the boot buried itself in Hanlon's iron-hard stomach muscles and the impact lifted her body off the ground and upwards. It drove all the wind out of her and left her gasping and retching, in a series of shallow, agonized pants, for breath.

A powerful hand grabbed hold of her wrist and dragged her across the tiled floor of the kitchen, to where Fuller was bound. Dimly, before losing consciousness, she heard the familiar click of a handcuff lock and then a second one. She was now shackled to the pillar next to the philosophy lecturer.

Her head was exploding with pain and she felt as if she was going to throw up, but amazingly, she was able to breathe. And then the pain in her head and the screaming agony, from the nerve endings in her stomach, reached a crescendo and darkness took her.

61

In the back of the taxi on the way to Bow, Huss outlined to Enver what Joad had been doing. She had no idea why anyone in the Oxford area might be interested in bribing an officer to find Hanlon's address. Huss didn't know about Hanlon and Arkady Belanov; Enver most certainly did. Joad, a corrupt officer operating out of Oxford and interested in Hanlon, was almost certainly their information conduit. Now he knew they had an address for her, Enver felt very worried indeed.

He never felt particularly Eastern in his outlook. The Demirels were fairly Western in their world view, and his mother, of course, was English. But he was acutely aware of the gulf between the sexes, outside of Europe, and he had appreciated what Hanlon had not, the extent to which the Russians would feel humiliated and enraged by her actions. Honour was something that you could kill over, and for the Russians, hardened career criminals, it would be bad business practice not to. Coming from a man her actions would have been bad enough. From a woman, a deadly insult. Or, equally plausibly, Hanlon knew but simply didn't care.

He suspected the latter.

He could imagine her not caring at all what they thought.

The angrier it made them, the better.

In his mind's eye he could see her careless shrug. He felt a visceral surge of affection for Hanlon crash over him and, like a wave with powerful back suction, a feeling of acute worry for her. She was stupidly brave in his opinion.

He had been trying since he arrived in London to contact Hanlon, and this was adding to his concerns. He had toyed with the idea of calling her from Leeds, but something had held him back.

He had called Murray and asked to have Michaels picked up for questioning, even though there was, of course, no actual hard evidence against him. Probably there was none whatso- ever. Hanlon had explained to him the philosophical theory of Occam's razor, that the simplest explanation was often the true one. Who else could have done the murders besides Michaels? He doubted the CPS would be so impressed. From what he had learned from Alison, and from his knowledge of the meticulous planning of the murders, he knew that Michaels would not be the kind of man who would obligingly leave hard evidence around, or crumble and confess at the first sign of trouble.

Anyway, at least Murray had sounded delighted. He tried Hanlon's phone again.

The lack of an answer led to his decision to try the address in Bow. Maybe she would be there. At least he'd be doing something constructive. He was beginning to feel slightly panic- stricken.

Now he was beginning to regret his not calling from the train. If he had, she'd have met him at King's Cross, anxious to talk. The fact that she was not answering the mobile was highly worrying. But how could he have known then about this threat to her from the Russians? The fact that he couldn't didn't stop him from blaming himself.

He looked at Huss sitting next to him in the taxi, sensibly

dressed for town in a stylish lightweight summer Barbour jacket and polished brown ankle boots. Their eyes met briefly.

Huss smiled reassuringly at Enver. God, he looks so worried, she thought. She had been watching his reflection in the glass panel that separated the passengers in the black cab from the driver. Occasionally a thunderous look would pass across his face and Huss intuitively knew that he was thinking about anyone hurting Hanlon.

He tried the phone again. Nothing. His worry for Hanlon ratcheted up a gear. She had no social life. She never left her mobile unanswered. If she was training or running, she'd have had the phone on. Tonight wasn't a boxing night. She couldn't be out with friends, she hadn't got any, or at least they were a luxury she took a morbid pleasure in denying herself. He was unable to shake off the image of Hanlon, injured, or worse, dead. Enver thought, if the worst happens I'll make sure the

Russians pay, and this bent copper Joad.

He wasn't quite sure what he hoped to achieve by visiting the address in Bow, other than it was something to do. It was a form of action, and action was infinitely better than doing nothing.

Huss, who had finished telling Enver about Joad and the PNC check, watched as one bearlike hand tugged on his moustache, while the other curled and uncurled into a very large clenched fist. He alternated between frowning in anger and worrying his lower lip between his teeth. She felt a resigned sense of jealousy at his obvious concern for DCI Hanlon, a woman she'd have thought more than capable of standing on her own two feet. It's always about her, isn't it, she thought bitterly.

Enver was checking a street map on his phone as they approached Bow, and he leaned forward and told the driver to drop them two streets away.

The taxi pulled over and parked behind a skip. They got out

and Huss looked around, while Enver paid off the driver. Bow, she had heard, was a fairly working-class area of London, but she could see what looked like the telltale signs of gentrification starting in the street. Soon, she thought, it would be sourdough, couscous, bicycle shops and chiropractors.

The taxi pulled away and she looked at Enver.

'We'll check on the perimeters first,' he said. 'Then we'll go to the house. Keep an eye out for her car.'

Check for what? she thought.

The two of them walked purposefully northwards along the pavement. Enver's face was like a stony mask. Other pedestrians gave them a wide berth. His muscular girth, but above all his expression, cleared the path for them.

As they drew near to the end of the road where Hanlon's address was registered, Huss suddenly slipped her arm around Enver's waist and buried her face in his chest. He could smell her hair and perfume, as she pushed herself into him.

He started in surprise and automatically pulled away, but Huss's arm tightened around him like a tentacle. He realized that he hadn't appreciated what a strong woman Huss was.

'What the hell do you think you're doing?' he hissed into her ear.

'You'll see,' said Huss, with an ominous calm. 'Keep walking.'

62

Hanlon's mind swam in and out of consciousness, until with a mental jerk, she snapped into wakefulness.

Her head was bowed and ferociously painful. She lifted it up, her surroundings still out of focus through her blurred vision, but slowly her brain began to work again and she started to piece together what had happened.

The first and most pressing feeling was one of agony, from her head and from where she'd been so savagely kicked in the stomach. She retched now and tasted blood in her mouth. She put her head to one side and spat it out. As her chest rose and fell when she breathed, she could feel a sharp pain in her side and guessed a rib was probably broken.

Her legs were stretched out in front of her. She had one shoe on and one shoe off. She glanced down and saw that the stitching on the seam of her tight dress, from her left hip up to her middle ribs, had given way during the attack. For some reason she found this almost unbearable. I really liked this dress, she thought sadly. Now it's ruined. Hanlon wondered vaguely where she was but her head hurt too much to think. Had she got drunk or something? She had no recollection of where she was.

She closed her eyes momentarily and reopened them, to find herself looking at a pair of legs in black cargo trousers.

'Hello, DCI Hanlon,' said Stephen Michaels.

63

Sam Curtis sat in the rented VW Polo, behind yet another skip, and looked again at the clock display on the dashboard. It was eight o'clock. He'd been here three hours now and his bladder was bursting. The skip was beginning to look good. It wasn't that full and he thought, in half an hour I'll climb in and kneel down and no one will see me.

There was a pub up the road with a toilet he could use, but he thought, if Hanlon arrives and I'm in there, Dimitri will kill me. And with the giant Russian that wasn't necessarily a figure of speech.

Curtis thought of being attacked by Dimitri. He had never met a more frightening man in his life.

He was incapable of holding a thought for long. God, I'm bored, he thought. I'll give it half an hour and then I'll have a piss in the skip. The evening stretched ahead of him like a long and dull road. He had a low threshold for tedium. He wanted to play games on his phone but he thought, if Dimitri comes along to check on me and sees me doing that I'll be well fucked. Plus he'll never use me again.

He rolled himself a joint, with some grass he had in his pocket. This'll help to kill the time, he thought.

A couple walked along the pavement towards him. He bowed his head and shrugged his body down in its seat, to appear less conspicuous, as he built his joint. They were obviously on some kind of date, she was clutching on to him passionately. He tried to see her face in the car mirror but she started kissing the guy she was with, some big, fat fucker. As they walked by the car all he could see of her was her hair.

There was something vaguely familiar about the woman, but he paid no attention. They were obviously local, nobody would come to Bow on a date.

He started thinking of his own girlfriend, Chantal. He lit the joint. Would it be better to have the window down so the smoke all billowed out at once, or open it a crack and have the car fill up with smoke?

It was a tricky question.

64

'So, it was you,' said Hanlon flatly. Her head was still agonizingly painful, but at least her mind was working.

Michaels nodded. 'Oh yes.' He stood looking at her, his hands on his hips. He was wearing a double layer of latex gloves on each hand and as he talked, he lifted each foot in turn and slipped on a pair of plastic, disposable shoe- covers like the ones they give out at swimming-pool changing rooms.

Hanlon said, 'Abigail Vickery was your daughter, wasn't she?'

The chef nodded. Hanlon's quick mind filled in the rest of the details, as Enver's had done.

'You must really hate him,' said Hanlon, jerking her head at the mummified figure of Fuller.

'Yeah, yeah, I do.' Michaels looked at him with real venom. 'Life's always so easy for people like that, isn't it. I'll just bet he had a privileged background. Public school, ponies, that sort of thing. You can always tell.'

Hanlon sensed, rather than felt, Fuller's body moving. She craned her neck to one side and saw his ribs shaking under the folds of cling film, as if he were laughing.

Perhaps it was hysteria, she thought. Neither of us is going to live that much longer. Of that we can be sure.

'How did you get him here?' she asked. Hanlon didn't really know why she was bothering to talk to Michaels. Like Belanov, she had settled to die with as much dignity as possible, while waiting for either a miracle to save her or, almost as unlikely, Michaels to make some fatal mistake.

'I texted him, saying it was you – I even bought a new phone for that – and that you'd give him a second chance. I think I added something like, only someone like you can know what I mean. Some trite platitude. What a dickhead.' He looked scornfully at Fuller.

Hanlon suddenly felt very sorry for Fuller. S&M hadn't killed him in the end; good old-fashioned romance had. Passion for Hanlon had. It was the thought of seeing her that had brought him here, and that alone. He'd fallen in love with her and was now going to pay a terrible price.

At least he had an excuse, which was more than she did.

How could she have been so stupid? She felt a surge of contempt for herself. And now you're going to die in your new party dress, she thought.

She suddenly thought of Corrigan, crossly looking at his watch and cursing her non-attendance. Typical Hanlon, he'd be thinking. Bloody woman. And here she was, a victim of a self-pitying murderer, bemoaning the hand that fate had dealt him.

'You'd have thought being a university lecturer, he'd have shown a bit more intelligence, but oh no, thick as pigshit,' he said. 'You know, I always wanted to go into teaching. Three lecture jobs at catering colleges I've been rejected for now, whereas privileged perverts like him can get anything they want.'

There was no mistaking the bitterness in Michaels' voice now. There was no mention in the list of complaints against Fuller of

Abigail Vickery. Hanlon suddenly thought, your daughter's death was just an excuse to hang all of this on, wasn't it? Your resentment in life has sparked all this off but you've cast yourself not as the embittered loser, but as the revengeful vigilante. Just to make yourself feel better.

You make me sick, she thought.

'I could do his job myself,' he continued in the same aggrieved tone. 'I'd like to see him try and do mine. He wouldn't last five minutes. Or that bitch Dame Elizabeth. Do you know what she was being paid? Nearly two hundred K, six times more than me and I do a sixty-hour week. She only worked, if you call it working, six months a year.'

He moved to stand directly in front of the trussed-up Fuller. His face was furious with resentment. 'And there was all the extra money she earned, on committees, lecture tours. She was minted. Yet ask her for a raise and it was a different story. Can you imagine that, the hypocritical bitch.' He looked Fuller up and down and balled his fists.

'I've worked at the Dorchester.' He hit the bound man bru- tally hard in the stomach with his right hand. His latexed fist thudded into Fuller's gut. The lecturer bound to the pillar took the full force of the vicious blow. 'The Georges Cinq in Paris.' Another savage punch with his left. Hanlon wondered if Michaels was going to beat him to death while working through a list of famous restaurants he'd worked in, like a homicidal San Pellegrino Top One Hundred restaurant award. 'And Claridges, and no one gives—' a last vicious right – 'a fuck. They just don't care, Hanlon. They couldn't fucking care less. Well, now it's payback time.'

Fuller couldn't move. He was a human punchbag. His head sagged. Michaels surveyed his handiwork with an air of satisfaction.

'And that upper-class whore McIntyre. I fucked her, you know.' He sounded aggrieved about his role as a sex toy. 'And you know what she called me? Her bit of rough. And that, Hanlon, that was supposed to be some sort of compliment. The perfidy of women, Hanlon, the perfidy of women.'

He took a filleting knife off a magnetized holding strip on the wall, walked behind the pillar and started cutting Fuller free. The lecturer's body was leaning forward and a couple of seconds later, as the support of the plastic holding him up gave way, he toppled forward, trailing cling film. He was on his hands and knees, as Michaels put the knife down and started gathering up the torn plastic around him and stuffing it into a black bin bag.

Despite herself, Hanlon found something beautiful about Michaels' movements. All those years in top-class kitchens had left him with an impressive ability to work fast, gracefully, efficiently and, above all, tidily. And the importance of meticu- lous planning had been beaten into him from an early age in his sixteen-hours-a-day, six-days-a-week apprenticeships in Britain's top restaurant kitchens. Hanlon had little doubt that when it was eventually discovered, the crime scene would look exactly how Michaels wanted it to look.

He approached her now with the knife and, despite herself, she swallowed. He squatted down next to her and lifted her chin up with his thumb and forefinger. His calm, brown eyes looked deep into her furious grey ones. Her throat was completely exposed.

He put the point of the knife into the material of her dress, about a centimetre below the collar, and ripped upwards, gashing the fabric. The razor-sharp blade left her skin unmarked. Michaels' expertise with a knife was unrivalled. Then he put the knife down and, using both hands, tore a rip in the dress so her collarbone and the top of her chest were visible.

He stood up again and put the knife down on a work surface, then he turned to look at Hanlon.

'The only person I feel sorry for, really, is that stupid girl

Hannah Moore. I thought killing her would be enough, what with putting Fuller's hair on her and everything. But oh no, I had to keep going. Well, that's why you're here, Hanlon. To lend credibility to Fuller's demise. If anyone's likely to kill a suspect in the Met, it's you. Nobody will be surprised. You've established a bit of a reputation. You should Google yourself. Full of alarming comments about you.'

He stood next to Fuller, still face down, and grabbed him by the hair with one hand and the waistband of his underpants with another. Fuller hung as motionless as a log in Michael's arms and Hanlon found herself staring at the crown of his head, where he was starting to go bald. Michaels braced himself and suddenly swung Fuller forwards like a human battering ram into Hanlon's face.

She could do very little about it, but she pushed her head against the pillar for the impact and tucked her chin in, so Fuller's face would smash against hard bone.

There was an audible thud as Fuller's face met her forehead. The pain was excruciating, but she was largely unscathed. Fuller's face, nose, mouth and the thin skin around his eye socket, however, already damaged by Hanlon's head from the university encounter a week or so before, exploded in blood.

Hanlon's face was covered in it. Michaels dragged Fuller's crimson face over her dress, holding his lolling head by a fistful of hair, smearing more of his blood down her. Then he took Fuller's right hand and scraped it down her exposed flesh, leaving claw-like scratches from her shoulder, to halfway down her breast.

He stood back and surveyed his handiwork with satisfaction. Then he pulled Fuller up by his hair like a giant rag doll, marched him over to the walk-in freezer, opened the door and

pushed him in.

He slammed the hugely thick door shut. The freezer door, like the fridge, had a hasp for a padlock and Michaels pushed a knife steel through it so the door couldn't be opened. Just like he'd done with Hanlon in the walk-in fridge. There was an LED display on the outside of the door, minus eighteen degrees Celsius, it read. Hanlon wondered how long Fuller would survive.

As if reading her mind, Michaels said, 'I think he'll last about half an hour. They'll find him tomorrow, with bits of your skin under his fingernails, where he tried to rape you. You fought him off and locked him in there, while you went to get help.' He walked over to where she was secured and stood over her.

'I am sorry about this,' he said. You don't look it, thought Hanlon. 'But you know, Hanlon, when you cook meat, say beef, if it's fifty-seven degrees it's medium rare, all lovely and tender and pink. Well, that's how my heart used to be, but when you heat beef up to about seventy, it's all tough and dry. I'm afraid that's me these days.' He shook his head regretfully. 'That's what life has done to me, I'm afraid.'

I don't give a rat's arse about cookery or beef, thought Hanlon. Or your pathetic self-justification. I want to kill you. He looked towards the internal kitchen doors at the far end of the room. The drain was still blocked and the resultant puddle was now wide and shallow, but in its centre, where the drain grill was, the water was probably a couple of centimetres deep.

He jerked his head in its direction.

'And that's where they'll find you tomorrow, Hanlon. Col- lapsed with your injuries, drowned in there. A tragic accident. You bravely fought off your attacker, only to die so needlessly, in a puddle of water. God knows I've submitted enough memos about that fucking drain. Did anyone listen?' He shook his head angrily. 'I've told them, time and time again, that it's a health hazard and a potential death trap, but would anyone do anything about it?' He mimicked a kind of mimsy voice. 'Oh no, we'll have to dig the whole floor up to fix it. It'll cost a fortune. We haven't got the budget. It's not covered by insurance. It's grade- one listed.' He shook his head. 'Well, I'll have been proved right, won't I! You won't have died wholly in vain.'

Momentarily she wondered if Michaels was entirely sane. He sounded genuinely aggrieved by the blocked drain. A decent man, pushed by idiots into unreasonable behaviour.

He looked down at her, grabbed a handful of her hair and pulled upwards. Back braced against the pillar, she straightened her legs until she was standing.

Hanlon looked bleakly towards the drain, her final resting place. Then she saw something that gave her the kernel of an idea, and hope blazed inside. At least she felt she had a chance and that might be all she needed.

A yes, a no, a straight line, a goal.

Michaels slipped the choke chain around her neck and held the other end behind the pillar.

'I'm going to unlock the cuffs. I want you to put your hands behind your back.' She heard a click, then felt one arm being taken out of the open metal bracelet. Docilely she moved her arms behind her back, as Michaels had demanded. She gasped as the chain bit into her neck. Michaels was taking no chances. She felt the cuffs tighten on her wrist as he relocked them, and now both her hands were secure behind her back. The choke chain was removed and Hanlon stepped forward. As discreetly as possible, she flexed the long powerful muscles in her legs.

Her legs felt good. They felt strong.

'Now,' said Michaels, 'over to the freezer door. Good, turn round, face me, touch the handle. Good girl, now the top of the steel, excellent.' Satisfied there were enough of her prints on the door, he looked her in the eye.

'Come on, Hanlon,' said Michaels gently, looking at the puddle. 'Time for your bath.'

65

'Put your arm round me and keep walking,' said Huss quietly to Enver. He did as he was told.

He wondered what on earth she was doing, but Huss was the kind of woman who inspired confidence. It was a long time since he'd been so close to a woman. Her springy hair smelled of some light floral shampoo as she pulled his head close to her, her powerful fingers twined in his thick dark hair. She could feel his breath on her cheek and the roughness of his thick, drooping moustache.

Huss had arrested Sam Curtis twice in her career and interviewed, or sat in on interviews with him, on three other occasions. All of these had involved crimes of violence, or intimidation of one form or another. She knew him as a thoroughly nasty little thug. To find him here was a genuinely unpleasant surprise. Curtis also knew her face well, or he should have done. He'd spat in it once when she'd nicked him.

That had been the time when Curtis had been employed by the

Russians to trash Paul Molloy's pub. It was a commission Curtis had carried out with exemplary zeal. Nobody had testi- fied against him, and he'd walked.

She had no doubt he would have recognized her immediately. They rounded the corner, out of Curtis's sight, and Huss let go of Enver, who almost sprang away from her. She was very disappointed by the alacrity with which Enver had let her go. Ed Worth would have clung on for dear life, his hands desperately trying to cover as much ground as possible. Of that she was quietly confident.

Quickly she told Enver who had been sitting in the car and why she had averted her face. There could only be one reason Curtis was there and that was Hanlon. Why else would he be in central Bow?

Occam's razor again, thought Enver. Why would an Oxford villain be in a car at the end of Hanlon's road? To wait for her, presumably.

There was one street for Hanlon's address: one road, two entrances to the road. Curtis at one end.

'Come on,' said Enver, turning into the street parallel to the one with Hanlon's address. 'Let's see if Mr Curtis has got a colleague.'

Huss smiled up at him. She did quite a bit of shooting in her spare time and she enjoyed stalking. Enver might have slipped out of her sights; time to find a different prey.

66

'After you,' said Michaels politely to Hanlon, indicating the other end of the kitchen, near the door of the walk-in fridge where Hanlon had been trapped several days before. She still had one shoe off and one shoe on. The slight imbalance made her bob up and down as they walked.

The further down into the kitchen they went, the louder was the noise of the extractor fans. They roared overhead. There was a peculiarly harsh, strong smell of chemicals and she noticed that the oven doors were open.

There were four of them, two banks of two, Hobart again, the same German make as the ones she'd seen when she had been with Michaels in the upstairs kitchen. These were much bigger, though.

She guessed that the ovens must be having some sort of deep clean and that the insides had been sprayed with a degreaser. That would explain the smell and the fans.

She stood, head bowed, by the work surface facing Michaels, outwardly awaiting her fate. In the centre of the kitchen the puddle spread out across the floor. In a minute she guessed he would stun her, either with his fists, or against some surface. She was already so badly bruised on her head, stomach and shoulders, from the choke chain and the handcuffs, that the pathologist would find it impossible to work out what had happened. Once she was half conscious, her slow death would begin.

She had a sudden vision of herself, lying pale and inert, naked on the morgue table, while her body awaited the Y-incision, so they could determine cause of death. Of the two bodies the police would have to deal with, she'd be autopsied first. Fuller would have to wait until he'd fully thawed out, like a piece of frozen beef.

Who would mourn her?

Enver, she thought, and felt a huge wave of affection for her gloomy colleague. Enver will be distraught.

Michaels would lead her to the centre of the puddle where the drain was and the water was deepest. He would sweep her legs away and lower her down face first, in a kind of baptism, and almost certainly sit gently on the base of her lower back while he held her face against the tiles. So long as her nose and mouth were underwater, it would be enough. Within two to three minutes she'd have lost consciousness, and he could afford to relax. She guessed that Michaels would wait around for a quarter of an hour to check she was quite dead.

She raised her head and looked into Michaels' brown eyes. His face looked as calm as ever. She turned her head to look at the water and he did too.

Behind her back was the waist-high electrical socket for the slicer machine. The one the sign had warned against, the one missing its safety guard. Despite the warnings, it was plugged in.

Unseen by the chef, Hanlon's fingers located the switch and she pressed it down.

Behind Michaels' back, on its steel work-table, the unguarded slicing machine started into action. There was nothing between the blade and the air, no guard, no protection at all. Its razor- sharp cutting blade spun so fast it looked almost stationary, any noise it made being drowned out by that of the fans. It was about a metre behind Michaels' back. He didn't notice it. His attention was focused on Hanlon.

She nodded at the water. 'Please,' she said imploringly, 'not that way, please, I beg of you.' She got down on one knee in front of him submissively. She bowed her head and kept her gaze fixed on the floor; she didn't want Michaels to see the look in her eyes. She made a weeping noise, or tried to. It wasn't a natural sound for her.

She heard him say in an exasperated tone, 'At least show some dignity, Hanlon. Whining won't do you any good.'

The blade of the slicer spun behind him. It was industrial spec. You could push a partially frozen ham as thick as your thigh through, using your little finger, and it would effortlessly cut it in two, it was that sharp.

'Please don't kill me,' moaned Hanlon, as pathetically as she could.

'Oh, for God's sa—'

He didn't get to the final syllabic 'k' of the word. With all the strength in her legs, all that power accumulated from years of cycling, running, swimming, endless punishing squats in the gym with heavy weights on the bar, she drove herself forwards and upwards into Michaels' chest.

Her shoulder smashed into him with irresistible force and the impact of her body knocked him backwards into the revolving blade of the slicer.

Michaels roared with pain and anger, as the razor-sharp steel of the spinning disc cut deeply into his flesh.

Hanlon, hands bound behind her back, took a step back- wards and watched as Michaels stood upwards and away from the machine whose shining silver blade was now a bloodsoaked crimson disc. Fine droplets of blood spattered the white-tiled walls behind him and the floor in front of him. He turned and stared in disbelief at the machine, before looking at Hanlon.

She was a fearsome sight, scarcely human. Until now, obsessed with his own plans, Michaels hadn't really paid her much attention. He'd been too preoccupied; Hanlon had been an abstraction.

Now she stood facing him, her dark corkscrew hair matted and covering her face, mottled with Fuller's blood. Her torn, blood-stained dress clung to her slim, muscular figure and her lips drew back in a snarl from her sharp, white teeth. Her feral grey eyes shone through her curly hair with hatred and bloodlust. There was no rationality there, no compassion, no humanity.

The right sleeve of Michaels' chef's jacket was now a very dark red, as the blood soaked into the fabric. His hand and arm hung uselessly at his side. He started to feel faint and sick. The blade had severed nerves and tendons. Every second that passed played into Hanlon's hands. The deep wound was not going to stop bleeding and the human body can only afford to lose so much blood before it collapses.

Michaels was now one-handed and weakening. Hanlon, of course, didn't have the use of either of her hands, so the advantage still lay with Michaels. Hanlon grinned savagely at him. Whatever happened, his plan to frame Fuller had now come to nothing. There was enough of Michaels' DNA bleeding out of him to paint this whole end of the kitchen, let alone cover a slide for a forensics specimen.

The chef looked around for a weapon. I need a knife, he thought. He blinked rather stupidly. Loss of blood, shock and the extreme pain in his back were slowing his thought processes. He shook his head angrily. I'm the head chef, he thought, I own this kitchen.

The obvious place to get a knife was the magnetized rack on the wall. It was full of them. But Hanlon stood between him and it, and in his weakened state he didn't want to get close to her. Hanlon continued to grin crazily at Michaels. All normal thought had more or less departed. She wanted him dead. She bared her sharp, white teeth at him and snapped her jaws. She didn't have her hands, but she had teeth, canines, incisors and Michaels had a throat.

Under the long metal table that supported the still spinning slicer and a couple of microwaves, was a long, metal shelf with steel mixing bowls, colour-coded plastic chopping boards and the huge, three-kilo plastic rolling pin that Hanlon had picked up the other day.

To see it was to act. He bent forward to grab it. You can suck on this, bitch, he thought, as his fingers stretched out for it. As his body reached a ninety-degree angle, Hanlon kicked him as hard as she could in the stomach.

Hanlon lacked the advantage of Michaels' steel-toed work-boots but she was kicking for her life and she put every fibre of her hatred of Michaels into it. He was unbalanced, slightly dizzy now. His blood pressure was falling and he was low to the ground, his centre of gravity off-kilter.

The force of the kick spun him backwards and his foot skidded on the treacherously slippery floor. Ordinarily, when you slip over, you put your arm out to break your fall. Michaels' arm was useless to him.

He fell on to the open door of the lower oven, which protruded outwards like a shelf. It was hinged at the bottom rather than at the side so it could open up and down. He crashed down hard on top of it, but it held. The Germans make very good kitchen equipment. He lay there momentarily on the glass door, winded, with his useless right arm trapped under his body.

The glass of the oven door was immediately slick with blood. He put his left palm down on the floor of the kitchen to help push himself up and Hanlon stamped as hard as she could on it. All her weight was concentrated on the two-centimetre heel of her shoe, which crashed down like an industrial press, squarely on the back of the chef's hand. She felt flesh and bone

give beneath her foot and she cried out in triumph.

Michaels shouted in pain and involuntarily curled up with agony, snatching his hand back towards him. Hanlon put her foot against his knees and shoved him backwards from the shelf, deep inside the oven.

His blood on the glass shelf acted like a lubricant and he slid further back across the glass on to the polished, steel floor of the metre-deep oven. Hanlon stepped back, placed the tops of the toes of her right foot under the lip of the oven door, and slammed it shut.

Unlike a walk-in fridge or freezer, there is no inside safety catch, no inside handle, in an oven. Why bother? You're not supposed to go in. The oven door is, however, designed to click shut and stay shut, so it can't be accidentally knocked open.

Hanlon stood for a second or two, breathing hard, then she stepped back and looked through the reinforced glass of the oven door. Michaels was an indistinct dark mass inside. She could see him moving as he tried to get some leverage. He was trying to squirm round inside so he could kick at the door, but there wasn't enough room. The door rattled gently, but showed no signs of giving way.

Hanlon looked down at her torn, bloody dress. She had looked so pretty wearing it in the shop. Now she looked like one of the living dead.

She suddenly thought of the 'Women in Policing' dinner she should be attending right then. Perhaps I ought to go as I am, she thought, they'll be impressed. She stifled a laugh of pure hysteria.

With almost hallucinatory clarity, she remembered the shop assistant asking her, 'Is it for a date?'

'Yes,' she'd said proudly. 'Yes, it is.'

Her stockinged foot idly traced a pattern in the water on the floor that had been destined as her final resting place.

She thought of Michaels' words to her, something along the lines of, you banged your head and collapsed. Well, I've taken enough of a pounding for that to occur, she thought. I guess round about now, amnesia will set in. That's what I'll tell everyone.

I can't remember a thing.

'This is for you, Michaels,' she said out loud.

She remembered Michaels showing her how the ovens upstairs worked. These were the same, just bigger. Hanlon pressed the power switch on with her forehead. The LED display for the oven temperature flashed, displaying 000. The inside light came on and she could now see his face.

The oven must have been soundproof. She could see his lips moving, but no noise came out.

'This is for Hannah and Jessica.'

She turned round, back to the oven, selected the steam function of the Hobart and pressed the on button. The machine made a loud, metallic *Kerchunk* sound as its function changed from fan oven to giant steamer.

'This is for Dame Elizabeth and my father.'

Michaels must have known what was happening. His face was agitated; she could see he was shouting and his body jerked frantically, as he tried to break free. It was a pointless struggle. The oven door was toughened glass. You'd have needed a sledgehammer to break it.

'And this is for me!'

Hanlon turned again and pressed the temperature setting. Michaels had told her he usually had it at a hundred and seventy degrees Celsius, so in tribute she selected that.

Her face was set and impassive while she calmly watched the

LED display on the oven change incrementally, recording the speedily rising temperature, as the scalding steam hissed into the oven.

In the breast pocket of his jacket, Michaels had placed Dame Elizabeth's letter to Hanlon. As the steam filled the oven, transforming it into a scalding coffin, he had clawed it out of the thick cotton material. Soaked in his blood and superheated steam, the paper dissolved into illegible shreds. In destroying Michaels, Hanlon had obliterated her past.

At fifty degrees Celsius, Michaels started thrashing around like a madman, trying desperately to move his skin away from the agonizingly hot metal. His mouth was open in a soundless scream.

At about seventy degrees Celsius, he must have lost con- sciousness, for he stopped moving.

She looked at the motionless body inside the oven and nodded curtly to herself.

Hanlon crossed the kitchen floor carefully and walked down to the freezer.

Her bag was on the floor still and she upended it. Make-up, tissues, purse, phone and keys fell out. On one of the key fobs was a small universal handcuff key and sitting on the floor, with great difficulty, and several false starts, she managed to get it into one of the locks and twist. She felt it give.

Her hands were free.

Quickly she opened the freezer door and dragged out the freezing, but still breathing, body of Fuller.

She wrapped him as warmly as possible in her coat and called the emergency services. Then still holding her phone, she walked back up to check on Michaels.

She looked at his dead body, gently cooking away. What was it he'd told her?

'It's as if my internal temperature was seventy degrees. I'm tough and dry inside.'

Her lip curled in contempt.

The oven purred along contentedly at a hundred and seventy degrees. She guessed he'd take a while to cook through.

Slowly, she walked down the kitchen to open the double doors so she could go outside and call Enver.

She could hear sirens approaching.

They hadn't got far to come.

67

Enver and Huss reached the end of the road paralleling the one with the Hanlon address, when his phone vibrated in his pocket. He took it out. It was Hanlon herself. Relief washed over him.

'Where are you?' he asked. The tone of his question, angry and concerned, jumped the memory of the twenty-seven- year-old Huss back to when she was a teenager, to those few occasions, mainly Young Farmers' Balls, when she'd worried her father. Enver sounded exactly like him. She half expected him to say something like, 'I've been worried sick.'

Huss watched intently while the conversation continued. She could piece together what was happening from Enver's side of things.

Fuller, alive, innocent. Michaels, dead, guilty.

Hanlon, about to be taken to hospital for her head injuries, but otherwise OK.

Enver's face was one of acute concern. 'I'll see you there in about an hour. What am I doing? Oh, nothing much. No, I'm having a walk with DI Huss, showing her London by night. Yes, I'll see you soon. Bye.'

Enver sat down heavily on someone's wall and passed his hands wearily over his face. When he put them down on his thighs, Huss could see his eyes were wet. She decided diplomatically not to notice.

'So what do you want to do now, Enver?' she asked. It was clear that whatever had happened, or was going to happen, Hanlon would be in no danger from this direction tonight. But the decision was Enver's to make.

She wondered what had happened to Hanlon, what sort of condition she was in. A part of her was extraordinarily jealous of the woman. How could she possibly live up to such a role model in Enver's eyes?

'What I want to do is send a message, Melinda,' he said, with finality. 'Let's go and find Curtis's friend.'

Enver hadn't been able to protect her from Michaels but the least he could do was protect her from Arkady Belanov.

He stood up and put his hand in his pocket, and took out a pair of soft black leather gloves. Huss looked at him questioningly.

'We don't want anything to get lost in translation,' Enver explained grimly. He took his jacket off and gave it to Huss to hold. His tie followed. Then he slipped the gloves on and flexed his fingers. He looked huge now in the darkness, lit softly by the glow of the energy-saving street lamps.

'Time for a little chat,' he said. His voice was quiet with menace, his eyes hard. Huss looked at him wonderingly. This was a side of Enver she had never seen. She knew his history; she knew he'd been a boxer. But she had never considered the innate brutishness that is necessary to reach the top flight as Enver had. When Enver chose to, he could be very violent indeed. They came to the end of the road. Parked diagonally across from them was a white Ford Transit with a huge, burly figure

at the wheel. It had to be Dimitri, thought Enver.

They crossed the road.

'Wait here,' said Enver quietly. Huss did as she was told and watched as Enver approached the van. He tapped on the window and the driver lowered it. She could see his face, a white blur, as he peered out at the thickset stranger with the heavy moustache.

Enver would never have made anything other than a good journeyman boxer, but he could hit unbelievably hard.

His best punch was a right hook and it was this that con- nected with the side of Dimitri's head.

Huss didn't see the punch, but sound travels at night and she heard it quite clearly. For the second time in just over a week Dimitri's cheekbone was shattered. Then Enver yanked open the door of the van and dragged the stunned Dimitri out on to the pavement. Another couple of blows and a savage kick to the ribs.

Enver bent over the figure now lying half in the gutter and said something, then turned and walked away.

A couple of metres away, he stopped and walked back to where Dimitri lay.

'Nearly forgot,' he said. He kicked Dimitri as hard as he could in the groin, then rejoined Huss.

'Time to go,' he said.

They walked a couple of streets away, down to the high street, and caught a taxi to Paddington. Enver was completely silent, wrapped in whatever thoughts he had. Huss respected his right to privacy.

Enver appreciated Huss's tact. He looked at the stocky young woman beside him and smiled apologetically at her. He hoped he hadn't alarmed her. Beating Dimitri up had left him feeling cleansed somehow. Huss smiled at him and patted his arm.

They pulled up outside the station and he decided to wait with her, until her train back to Oxford was ready for boarding.

He liked Huss. They sat at a table outside the station bar and had a drink, while they waited for her train.

Now that the earlier tension of the evening was draining away, Enver was funny and warm and considerate. Huss stared at him mistily. Ever the optimist, she thought, it's like a date, sort of.

'Do you like ceviche?' she asked Enver suddenly. He stared at her with some surprise.

'What, that raw fish with lime juice on it?' 'Yes,' said Huss.

'No, no, I don't,' he said.

'I don't either,' said Huss, pleased. 'What do you like to eat?' I wonder what she's on about, thought Enver. 'I like köfte and shish kebab, that kind of thing. Stereotypical, I guess, but, well, it's what I like.' He paused. 'Grilled meat, and cake.

I do like cake.'

'I'm glad,' she said. 'I like cake too.'

She nodded, satisfied. She stood up to go.

'I'll walk you to the barrier,' he said. There they halted awkwardly. They stood looking at each other, almost in embarrassment.

'Well,' said Enver lamely, 'it's been lovely to have worked with you.'

Huss smiled at him. Sod it, she thought, then, 'I like köfte too,' she said.

'Good,' said Enver.

Huss shifted her weight awkwardly from foot to foot. Enver tugged his moustache. The enormous station was brightly lit and had very few people around. It felt almost hallucinogenic. 'Is it true that DCI Hanlon stabbed a man to death on that island?' she asked.

Enver looked at her in surprise. 'Oh no. Not at all. She didn't stab him. She killed him with a spear. It was there,' he made a sketching motion in the air, 'hanging on the wall. She didn't bring it with her.' He shook his head emphatically; that would have been weird, the gesture implied.

'Oh,' said Huss faintly. How can you compete with that, she wondered. 'Well, I'd better go.'

She passed through the barrier and walked towards the train. I won't look back, she thought. She did, though, and saw Enver's broad shoulders as he slowly lumbered towards the Underground. Off to see Hanlon, she thought bitterly.

With a spear. She shook her head.

She settled down in the carriage and took her phone out. And a book. Fiction is a great consolation, she thought. Huss never gave in to self-pity. She always made the best of things.

To her delight and amazement, a message appeared on the screen of her Samsung phone.

I'm glad you like köfte. Would you like to come to my brother's restaurant some time, if you happen to be in London? Enver.

Oh, I think I can happen to be in London, thought Melinda Huss. She frowned gently to herself as she answered, and smiled.

68

Corrigan sat in the visitor's chair beside Hanlon's bed, looking at her with affectionate concern. He was formally dressed in black tie, but with his size and battered face he looked more like a doorman than a senior policeman.

Her dark, curly hair contrasted with the white of the pillows, and the bandage that ran around her head looked almost chic. She was wearing a hospital gown and seemed frail and childlike in the bed.

Fuller was making a good recovery in a separate hospital. Parts of him were frostbitten, there was a certain amount of internal bleeding and his skull was fractured, but it seemed he would survive intact.

Hanlon's mobile was charging next to the bed, when Corrigan's phone rang.

'Excuse me,' he said and left the room, closing the door behind him.

Enver had spoken to him briefly about a threat to Hanlon from some Russians. The Russian mafia, he'd said. Corrigan had groaned to himself. Not content with home-grown may- hem, Hanlon was casting her net further afield. To Enver's huge relief, Corrigan had told him to fill him in later. The assistant commissioner had watched the expression on Enver's face and rightly guessed that the DI would be busy trying to airbrush whatever facts made Hanlon look bad, out of the report.

In the interim, for security reasons, Corrigan had Hanlon transferred from University College Hospital, where she'd been initially taken, to the one at Seven Sisters where Whiteside was being looked after. In fact, he was just down the corridor. Hanlon was high on a cocktail of medication and felt warm, comfortable, safe and grateful to be alive. I could be face down in that drain, she thought drowsily, sleeping with the microbes,

not even the fishes.

She propped herself dozily up on one elbow and saw that Corrigan's long black overcoat with a velvet collar, the one that made him look like a successful bookmaker, was draped over the back of his chair and his briefcase, a kind of man-bag that rather surprised her, was there too. He had been wearing a dinner jacket; only now did it occur to her that he must have come straight from the Mansion House.

She thought, I wonder. She took her phone from the bedside table next to her and scrolled through the menu, until she came to the number of the unrecognized mobile that had been giving her the information on Whiteside's family. She pressed dial.

A phone rang from the overcoat pocket. One ring was enough. She pressed end call and put her phone back.

Corrigan knocked and re-entered the room.

'I'm off now, Hanlon. I'm sure DI Demirel will keep me up to speed and you can come and see me when you're up and about.'

'Yes, sir,' she said sleepily. 'I'm sorry if I messed up your evening.'

Corrigan smiled. 'It was very dull, Hanlon. You'd have hated it.'

She smiled woozily at him. 'I'll have my report ready as soon as I can.'

'You do that, Hanlon, and concentrate on leading as dull a life as possible, please,' said the assistant commissioner.

'Yes, sir.'

'No more excitement, Hanlon. I'm on pills for that kind of thing, understand.'

'Yes, sir.'

Corrigan turned to go. 'Sir?' said Hanlon. Corrigan stopped and looked at her.

'Thank you,' she said simply, and closed her eyes. Corrigan nodded curtly and left the room. A wave of con-

flicting emotion washed over him. It was the first time Hanlon had ever thanked him for anything. He felt very moved. He closed the door quietly behind him. Hanlon waited five minutes. She had one more thing she needed to do, before she could sleep. She slipped the heart-rate monitor and blood-pressure counter off the fingers they were attached to. She had canulae in the backs of her hands but they weren't yet attached to any lines.

She swung her feet down on to the cool, beige lino of the floor. She picked up the book she'd asked DCI Murray to bring in. It belonged to one of his daughters and the request had puzzled him greatly, but he'd done as she asked.

Hanlon padded in her bare feet, two doors down to Whiteside's room, and let herself in. The nurses' station was the other side of a partition with a window and allowed enough light to read by.

Whiteside lay asleep in his coma and he stirred as she watched. She could see a muscle move in his powerful forearm. She whispered, 'It's not called *Sleeping Beauty* in the original, Mark. It's called

Briar Rose. I'll read you the opening sentence. Just like I promised you. Everything's going to be all right, I swear.'

She opened *Grimms' Fairy Tales* and started reading. 'A long time ago there lived a King and Queen . . .'

A little while later she leaned forward and kissed his fore- head. 'One day, Mark, one day.'

MORE FROM ALEX COOMBS

We hope you enjoyed reading *The Innocent Girl*. If you did, please leave a review.

If you'd like to gift a copy, this book is also available as an ebook.

Sign up to Alex Coombs' mailing list below for news, competitions and updates on future books.

http://bit.ly/AlexCoombsNewsletter

Explore the next book in the The DI Hanlon Series, *The Missing Husband*.

ABOUT THE AUTHOR

Alex Coombs studied Arabic at Oxford and Edinburgh Universities and went on to work in adult education and then retrained to be a chef. He has written four well reviewed crime novels as Alex Howard.

Visit Alex's website: www.alexcoombs.co.uk

Follow Alex on social media:

facebook.com/AlexCoombsCrime

twitter.com/AlexHowardCrime

bookbub.com/authors/alex-coombs

ALSO BY ALEX COOMBS

The DI Hanlon Series

The Stolen Child

The Innocent Girl

The Missing Husband

The Silent Victims

The Hanlon Private Investigator Series

Silenced For Good

Missing For Good

Buried For Good

ABOUT BOLDWOOD BOOKS

Boldwood Books is a fiction publishing company seeking out the best stories from around the world.

Find out more at www.boldwoodbooks.com

Sign up to the Book and Tonic newsletter for news, offers and competitions from Boldwood Books!

http://www.bit.ly/bookandtonic

We'd love to hear from you, follow us on social media: